ALMOST GUATEMALA

A NOVEL

RR CARROLL

PUBLISHED BY

4T2 BRAND, LLC

NEOSHO, MISSOURI

I remember the first time I met Dr. Norman Borlaug. It was at Texas A&M in a well worn university meeting room. He was seated at the far end of a long conference table, dressed very casually. I didn't know who he was and thus didn't think much of him at the time.

The next two years changed my mind drastically about Norman (he insisted that I call him that). As we worked intermittently together on a project to preserve the small remnant rainforest in Chiapas, Mexico, I came not only to respect the man and his many achievements in life, but also to truly like him.

This work of fiction was created out of the memories of that time and of Professor Borlaug. I will remember him always with a warm fondness and will be forever glad I had the opportunity to know him briefly.

This story is dedicated to

Dr. Norman E. Borlaug
(1914-2010)

Cover & interior design by the art department of

4T2 Brand, LLC

Editors

Sandra Sargus

Cheryl Carroll

ISBN: 978-0-9802014-5-1

ALSO BY RR CARROLL

‡

The Big Lost, novel
The Old Cowboy's Box, short stories

Chopo My Pony, children's book
Mustang Ghost, children's book

Rounder, The Tales of Rounder M. A. Dilla,
narrated compact disc.

Visit: 4t2brand.com
& 4t2brand-tex.com

ALMOST GUATEMALA

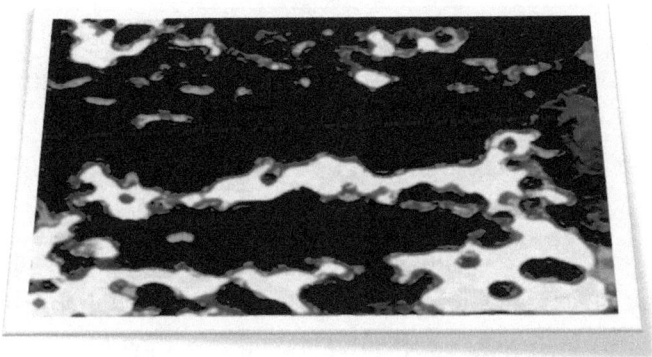

PROLOGUE

THE SONG OF THE OWL

IT WAS A MISERABLY HOT DAY and I walked slow as my boots stirred the dust on the dirt road that led from the hay barn to the screened-in porch. As houses go this one was not much, only a ten by twenty structure. It was one of the nine houses and shacks that were scattered over the sprawling Running~Bar Ranch. The ranch was about thirty miles north of San Antonio, and it had been my refuge for just over a year.

My casita, as I called my quarters, wasn't roomy but it was comfortable. The cramped space inside wrapped around me like a cocoon and the dampness of the cool naked limestone walls felt good in the summer months. The little house was stuck out on the back section of the ranch with only the one unpaved road leading in or out. I'll tell you, after the last couple of years of a troubled life, the notion of privacy, if not outright seclusion, was a sight more appealing to me than luxury. Divorces, bankruptcies and the harassment of the IRS can certainly do that to a man.

I had reached my sanctuary and was just about to open the screen door when I noticed that the cows had again knocked my bird feeder off its hook. The troublesome bovines didn't care about the birdseed, they were merely curious but none too delicate. I was busy scraping up the loose hulls and hanging the plastic tube back up on its nail when I noticed the fire ants had also been hard at work in my absence. Their ugly black mound had abruptly erupted like a volcano and was right next to the outdoor shower I used in the summer to rinse the Texas sweat from my back. They appeared to appreciate the fresh water supply as much as I did. From experience with these little devils though, I thought it prudent to discourage their construction project at the get-go. If I didn't, eventually they would make my sugar bowl look like a jar of black pepper.

I was intent on seed collecting when something large and quick swooped almost noiselessly about six inches above my head. I reacted like a cowboy that had backed into a cattle prod by involuntarily redistributed the seeds about the dry rough ground. As I jerked my head back, I saw the dive-bomber. It was a magnificent barn owl settling itself with some pomp on the oak limb that supported my wood swing. The owl's regal and serious looking curved beak and prominent yellow eyes were no more than five feet from the end of my nose. The way the bird's gaze was fixed on me you'd have thought I was a field rat. I was a little surprised to see an owl this time of day. Every now and then, you'd catch one late in the evening about fifteen minutes before sunset, but rarely ever in the bright light of day did you see the predator at his work.

Rarity or not, I was now face to face with the biggest feathered creature I had seen in a while. And as the staring match continued something happened that I neither can explain nor, up until now, have told anyone about. If I had, I reckon probably with good reason, they would think I had been living out on the back section a bit too long with the cows.

You see this owl seemed to motion to me with its head. It would first look my way with one open eye and then the other. Then, I swear on things most holy, it would swivel its head as if requesting that I come a bit closer. The bird's behavior was so unusual that it took me a moment before I made the connection. Nevertheless, the owl was persistent. It continued the gesture until I finally got the message.

I took a couple of steps toward the bird, fully expecting the creature to fly off on my approach, but it didn't move. It just kept rotating its head back and forth. I got close enough that I swear it could have snatched a fly off the brim of my hat.

There was no way I could have understood the bird's behavior that day. Nonetheless, a year later and a thousand miles south of the Rio Grande, in the thick greenness that is the Mayan Selva of Chiapas, Mexico, I would finally begin to see the connection in the starkest of terms.

CHAPTER 1

POINTED SOUTH

THE TIRES OF DREW'S JEEP Wrangler vibrated violently as they rattled across the cattle-guard between the rocked corner posts of the ranch gate. The barrier guaranteed that the cattle stayed on the tall grass and off the highway that bordered the south end of the Running~Bar Ranch near Bulverde. Drew's hands mimicked the shake of the steering wheel and he tightened his grip.

As he cleared the gate, he took a look east, then quickly back to the west. All was clear. He pinned the gas pedal against the fire wall and all four drive wheels chewed at the loose pea gravel as his rig climbed noisily onto the pavement of Texas Ranch Road 1863.

The sun had warmed early for a spring morning and forced the haze to retreat. Drew's rig came up to speed and he rounded the first curve. He shifted into fourth gear and stuck his left arm out to fret with the oversize mirror. On the curve, the Kit Carson trailer angled back on the Jeep and he couldn't see around the fifteen feet of sheet metal. Just ahead he spotted road-kill growing in his path and decided to abandon the mirror adjustment.

As he approached the remains, Drew could see that it was a deer sprawled across most of the right lane. One leg with a hoof partially detached extended skyward in what appeared to be a misshapen plea for mercy. Drew slowed to give the on-coming traffic time to clear, but his timing was off and he was on top of the blood and guts before he wanted to be. At the last second, he jerked the steering wheel a quarter turn one way and then the other; he crossed the center-stripe and re-crossed it again. The trailer made known its protest. Drew squinted and tightened his shoulder muscles waiting for the consequences if he plowed into the heap of inanimate flesh. Luck held and the Jeep and trailer missed the remains.

Drew let out a whistle to signal relief. As he did he noticed a black crow pumping its wings heavily up ahead. The bird power-dived just above the mustang grape vines and settled itself on the five-strand barbwire fence along the road. The crow was the size of a red-tail hawk and just as graceful as it glided to a rendezvous with its shadow above the freshly planted Sudan hay field. As his eyes surveyed the land, Drew noted that the Running~Bar Ranch looked promisingly green for south Texas this time of year.

At the US 281 junction, he slowed his equipment to a crawl, not bothering to come to a full stop at the sign, as he crossed the two northbound lanes and the wide median and turned to head south. He veered back to the right and crossed the asphalt driveway at Luke's Grocery. His brakes squealed and bounced an echo off the outside row of pumps as they strained to stop the rig.

For a second Drew sat behind the wheel and thought about the near miss with the deer carcass. A small brown spider dropped off the visor and broke up his thought. Its flimsy lifeline yo-yoed the little critter eye to eye. Drew reacted like a turtle caught by a schoolboy and quickly tucked his head into his collar. The glutinous string stuck to his forefinger as he made a swipe at the filament but the spider ejected line faster than he could reel. The small creature hurriedly vanished between his boots under the front seat. Drew scraped the filament on his jeans and paid the critter no more mind.

He made a note in pencil of the odometer mileage on the edge of the Rand McNally Road Atlas & Trip Planner map he had torn out of the '89 edition. Somewhere near seventy-four thousand was the number he scratched in the margin. He'd had to splice the front of page 76 and the back of page 95 together to get the entire route for his trip. He had applied both pages to the green metal dash with duck tape. An orange highlighter traced the highway branches along the length of his predicted route to Chiapas, Mexico.

He noticed his cheap compass was still trying to find center. When Drew had bought it the little ball seemed like a bargain. The round bubble on a stand was only $2.39 at Albertson's on the auto supply rack. Soon after installing the gadget though, he noticed that hitting a pothole made the degree ball imitate a kid's top, becoming more gyroscope than compass. Under the erratic apparatus, Drew had placed a piece of carved ivory he figured was some kind of Buddha. Its stomach was shiny from rubbing. Its crude toes quoted the word happiness chiseled on the base. Drew had bonded both navigational aids in place with wood glue next to his radio with no knobs.

As he pumped unleaded into the rear tank, he watched the working mothers rush in and out of Luke's frantically trying to begin their day. After the tank had its fill, he stuck the nozzle into a plastic emergency red container with built-in pour spout and pumped another five gallons. He cinched the extra container to the roll bars with stretch rubber ties.

As he entered the store, Drew held the front door open for an oversized woman in a velour sweat suit. It was obvious, to him at least, that the outfit wasn't for aerobics, just comfort. Tiny cloth balls clung like little stars all over the blue fabric. The galaxy of those just above her right cheek, he figured, was formed from watching the soaps on a couch. She convoyed three kids with matching suits. They moved about like the Three Stooges, bouncing off display racks, a washtub full of ice and beer, and a stand full of the latest edition of the *Pick-Up Buyers Guide*. Finally the whole brood funneled out the door. He stood patiently thinking how grateful he was they didn't belong to him.

Drew poured a Styrofoam cup full of coffee and stirred in a half-packet of Sweet 'n Low. The plastic no-spill lid cracked as he snapped it on the cup so he tried another one, it cracked too. He noticed that the pot sitting on the back burner of the Bunn had coffee remains boiled to lava rock so he set it off and went to the counter to pay.

"Mornin' Debbie. My rig took $14.50 worth of unleaded. Got a small coffee too," he said as he moved his eyes over the girl at the counter while poking around in the front pocket of his jeans for change.

"That's $15.10 with the coffee. How you doin' Drew?"

He forced his gaze upward. "Fair to middlin. I think I have a dime in my pocket ... yeah, here's one ... kind of busy? Oh, I'll take one of these doughnuts too."

"$15.60. Not too bad, just normal for Friday. How's the midget Mexican doin'? Haven't seen Ruben lately."

Before Drew could answer and tell her the story of how Ruben lost two fingers between a rope and a saddle horn last Saturday night, a trucker wearing a tee shirt lettered *Meat: the Real Food*, shouted angrily at Debbie to turn on the diesel pump. Debbie gave him a screw-you buster kind of look and ignored the request for a few more seconds, hard staring all the while just to be mulish and make her point.

The distraction cleared her memory of her last question so Drew took the advantage and backed out the door with his coffee in one hand and a doughnut in the other. He stopped short at the back-end of the Jeep and took a long look across the highway at the southwest corner of the ranch while carefully sipping the hot liquid through the crack in the lid.

"It was for the most part a good three years," he said aloud, to himself.

As he took another sip, he could just make out Ruben's red Chevy dually cutting across the west pasture. Drew figured Ruben was checking for spring calves that the mamas were trying to hide in the cedar breaks and honey locust. They had had some good times on that ranch, that they had. The little Tex-Mex Indian had been a real friend. Nonetheless, Drew was glad it was Ruben's fingers that were lost and not his.

All Drew had lost in his stay at the ranch was a few cattle dogs, now planted randomly around the 3000 acres in shallow graves that showed no sign after the first rain. Some got themselves kicked to death by livestock and others were put-down by a .22 long rifle behind the ear when they either went crazy or got too old to work. The ranch was hard on dogs. Old age was not a common cause of death. He still had one of the best with him though, her head now extended out the back of the Jeep and her deep black eyes begged for an ear rub or a treat of some kind. Drew complied with the rub while he finished watching Ruben's quest across the highway and gnawed at the doughnut.

The early morning traffic on State Highway 281 was thick but moving steady. Damn good morning to head out, he decided. He redirected his gaze from where he had been to where he was going. The temperature was about 70 degrees and there was no sign of rain. The wind would be a problem though. Already it came in hard gusts out of the south and made him keep the bill of his baseball cap aimed downward.

The engine cranked and he stuck the cup between his legs and watched the needle on the oil pressure gauge creep up. Finally, it split the middle where the word normal had faded beyond recognition and Drew slipped the clutch to soften the shock as the first of the five gears completed the transfer of power to the wheels. The Jeep forced the trailer to follow and they rolled down Luke's blacktop driveway.

As the short trailer cleared the gas pumps, he pushed harder on the pedal. The extra weight tugged at the straight-six forcing it to struggle on the first hill but he didn't pay much attention. The noisy valve rattle of the engine was one of those nuisances that he had learned to accept. It was the price one paid for driving old cars. Without too much trouble the coupled rig melded in between a Wal-Mart 18 wheeler and a Comal County school bus with the words *Emergency Exit* painted in international orange on the rear door. A bumper sticker that read '*Save the Fire Ant*' was applied at an angle on the back of the bus. Drew figured it was a school kid's idea of funny.

The three vehicles crested the first hill together and accelerated in harmony into the Cibolo Valley below. The muddy creek, swollen with the recent rains, barely caught his notice as he and his cattle dog passed over the bridge. They were only twenty-five minutes north of downtown San Antonio, burning daylight on a southerly course that would take this middle-aged, down on his luck cowboy, on the adventure of his life.

Drew looked into the rear-view mirror at Chica hanging out the back and wondered what the little dog was thinking. He also wondered if she sensed that they were not coming back to the Running~Bar Ranch.

WARMNESS OF A BLIZZARD

DREW HAD BEEN RIGHT. The head wind was a problem. It dogged his consciousness as it resisted the torque of the engine at the same time. The Jeep's speedometer kept a running account of the struggle but never made it above sixty. It would display forty up and sixty down the undulating dry land swells of south Texas and somewhere in between on the flats.

He kept hearing engine noises, strange ones. They came in no particular order and obligated him to constantly monitor the oil gauge. Normal, it always indicated normal. Drew didn't believe it so he repeatedly tapped the glass with his knuckle, beseeching the truth. The gauge never budged. It appeared to be stuck on normal.

The upshot was that the driver carried a traveler's paranoia along every mile. He mentally visualized the inside of the old engine churning not three feet in front of him like the cut-a-ways they did on the TV commercials; cracked pistons, worn out rings, all held together by carbon buildup is what he conjured. The mechanical whole would most likely vomit its metallic guts along some Interstate, or worse, some jungle trail he thought. Nevertheless, Drew pressed on, choosing to ignore the odds.

The city limits sign at George West interrupted the mental fog and made him realize he had already covered three hours of road surface. His eyes again cut to the rearview mirror to check on his compañera. His dog, stretched out on her side next to his duffel bag, had one leg awkwardly pushed through the bag's strap-handle. Now there is God's definition of peace he thought. The duffel, an Arctic Dream sleeping bag and a Coleman stove, were the only luggage in the back. The dog had plenty of room and a good ride.

"How about a treat?" Drew shouted over the rattle of the loose gravel against the Jeep's under belly.

Chica jerked her head off the green carpet remnant; both ears straightened to a point. The tires fabricated dust devils as they rolled along the shoulder in front of the big red sign. Chica stuck her head between the front seats to check it out, her white tipped tail swinging from side to side in a dog's anticipation.

Drew looked at his dog and thought how ugly she was, ugly as a mouth full of green teeth. But Chica knew how to travel and was steady and he admired her for it. During the last year, he had taken his cow dog everywhere with him. Put traveling handles on the dog as Ruben would call it. Now she was like a four-legged accessory, indispensable, and if not in the Jeep then she was trailing Drew just to his left and slightly behind.

"Watch the rig girl," he said as he walked away toward the drive-in.

He had positioned the driver's side under the shade of the Dairy Queen sign and set the parking brake. DQ's were good places. Gave him a chance to take a break from the highway and check out the locals. Mostly high school girls and sorghum farmers. It was too early in the season for the tourists to be coming through on the way to the third coast. The counter girls were usually nothing to look at either, but the ice cream was the best. He settled in a front booth with a Blizzard sprinkled with M&Ms, Drew's favorite. From the front, he could watch his rig and eat with a commodious separation from the buzz around the order counter.

Drew poked his spoon into the soft cream and came out with twice its potential. The journey from cup to mouth was quick. He did not want the overload in his lap. As his cheeks spread to accommodate the ice cream, he started to count the little pieces of candy that made the crunch, turning it with his spoon to stir the bits up from the bottom.

"Hi, is that Jeep parked out by the sign yours?"

The unexpected voice gave him a start and made his head turn with a snap. Drew spoke before he was ready and sputtered the words through the cream.

"Yeah, it is." A portion of the hard candy popped out of his mouth and stuck to the table, hanging on the edge.

"What kind of dog is that? She's mighty cute," the stranger said pretending not to notice the wayward remnant.

Drew force swallowed the lump of cold cream and candy and it burned his throat. The sudden jolt triggered a memory of a kid sucking on a big cube of ice in the back seat of the family Chevy headed to Sulfur Springs to see his uncle Ernest with his folks. He had laughed too hard at a stupid joke his daddy told him and swallowed the jagged chunk. It wedged stubbornly in his throat and he damn near choked to death before it melted. The pain was the same as now, and the burn had lasted two days he recalled.

"She's a cow dog," he said. His vocal cords already hurt. This woman must want something, he figured, why else would she call his dog cute. He could feel the extra blood in his face and he wished the piece of candy would fall off the damn table.

Drew noted that the woman was short, maybe 5 foot 2. Out of habit, he tried to look around her to see if she was alone. He couldn't tell.

"I like dogs like that a lot," she continued. "A friend of mine had a cow dog once, but he didn't know what to do with it. He kept him chained in the back of his pickup. Rain or shine in the back of that pickup. I always thought what a poor existence for a proud working animal."

The woman shifted her weight. Her Wrangler jeans clung to her hips and rounded up to a narrow waist. She wore a conch belt. It

13

looked like real silver. Since the belt was at eye level, he studied the design. Drew had seen similar in Santa Fe.

"That so?" he responded keeping his gaze on the buckle. Drew wasn't too happy about his throat.

He decided he had better stop staring and diverted his eyes toward his rig. Chica perched on the top of the outside spare tire returned his attention. She was suspicious of strangers and he could tell by her look that she had taken note of the woman.

"I'm from Canton. Well really from Lancaster, but my parents live in Canton. Where are you from?" Without invitation she slid into the other side of the booth and balanced her body on the edge of the bench-seat only half behind the table.

"Just up the road north of San Antone."

"My name's Ree. Ree Taylor." She began to extend her hand but seemed to think better of it and pushed it timidly back under the table.

"Hello, I am Andrew Grady Cotton," he said formally while anchoring the spoon in the cream and extended his hand.

"Where you headed, Mr. Cotton?" she asked, but her voice wavered through a pronounced hoarseness. Her hand reappeared and gladly responded to his offer.

"The valley," he said. "People call me Drew."

He looked at his dog again. She was still watching the same way she kept her eyes fixed on a cow moving across her territory. Watching but not moving unless the animal crossed some boundary only she recognized. Most times the beast understood and paid tribute to the limits and the world remained calm.

"You wouldn't be going to McAllen would you Mr. Cotton?"

"As a matter of fact, I am," he said. Drew uttered the words before reason could take hold of his tongue. He quickly realized that he had missed a chance to lie and regretted it.

"Mister I know you don't know me but I sure could use a ride to McAllen."

Drew took a moment before answering and took another bite of the Blizzard. He shifted nervously on the bench while he moved the coldness around in his mouth trying to decide when to swallow. She was not bad looking he thought, so he rechecked the inside of the Dairy Queen. For what or who he wasn't sure. He was just not comfortable; a girl that damn pretty is not just stranded. There has to be a story.

"Go ask my dog," finally he said, with a quick nod toward the Jeep. "If she takes to you, I'll give you a ride." Drew hid his uneasy partial grin under a bushy mustache.

Without hesitation the woman got up, walked out the front door, and took deliberate long steps toward the Jeep. As she moved away, Drew got his first good look at the entire package. His spoon scraped the last of the ice cream off the bottom of the cup and he licked at the plastic while he studied the subject. She had long hair tied back in a single brown braid. Around twenty-five, maybe thirty, he guessed. What the hell am I doing he thought as he licked the spoon that now tasted more like plastic than ice cream. He stuffed it along with all the dirty napkins into the empty cup, using his index finger to flip the candy remnant off the edge of the table.

On his way out, Drew waved and smiled at the ugly counter girl which was his habit. He wiped at the front of his beard with a paper napkin. The ugly counter girl smiled back. Drew turned and pushed through the double glass doors flipping the last napkin in a relaxed arch toward the waste barrel; two points he whispered. It was time to get on to Mexico with a quick stop in McAllen. He hoped the unexpected passenger wasn't a chatterbox.

CHAPTER 2
DARK

HARD MINUTES HAD PASSED since Buddy had violently slammed the screen-door on his way out of the next-to-last frame house on Cherry Way Street. The anger in the powerful man had magnified his force so that the doorframe separated from the jamb. Only partly freed but crippled, the wood swung back and forth by a single hinge taunted and pushed about erratically by the wind that came in hot gusts from the south—gusts that toyed with anything loose on the front porch.

Just inside the front room, Ree lay face down in the brown carpet. She hadn't moved since Buddy splintered the door. Blood trickling from her nose had formed a small dry lake in the dirty shag while she listened to the rhythmic beating of the screen door against the outside wall. Each slap produced a resonant wave through the floor that reached her ear as a muffled thud. The vibration was slight but annoying, like a call for help from one broken thing to another.

Ree's pain martyred her in-place. She used the time to stare at the blood on the matted carpet, to focus on the tiny details seldom seen at this level. The fine dirt, more like powder, clung at the base of the carpet fibers; dirt that mocked the sucking power of the Hoover. And, look at this she thought, a straight pin lost in a long ago sewing task waiting to ambush a bare foot.

After a while, the pain began to yield slightly. Ree wanted to get up. Slowly and deliberately, she flexed her back and thigh muscles and pushed up on all fours. Her knees gave some stability and she shuffled in syncopated sidesteps that moved her rear-end on a pivot until her head pointed towards the wicker rocker in the corner.

That dark corner was her favorite place in the clapboard house: the corner with the rocker. The meeting of the walls is where she watched the neighborhood from the double frame windows that looked out onto the street. Activities along its length were mostly slow, just old people lived here now. They stayed inside mostly and to themselves. Except Ree had noticed how a car moving slow down the street seemed to always trigger a rash of separated Venetian blinds in sequence with the progress of the vehicle. Blue jays intimidating the squirrels and the cardinals normally provided the entertainment. That was all right. It is where she did her thinking, her deciding.

18

The rocker frame was made of dark mahogany, stained and hand-rubbed almost black, thick and heavy. The wicker, tightly woven in small delicate hexagon patterns still held up. The original workmanship had fought off the years, so far.

Ree sat for long spells in the rocker, usually when Buddy had gone off to work or was out with the guys. She enjoyed putting her hands in the worn spots on the arms. They fit perfectly. There was a natural place for her to position her hands on the worn spots. Weaver had worn these places on the arms. The old man spent every night of the last days of his life in the rocker. Ree liked to think about their arms being the same length. It was a way to keep the connection with her grandfather.

She especially liked the story he told about the rocker. Weaver had carried it home on the bus, brand new. He did not get a scratch on it even though the coloreds had to climb around the chair to get to the back seats. He bought it on impulse in the 30's at the pinnacle of the depression years. It was to be a gift for Mama. Three dollars and a quarter it cost. A fortune then according to the stories he told about that time in Texas.

"I made ten dollars a week back then," he had said. "Ten for the week at Simmons Mattress Co. Them was damn good wages too."

But Mama never used the luxury. She was too busy with the house to sit, she would say. The house, the cooking, the grand kids were Mama's life, not sitting. Weaver liked to chide Mama about it.

"Come on woman take a rest in the chair," he'd say after the evening feed. "I've kept it warm for you." She never did.

But Ree did, especially when she hurt. Like now. She felt the old man's presence through the arms. The tears signaled the link.

19

Not crying tears, but remembering tears—the ones that glazed the eyes but didn't run down the cheek.

Stiffly Ree eased back against the upright, against the perfect angle. *Weaver I need to lean against you. Help me, just this once.*

She called out for a wisdom that would tell her what to do. That was Weaver's strength. In Ree's eyes he always knew what to do. She had learned to appreciate the old man's wisdom in her late teens shortly before he died. Eighty years on this earth helps a few to see things clearly. Sometimes they just sat together. Ree never noticed a slowing of his mind. Not even on the last day he spent on this earth. His body moved inexorably toward the end time but his mind never changed.

His clear blue eyes, as much as his words, were the gateway. Ree never had forgotten the light they cast, the brightness they shown. She never ceased to see their spiritual health. Weaver's words, particularly the advice, were vital to her but always secondary to his eyes, which portrayed truth without words.

She recalled now her last question of the old man. She was standing behind Mama's rocker brushing his thick white hair with her fingers before supper.

"Weaver, do you think I should be a nurse?" she asked abruptly.

His response came in-kind with no hesitation. He merely raised his head and folded over the newspaper. Ree had the sense that he had anticipated her question, had given long thought to his response even before being asked.

"Ree darlin', I think you should be many things and a nurse is one of them. You are meant to care for others."

That's all he said. She did not press for more and Weaver never volunteered to explain. His answer had always been a puzzle. Not the part about being a nurse or caring for others, but the part *you should be many things.*

HUSH DOG

THE CARPET ODOR LINGERED in Ree's nostrils making her slightly nauseous. She pressed her chin to her chest and looked at the front of her shirt. The head of the embroidered white horse was deep magenta.

Another hour passed. Her mind came full circle and returned to the pain of the body. In small increments, Ree gave in to it, enough to clear her thoughts, enough to help her decide. *What to do now.*

These small impulses, messengers that joined the body to the mind, underlined her thoughts, her logic, highlighting the practical, and the doable. Occasionally the intense bark of Buddy's pit bull pushed through her shell. Like the random beat of the door, the barking became a variable to be factored.

The dog, tied to his 20-foot length of chain in the back yard near the trashcans, became Buddy's advocate in Ree's debate. Savage barked at anything that moved so his contribution was frequent.

Ree rocked, listened to the messages from the back yard, watched the door rotate in the wind and thought. The rocking was slow and steady, effortless. Back and forth, back and forth. There was no urgency in it. She only had to move her toes slightly. The chair did the rest. It soothed.

The more she traveled back and forth in the short little arcs, the safer she felt. This time in her life seemed less real, less important.

"Weaver I have another question." she whispered to herself.

Nervous

A NEW NOISE JOLTED REE. It rang again. She jumped but the soreness assaulted her muscles and took her breath. Reflexively she bit down on her bottom lip and settled back against the chair. The ringing would not stop and it made the door bang louder. Each long jangle seemed to form a raucous chorus with the door and the backyard dog.

Finally, Ree made the effort. It took four more rings to reach the phone.

"Hello."

"Hi honey, what are you doing? Did I get you out of the shower? The phone rang for an eternity."

Ree studied herself in the mirror that hung over the table in the hall. A thin red veneer covered her nose, mouth and chin. Her hair was matted and stuck out like the nap on the shag carpet. One puffy eye peeked back from the reflection. Ree cringed at what she saw and turned around to face the opening in the hall.

I can watch the front door from here.

"Ree, you still there honey?"

"Hello Mom," she answered in a monotone.

"What time are you coming over in the morning honey? Father is going to be working in the yard most of the day. He wants to get down the lawn food before the rains dry up. I thought we could go into town and get lunch. You know you can really help me look through the new pillow patterns at Stitches. They have so many new ones. I already have the material, it's a chintz. You'll just simply love the design; it almost matches the drapes in the living room... Ree?"

"Mom, I'll call you back in a minute."

"Ree. There is something wrong, isn't there honey? You don't sound like yourself. Ree are you all right? Is it Buddy again?"

"Mom!"

"Ree, when are you going to listen? You know what your father told you. "

"Mom! Please! I'll call you back in a minute." Ree lowered the receiver.

"Ree? Honey!" the voice fell silent with the click.

Ree moaned softly as she tugged the stained shirt over her head and maneuvered down the hall to the bath. The tight jeans took more effort. She sat down on the toilet lid and weakly pushed the right pants-leg over her calf. Her left foot resisted her effort and she became entangled in the denim fabric. Ree stopped struggling and let the one leg stay in the jeans. She folded at the waist and lowered her face into her hands. The damage went deep this time, she felt exhausted to the soul.

Why am I doing this? she thought as the sobs, coming without noise, were muffled by wet fingers. The salt tears ran down her forearm and dripped off her elbows. The water trickled through her toes. It tickled.

When Ree finally made it to the shower her head directed the warm streams in cascades down her body. It was therapy, the best kind. She stood there for fifteen minutes barely moving. Then the hot-water heater reached its limits and began to offer tepid streams. Then cool.

The last thing she wanted was to be cold. She flipped the little plunger and turned the valves. She slid a white cotton towel through the rack and stepped out onto the mat.

From somewhere outside, she heard a car door slam. Quickly Ree wiped the mirror with the towel until she could see herself. She looked like a soft focus studio portrait filtered by the water vapor, prettier than she really was. Her nose was red but OK. The worst was still the swollen eye. She finished drying her smooth skin.

God I hope that's not Dorothy, she thought.

Suddenly Ree became aware that the screen-door had gone quiet. Then she heard heavy steps in the hall.

"Ree" the voice penetrated the wall and bathroom door. It was soft, slightly feeble.

"Ree, I'm sorry honey. Are you all right? Guess I got a little carried away, huh? ... I'm sorry, are you OK? ... Ree, you just made me mad. You know my temper. Come on out and we'll talk a while, before I have to go to work ... OK? ..."

Ree just watched the door and tried not to speak or scream.

Why am I doing this?

She had checked out the books from the Dallas County Woman and Children's Resource Center. She read the theories, the psychological jargon, and the criteria of abuse. The why. The reasons. The explanations derived coldly after the fact.

Low self-esteem; inability to express anger; jealously; substance abuse; stereotypical thinking; denial; lack of impulse control. After the third beating, Ree realized that Buddy was the model for that profile.

"Damn Ree, say something!" Buddy let his growing impatience show through his voice.

Ree likewise saw herself in the literature.

24

Wants the relationship to work; stereotypical feminine role of inferiority and passivity; low self-esteem; isolation; fear of physical harm or death as a consequence of getting out.

She looked at the door and wished it were made of bricks. Solid, unyielding, a fortress. *The stupid thing didn't even have a lock.*

Old houses never had locks on the bathroom. Ree wondered *if privacy was not necessary in Weaver's time. Or maybe, you did not have to guarantee it with locks.*

She turned and leaned against the door with her back. She pulled the wrapped towel tighter and tucked the loose end under her arm. Her lips began to quiver uncontrollably.

Why don't I do something?

Ree had figured this one out too.

Fear of the unknown. Fear of consequences.

"Buddy," her voice cracked, the normal hoarseness of it deepened when she got emotional. "Buddy, please leave me alone. I need some time, you hurt me."

"Ree, I said I was sorry. You know I didn't mean it. Why don't you ever see my side? Ree come on out, I need to see that you're OK"

"Buddy just go to work. We'll talk tomorrow."

"Now! We can talk now. Shit, Greg ain't going to be here for another hour-and-a-half. Let's settle this thing now. Come on, open the door."

Buddy put his hand on the doorknob but didn't turn it.

"Ree, I promise I'll make things different. You know the pressure I've been under. For Christ sake! None of us know about our jobs with all the layoffs. I just get upset that I can't give us more than we have."

25

"Buddy, it's all right. We'll talk later, OK?"

"Ree, I want to talk about us getting married. I think that's part of our problem. What about it? Ree, come on, let's talk."

The plea didn't work. Usually Ree felt sorry for Buddy. Especially when he said, he was sorry. *I'm sorry* made her feel responsible for what had happened, responsible for his anger. If only she would try a little harder things would change.

The violence shook something loose this time, rearranged some little something, changed the cause and effect. A message, a sign, a bit of power, a cleared vision. Ree wasn't sure what was in her.

Now the boots moved away, down the hall, away from the door. The sound went towards the bedroom. *Oh, please make him leave me alone, please God. Just a little time, just this day.*

The house was quiet. Only faint noises came from the direction of the front of the house. Ree heard Buddy rummaging in the chest-of-drawers.

From her stronghold, she thought about that chest. She had bought it, and the bed, both made of cherry wood, last year with her Christmas bonus money. She loved the *Lillian Day* furniture. It was so elegant, solid. The kind of furniture that is passed along to the children; that link families. Like the rocker. Then Ree remembered how mad Buddy had been when Haverty's delivered it.

"You spent all the bonus on a bunch of sticks," he had yelled. He was drunk again. He had been for two days before New Years and a day after. It was the second time he beat her. It was his New Year's Day gift.

She remembered that night, lying in the bed and just looking at the chest. Buddy had gone out with some guys from work. *Why did I buy such a good piece of furniture?*

Then the boots marched back from the bedroom. Again, they were outside the bathroom door. For a few hard moments, there was nothing but silence.

"Ree, I'm coming in!" Buddy turned the doorknob but felt the obstacle behind the door and didn't push very hard at first. Just enough so that Ree reacted, setting her bare feet against the linoleum floor. Her toes curled, blood showing at the joints, trying to get a grip.

"Ree, goddamn to hell, why are you being so damn stubborn ... I said I was sorry; Jesus fucking Christ Ree!" The words came slow, chopped into brittle pieces.

Every muscle in her body constricted violently to Buddy's tone. She knew that tone. When he couldn't get his way, after his brooding ended, his voice took the edge that warned explosion. Like a smoke detector. Danger!

An uncommon memory forced Ree to desperately scan the bathroom, her refuge now a trap. No phone, no exit, no hope. She looked from the small window to the mirror, begging silently for help. But the image was now an animal, a deer caught in the headlights of a car. Or maybe this time a train. The eyes reflecting the light, disengaging mind and muscle, joining unthinking, hard metal to soft flesh. The final collision guaranteed.

Buddy's power swung the door into the bathroom. Toes as foundation gave up easily to his force and her bare feet scooted across the wet floor and went horizontal. She folded up like a jack-knife landing on her butt. Meeting the floor took her breath. The scream was in Ree but there was no air to vibrate the vocal chords.

Buddy stood over her for long seconds, looking down. She didn't try to meet his gaze. The triumph would be there, she knew.

His will and strength captured in a self-satisfied half-smile. She felt cold air on her skin as the towel jerked away. She tightened into a ball to stay warm. The curve of the commode between base and bowl cradled her head.

Buddy bent down over Ree and put the black Glock .40-caliber pistol to her head. The floor felt strangely warm and comfortable. In the back yard, Ree could hear Savage barking, continuing the debate.

Mortality's Call

As usual, Greg picked Buddy up at the curb for work. Ree was still sprawled crossways on the bed with the covers tangled around her shoulders. She had not moved for almost an hour while Buddy took a shower and got ready. She stared at the brass ceiling fan rotating slowly directly above.

Ree remembered buying the fan at a sidewalk clearance sale at Wal-Mart. It was on a Saturday morning right after they moved in together. One of Buddy's friends said it would help move the air in their old house that didn't have air-conditioning.

The blades turned slow. The cheap motor rattled too much on medium or high. Ree could see the accumulated dust on the leading edge as the blades rotated like carousel horses. The fake brass plating was flaking off in irregular chunks exposing the extruded plastic. It had cost $49.95 unassembled, marked down from $99.95.

The phone rang again four times before Ree made herself roll over and get up. There were small patches of a white crust on her shoulders and on her thighs. She felt dirty. She shuffled to the bathroom, ignoring the phone.

It took forty-five minutes to bathe and dress, loose braid her hair, smooth away the hardness around her eyes with *Clinique* powder and pack a small black canvas tote bag.

The bag had both straps and a handle. In it she stuffed two extra pair of jeans, two blouses, three tee shirts, her shorts, tennis shoes and a small make-up bag. Without thought, she slipped into an outside pouch the small first aid kit that she liked to carry. It was a habit she developed in nursing school.

In an ashtray in the top drawer of the dresser, she found the keys to Buddy's truck. Next to the ash tray, slid under Buddy's jockey shorts, was the ugly pistol. Ree covered it up and sat on the edge of the bed. She deliberately dumped her purse out and counted the cash, two hundred and ten bucks and change. One of the quarters had red nail polish on it. It had come out of the bill changer at the Suds & Scrub Laundromat next to Fuddruckers downtown. Ree put it in the little coin pocket of a fake alligator wallet. The wallet, along with her ATT calling card, her Visa and Buddy's Mobil credit card went back into the small leather purse.

Ree slipped the tote bag strap over her head letting the bag swing around and rest on her hip. Then she grabbed the keys and her purse and walked to the door of the bedroom that opened to the living room. Before she reached the front door she stopped, looking straight ahead, standing still.

Ree turned her head and looked at the rocker for a moment. She then spun on the hardwood floor and went back to the bedroom. Again, she stopped just for a moment in front of the chest-of-drawers. She slid the top-drawer open. Without looking, she reached under the cotton jocks and put her hand around the pistol. Ree pulled it in front of her feeling its weight. She unzipped her purse and let the gun fall from her fingers in among the jumble.

Ree walked out the front door and shut it behind her without bothering to set the dead bolt. Buddy had pulled the screen door off the bottom hinge before he left for work so it now stood against the wall. He'd probably fix it tomorrow she thought. *The Dallas Morning News* hid down in the tall Bermuda grass in the yard. Ree tossed it towards the front door. The rubber band broke but she didn't notice.

Savage began to bark as Ree's shadow moved ahead of her down the side of the house toward the back yard. The squeaky gate drew the dog's attention and Ree walked to just outside of the range of Savage's chain. She stood there staring at the dog as it barked and lunged forcefully against the restraint.

Buddy had bought the pit bull over a year ago and still the dog barked at Ree. When they first got him, Buddy had let Savage roam the back yard.

"By God no one's gonna come in this yard," Buddy has told old man Ferguson who lived next door.

Savage's freedom lasted all of two days. Until right after the Lancaster police were forced to rescue the little man who read the gas meter. He had been marooned on top of the tool shed for two hours. But he was lucky. At least he had made it out of the dog's range. The gas company said they wouldn't read the meter unless the dog was restrained.

Ree had begged Buddy to give Savage away.

Buddy said she was crazy. "I'm not going to give a $250 dog away. Hell, I'll just tie him up until I have a chance to train him," is how his logic went.

I'll just tie him up. For a year now, waiting for training, Savage spent day and night lying at the end of the force greater than he was. To Ree's way of thinking that just made the dog more dangerous.

Ree often watched Savage from the kitchen window. So much power and anger at the end of a tether she thought. Her feelings went from disgust to sympathy. *Why do men manipulate nature to create these things?*

When Ree reached into her purse and came out with the pistol, Savage strangely calmed. He moved his head from side to side at rotating angles, displaying curiosity. Ree held the gun sideways and wondered if it was ready to fire. She had never fired a gun in her life, but she had seen it done many times on TV. Characters, good and bad, holding the gun steady with their opposite hand, feet spread for balance. Eyes serenely focused on a target. Then, shooting with no thought, no hesitation, and afterward, no obvious remorse.

Was it really that easy, that clean? She stiffened her arm straight with the gun and aimed it at the dog's square head. Her finger found the opening in the trigger guard and embraced the metal lever protruding from the gun's body.

Savage split the sight. *It is easy.* The dog watched, graciously not moving.

"It's for your own good," Ree said softly; the words came back to her ears hollow and void as soon as she spoke them. She moved the site to the middle of the massive ridge of bone over the eyes. Savage tried to wag his stub of a tail. He obviously liked the attention.

31

With increasing pressure, her finger pressed on the trigger. She wondered at what point the explosion would occur. Ree braced for the recoil and hoped it wouldn't hurt. But the trigger wouldn't move. Ree pulled harder but nothing. A quick look at the gun offered no clue. It just would not fire.

Ree turned her back to Savage and let out a long breath. She jammed the pistol back into her purse and turned around. Savage calmly watched her.

Ree took the dog's lead from the oak tree where Buddy kept it and snapped the quick release to the dog's choke collar. Savage sensed with enthusiasm that his restraint was not as permanent as the tree. The exuberant dog led Ree forcefully to Buddy's truck.

As always, when he got near Buddy's black Ford pickup he jumped in the back. The dog lived to ride in the truck, to ride and bark. First one side then the other, barking at the world as it moved quickly past. Ree snapped the dog's lead securely to the metal eyehook bolted to the chrome rail on the right side of the truck bed.

FINITENESS

IT WAS ALMOST 3:30 IN THE AFTERNOON when Ree pulled into the parking lot of the Gibson Veterinarian clinic just off IH 35. There was one truck in the parking lot pulled to the farthest corner. When Savage sensed their direction, he again powerfully dragged Ree to the front door. The dog was hyper. His underused muscles needed exercise. They crashed in tandem through the door and into the waiting room.

There was a faint smell of urine; a fact that Savage sensed immediately. The dog raised a leg and pissed on the end of the coffee table. Ree made no effort to stop or scold the dog.

Strewn haphazardly on every flat surface were stacks of pet magazines. Bags of Science Diet dog rations leaned against the walls along the baseboards and protruded from what was once a coat closet with a bi-fold door that was now permanently open.

On the back wall, there were a few certificates and diplomas. All the frames tilted at opposite angles. Next to the frames was a small bulletin board covered with ads and notices for lost pets. Many were family pictures taken at picnics or bird hunts. Ree stood in front of the board reading. She wondered how many of the animals were now dead meat in some kind of medical research program. Had their hearts preserved in a beaker for the good of science.

A voice interrupted her thoughts. It was lively, cheerful and came somewhere from the back, "I'll be with you in a minute."

Ree stood stiffly with Savage straining at the lead. He nervously continued to smell the bags and what must have been traces of territorial marks sprayed by other males. Doing this work required Savage to circle, first one way and then the other around Ree's legs. Savage entangled the leash like a kid around a Maypole.

"Hi, I'm Doc Gibson, what can I do for you?" the vet was dressed in Levis and a dirty white cowboy shirt. His boots were caked with dried mud that looked permanent.

"Got a problem with your dog?" the vet offered a big smile but kept his eyes focused on Savage who returned the glare. Ree ran her hand down the lead and tightened her grip. She set her eyes on the doctor, "Do you put dogs to sleep?"

Gibson looked quickly up to Ree and then back to the dog, he seemed not to be ready for such a request. "Ah...well yes I do. What's the problem?"

There was no hesitation, "I would like this dog put to sleep."

"Has he hurt someone? I know pit bulls can be a little unpredictable..." he kept shuffling his gaze between Savage and Ree.

"Yes he has," Ree stretched the truth but didn't waver, "I want him put to sleep," she said forcefully.

"Possibly you would like to leave the dog for a few days for observation?"

Ree ignored the vet's argument for a reprieve.

"No, thank you, I want to do it now. Please, I'm in a hurry."

Doc Gibson changed his expression. The smile disappeared. "Well alright, can you follow me, please?"

The procession moved down the hall and turned into a small cramped treatment room. It had a waist high stainless steel table and a bright light. The shade of the light was covered with dust. Gibson reached in the drawer and fumbled through a hodge-podge of utensils, medicine samples, stirring the mixture like a stew. Finally, he produced the object of his search, a well-worn brown leather muzzle.

"Think we can get him to accept this?" Ree nodded and grabbed Savage under the collar. Doc Gibson talked to the dog in soft slow tones.

"You know, the only dog that ever bit me was a chow. A black chow with one eye. The owner said he wouldn't harm a flea. See this scar. Pretty bad dog wouldn't you agree? Name was Jack." Ree didn't look at his hand and the vet gave up the small talk.

34

"We need to lift him up on the table. Hold his head steady so he won't turn on me. Now, you may wait outside."

"No, I'll stay."

"OK... if you wish ... shouldn't take long."

Ree watched the syringe fill with red liquid. It was a deep strawberry color. Gibson squirted a few drops of the heart-stopping drug and lightly tapped the syringe body with his index finger. Savage dripped saliva from his extended tongue. The vet turned to the pit bull and grabbed a small amount of hide just below the dog's oversize shoulders. He looked at Ree to give her a final chance to do something besides kill the dog. She just glared at Savage.

Gibson put the needle slowly just underneath the skin probing for a vein. He drew a small amount of blood back into the syringe. Ree's eyes followed the plunger as it pushed the liquid steadily into Savage.

An instant before the energy flowed out of the dog; Ree reached out and put her hand on his head. The dog's eyes hollowed and the nervousness of his massive body changed to dead weight. The metal table supported the melting animal as his head flowed over the edge.

The vet put a small mirror in front of the dog's mouth and waited a few seconds. He looked up at Ree, "What do you want me to do with...what was the dogs name?"

"Buddy," she answered still with her hand on its head. She raised her eyes to Doc Gibson, "Can you take care of it for me?"

"Sure."

"How much do I owe you?"

"Thirty bucks. I'll write you a receipt."

THE FORD PICKUP MOVED QUICKLY onto the IH 35 entrance ramp and joined traffic blending with the commuters making their way slowly out of the metroplex. In a few minutes, Ree passed the Owens-Corning plant. She alternated her glances between the strange building with the black inverted scoop on the roof and the bumper 10 feet in front of the pick-up. Frequently her eyes darted to the rearview mirror to gage the distance of the white diesel pushing her south. All she could see was chrome grill works. Ree used quick taps of the brake pedal to back the trucker off.

As she drove by the plant, Ree could feel Buddy watching her from the huge doors of the loading dock. She imagined that her fate would make him raise his eyes to the highway just at the moment she passed. It would have him see her in his truck and he would instantly know she had left him, had taken his gun, and had killed his dog.

She was afraid to look toward the factory. She didn't want to see Buddy racing to Greg's truck in the parking lot intent on catching her. She quickly opened the glove box and glanced at the gun. *I'll get someone to show me how to shoot,* she thought.

The traffic moved with incredible agility down the interstate toward the series of exit ramps from Red Oak to Waco. As Ree passed each exit, sanity gradually retook the highway. By the time she had passed the signs for Bardwell and Italy she was able to relax her shoulders a bit.

The rearview mirror gave her some relief too. There was no sign of Buddy and there were at least twenty-feet between each car. She had time to notice the sign in the right-of-way a quarter mile ahead. Typical Texas chamber of commerce, she thought. *Milton, home of 457 friendly people and 1 old grouch.* Ree found herself thinking about the one old grouch—probably the only one worth meeting.

Austin 174

Hillsboro 34

As she drove, Ree took notice of the central Texas prairie. Already the spring corn, hay and cotton crops were well along. She felt relaxed. With her right hand, she changed the angle on the rearview mirror to see her face. The swelling had mostly disappeared. She liked her hair pulled back in the braid. It gave her face prominence. It looked OK. She would be OK.

The green interstate sign read Exit 242 to Hillsboro. Ree headed the truck down the ramp and pulled into the Mobil station; one of the few still offering full services.

"Yes ma'am, can I hep ya?" the attendant greeted Ree with a big grin. He was a young lanky kid so tall that Ree had to pivot her head unnaturally back on her shoulders to meet his eyes. The movement caused a flash of pain but she smiled anyway.

"Fill the tank and check the oil please. Do you have a phone?"

"Yes ma'am. On the back wall by the map rack."

"Could you also check the air in the tires for me?" The kid nodded without looking up.

"Hello." Ree hated her mother's voice.

"Hello Mom. It's Ree." She said as she turned and rested her back against the map-rack looking through the station's grimy plate glass window. The kid giant had his long frame halfway under the hood of the pick-up but amazingly, his feet were still flat on the pavement.

"Ree? Where are you? I have been calling you for hours! Are you all right?"

"Yes Mom, I'm OK."

"Where are you?" Dorothy repeated.

"Mom I need you to listen to me for a minute," Ree's voice was calm but forceful. "I want to..."

Dorothy's nervousness forced the woman to break in. "Honey, where are you? Your father and I have been so worried."

Ree put an edge on her tone, "Mom, just listen, please. For once just listen."

Ree's tone caught Dorothy by surprise. "Sure, OK, honey."

"Buddy and I have had a fight. A bad fight. I need to get away for a few days. I've taken Buddy's truck."

Ree was not sure how much to tell her Mom. It didn't matter that Dorothy disliked Buddy because she would eventually tell him anything he wanted to know. Ree suspected that both her mother and father were frightened of him.

"I'm going to see a friend for the last few days of my vacation. It's a girl I went to nursing school with." Ree stopped short of saying where.

"Well ... Are you alright, honey?"

"Mom, I'm fine, really. Don't worry. Please don't worry. When Buddy calls just tell him what I have told you. He's going to be very upset. Especially about me taking his truck. But don't let him scare you. OK?" Ree didn't wait for Dorothy's response.

"Just tell him I said he would get his truck back. Nothing more. Do you understand what I'm asking you to do?" she waited.

Ree turned back around and looked at the rack of maps haphazardly arranged on dingy metal shelves. Texas, New Mexico, Arizona, Oklahoma, Dallas-Fort Worth Metroplex, Mexico. "Mom?"

"Sure, honey, I understand, but...but, I think you need to talk to your father." When Dorothy got confused, she always wanted Horace to take over. Horace was a quiet man. A gentle man who practiced the philosophy of live and let live. He spent his time, now that he had retired, tending to an immaculate yard and garden. Occasionally he'd fix a broken piece of furniture or an antique for the widows around Canton. He and Dorothy had lived in Canton for the last 40 years.

"Let me go out to the shop and get him, hold-on." Dorothy said.

"Mom! ... Mom! No! I don't have time now. I'll call you back when I get to my friend's house."

"Ree, at least give us a number where we can reach you."

"Mom, I'll call you when I get to where I am going, don't worry. Oh! If Buddy asks, you about Savage just say you don't know. Understand?"

"Where is Savage, with you?"

"Mom, don't worry. I've got to go now."

"Honey, please be careful. Ree I'm worried about you."

"Mom, don't...I've got to go. Call you soon. Bye." Ree didn't wait. She hung up and went into the ladies room.

When she came out the giant was standing by the register wiping his hands with a red rag. "That'll be $18.42. Do you save *Fill'em Up Stamps* lady?"

"No. Put it on this card, please. Do you know how far McAllen is?"

"'Fraid not, but we have some maps right over ..."

"Give me a Texas one please."

"They're a dollar. Oh, I've got one here that's been torn a little. Let you have it for seventy-five cents."

The 353 engine accelerated the pick-up down the entrance ramp and slipped it onto the interstate at sixty-five mph with little effort. The traffic was light, still too early for the semi-tractor trailer rigs to take over from the commuters. Ree turned her wrist to look at her watch. 5:30. The digital clock in the dash read 4:30.

As she took the first curve where IH 35 South joined IH 35 Alternate, Ree converged with the cars and trucks coming out of Fort Worth. They pointed south to Waco together.

CHAPTER 3

TRANCE ROAD

HIGHWAY 281 BETWEEN GEORGE WEST and Alice is straight. Really straight. This is flat south Texas brush country. Above ground, it looked useless and forever. There was nothing but scrub mesquite competing for what water there was with the cactus, purple sage and the agaritha that crowded around the meager shade of the scrub oaks. Everything in and on the land bit, scratched, stung or poked. The thorny vegetation housed the rattlesnakes; the little pigs called *javelinas*, and provided refuge for the new fawns in June. Of course there were the coyotes, the perennial bookkeepers who made sure the number of tenants matched the capacity of the available dwelling places.

This sameness meant monotony when you were driving. Except for what Drew called *the riddle of the fence*. Miles of it, endless barbed wire tacked on juniper post. Every time he came this way, he spent more than a few miles wondering about the cost-benefit ratio of all that wire. Most of the cows behind the cruel barrier, at least the ones he saw, were nothing but packer animals. They'd bring maybe forty cents a pound at market, and that's on a good trading day. Their bitter meat barely visible on boney carcasses was produced from the scarce nutrients in the buffalo grass and mesquite beans. Most hadn't seen a good protein source since their mama head butted them away from the tit. They made good meat for greasy fajitas or dog food, but not much else. Hardly worth, at least by Drew's reckoning, a five-strand fence that went on forever.

The answer to the puzzle, as Drew already knew, was scattered out in the scrub. The black pumpers that went up and down like perpetual bird toys dipping in a glass of water. The counter-balanced mechanical dinosaurs hiding in the mesquite gave a clue to the real value of this land. The cows were just part of the Texas myth, an old story that stubbornly refused to die. After all this was Texas and Texas without cows would be like a bull without balls. So the oil built the fence and the cows ate prickly pear during the droughts.

Other than the mind game there was little else to do but drive. Highway 281 was a trance road. Kick your head out of gear and hopefully wake up in the next town. However, there is a fine line between trance and sleep. A driver could leave the road dead if he confused the two. Some travelers on this lonely route did. Small white crosses tucked neatly up against the fences often memorialized the tragedies. Most were just out of the right-of-way and off state property. A few were encircled by artificial flowers of white, red, and violet. Their plastic nature kept them fresh making it appear that someone had just been there and offered a eulogy. They made effective warning signs for a weary or bored traveler. These random commemoratives, especially if there were more than one on a spot, always made Drew shake his head several times to clear the fog.

Damn to Hell!

THE NEW RIDER HAD SAT SILENT for the last twenty miles as the engine took advantage of the flatness and maintained a steady r.p.m. at sixty-two miles-per-hour.

Before he had pulled out of the parking lot of the Dairy Queen, Drew had removed the Jeep's plastic windows and stowed them next to the spare tire. The south wind took immediate advantage and made its way through the interior with a consistent roar, creating a steady hum in Drew's ears.

Chica's curiosity now was peaked with the new passenger. Her front paws were firmly planted on the console between the two front seats and made a bridge, or maybe it was a barrier, between the strange woman and the driver. Drew wasn't sure. Chica took to the stranger right off. She kept twitching her nose like a beacon in Ree's direction. Judging by the constant movement of the dog's tail, Drew figured there was something there of interest.

This woman has been around a male dog recently, he figured.

"Been to McAllen before?" Drew finally spoke over the wind noise.

"What?" Ree's head came around quickly, her expression tense.

"McAllen? Got relatives there?" Drew repeated.

The woman deliberately adjusted herself in the seat, swinging her left leg up under her right and placing her upper body at a 45-degree angle in the driver's direction. She placed her left hand on Chica's back and began pushing the dog's hair against the grain. Chica's tail went into high gear slapping the back of the seats. Drew slowed the Jeep down a bit so he could hear her answer.

"Chica! Leave the lady alone. Go back there and lie down."

"She's not bothering me. I'm...I'm going to visit a friend," Ree's voice squeaked as she tried to match Drew's volume. They both grinned.

Drew cocked his head halfway towards the woman and cut his eyes the rest, just long enough to take a read of her expression.

"You always travel this way?"

Ree did not answer or even smile.

Another couple of miles slipped under the tires before she again adjusted her position and faced Drew directly. Chica interpreted the movement as a sign for more attention. She poked her nose close to Ree's face and wiggled her furry frame.

"No, I don't," she said finally.

Drew again glanced from the road to the passenger and then to the dog.

"Chica!" he extended the sound and changed the pitch to indicate a warning. Ree's eyes were fixed on Chica so Drew didn't make the dog mind.

Women sure can ruin a good dog quick, he thought.

He waited for more of the answer. Instead, Ree rotated her head and looked down the highway.

Drew let it go and did the same. He made note of the Jim Wells county highway sign with its close pattern of bullet holes in the middle. *Only in Texas* he thought.

Damn, we're already half-way to Alice. Making good time ...ought to make McAllen before dark, Drew thought to himself.

The steering wheel jerked, without warning. The front-end left the road surface. The right tire dropped violently off the pavement into the loose gravel.

"Shit! Hang on!" Drew shouted.

The rigid muscles in Drew's forearms formed deep rows as he squeezed the steering wheel with all his strength. The rig took a millisecond to hit the low spot in the bar ditch and began to plow up the other side. Chica, who had gone airborne at the first impact, was on her way down from the roof. Ree gripped tightly the hand bar on the dash and pushed hard at the floorboard with her tennis shoes. On the other side of the ditch, they leveled out. Drew took sight on four strands of barbwire in between two massive cedar H braces in the fence. He climbed hard on the breaks. A thick envelope of dust shut out the world as they finally stopped.

It was quiet. Chica hung half out of the Jeep with her back legs dangling just above the running board. Ree lowered her head slowly until her forehead rested against the dash. Drew pushed open the driver's side door and put one foot on the ground but he didn't move to get out.

He looked over his shoulder, back at his passenger. "You OK?"

Ree looked up but didn't turn her head. She just watched the dust swirl around the hood, "Think so," she answered softly.

Chica at last gave up her hold and slid to the ground. She sniffed around while Drew got out and walked to the back of the trailer and up the other side assessing the damage as he went. The bumper had pushed into the barbed wire. The ugly strands were stretched tight, like a bowstring, but not broken. The tire was something else again. It looked like a grotesque Christmas wreath.

Drew went back to the trailer and opened the door. The neat packing job he had done at the ranch had been a waste of time judging by what he saw. Under a seat cushion, he found and pulled out the water jug. He walked back to where Ree was sitting and handed her the container through the open door window.

"Guess we're pretty lucky," he said finally. "The trailer's a mess but nothing seems damaged other than the tire. I'll back the rig up to get it out of this guy's fence. Why don't you move around a little?" Drew opened the door.

Ree swung her legs out. "Hope I can walk." she smiled, "What happened?"

"Not sure. Just looks like the tire came apart. Something in the road, who knows? Would you see what you could do with the disaster in the trailer? It would help me out."

"Sure," she passed the water jug back.

"Thanks. My mouth's full of that good Texas dust," he took the jug and a big swallow as he walked around the Jeep to the driver's side looking back at the tracks. They were straight. They came up through the bar ditch and across the distance between the road and the fence, a good fifty yards. He pitched the water jug in the back and crawled in behind the steering wheel.

He looked in the right side rear view mirror to see where the woman was. "I'm going to move the Jeep," he shouted. Chica reflexively jumped into the passenger's seat.

"OK," Ree responded.

46

As Drew cranked the engine, he kept his eyes on Ree in the mirror and slowly moved back away from the wire. Even in four-wheel drive, it was a struggle to push the trailer back in the soft dirt. Drew eased it back and began to look over the ground for a solid spot to set the jack.

At least it's not raining he mumbled as he killed the engine and stomped down on the emergency brake. Ree climbed into the trailer and shut the door. Chica curled up in the front seat as Drew broke out the toolbox.

IT WAS ALMOST 5 P.M. by the time Drew and Ree made it to Alice. The road trouble had pushed the schedule back by several hours. McAllen was still many long road miles away.

"Welcome to Alice," Drew said to himself more than to Ree.

The words broke the silence that had held up for over an hour. Still nervous from the unexpected adventure, Drew and the rider had talked only for a few minutes when they pulled back onto the highway. They laughed and said something or other about *fate. It's your time or it isn't; karma,* as they got back up to speed. Within 10 miles, they had both drifted back into silence.

Maybe I ought to turn this thing around ... nearly hit a deer, could've flipped the trailer ... picked up a stranger, what's got into me... damn tire lets go without warning ... what's next the engine? ... Damn, Chiapas, Mexico is still 1500 miles away ... through who knows what? ... I had a safe place to stay at the ranch ... I'm getting too old for this shit ... where's that fuckin' spider anyway? ... To hell with the "call."

47

What am I doing here ... in this car, with this man? ... I could've been killed back there ... who is he, anyway? ... God, I'm in a lot of trouble ... I wonder where Buddy is. ... I've got to go back ... in a few days ... straighten it all out ... things will get better ... just need to put more effort into it ... maybe Buddy's right ... maybe we should get married ...

Spotting a Firestone Service Center, Drew cut the wheel sharply and pulled up the service ramp.

"Got to see about a spare." He shot a grin toward Ree. "Be back in a sec."

Ree and Chica watched Drew push through the double glass doors and then Ree grabbed her small bag out of the back and went to look for a restroom. As soon as she abandoned the front seat, Chica quickly spilled into the void doing her circle dance until she found the comfort zone and settled.

The temperature in May is either summer or spring in south Texas. Today was a good day. It was spring. When Drew came back, he pulled dirt clods out of the winch motor on the front bumper and then sat down. He tilted his head back to take the sun on his face. Then Ree crowded into his thoughts. He liked her toughness. No panic.

Drew got up and walked to the passenger's side. "Where's Ree, Chica?" Chica jumped up and began her customary body shake.

Ree appeared around the corner. She had re-tied her hair and put on a soft shade of rose lipstick. She was a woman who didn't use or need much make-up. Her skin had a slightly olive tint to it, and except for a few shallow crows-feet, was flawless. Her eyes were deep chestnut, almost black. They reflected any highlights available. Her body moved easily and Drew stared as she came toward him.

"It'll be an hour or so before they can mount the tire," Drew said. "Let's get something to eat. You hungry?"

"I guess ... sure."

"Saw a restaurant back down the main drag. What do you think, sound OK?"

"Sure ... whatever," Ree answered.

They pulled slowly into the parking lot of the Black Gold Cafe and looked for enough spaces to park the rig so as not to be blocked in. Drew backed the trailer up to the dumpster near the back and cocked the front end to assure an exit. He got out and pointed his finger at Chica *¡Quedate!*

"What's that mean?"

"Means to stay put."

The outside brightness had closed their pupils to the max. It took awhile to adjust to the low-level light in the restaurant. Finally a few details appeared. No surprises. Mostly oil field memorabilia, pictures, pipefitting, wrenches. A replica of a derrick made out of kitchen matches sat on the crowded counter next to three bowls full of mints. The stuff covered every wall and shelf in the place.

A front page of the *Alice Beacon* was framed and hung on the wall behind the cash register. The 120-point headline read "Iraqis Torch Wellheads." For this part of the world, Drew figured that had been good news.

Alice, Texas had been in the center of the many an oil boom. Sixteen-dollar-a-barrel oil had abruptly put an end to the last one in the early 80s. But the main drag through town was still lined with pumping services, drilling outfits, pipe fitters, seismologists and mudding services. All were waiting and praying for the Middle East to blow up again which most old hands in the business knew was a given.

Drew and Ree didn't wait for the waitress to greet them before they took a seat. The cafe wasn't busy. Maybe half dozen customers were scattered about in the dark corners. The place could seat twenty times as many.

The good business now came from the *snowbirds* as they made their way from the cold country of Minnesota and Wisconsin to the winter warmness of the Texas Valley. But most of the rich itinerants, queued in caravans of ten or more trailers, had already beaten the trail back home before the Texas summer melted their tires. So Alice was quiet. With the locals anticipating the next war or winter, whichever came first.

Ree and Drew slid into a booth close to the door. The view of the highway filtered through the front window. Drew figured the glass had been washed the last time back in the 50s.

"I sure could use a big glass of iced tea," Drew said.

Ree nervously looked out the window and didn't reply.

The Coors's truck man who stacked cases of Colorado Kool-Aid 10 high on his dolly entertained them both. He was a little shrimp of a *Latino* ... maybe 110 pounds if he was wet. The beer had him two to one, easy. They waited for the crash.

Breaking the spell, Ree said, "Drew, I have to... I have to tell you something."

Drew blinked and looked around. For the first time he caught Ree's eyes head on.

"Hi folks! Want to see a menu?" The waitress appeared out of nowhere dressed in a black knee-high skirt and a wrinkled white blouse.

"Can I get you something to drink?" She pushed two worn menus across the table. They had the history of the oil industry on the covers. Jenny Lee was on her nametag. She had black hair, cut short and streaked with gray. Her eyebrows grew together in the middle. Under the second button of her blouse was a dull yellow stain. Looked like mustard, old mustard.

"Iced tea," Drew answered as he stared at the stain.

"Me too," Ree nodded.

"Two iced teas. Be right back honey."

The waitress spun on her toes and crashed through swinging doors to the kitchen. Drew turned back to Ree but he did not speak. He wanted her to continue where she had left off. But, Ree had turned and was looking out the window back to the north.

CHAPTER 4

REGRESA

THE GREYHOUND COACH PULLED to the shoulder on a straight
stretch of highway between Brawley and El Centro, California. A
thick white cloud was moving slowly across the road. The mass was
so thick that it obscured the chauffeur's visibility and forced him to
take a break on the shoulder of the highway. From the window
seats, the passengers stared at the gathering. It was feeding time
and the sweet-potato whitefly was hungry. The bugs worked one
fresh field after another. They took the sweet juices from the
vegetables and left the farmers a nightmare and a mess.

Tuna peered down from the safety of the bus onto the swarm.
In the eight years he had worked the valley this was the worst he
had seen. The flies were not giving up to the strong chemical sprays.
Instead, they seemed to thrive on the insecticide. They bred as if
they were on vitamins.

A white film obscured the fresh field of iceberg lettuce off to Tuna's right. He guessed that the leafy balls had been about ready to pick. The insects were fascinating. They would dissolve into the green vegetables and then suddenly reform when the destruction was completed. Tuna was very happy to be on the bus. He was happy to be leaving this place. He felt a sickness all through this valley. The voracious winged feeders were only one of the signs. All around him life was changing.

The show of the frenzy combined with the gentle vibration of the diesel engine of the bus had a calming effect. Tuna's mind wandered. Images of the first trip to el Norte appeared out among the pests in the fields forming on their flowing patterns like a movie screen.

Diez y siete y media de edad. He was only seventeen then. The first time he made the crossing. Tuna pressed his back into the comfort of the seat and let that time come back to mind.

NORTH IS WHITE

IT TOOK ELEVEN DAYS for the three hombres, Rafael, Goy and Tuna to reach la frontera. They started from Zapata by walking to Ocosingo the closest trading city in the valley of the Rio Jataté River. For the next sixteen hundred kilometers, the small band hitched rides with truckers and sugarcane haulers until they made the port city of Tampico. From there the trio used some pesos from a little cloth bag that Rafael carried to buy a bus ticket for the last leg to the Rio Grande river and the Texas border.

For Goy and Tuna, it was the first time away from the pueblo. Rafael was the only traveler of the three. He had gone to Villahermosa in Tabasco once with his father. They had sold some palm fans in the big city that were made by the women of Zapata and two other villages close by.

So Rafael had to be the guide. He had the road-wisdom. And besides it was Rafael who had convinced the other two of the treasure and adventure waiting in the north for those con huevos.

Podríamos tener todos mis compañeros, he said many times.

Having it all was not on their minds this day as they arrived in Reynosa. The city looked dirty and ugly. There was nothing there they knew. Goy told Tuna he was scared. Tuna assured him that he was only tired and hungry, but he too was anxious.

As soon as they stepped off the bus at the depot next to the Blanco Supermarket and Department Store on Cardenas Street their mood changed. The activity around the place was frantic. People were everywhere. Going everywhere. Doing everything. Tuna saw gringos mixed in with the Mexicans. More gringos than he had ever seen in his life. And there were other Indians like Tuna and Goy and Rafael. Vendedores in todos los partes. More vendors with more plastic things than Tuna thought existed. The world suddenly became large; it exploded with activity in every direction.

"Vamonos con prisa," Rafael shouted. "Let's go see it, hurry." The North was close. Goy took the lead. He was pointing to the big green signs spanning the street like a youngster at Disneyland. They eagerly paid the fifty-peso fee and pushed through the turnstiles at the bridge. Falling in step with the foot traffic on the bridge, they walked to the center on the Mexican side of the International Bridge. Tuna watched the mud-red waters of el Rio Bravo without sound move below. Dusk was approaching quickly and Rafael was the first to see the lights of the other side.

"¡Mira, mira! ... el otro lado." Rafael resumed his role as guide and pointed out the landmarks as if he had seen it all before.

"¡Dios mío! un McDonalds." They shared nervous laughter and quick glances at the men of the U.S. Border Patrol, el Migra, up ahead.

PLANET BRAIN

THE COYOTE HAD DEEP UGLY holes in his cheeks. New red pregnant eruptions filled the gaps between the holes. Tuna thought the man's face looked like the moon on a clear summer's night. But he was friendly, reassuring. He had a quick smile and more confidence than Tuna thought this place could offer a man. He knew his territory well.

It had taken Rafael two days to track Pepé down. A man back in San Quintín, the pueblo next to theirs, gave the name to them. The man said he made the crossing many times and he always used Pepé Morales. He told Tuna's father that Pepé could be trusted "un buen hombre," he said. On the piece of paper, the man copied the letters from a notebook he had carried for years. He told them to show this paper to people in Reynosa. People around the Plaza Central. They will help you find him he said. *Pepé Morales - Farmacia Hidalgo, Aldama y Bravo. Reynosa, México*, the message read.

Pepé didn't waste words in their first meeting. "Escucha me con mucho cuidado cabrones. There are many dangers in the crossing my friends," Pepé told the trio as they watched the photographers on the plaza lift the gringo touristas and their kids on the grotesque stuffed remnants of real horses taking their pictures with Polaroid cameras. "There are dangers on both sides, Pepé cautioned in a soft low voice."

Tuna liked moonfaced Pepé Morales from the beginning. Even when he told them about los rateros, the robbers, the ones who rape the women and take all from the "emigrantes." He gave them quick survival lessons.

"Stay away from la policia y los federales too. They will take all you have. Anything of value. Do you have a place to stay until I can put together a group of pollitos for the crossing?"

Tuna didn't think he liked being called a little chicken. But Pepé said it with a smile and everyone else smiled back so he thought it must be OK.

Rafael explained to Pepé how they could stay with a cousin of a man they had met on the bus ride from Tampico. Raul was his name. Raul Villareal. He had built frame huts out of discarded television packing crates he pilfered at the Zenith plant. He hauled them from the maquilladora on a little wagon pulled by a burro and covered them with plastic sheets. There were about fifteen or so of these casitas as Raul called them. They were located not far from the train station near Colon Street. They held a little high ground just on the perimeter of the flood plain in the Andzalduas Canal.

When the rain was not too heavy, Raul rented them out to the viajeros coming from the south. All three could stay for only tres mil pesos a night, about one gringo dollar. He told Goy he gave a cheap rate to the Indian boys, the puros he called them. Raul's mother had some Chol blood in her he said. He always gave the Indians a break. Frijoles and tortillas were included. But, you had to get them for yourself out of the black pot that rested on the open fire in the back.

Best of all, the casitas were safe. The Mexican police didn't come into the canal unless there was a riot. Raul explained to Tuna that la pendejos policia didn't want to get the mud on their shoes. He laughed hard as he made fun of the police.

"Que bueno," Pepé responded, "Stay out of the way until Tuesday. We cross Tuesday night." Pepé had a theory. He only crossed his people on Tuesday. He said that he figured the immigration people didn't like to work too hard on Tuesdays after the hard weekend and Monday. Monday was always a butt buster on the river. "They let a lot of things go by on Tuesday," he said, "we will have an easy time. No problemas, yo lo prometo."

BOUND FOR THE RIVER

PEPÉ'S CHICKENS GATHERED IN SMALL CLUTCHES of four or five early in the afternoon on the appointed day. Tuna could see other small groups scattered all along Echeverria Street just as Pepé had told them there would be. He wondered how many were Pepe's. How many would attempt the crossing that night. How many would be caught by el Migra.

They could see the river stretched out some three hundred yards in front of them. There were two others in their group. One was a Guatemaltecan who was no more than thirteen. The kid was beyond nervous. Tuna felt sorry for him. He tried to exchange a few words but the youngster was shaking so bad Tuna gave up. The other one was a woman. Tuna figured she was in her twenties. He couldn't believe women crossed this way. She was pretty but kept to herself.

They crouched behind piles of sand used for street repairs and waited for the signal. The mood was somber, but Tuna felt happy. He concentrated on what life would be like on the other side.

I will work. Make money and save for the future. I will send money home to my ejido. I will help them build a school with this money. Oh, yes, I will learn to speak English and learn to read. I will learn the good farming of the north so I can teach these skills to my people when I return to Zapata. I will become a man in el Norte.

Finally, the darkness moved among the gatherings. Goy nudged Tuna with his elbow. "Wake up! Pepé is here. We go soon." Tuna had been dozing balanced in a squat position with his feet down in the soft sand. He came to attention. Tuna could feel his heart begin to pump harder.

"Muchachos, vengan conmigo."

There little group fell behind Pepé in a single file. Rafael was in the lead behind Pepé. Then followed the woman. Goy said her name was Julia. Goy followed her, and Tuna and the boy from Guatemala completed the train bound for the river.

They walked for over an hour along the water's edge moving west. On the other side in the darkness, Tuna could see the lights from the Migra helicopters patrolling the north bank.

The going was getting rough. Debris lined the banks of the river. Rocks, old cars, household garbage was scattered in the dark. Tuna could hear the boy behind him crying softly. He pulled out his shirttail and turned, "Here take this so we don't get separated." Tuna felt the boy's tug. It made him feel better, too, about his own fear. He had to brave for this little one.

Then Tuna heard the coyote give several low whistles. They all stopped and waited. Five minutes seemed like five hours. Then two whistles came in return. Pepé turned and smiled. "Muchachos, es la hora de cruzar."

Tuna's mouth turned to cotton. He thought the fear would gag him. There was nothing in his stomach to throw up. All the men took off their shirts and shoes and wrapped them in tight little bundles. They balanced their belongings on their heads and began to wade. The crossing was easy just like Pepé had promised. "Guarantizado."

They all sat in the cenizo shrubs for a while after they cleared the north bank. The Guatemalan was still shaking but his bright teeth shown through a smile. The muchacho's eyes could have lit the trail in the dark.

Tuna shook hands with Goy and Rafael. They could not believe they had made it. They laughed quietly among themselves and whispered of the work picking the Texas Ruby Red Grapefruit and the Yankee dollars that would come from the effort. Tuna felt good. He would be a champion and much admired in Zapata someday.

A few Migra jeeps passed within a couple of hundred yards but nothing happened. They just kept going. Pepé said they would double back and go through the McAllen Airport.

"Stay off the runway and stay low," he cautioned sternly but still with a smile. "Once we get to the IHOP restaurant on the north side of the airport, I have a man who will take you to a safe-house for the night. Tomorrow another man will pick you up and take you to a grower who will give you a job."

"El norte, estamos en el norte," Tuna hugged Rafael and Goy otra vez.

FRUITS OF THE EARTH

THE FIRST YEAR IN THE NORTH was good, it was very good. The Border Patrol never found Tuna or his friends in Texas. As long as they stayed in the orchard and worked, it was safe. They were part of an important economy. Legal or illegal it didn't matter. The growers had to have them. Gringos wouldn't do this work and, if they did, they complained constantly and worked slowly, costing the grower more than they were worth.

But not so with los emigrantes. Tuna and his kind worked hard. He put his whole energy into the work. There was nothing else of importance to him during this time. Tuna's greatest pleasure came on the days they all went to the Western Union office and sent the money home. Nearly five hundred dollars a month made its way deep into Mexico from each of the three. This was a fortune for the pueblos in the south in the state of Chiapas.

José, a cousin, once a month traveled the long road to Ocosingo from their ejido to receive the dollars. He put most of it in a small bank in town and stuffed the rest in his shoe. He walked an uneven pace as he returned to Tuna's family in the mountains near the border with Guatemala. At eighteen Tuna was a hero, una valiente real.

The following year was good as well. They had experience now. They knew the territory too, like Pepé. Tuna was learning some English from a teacher at the Catholic Church. He was no longer afraid of the gringos he met. On the contrary, he was outgoing trying to talk to anyone who would let him use his halting English.

Goy too was contented. He had a chica in Reynosa. Elizabeth was a cook at the orchard where they picked grapefruit. Elizabeth's mamacita let them all stay over at her house when they were coming or going from Zapata during the spring planting in Chiapas. The trip home was easier now too. They had the money to ride the whole way on the bus. The journey only took four days. The money made everything easier.

They were also river wise. The crossings were easy for them. They still used Pepé. But he didn't charge them much, only a quarter of the regular four hundred dollar fee. They helped Pepé cross the others. They gave them courage, the ones who were scared and nervous. They had been caught only one time. The helicopter lights had illuminated their little line in mid-river. It was no big deal as Tuna related his story to the fascinated muchachos in Zapata.

La migra only kept us for two hours. They only took our names and where we were from. Of course, we all gave different stories, and then they bussed us back to the bridge. The next night we made it across with no trouble.

The money was good. The life was good. Then the change came to south Texas. It came in the winter of 1983.

The weathermen called it an arctic express. They said it was a result of the El Niño cycle, an aberration. But this aberration within a few days brutally mutated the lives of poor and rich alike in the fertile valley. A valley that could go through a winter with temperatures that would seem resort like to someone from Akron, Ohio: where in some years fruit trees missed the dormancy cycle altogether.

This year the cold was unstoppable. It bit at exposed skin. Even the semi-arid region between San Antonio and the Valley could not slow it. The temperature assaulted everything alike, people, animals and vegetation. The bitter air forced its way across the Rio Grande ignoring the sovereignty of the border, pushing far into northern Mexico. One hundred twenty-three Mexicans as far south as Sabinas Hidalgo and north of Monterrey froze to death.

There were cases of frostbite in some of the barrios of south Reynosa where Goy's girlfriend lived. People there didn't know what it was. They had never seen skin turn ugly colors from the cold.

When the three waded the river again for the spring work, leafless fruit trees greeted them. "There will be no fruit this year," Jesus, el jefe for the orchard told them somberly. No fruit until new trees could be planted and allowed to mature. No fruit meant no work, it was a simple equation.

"No regresamos a México," Rafael had been so determined that night as they sat around the kitchen table in Elizabeth's casa and talked. There was nothing there for them, no money he argued.

Goy and Tuna had to agree. Besides, Tuna now had a girlfriend, a novia. He wanted to marry her the next time they went back. He wanted to make an inheritor. Have niños. He wanted to raise them properly. Tuna could do it with the money. The money was important. The money was the only way. All he needed was one or two more seasons in the fields. The cycle of poverty of his father and his grandfather could be broken with the money. He could show the pobrecitos how to raise more than corn and chilies. How to do more than just survive.

"We'll be pulling out in a minute folks ... It looks like the worst is nearly over. I'll try to make up the time so maybe we will make it to El Centro on schedule. Thank you for your patience." The bus driver's message broke into Tuna's thoughts.

The power of the money. Tuna smiled as he again looked out the window and watched the blur begin to break up and scatter. He could pay now for the ride on the bus. He could ride in comfort from here to south Texas and then on to Tampico, Veracruz, Tuxtla-

Gutiérrez and finally Ocosingo. The Greyhound coach was heaven. Money is what made life easy. Good.

Seven years ago, it was different in Reynosa. The money from the last year of work was gone to the account of the ejido in Ocosingo or spent in travel from Zapata. The decision was simple. Go back home or search for work farther west.

Tuna remembered how hard it had been to leave his known world. To leave Reynosa. It would be like starting over. Like the time of the first crossing.

But, Rafael was right. They made up their minds to go to California. There would be no freeze in California. The huge fertile valleys demanded pickers for the lettuce, for the asparagus, for the spinach. For the things that make America and the gringos happy.

On the journey west to California, they walked only at night, a hundred yards off the interstate. The rattlers kept them awake and alert but they seldom saw the snakes. They developed bat-like radar to avoid the sound. But the cactus was worse. It was everywhere, poking and stabbing trough trousers into leg skin in the dark. Rafael stepped on an armadillo the second night out, somewhere near Fort Stockton. Both jumped backwards in the darkness. A four-foot cholla cactus embraced Rafael's backside.

They stopped and waited for morning and enough light to pick the spines, hundreds of them, out of Rafael's tender back and butt. Rafael laid on his stomach for five hours in the darkness waiting. He never cried out. Tuna smiled again thinking about the bravery. They kidded the pobrecito. Called him porcipelo. Rafael did resemble one of the scrawny pigs in Zapata with its stiff black hair bristled on its back.

The days were spent out of the sun watching the horizon for the helicopters. Two slept in shallow pits they dug under a Sequoyah cactus while the third watched.

Near Tucson, Tuna heard the familiar pop-pop-pop of a Border Patrol helicopter. He remembered the sound well from the time they were caught in mid-river. It penetrated his ears. The sound was far out front of the machine. The three offered wordless prayers to the Virgin of Guadalupe as they waited. When the rotors moved past the noise faded quickly. The only sound then was the blood pounding in their ears.

Tuna still didn't understood why the Norteamericanos spent so much money on such poor Mexicans and Central Americans. They only came to work. Who would pick the fruits and vegetables if la pinche migra were good at its work? He had put a sticker on his travel bag. One he had noticed his first night at the safe-house in McAllen. It read: *Ningún ser humano es ilegal.*

PATTERN OF NO TIME

AS THE GREYHOUND BUS pulled back on the highway Tuna pushed his back against the seat. The black man next to him leaned a little his way. "Mister...mister. You got the time? We're not goin' to be late to El Centro I hope. My daughter is waitin' for me. Sure hope we're not going to be late to El Centro," he said. Tuna was polite but said he didn't know and turned back to the window.

His mind returned from the mental trip and he removed a paper from his shirt pocket to read it one more time. The form was beginning to tear along the creases. Tuna stared at it. The first line read *Patient: Angel de Jésus González Ramos.* Most of the medical jargon was beyond his ability. A bilingual social worker from the county hospital had explained the rest to him.

"Señor González," she said calmly, "the doctor wants me to tell you the nature of your illness."

Tuna thought she was pretty. Her voice was kind and soft. Reminded him of his girlfriend Carmen in Mexico. She fumbled with a few papers making a little show of putting them in order before she went on. He could see that she was uneasy. She studied the papers, speaking without making eye contact.

"Señor González...I am here...Señor González I must tell you Señor that you have a serious illness. The doctor wants me to explain to you... explain about your cancer," she waited.

"Señor González?"

Tuna understood the word. It was the same in both languages. His expression did not register any impact and the social worker seemed to need a reaction to continue.

"I am here to explain what this means and what can be done for you. ¿Entiende me? Señor González."

"Sí, Señora." Tuna looked away from the kind woman and over the dividers that were intended to give privacy to her work. The rows of chairs were at least ten deep and a dozen wide and all were occupied by brown men and women. Some of the patients spent the entire day waiting to see the doctor, a lone volunteer who came on Mondays, Wednesdays and Fridays to see to the workers. Tuna recognized many of the trabajadores from the fields where he and Goy had worked for the last six seasons. *There were so many sick now,* he thought.

"Señor, the doctor says that the disease has spread from your lungs where it began. It is called oat-cell cancer. Lo siento mucho, Señor. I'm sorry, Señor González, it is very serious."

Tuna traded glances with Goy. He was in the third row waiting his turn. He too was feeling bad. The cough was slight but persistent. Goy used a handkerchief to muffle the sound as his eyes met his friend.

"The doctor says that we can treat your cancer with chemotherapy immediately if you choose. But you will not be able to return to the fields. The treatment will make you sick for a while. The county will help you with some of the medical expenses. Do you have family here, a wife or father?" The lady knew the answer to that question before she asked.

"No, Señora."

"Do you go back to Mexico after the season?"

"Sí Señora, to Reynosa." Tuna did not want to explain that they traveled all the way to Chiapas. He didn't want her to know that he was an Indian.

"Señor, the doctor says that you should know that this disease is very difficult to treat with present medical technology. It will help but you must understand that the cancer may continue to spread in your body."

"Sí Señora."

Tuna's stoicism made the social worker uneasy. *Why don't they show emotion at such terrible news?* she thought. They never react or become angry, or cry, nothing. They are always so calm and resigned. These people made her feel weak.

"Por favor, Señor," she hesitated again. Señor...the doctor says...that with treatment you may live..." this was the hard part of the job.

Tuna broke in, "Sí, señora, yo entiendo todo, muchas gracias."

"Señor, I must know what you wish to do. About the treatment."

"Señora, I will speak to my friend and come back to the clinic soon." This was the first time Tuna had used English and it caught the woman by surprise.

Her tone changed slightly, less sympathetic than before. She responded to Tuna in English, "That will be fine Señor, thank you."

Tuna offered his hand to the woman then walked over to where Goy was seated, watching everything with wide-eyes, like a kid.

"I will wait for you outside Goy," Tuna said.

He sat under an Arizona ash tree. A native stone planter surrounded the base of the tree with seasonal plants distributed haphazardly. All were nearly dead. Quietly Tuna sat and watched the workers come out of the community hospital. Occasionally he would wave at a familiar face but he did not want to talk. They were all Hispanic or Indian, mostly from Mexico but a few from Guatemala or San Salvador. The nervous one on the first crossing came to his mind. He wondered what had happened to him. He hadn't stayed to work in Texas. Tuna thought maybe he had gone to Chicago. He wasn't sure.

It was getting warm. The sun was almost overhead. The rash on Tuna's forearms itched when it got hot in the afternoon. The rash was worse after they sprayed the fields. Tuna tried not to scratch. Scratching made the skin swell and new bumps followed quickly.

They sprayed more now, Tuna thought. It seemed almost constantly. Last week, he and Goy had been caught in a field of cabbage when the planes sprayed the field next to them. The gentle breeze changed quickly to a stiff wind and carried the vapor over everything. Tuna and Goy kept working through the mist.

MEMBER OF THE FAMILY

GOY CAME THROUGH THE FRONT DOOR, crossed the small courtyard, and approached Tuna deliberately. His friend smiled as he neared. Goy always smiled. Tuna cared for this man a great deal. They had been through much together in eight short years. It made him think again of Rafael. Where was he? What was his life like now? Three years before Rafael had boarded a bus in Brawley and went to East Los Angeles. He became another drop in the brown sea. Goy and Tuna had stood silently at the bus terminal and waved until the bus was out of sight. They had heard nothing of Rafael since. They both wondered if he had become a documented worker, as they had after the new immigration law passed in 1986. Rafael wanted to stay in the U.S. very badly. He always made a joke about marrying a gringa, raising light skin muchachos and being a citizen of America.

"What happened?" Goy said as he sat down on the edge of the planter. "What did the lady tell you Tuna?"

Tuna did not look up at Goy. "The doctor says I have a cancer," he continued to watch the workers come and go from the entrance.

"¡Dios mío!" Goy replied.

"The lady said I can take treatment but I cannot work the fields."

Tuna and Goy both looked back toward the valley and the crops that covered every available inch of farmland. They did not speak for a while. Tuna had pulled a small leather sack from inside his tee shirt. Slowly, rhythmically he rubbed the pouch.

"Goy, I must tell you. I have decided to go home." Tuna moved his eyes to the bag and continued to rub it gently.

"It was a mistake for us to come here Goy. We have been pulled from our people and our place for this." Tuna pushed his index finger and thumb into the leather bag and withdrew the money. It was tightly rolled and wrapped with a rubber band used for tying the asparagus together.

His fingers pushed the rubber band off one end and Tuna unrolled the bills. "Goy, there is one thousand dollars here."

Goy quickly looked around the courtyard to see if anyone was watching. The sight of that much money, out in the open, made him nervous.

"I am going to give you half of these dollars Goy. I want you to take it and come with me back to Mexico."

"Mi hermano, we cannot go back now. There is still much work to do. The season is only half over."

"Goy, the doctor thinks I will die from this cancer. I know what caused this to happen to me. The same is happening to you now. I wish us to return to Mexico, together."

"But why can't they cure this disease, Tuna...this cancer?"

"For the same reason they cannot kill the bugs in the field anymore Goy. They do not know what they are doing with these chemicals. Don't you see the people that are sick in this hospital? Do you remember seeing so many before; when we first came here? No, I am sure that you do not. Yet still there are the insects. More than ever. And the spray for the insects, it comes more often than ever before, no?"

"Goy, in Chiapas we do not have much I know my friend. Only our land. Only our family. There is much need there. There are many problems. But cannot you see we are selling what we do have for so little. I have traded my life for dreams of the gringo. For this." Tuna held the green bills up to Goy.

"I must go back to Zapata. And you must come back with me."

Goy looked away from the eyes of his friend and moved the loose pea gravel around with the toe of his shoe. "You do not think that our lives are better now? Have you forgotten so soon?"

"Do you think I am better off now my friend?" Tuna countered. "Yes, I agree we have more money. Our families think we are successful in this country. We send them dineros. We send them comfort and security. We have our work papers. We plan for the next year and the next. This is true. But I wish to ask you Goy, are our lives better? What have we given in exchange for this roll of bills? What do we pay to be the big men to the people in our pueblo? What have we paid Goy?"

"I think the doctors are wrong about your sickness Tuna. When we go back to Mexico after this season, we can see Socorro. She will tell us the truth about your illness, no?"

"Goy, listen to me. The old curandera will tell us nothing. The gringos can make the diseases better than they can cure them, but they do know them well. The doctor is right about this. I am sure. I believe him.

Goy could never argue with Tuna. Tuna thought about things too much. He was the first to learn to speak the language of the north. He listened to the radio to practice. Tuna, in his way, studied the Norteamericanos closely. He worked the hardest at the amnesty classes. He knew more about the history of the United States than

70

most high school students did in the valley. When they returned to Zapata, Tuna was the most popular. He could tell the stories of the North.

"We have been together for a long time, Goy," Tuna continued. "We have learned much and seen more. Together, we could take some of this knowledge back to Zapata. Use the best to improve things on our land, for our own people. For the past two years, I have thought of this but always the money brought me back to pick. Always the money, always for just one more year. Now, I discover that I have little time to me. Goy, I am only twenty-six. I must live the rest of my life quickly. Should I spend the rest here or in Mexico? You tell me, diga me Goy."

"Tuna you ask too much of me. I do not want you to go back to Zapata. We have always been together. Stay here and take the treatment. These gringos are smart; they will make you well."

Tuna took five of the hundred-dollar notes and folded them in half. Gently he pushed them into the shirt pocket of his friend and stood up. Goy reached quickly for the money, but Tuna had already turned and was walking toward the bus stop at the front gate.

Goy watched his friend for a while and then looked toward the distance, toward the crop dusters working the cantaloupes below. The swooping yellow planes and their sudden bursts of vertical power that skimmed their strutted wheels just out of the grasp of the high-line power cables fascinated Goy. The planes reminded him of the Harpy eagle of the Lacandon Jungle. He used to watch the eagle in the rainforest when he was a young boy. Once he saw that powerful bird take a sloth out of the top of a ceiba tree in full flight. Now he watched the powerful planes with the same fascination.

Chapter 4

Goy loved California. He coughed slightly and thumbed the money as he watched Tuna board the company bus. Goy could not leave California. He would stay in the North to live, or to die.

CHAPTER 5

WE CAN DO THIS

ONLY ONE DAY ON THE ROAD and already Drew had broken two of his three travel rules. The first, never pick up strangers; the second, never eat enchiladas at a restaurant with catfish on the menu. At this moment, he regretted breaking the second more than the first. Drew shoved the remnants, still half submerged in red grease, to the far-reaches of the table. The chipped white porcelain plate wedged its way into the hodge-podge of condiment bottles and two napkin holders next to the window. A chili-pepper bottle, which held toothpicks, fell over. Drew picked it up and started poking one of the sharp sticks back in the small hole.

"How'd you end up in George West?" Drew collected the wrapper and napkin litter and piled it on top of the greasy remains as he attempted to restart the conversation. Ree, for her part, constructed little salt piles nervously on the table with her middle finger as she pondered Drew's question.

"Well, after I made it through Waco there were a couple of hours of daylight so I decided to keep going. Never driven that part of Texas before so I wasn't sure of the distances. All I could think about was getting to McAllen and Jane's house for refuge. Then for some reason I got off the interstate just south of Waco. That's not like me. I don't even know why I did it. Maybe I was afraid Buddy was following me, I don't know."

"Let me guess ...Highway 84, right ... heading west."

"That's it. How did you know?"

"I've traveled that stretch before myself. It's a more scenic route between Dallas and San Antonio. So then what?"

"Oh ... well, there wasn't a whole bunch of places to stop, so I kept driving. When I saw the 281 sign south there at Ev ... Event?"

"You mean Evant, you turned at Evant?"

"That's it. I turned there and headed toward San Antonio. I just continued to drive until I got to Lampasas. I stopped to get gas in there and there was this counter lady at a Stop-N-Go, she was very friendly. I think she could tell I was nervous, and not from around there. Anyway, we talked for a while. Her name was Agatha. It was real slow in the store so she made some fresh pop corn and helped me mark the right highways to get me to McAllen."

"Did you really think you could drive straight through from Lancaster? That's about 600 miles; that's a hard trip lady."

"I know, that's what Agatha said too. Drew I wasn't thinking about it much. Well, anyway I went through San Antonio at close to midnight. Felt pretty good then, but when I got out of the city and away from the lights I started getting sleepy."

"I guess so." Drew held his glass up as Jenny Lee went by. She bobbed her head and grabbed a sweaty tea pitcher off the adjacent table.

"It was nearly 2:30 in the morning," Ree continued. "When I came to George West, I had to keep hitting my forehead on the steering wheel to stay awake so I pulled into the parking lot at the DQ. The whole town was dark except for the Texaco truck stop across the street and the trucks were coming through regularly so I thought I would be safe there. I rolled up the windows and locked the doors and stretched out in the front seat."

"I remember that pick up, a black one right, Ford 150? I parked right beside it when I stopped...right?"

"Yes you did. That's what made me notice you when you drove up. I had been drinking coffee and staring at that damn truck all morning trying to decide what to do next."

Jenny Lee filled their glasses for the fourth time and laid the check on the cracker basket. "Want me to take that?" she pointed to the mess on the far side of the table.

"Please, if you don't mind."

Ree paused and deliberately watched the waitress collect plates, utensils and trash. The stack was a work of art, everything in one pyramid. You could have balanced the universe on top without a wobble.

"Don't laugh, but when I saw you and your dog, that helped me make up my mind. I wrote Buddy's address and phone number on one of the napkins and took it out to the truck. I stuck it to the steering wheel and put the keys under the front mat. Don't ask me why, but I decided that I wasn't going back to Buddy."

"You mean that's when you made up your mind to ask me for a ride too? How did you know I was going to the Valley?"

"I didn't. Now don't take offense but you looked harmless. Sort of like my grandfather, very gentle-like and caring. So, I thought I'd take a chance."

"Well looks can be deceiving lady...what do you mean grandfather?" Drew smiled broadly and pretended to look at his reflection in the window.

"I meant your eyes. Your eyes are kind, like his were. Same deep blue, same cheer."

"What did you think would happen to the truck?"

"Oh, I suppose I really didn't care. I figured the sheriff would eventually find it and call Buddy's number. Buddy could get one of his friends to bring him down to pick it up. I don't know what I thought."

"So what happens now?"

Ree shrugged and tapped the iced tea glass, the ice slid into her mouth. "I'll sort it out when I get to McAllen. Jane has always been my sounding board. I can't go back now. I don't want to go back, wasted too much time as it is. Do you understand?"

"I think I do."

UP AN OCTAVE

WHATEVER HAPPENED TO CASUAL RELATIONSHIPS, Drew wondered as they both fell silent and looked out the nearly opaque window. *Everything these days is so damn quick.*

But Drew always got involved with people quickly. *Everybody looking, nobody finding, experimentation with others, who has the answer?* Now it happened again, with Ree. He knew more than he wanted. There was no turning back, no unknowing the things now known.

"Relationships with people, especially women, are like education; it sticks to you," he once told Ruben at the ranch. Ruben, as usual, was in love with too many women at the same time.

"Once you have one, that's it; you can't get rid of it." Ruben just laughed and kept at cutting the back strap meat away from the deer carcass. Drew let the lesson drop. He didn't think Ruben picked up on the connection. Drew wasn't sure himself, but it sounded good.

Drew broke the short lull of silence, "I guess we ought to go get the tire, you ready?"

"Sure."

Drew dug through a big bowl by the cash register as he paid the check. He fished out three miniature Tootsie Rolls from the assorted candies. As they crossed the black asphalt to the Jeep, he handed one to Ree and unwrapped another. Chica went explosive when they got in. Drew held the candy out and Chica gracefully took the piece of chocolate between her front teeth and retreated to the back to savor and guard her prize.

"Listen Ree," Drew spoke before he turned the ignition key, "I don't want to drive to McAllen tonight. There has been enough excitement for one day. Think I'll stay here in Alice until morning. You're welcome to stay with me if you want. By the way, that's not a proposition either."

"I didn't think it was."

77

"I saw a trailer park just before we hit the city limits. We could park there for the night. You can sleep in the trailer, Chica and I will bed down in the back of the Jeep."

"What a gentleman. I guess I pegged you right back at the DQ. It won't be necessary for you to sleep in the Jeep...doesn't the trailer have more than one bed?"

"Yeah, the dining table folds into a bed. I just figured you might want the privacy?"

"We can work that out as we go. OK?"

"Sure."

Twenty-three of the twenty-five concrete pads at the Lemon Grove Trailer Park were empty. The sign out on the highway read *All Hook-Ups & Showers*. Drew didn't bother to stop at the ramshackle pre-fab tin building with *Office* painted in orange letters on all sides. He maneuvered the trailer onto a pad toward the back.

"I'll go find somebody and pay, be back in a minute."

"Can I do anything in the trailer?"

"Sure, why don't you put on some water for coffee? Everything's in the cabinets over the sink."

"Done."

The office was empty. A 'closed' sign with a small manual clock hung in the door window. The hour hand of the clock was missing.

"Howdy," the voice came from behind, somewhere from over Drew's left shoulder. "Not much need this time of year to stay in the office; all the birders are back in their northern nests." The words came through a toothless grin. "Rough-neck?"

"Pardon me?" Drew responded.

"No, you ain't no rough-neck. Just passing through or did some slick tourist agency talk you into spending the summer in Alice?"

The old man slapped his overall leg and chuckled as he fumbled with one of the fifty keys on a large round ring. Finally, he made the match with the door lock and swung the office door back until it bounced off an army surplus filing cabinet.

Drew smiled politely, "We just need a spot for the night, on my way to the Valley. We'll use all the hook-ups though. What about the shower; is there hot water?" Drew thought to himself that a hot shower would set the night up just perfect. The Texas road film had stuck to him, glued by the sweat from changing the tire. He didn't want to wake up smelling himself first thing in the morning; and he did have gentle company.

"Sorry, turned the heater off last week—no use spending the money in the off-season. I'll give you a discount though. That'll be $17.50. It'll get you lights and water. You can use the shower if you want, it ain't that bad pad'ner, you look like you can handle it?"

"Probably, but I've got a lady with me. That's all right, we'll manage. What time's checkout?"

Drew completed his business with the Gabby Hayes look-a-like and on the way back to the trailer he stuck his head in the shower room. They were clean but reminded him of his navy days. The showerheads protruded out of a concrete block wall, no dividers, no privacy. He felt the chill already.

"Coffee's on."

"Good, I could use a cup to dilute some of that Tex-Mex grease. Say, if you want a shower you better go now before the sun goes down. There's no hot water."

"Maybe we ought to complain to the Chamber." Ree grinned and put the sugar jar and spoon on the table that made into a bed.

"Even a cold shower sounds good to me. Is that it over by the office?"

"That's it, the little concrete building, should be private. There's no one else in the park besides us and the inn-keeper."

"Can you watch the coffee? I'll be back in a minute."

"You bet. I'll hook us up to the power...say do you know how to play chess?"

Ree turned and looked over her shoulder and spoke through a smile, "Say, you really are a gentleman aren't you?"

"Maybe. Haven't you heard of strip chess?" Drew displayed a sheepish grin.

INSPIRATION

DREW TOOK HIS COFFEE AND A LITTLE RED CHAIR he kept in the tiny closet out of the trailer. After he plugged in the power cord, he leaned back until the back caught against the light pole and looked out on what must have been the lemon grove that park was named for. There were only two trees with branches in a line of ten. Stumps showed where the rest had lived their brief life. The two still standing were dead but hadn't rotted enough to shed their primary branches. Drew wondered if they ever produced lemons this far north.

Typical deal he thought, a man's dream of retirement. A little trailer park to tend along with the lemon trees; spend the years talking to the snow-birders as they pass through and offer them fresh lemon-aid. The freeze of '83 took care of the trees. The concrete and a cold shower were all he had left to offer.

"Your turn. Burrr, my teeth are still chattering. You should have saved that coffee until you get back from the Arctic. You're going to need it."

"Pretty cold, huh?"

"That's not the word for it."

Ree bent at the waist and shook out her hair. She let it hang down and rubbed the braids out between the folds of one of Drew's dishtowels.

Drew sipped at his coffee and watched. There was something about a woman just out of the shower that gave him a good feeling. Cleanliness, familiarity, who knows.

"Guess I better get with it," Drew eased the chair legs back to the ground. "Cold, huh? He repeated."

"You know about the well-digger's wallet?"

"That cold?"

"That cold."

THING OF MYSTERY

"I'LL SAY ONE THING FOR A COLD SHOWER; it really gives you an energy boost. What about you?"

"I'm OK, didn't get much sleep last night." Drew noticed Ree's mood had changed a little. She seemed tight again. The way she was at the DQ.

"Maybe I'm being paranoid Drew but I'd swear I saw Buddy's truck pass out on the highway while you were in the shower. Do you think that's possible?"

"Anything is possible. Does that scare you?"

"A little."

"Does he know your friend in McAllen, what's her name?"

"Juanita, everybody calls her Jane. Yes, he knows her. Jane spent a couple of weeks with us last summer. Buddy never liked her. He hardly talked to Jane. He didn't like my friends much. But he does know how to get in touch with her and where she lives in McAllen."

"Have you talked to her since you pulled out of...what was that place?"

"Lancaster. No I haven't called her yet. Maybe that's a good thing, what do you think?"

"Maybe. How do you know she'll be at home when you get there?"

"I don't. I think I'll go call her now. Is there a phone in the office?"

"I'm not sure. Want some advice?"

"Sure. Listen Drew, I didn't mean to pull you into this. Maybe I should catch the bus out of this place in the morning and let you get on with your trip?"

"That's up to you, but that's part of the advice. Why not just relax for a while. We're settled in pretty cozy for the night and things may look a little clearer with the morning sun. How's that sound?"

"That sounds pretty good. Want another cup of coffee?"

"No thanks. Don't want to catch a case of the big-eye tonight."

"Where's Chica going to sleep?"

"Oh, she'll curl up in the back of the Jeep. She'll be fine, probably sleep better than we will."

"She's a good dog. I haven't heard her bark once."

"She'll bark when it's called for. You about ready to turn in?"

"Yes, show me how to make the beds. Hey, what about the chess?"

"We'll save that for another time. My eyes are looking more Chinese every minute. Think we should give-it-up for now."

THE STORM GENERATES ITS OWN SEED

THE EARLY SUN RAISED THE TEMPERATURE rapidly in the cab of the pickup. The night had been uncomfortably cool but the day was going to be hot in McAllen. Already a southwesterly breeze was blowing in from the desert on the Mexican side. At first light, the traffic moving up and down Pecan Street consisted mainly of trucks and vans making the early morning deliveries to the convenience stores, bread, milk, beer, and the like. It was still too early for the commuters.

Buddy raised himself from the seat and looked around. He yawned and took the folded city map off the dash. Sixteenth and Pecan was only four blocks away. He had marked it before leaving Lancaster. Forty-two, forty-six, Sixteenth Street was the address that interested him. According to the little red numbers on the map, the house should be two blocks off Pecan and about in the middle of the block.

Buddy started the truck, pulled out of the Valley Shopping Center parking lot and looked for a McDonalds. Coffee and a pit stop were his first order of business. As he pulled into the lot and hit the brakes, his right leg cramped. The drive took almost all night. He had slept the rest in the truck.

The sheriff's call had come before noon from Falls County. The conversation still moved through his thoughts while he sipped at the black coffee.

Is this Mr. Skinner? Mr. Charles Edward Skinner? We believe we have your truck down here in George West. Is the license number AKB-667, a black Ford, right? Was it stolen? A lady at the DQ gave us a good description of a woman that left it there. There was a note with your name and phone number. Sorry we had to pry a little on the wind-wing glass to get in. The keys were under the front mat. You can pick it up at the sheriff's office on Randolph and 281. Be sure to bring proof of ownership. Oh, by the way, the counter girl said she thinks the lady left with some guy ... maybe in a Jeep with a camper attached.

"Greg, this is Buddy. Man I need a big favor. I need a ride to George West, now."

"What the hell is George West; what's the deal Buddy?"

"Hell man, it's one of those little cow patty towns south of San Antonio, how should I know. It's about six, seven hours from here."

"Shit man! what about work?"

"Greg, fuck work, we'll call in. Listen this is important. I need this favor, come on Greg. I'll pay for the frigin' gas. I need to go right now."

"You having trouble again with your old-lady? Where's your truck?"

"The damn truck is in George West. Hey Greg, you owe me, what about the ride. Yes or no?"

"OK, OK. Let me get my shit together. I'll be there in 30 minutes. I'll have Betty call work for me. You better do the same man."

"Hello."

"Dorothy, this is Buddy, do you know where Ree is?"

"Well, Buddy, she's not with you? Buddy we've been worried about ... "

"Listen Dorothy don't play that shit with me, she stole my fuckin' truck and took off. I want to know where she's gone."

"Buddy, please, there's no need to talk that way, what do you mean, she stole your truck?"

"Goddamn Dorothy I don't have time for this. I got a call from some John Wayne sheriff down south of San Antonio. He says he has my truck. That's where Ree left it and I want to know where she's gone. Now, what did she tell you?"

"Buddy ... I haven't talked with her."

"Holy shit! Dorothy ..."

"Buddy, calm down son, what's the problem?" Horace took the phone from Dorothy who was trembling.

"Horace, listen to me man and listen damn close. I've had it up-to-here with your fuckin' family. I'm going to find Ree with or without you and there's going to be hell to pay when I do. You can count on that old man."

"Buddy threats won't help, now calm down and tell me what has happened between you and Ree."

"You know goddamn well what's happened, you sons-of-bitches. Your daughter has split and taken my truck...and...what has she done with Savage...she took my frigin' dog too."

"Buddy, we don't know where she is either but..."

"Horace, you better pay attention you fucker, I'll find her for you, you can bet on it."

The receiver bounced twice before coming to rest on the phone stand.

Chapter 5

Chapter 5

THE COFFEE STEAM FOGGED BUDDY'S SUNGLASSES as he cruised slowly down Sixteenth Street. The street was wide and lined with brick fronts that opened through iron gates on Spanish-style courtyards. Most of the house numbers were of letters made from twisted wrought iron and attached to the façade. He drove slowly past 4246. Bougainvillea grew through ironwork that topped the brick and Buddy could see nothing of the inside of the house. There was no hint of life. Buddy hated this place already. A bunch of upper-middle class Hispanic south Texas bullshit he thought. Everything neat and well protected from the street drug-dealers by rear-entry garages and alarm systems. He parked four houses down from Jane's in front of a plumber's truck.

Buddy intended to stay right here until Ree showed up or Jane came out. He'd find out where Ree was from Jane, he knew it. Jane was the only friend Ree still kept in touch with.

The sun was getting high and the glare through the front windshield was giving Buddy a headache. He reached up and pulled the sun visor down to shade his eyes. As he did, a piece of paper floated down and stuck between his legs. Buddy picked it up and looked at the bold type of the heading.

Dr. Billy A. Gibson, Veterinarian. "What the hell is this for?" he said aloud. Buddy looked at the charge description. *Euthanasia.* Then he saw it. *Buddy, pit-bull terrier, approximate age 3, weight 75 lbs. Charge $30.00.*

Buddy's jaw tightened as he kept reading and re-reading Dr. Gibson's receipt for services. He glanced at 4246 Sixteenth Street and back down at the paper. Nervously he started the engine and then turned it off.

Patience, that's what I need patience, he talked to his contorted image in the rear-view mirror. Buddy folded the receipt and opened the glove box to stuff it in with the insurance papers. That's when he saw the pistol grip of the Glock sticking in among the papers. Buddy often carried it in the glove compartment, but he had been in such a rush to get away from Lancaster that he had forgotten to take it out of the chest-of-drawers. How in the hell did this thing get here, he asked himself. He took it out of the compartment and held the space-age plastic gun in his hand. He began to work the action back and forth. Run the hollow points in and out of the chamber. Reload the clip and do it again. It calmed his emotions, gave him something to do. Something to pass the time while he waited for Ree.

JUST A HALF CUP

"DID I SNORE?" Ree handed Drew a cup of coffee and sat down on the steps of the trailer.

"You couldn't tell it by me—I slept like a dead man." Drew tilted the red chair back, took his sunglasses off his cap and put them on. The morning sun was at least ten degrees above the horizon. This part of Texas was so flat that the sun made its presence known quickly after first light. There weren't many trees or hills to postpone the daily evolution of light and heat.

Ree sat down in the doorway of the trailer, reached up and retrieved her coffee cup from the countertop next to the four-burner stove.

"I dreamed all night long. Crazy dreams. One was more than strange. I got into this elevator and there were a bunch of people. Most of them were overweight, you know real fat. We all were going up and then suddenly the elevator car, whatever you call it, began to fall. There was nothing we could do, we pushed buttons, one woman even picked up that little emergency phone and calmly told someone that we are falling. That didn't matter, the car just kept falling. Then I was alone in the elevator...but it kept falling. I remember watching the floor as the thing shook. I couldn't tell the whole thing was moving except I could feel the shaking. Then it crashed and I died. I saw it so plain. It was so bright. There was a lot of light. I died. But it didn't hurt. I remember thinking in the dream that I would wake up before the elevator crashed. But I didn't. Drew, I've never died before in a dream."

Drew looked at Ree quizzically for a moment. "I heard or read somewhere that if you died in your dream you really died. So much for that theory I guess...you are alive aren't you?" Drew asked through a half-smile.

"Yes, I think so. At least I have a headache. I wouldn't think you'd have a headache after you died." Ree smiled a little and watched the steam rising off the cup. She tried not to think about Lancaster and Buddy, about her mother and her job and her life back there. Ree looked up slowly at Drew and studied his silhouette. He looked comfortable, relaxed, at peace. The sun was directly behind his head, which formed a shield between the brightness and Ree's eyes.

"Tell me something Drew. How come you were so nice to me yesterday, listened to my tale of woe?"

"My mother always taught me to be nice to strangers," he responded with a dead-pan expression.

"Seriously."

Drew sipped at the coffee and kept his gaze directed at the lifeless lemon orchard. "Oh I don't know. Suppose I was just trying to be sympathetic to someone in need. I'm not always like that. Most times, I'm selfish. The fact is that if you weren't so attractive I'd have turned you down for the ride."

"So you think I'm attractive?"

"That I do."

Ree got up. "Want another cup?"

"Sure."

"You don't strike me as a selfish person."

"Wait a while, it'll come out. Just a half-a-cup, that'll do it, right there."

"Need some more sugar?"

"Sure, poquito. Just a little. That's part of the reason I'm heading south. I'm looking to find a place to give a little something back." Drew sipped at his coffee and went quiet. "You know we really need to get on the road, you about ready?"

"Sure, just let me get the stuff on the stove stored. I think I'll call Jane before we leave town. That all right?"

"Of course. There's a store on the next corner. We'll get some sweet rolls and you can use the phone there."

"Drew did you see Chica's ears when you said sweet rolls?"

"That little bitch knows all the words that go with treat. Get the trailer ready and I'll unhook the power and water. We'll stop by the old man's trailer and say adios on the way out. Hand me a couple of those lemons out of the cooler will you?"

"NO ANSWER. I GUESS JUANITA HAD THE LATE SHIFT." Ree reached into the bag and pulled out a roll covered with sugar. White granules sprinkled across her lap as she tried to take a bite.

"We'll try again down the road, maybe in Falfurrias. It's about an hour, maybe an hour-and-a-half from here. Can you hold this coffee for me until we get rolling?"

Drew was glad to get back on the road. The events of yesterday and Ree had taken his mind away from the road. Away from the change. The sun felt good coming over his left shoulder, warm but not yet hot. Fresh and clean. Everything was clean this morning. The mornings were Drew's favorite time. He loved the morning. A time of hope renewed every twenty-four hours. His mind was clear in the morning, uncluttered with the sights, sounds and news of the day that he couldn't seem to avoid. It all built up during the day and reminded him of impending calamity by the time he fell asleep at night. Then doom turned to hope again in the morning.

It was quiet now in the Jeep. Like before the blowout yesterday. Ree continued to crumble sweet roll sugar on her lap and sip coffee. Drew watched the road and concentrated on rebuilding his image of Mexico. It was an exercise he had repeated over and over for the last six months, ever since deciding to make the move.

He never could seem to get it right though. It was a world that he had no clue about, any experience. As a Texan, Drew had made the obligatory trips across the border; to Piedras Niegras, Acuña, Reynosa, but he knew that they weren't Mexico. Kind of like going to New York to find out about the United States. He had tried reading the Mexican newspapers but he suspected that they, like there counterpart in the U.S., gave only a piece of the picture, an urban picture of Monterrey or Mexico City, not the rural Mexico, México profundo of the Indian south.

He glanced at the little map on the dash and wondered why Ree hadn't asked about it. The line was clearly marked. Maybe she was being polite. Maybe she didn't care. Simply caught up in her own troubles and trips. That made sense. She was in crisis, immediate and tangible. Drew's destination was remote and foreign, it wasn't important.

"Drew."

When he didn't answer, she repeated herself. "Drew."

"Yeah." Drew's head reluctantly came back to the moment. He reached for the cold coffee sitting on the dash.

"You were a long way off."

"I suppose."

At the sound of voices, Chica moved to her station between the seats and curiously gazed down the road as if she was needed to confirm their direction was the correct one. Drew stuck his hand in the sweet roll bag between his legs and pinched off a piece of the sugarcoated dough. He offered it to his dog. Chica accepted the sweetness quickly and retreated.

"Where are you going Drew?"

"To McAllen, I told you that yesterday."

"No, I mean from the Valley. You're crossing over, into Mexico, aren't you?"

Drew wondered if he had mentally steered Ree to her question. He did really want to talk. Explain his trip, the events that led to the changes. Drew needed to talk about his plans. The echo of his words provided a test of logic. If the idea didn't sound right, it probably wasn't.

"Yes."

"Why?"

To Drew the tone in Ree's voice didn't suggest just a polite question. It was warmer, deeper. The kind of sound that makes a man want to launch into his story. Hoping for sympathy or a connection.

Drew turned towards Ree who was smiling. "You want the short or long version?" he said.

AT THE GATE

"WHY?" DREW HELD THE LITTLE WORD mentally up in front of him for a moment. It was a simple question.

Why am I going to Mexico?

Then the branching started, pushing the simplicity out of the way, buried in mind clutter.

Why am I going to Mexico? ... well ... well because ... because I need to. What other reason do we need? But, then, why do you need to? I need to because I want to avoid the alternatives. I need to because all the things I've done in forty-nine years have put me here, in this Jeep, in this place. But, why did you do all those things in those forty-nine years ... that have put you here, on this road to Mexico?

Yes, it was the search. The search that eventually everyone says is the reason for what they do in this life. The search. Well, the search for what? The search for the easy life? ... a different life from the one you have now? The life already created and built on, invested in? or the life you think you deserve? The life that includes all you believe you want? Security; the perfect love ... blah, blah, blah.

Or, perhaps, it's only avoidance, running from the troubles. You know the third failed marriage, the business collapse, the bankruptcy. The overbearing reach of the IRS? Isn't that it?

No, it's the feeling of time moving. Movement that begins to limit choices until recently, I took for granted. The movement is so real at forty-nine, so much more than before, maybe my last chance. A real adventure; few get that...right? I need to create something; something I don't have, never will have if the pattern isn't broken. This pattern wasn't ever mine anyway. It was given to me, dictated, by others, by the momentum of history, a culture, my people; handed to me, a part to play. Do your share. Contribute. Be like us.

That's it! That's why.

NO! That's only a part. Only a part. There's more. There's another reason. There's more to it.

"A friend asked me to come to Mexico to help out with a project." Drew started.

"He's got this idea that we can save a piece of a tropical rainforest that still exists in southern Mexico. It's not big like the one in the Amazon but he thinks it's important."

Drew stopped there and pointed to the map on the dash. "It's called the Lacandon Jungle...it's down here. His finger touched an irregular green patch on the map. "Here, right here, in the Mexican state of Chiapas. Almost to Guatemala."

"Are you some kind of scientist Drew?" Ree bent forward to make out the small detail on the map.

Drew smiled. "No, but there will a bunch of those types working on this thing when I get there. No my job, at least from what I have been told, is to help them raise money. From what I know, they want to build some agriculture experimental stations around the rainforest. Help the Indian people grow more food, something like that, stop cutting the trees so fast. I really don't know a whole lot right now. He asked me just to come to Tuxtla-Gutiérrez, that's where my friend lives. My friend said he would explain everything when I got there."

"Tu ... Tux ... whatever, is here, right?" Ree stuck the city point with her fingernail."

"That's it ... the capital of the state of Chiapas, Mexico."

"Who is your friend?"

"Joaquín?" Oh, he's a Mexican rancher. I've lived on one of his ranches the last couple of years. He has cattle operations in the States, the ranch I lived on near San Antonio and a couple more out near Uvalde. His big operations though are in Mexico, in Chiapas. That's where his family lives. Joaquín is quite a story, but I'll save that for another time. That's part of the long version."

Drew didn't want to open that can of worms with Ree. It would be too hard to explain. Drew had known Joaquín for seven years, ever since he did ad work for one of his high-dollar cattle sales. Joaquín and a small group of corporate ranchers played tax games with their purebred cattle. They sold the same Santa-Gertrudis cattle back and forth among themselves, raising the stakes as they went from one ranch sale to the next. Some of the bulls went for over a million bucks. It was a hell of a good tax write-off until the Congress changed the tax codes. Caught a lot of the condominium cowboys with their chaps down around their boot spurs. Joaquín was one of them. He lost over a half-million on a single animal.

Drew remembered that bull well. They called him Macho. After Joaquín took the loss, he had as much semen collected from the poor son-of-bitch as possible in a ten-day period. Drew could still see the animal in a collection squeeze pen the last days of his life. He was a magnificent thing, went about two-thousand pounds, all muscle. But he was rendered immobile by hydraulic pistons pushing against two tube steel sidewalls with an electric prod stuck in his ass. Once a day a little guy named Roblés would flip a switch and the jolt of current made Macho empty his scrotum into in a quart bottle and squirt liquid shit about two-feet out the back end. The big monster just shook like a piece of Jell-O and bellowed every time Roblés passed him the juice. By the third day, Macho would start to shit when he saw the little Mexican come into the barn. Drew remembered how Roblés seemed to take pleasure from making Macho blow his product.

The process filled about three large nitrogen bottles with preserved semen straws. Enough to raise countless generations with Macho's genes. Joaquín wanted to make sure, that if the U.S. Congress changed their mind about the tax write off he'd be ready to re-coup his loss.

Joaquín then had Macho butchered in San Antonio and distributed a box of Macho steaks to all the hands on the Running~Bar. And so he wouldn't forget the lesson learned, Joaquín had Macho's balls bronzed. The orbs protruding through a deep golden, but cold metal sack now resting on his desk holding down the monthly bills to be paid.

"Wait a minute Drew. You've lived on a ranch, right?" Ree didn't wait for the response. "Are you a cowboy?"

"No...I'm not a cowboy either. Oh, I helped out sometimes but I wouldn't call myself a cowboy. No, I've done a lot of things in my life. Guess I haven't really decided what I want to be when I grow up." Drew paused and took in a deep breath.

95

"The best handle I can give you is that I have a worthless Master's degree in Political Science; worked at city planning and that kind of stuff for a number of years. Then I got tired of the bureaucracy and the bullshit and got into graphics, proposal writing for grants, advertising, anything to make a buck on my own. I had a small company for a while until the Texas oil-based economy went belly-up in the early 80s. The only thing left after that was a bunch of bad debts and a bankruptcy. Oh, and the IRS on my tail. That's when I moved the few sticks of furniture I had left in this old Jeep to the Running~Bar Ranch. Just wanted to hide out for a while. You know, lick my wounds?"

"Yeah ... I think so."

"This is my chance to break out. I'm ready to get back in the fight, I guess. Mexico seems like a good place to start."

"What about family? Are you married? Kids?"

Drew stuck his tongue in his cheek and grinned at Ree's question.

"What are you grinning about?" Ree returned the smile.

"Oh ... nothing. One kid, a girl, she's grown and three ex's, all from Texas. You know the George Strait song 'All My Ex's Live In Texas', that's me. Remember what I told you about being selfish?"

"That's why you're divorced?"

"A big part of it."

"What's your daughter's name?"

"Jeannie."

"Where does she live?"

"Just up the road from where you came from yesterday, North Dallas somewhere." Drew's voice was a little softer, his words more deliberate.

"Hey, we're almost to Falfurrias. You want to make that call?"

"Yeah, sure."

REPTILIAN BRAIN

BUDDY WAS RESTLESS just sitting in the cab of the pickup. He was beginning to doubt his strategy of waiting. Maybe she wasn't coming to see Jane; maybe she was already back at home. Maybe he should call. *Shit, I'm not getting anything done here,* he thought. Buddy didn't have much patience for waiting. He wanted to be doing something about this mess now. He wanted to confront Ree. He wanted her in the truck, right now, out on the road, getting it straightened out, once and for all. Talk some sense to her. *Why in hell did Ree kill my dog?*

Just as Buddy was about to start the pickup, Jane came out in the front yard in her bathrobe. She reached down to pick up the newspaper and snapped the rubber band. Buddy watched her intently, trying to decide what to do. He had two choices as he figured it. Go intercept Jane now in the front yard, find out what was going on...maybe Ree was already there, inside drinking coffee...or maybe he should wait. Watch for signs, be sure first. Not warn Jane that he was here in McAllen waiting for Ree. Jane might tell Ree not to come.

Jane looked up from the headlines and glanced down the street. Buddy slid down in the seat a little. He thought she looked right at him. Did she know it was him? Did she recognize the truck? He wasn't sure. He decided to wait it out. Just then, as Jane seemed to be looking his way, he saw her head turn around toward the house abruptly. Jane bent over, picked up a stray paper soft-drink cup quickly from the yard and moved hurriedly towards the front door.

Buddy couldn't wait anymore. He lifted the door handle and slid off the seat onto the pavement. He had to find out what was going on, what Jane knew. He was about to walk over to the house when he realized he still had the pistol in his hand. Buddy turned to throw it back in the truck but stopped. Instead, he stuffed the gun in his belt behind his back. He pulled his windbreaker jacket down over the handle and began walking toward the wrought-iron gate Jane had left open as she went back into the house. Buddy figured she had heard the phone.

He walked along the curb in the street until he came within one house of Jane's. The neighborhood was still and quiet except for a small dog barking from one of the townhouses. There wasn't any way to know if he was being watched. Buddy didn't really care. He just wanted to get on with this business. Get Ree back. He stood in front of Jane's house for a moment. He could see she had not closed the front door. He strained to hear inside. That's when he noticed the snake. It was about as big around as a man's forearm. Buddy couldn't tell how long it might be because it was coiled around one of the small stone yard statues. It was right where Jane had picked up the paper. Buddy couldn't tell what kind of snake it was either. It had some markings on its back but he wasn't sure if it was a rattler. He wondered what the hell it was doing up here in the neighborhood. So close to people.

The snake was stationed on a line between Buddy and Jane's front door. He reflexively reached under his jacket and fingered the pistol. The snake didn't move. It captured Buddy's attention completely. *Hell, maybe it's not real...some rubber imitation...to scare the squirrels or something stupid like that.*

98

Buddy stepped up on the curb and took a couple of steps toward the door when he saw the forked sensor shoot from the coiled monster. He jumped sideways and held onto the handle of the gun. Jane laughed from inside the house. Buddy stopped, eyes still on the snake, he listened, straining to hear. He could only make out bits and pieces of the conversation. He couldn't tell who she was talking to, but he thought he heard her say something about the front door key. He wasn't sure. The snake's tongue was continuing to evaluate its immediate environment and capture Buddy's heat signature.

"Shit on this," he mumbled and began to move in a precautionary arc towards the door. Buddy's eyes stayed in contact with the reptile and watched the tongue for signs of movement. He kept his upper body turned toward the danger. He was almost to the front door when his left boot caught in the green garden hose curled deep in the Saint Augustine grass. He looked down instantly and saw another snake. His right boot stepped on the same hose and made him pitch forward violently. He caught himself with his left hand and his forehead on the gate. The pistol was in his right hand as it hit the gate, which slammed shut with a loud clank and locked. His right arm slipped through the bars, he lost his grip on the gun, and it flew toward the front door and clattered on the front steps.

Buddy pulled himself up and spun around to see where the snake was. *Where is that damn thing?* He jerked his head around and looked at the pistol, now out of reach and lying just inside the front door on a mat. Buddy scrambled for a way to open the gate, it only had a key latch, no handle. Then he heard Jane say something into the phone, something about a noise. Buddy went on a run to the truck.

"DID YOU GET JUANITA?" Drew could tell before he asked that she had. Ree's face reflected something different from when she had gone in to use the phone at the Tastee-Freeze Drive-In just off the square in Falfurrias.

"You're not going to believe this." Ree flopped into the front seat and didn't bother to close the door. She stared straight ahead for a moment through the windshield and then turned to face Drew. "I was right," her voice was a whisper.

"Right?...about what?"

"You remember when I said I thought I saw Buddy's truck go past back at the Lemon Grove trailer park?"

"I do."

"Well, I think it must have been. This is strange. You know just now when I was talking to Juanita; we were making plans to meet when I got to McAllen...and, while we're talking, Jane hears her front gate slam. She tells me to hang on a minute so she can see who it is. When she gets back on the line she is breathing fast and she's excited about something. Drew, this is the strange part. She tells me she's got some kind of gun in her hand...says it was lying just inside her front door, right there on the foot mat."

"Let me take a guess. It's a Glock pistol?"

"Exactly. Buddy must have been right there while I was talking to Jane. But, why would he throw the gun into her house? I'm getting frightened Drew. Buddy can be strange at times but this sounds too crazy even for him."

"How's Jane taking it?"

"She just laughed when I told her the story and why I was coming. She said get your butt down to McAllen, right now. It is just like her. She told me that we would get my life straightened out muy pronto. They'd do it together."

"She's not afraid of Buddy?"

"Drew I don't think that Jane's afraid of the devil himself. She does a lot of community service work in the barrios, some tough neighborhoods. She even counsels gang members, helps them to make the break with that kind of life. No, Jane's not afraid of Buddy. She said she'd shoot the son-of-a-bitch with his own gun if he caused trouble. She thinks it's all a joke. Jane thinks he's playing mind games with me. Trying to scare me into coming back."

"Well, at least you know where Buddy is. So what now?"

"Damn Drew. What have I started? I don't want anybody to get hurt or in trouble. Maybe I should just find Buddy in McAllen and try to turn this mess around myself before it gets completely out-of-hand. What the hell do I do?"

"As I see it Ree you've got two choices. You can catch a bus and head back to Lancaster, deal with it there, stay with your parents until Buddy gets back and talk to him at their house. Or, you can go on to McAllen with me and I'll drop you off there with Jane; your friend can help you sort this thing out."

"What would you do Drew?"

Drew spread a big grin across his face and reached over and touched Ree's hand lightly, "Hell lady, I'd go to Mexico." Ree gave Drew's hand a squeeze, reached out and pulled the door shut. She turned loose and pulled the seat belt across her lap. "Guess we better get going, uh?"

"Guess we'd better."

CHAPTER 6

PEACOCKS IN PARADISE

THE SCREECH OF THE PAVOREAL shattered the pre-dawn silence. It was still pitch black outside. The sun would require another thirty minutes to make its appearance, and then another two hours before its direct light climbed the backside of the jungle mountain that shielded the eastern flank of Rancho Julieta.

Joaquín abruptly opened his eyes and stared at the ceiling. He barely could make out the faint lines of the slats that crossed the massive wood beams. The ceiling was a lofty twelve feet from the highly polished hardwood floor. All of the woodwork in the ranch house was hand finished from Joaquin's stock of rare tropical hardwoods that he kept hidden in an old storage barn at his ranchito in Tuxtla-Gutiérrez. The tropical hardwoods were contraband in Mexico. Logging had been declared illegal and all the mills closed in Chiapas in a faint-hearted government effort to deal with the deforestation that was rapidly denuding the mountain sides all over the state.

Joaquín loved this ranch house. The rough tan adobe walls and reflective rich woods melded into simple elegant lines. The type usually found only in Mexico City or in Phoenix. Joaquín was proud of his ranches, all of them. He was proud of the way he took them and polished the raw material into jewels. But in the darkness, Joaquín wondered why he had brought those obnoxious birds to the ranch. Their piercing calls in the pre-dawn darkness shattered his nerves.

Joaquín rolled his head on the pillow and squinted to see something in the darkness from the window. The transition was beginning and the obscurity was yielding to shapes. He thought he saw Ernesto heading up to the milking stalls in the corral at the backside of the ranch. It was either Ernesto or Cruz or Jorge. They all had the same gate when they walked. Joaquín could not tell one from the other in the dark. He thought about shouting out an order to capture the peacocks before the first light but thought better of it.

Instead, he watched some movement in the trees. It was the gangly images of the spider monkeys already at their work. They were swinging in the dimness on the end of restraining ropes from one mango tree to the next. Joaquín preferred to watch them in the daytime, mostly in the hot afternoons when the ranch was quiet and sleepy. He would take a chair from the house and sit near the changos, to watch their acrobatics. It was like a circus next to the ranch house. They never seemed to tire of the swinging. The monkeys spent the day swinging; occasionally they grew quiet and slept or diligently tried to untie their binds. Usually it was only the females who figured out how to do that. Then they would head for the big house with their tether coiled up vaquero style in their prehensile tail. The smart ones held the rope just out of reach from danger of capture. If their luck held, Joaquín would be at the ranch house, the monkey would sit on his lap for a while and Joaquín would offer the fugitive cut-up pieces of mango while he rubbed their backs.

The roosters now began to pick up the pre-dawn tempo. Their calls blended with those of their wild cousins the chachalacus in the nearby jungle. They were great noisemakers too, almost as good as the peacocks. They lived in the small remnant clusters of rainforest trees on the slopes of the encircling mountains and competed with the roosters for the privilege of waking the dead.

Joaquín finally gave up and swung his legs off the edge of the bed as he tried to focus his attention on something besides the cacophony. He studied his belly for a moment as he sat on the edge. His chin rested on his chest. It was getting out of control he thought. Joaquín considered a walk to the front gate before breakfast but decided against it when his sense of smell detected coffee. The exercise and the growing bulge around his middle would have to wait for another time.

Anna Marie had quietly come and gone in the dark before all the excitement began. She, like all the indígenas on the ranch, moved noiselessly. Even during the busiest part of the day, they went mostly unnoticed. Like apparitions, only the consequences of their coming and goings stood out. The flowers watered, fresh tortillas on the table, the dirty clothes no longer in the corner but cleaned and neatly folded in the drawers of the carved bureau dresser in Joaquín's room.

Joaquín did notice the women of the ranch when they walked to the highway to catch the bus to Coita. Someone from each of the families that occupied the three vaquero houses went shopping once every couple of weeks. Normally just the women journeyed the 24 kilometers to the market town and bought the families' staples; the frijoles, the masa and chilies. The men only went to town when there was a fiesta or a meeting of the cattlemen's association. Just the women with their miniature people along side or wrapped in a cloth bundle slung across the shoulders walked the dirt entrance road. Joaquín was fascinated with the Indian children. They appeared not to be children at all but more like undersize adults. They reminded him of armadillos, five small adults following behind the mama, no difference in their manner except for scale.

The entourage would crawl through the fence that lined both sides of the ranch road and deliberately move down one of the gravel tracks that led straight for a mile to the gate. All without fanfare or circumstance, not even a look back or a wave goodbye to those left behind. Every few minutes Joaquín would look up from his work or reading and peer at the figures as they became slowly smaller in the distance. Then finally he would look up and all had vanished.

The men likewise were quiet. The vaqueros moved the cattle between pastures, put a stud on a mare, or prepared the cornfield for planting without undue commotion or distraction. The three thousand hectare ranch absorbed the ten of them, the men, boys, and their daily routines. They were seldom seen around the main house. Only the peacocks and the undisciplined dogs who barked at imaginings or out of boredom invaded the quiet of the day. Joaquín pulled back the large double wood doors and stepped out onto the covered porch to take his morning coffee.

This was going to be a big day or so he hoped. He had come to Julieta the night before to calm himself. Joaquín left Felicia behind. He did not want to talk to anyone, least of all his wife. Felicia didn't like the Rancho Julieta anyway. She didn't like any of Joaquín's other houses. The house in Tuxtla; that was her house. The rest carried too many ghosts. To Felicia they were Joaquín's houses or Joaquín's dead father's houses. In Tuxtla the house belonged to her, she ruled the rhythm there. She said who came and went and how they were to be treated. She gave the servants the orders and presided.

However, this morning there was just Joaquín and his coffee. The nervousness was returning as he thought about the trilogy of communications he was to have on this Monday, all critical, all dangerous. Dr. Solomon E. Boxxloader would be the first via phone to Texas A&M. Sol Boxxloader, crusty old Sol Boxxloader. He had been like a father to Joaquín when he studied crop pathology twenty years ago in the United States. Boxxloader was a miracle man to Joaquín. He was a Nobel laureate. It was Boxxloader's work in Mexico that Joaquín respected most. The old teacher had spent most of his professional life in Mexico and was as much Mexican as American; a fact Boxxloader boasted of often. Now Joaquín needed him again; needed his name, his prestige and respect, needed his ability to open doors and attract money.

The need for influence and power was the reason for all the discussions Joaquín would have this day. Father Pedro Ortega

Sanchez-Roblés, Bishop in San Cristóbal de Las Casas and Patrocinio Rodolfo Gomez Santo, Gobernador de Chiapas, were both on his agenda. The cup shook imperceptibly in Joaquín's hand as he went over the mental speeches he had prepared for each.

"Buenos días, Don Joaquín." Gilberto had come up on to the porch and taken his hat off before he addressed the Patron.

"Buenos días, Jefe, ¿cómo estás?"

"Aquí estamos Don Joaquín."

The conversation would not be different from any other morning between the two men. There would be the normal exchange of pleasantries; then asking for and receiving the status of the herd; a complaint or two about this fence or that untended flower bed. In Mexico, the rituals are important and rarely vary. Except for last month, when Mariano was killed.

His sudden death still bothered Joaquín. If Gilberto had told him about Mariano's drinking, had deviated from the ritual and talked about Mariano driving the tractor drunk; or told him of the beatings Mariano administered to Calenderia and little Mauricio, maybe Joaquín could have done something in time. Something, maybe moved Mariano and his family to the remote ranch near the jungle at Las Palmas or fire him or something. But Gilberto, in his quiet way, protected Mariano until Mariano stumbled into the path of grain truck at night on his way back from the bar at the ranchito Aguilita. Mariano's body had been slammed far off the road into the acahual; the weeds shrouded it for three days unseen. The truck driver hadn't stopped. He probably thought the sixty kilo Marianno was a dog or deer that bounced off the massive metal cattle guard. The men of the ranch never found Mariano's head. Gilberto said that the dogs probably carried it away. They never let Calenderia see the body.

Now Calenderia, Mauricio, Maria, Hugo, and the six month old Elizabeth had moved in with Ernesto's family. Joaquín couldn't force them off the ranch but he didn't know what to do with them either. There was no work on the Julieta; Anna Maria took care of the main house.

But there were more immediate matters to deal with this morning. Joaquín forced the thoughts of Mariano's abandoned family out of his head. There would be another day to consider the fate of Calendería and the children. The Indians could wait; they weren't going anywhere.

"Gilberto, tell Anna Marie I'll take my breakfast earlier this morning. I have to leave for Tuxtla before eight o'clock."

"Sí ingeniero," Gilberto turned and left for his small house through the lime trees. He felt one of the fruits as he passed. The limones would soon be ready, as would the mangos. The fruit would be welcomed by humans and animals alike. They would add variety to the tortillas and frijoles, a good change.

CREATIVE EMPOWERMENT

JOAQUÍN DROVE PAST HIS RANCHITO in Tuxtla and headed straight to the city and his office. He was anxious to talk with Boxxloader, and Boxxloader's secretary had promised that the old man would be in his office at exactly 9 a.m. in College Station.

He made an illegal u-turn across the boulevard median, dodging two overloaded colectivos as he crossed two lanes of traffic and darted into the last parking place in front of the building. Joaquín glanced up at the second story office window of the

Consejo and offered a quick prayer that all the papers and reports were ready for tomorrow night's meeting with the state producer's organization. Everything had to be perfect. He had to have a consensus from this group. One more piece in a complex puzzle.

But for now, Joaquín forced his thoughts back to Boxxloader. He had to practice his argument. Boxxloader wasn't going to be an easy sell and he knew it. And without Boxxloader's help, Joaquín's grand scheme for the Selva Lacandona would be dead upon arrival.

"Buenos días, Marta," Joaquín said as he entered and without waiting for a response continued through the office. He shouted back to his secretary and heaved his heavy briefcase onto his desk, "Marta, place a call to Dr. Solomon E. Boxxloader at Texas A&M in College Station, Texas por favor."

Marta had learned Joaquín's ways in the last year that she had worked for him. She could tell that polite conversation was not important this morning so she turned to the personal phone directory and began the search for the number.

She did her job calmly, but like the others in the office, Marta was frightened. The next two days were critical. The meeting and phone calls would determine whether she could keep her job or have to look for another one. In Tuxtla, the latter meant trouble. Women from all over Chiapas came here to work. It was the capital of the state and it was where the clerical jobs existed. There was only one other city anywhere close that offered these types of positions for women but Tapachula was too far from her family; it might as well be at the end of the world.

Marta dialed the phone. She hated calling to the United States. No one spoke Spanish. If the conversation had to go beyond a simple request, she would have a hard time making herself understood; she would have to turn it over to Joaquín, she would be embarrassed. It made her feel inefficient and vulnerable. It is why she studied her English dictionary at night.

The phone clicked through the connections and rang. Marta glanced at the clock. 7:52, 8:52 in College Station, Texas. *Please be there Dr. Boxxloader*, she thought.

"Hello."

""Good morning, how are you? Dr. Boxxloader please."

"Can I say who is calling please?" Marta recognized the word who.

"Sr. Joaquín Villa in Mexico, a call for Dr. Boxxloader please."

"Just a minute I'll take a peek in his office, I haven't seen him yet but maybe he snuck in on me, just a minute." Marta only understood the word office. She waited nervously.

"Hello," the voice belonged to Dr. Boxxloader. It was sharp and quick, no invitation to talk. But Marta was thrilled with the sound of it anyway. The professor spoke Spanish.

"Buenos días Doctor, tengo Sr. Villa para usted, un momento, por favor."

"Good morning Solomon," Joaquín tried to raise his cup of coffee to his lip but his hand was shaking so he slowly lowered it back to the desk; a few drops of coffee slid down the side of the cup.

"Good morning Joaquín, what have you got yourself into now. Dr. Mañcheco called me last night from Mexico City and said you were up to your bald cabeza in a new project. He said it was something to do with the rainforest. What the hell is going on?"

Joaquín broke into a smile. When the old man carried on, he was in a good mood. It was when he didn't talk that you knew you were in deep trouble. Once, many years before, Joaquín had

111

impulsively questioned one of Dr. Boxxloader's orders in the field; he was a graduate student at that time working on one Dr. Sol's projects in Mexico. Boxxloader just stared at him with his cold blue Norwegian eyes and walked away. It was two weeks before Joaquín so much as enjoyed a word in response to good morning from Dr. Sol.

"Solomon, I need you to come to Chiapas."

"I don't have time to come to Chiapas. As soon as I finish grading these exams, I'm supposed to go to Chad and try to straighten out the unholy mess they have going on over there. Now that we have them producing more grain than ever, they cannot find the places to store it. If it's not one thing, it's another. You don't grow it they starve, you grow it and they still starve. They can't even store it and distribute it. And now, you want me to come to Chiapas. There's no way."

"Just for one week Solomon, only for one week."

Somehow, the ranting and raving of Dr. Sol had calmed Joaquín. He raised his coffee cup and took a sip. It was cold but he didn't care.

"Solomon, I need your help. It's going to be difficult for me to give you the whole picture over the phone but permit me a few minutes to boil it down."

"I'm not ready to start grading these exams anyway so go ahead. But don't count on me when you finish, Joaquín."

"Solomon, being an old Mexico hand, you'll appreciate the story. I'm going to save the personal side of all of this for the future, maybe over a Scotch. But for now let me say that for the past year I have been putting together a statewide group of cattle raisers and agricultural producers to form a small power base. We call it COPA, the Consejo de Productores Agropecuarios. I am the president of the consejo. It's similar to the group you formed forty years ago in Senora for grain production. Well Solomon we had our 12th meeting last month and the topic for discussion was the ecological future of our state. The damn place is burning up."

Joaquín motioned for Jorge to bring the stack of reports Jorge kept neatly on the corner of his desk. Jorge moved quickly, as usual. Obediently.

"I've got the report right here; let me give you a sample. Let me see, here it is...1986 to 1988; average loss of primary forest to slash & burn agriculture, 15,000 hectares."

"Joaquín save the statistics, get to the kernel."

"OK, Solomon, this is my point. Some of us in this state realize that if we do not take some action, and soon, this whole state is going to become a desert. The migrants and campesinos are cutting down the rainforests at a rate that will produce total destruction in something like 15 years. Normally the producers could give a damn about the campesinos, but now Solomon, most are beginning to notice the change in climate...the change in rain patterns is beginning to make them nervous."

"It's the quickest way to get action, kick somebody in their pocket book and they get a social conscience and become born-again ecologists ¿muy pronto, no?"

"That's about it Solomon, but there's more. It seems like the whole of southern Mexico is turning green. Last week, I got calls from both ends of the political spectrum down here. The first one came from the governor's office. Some bureaucratic assistant calls me and tells me that none-other than Patrocinio Rodolfo Gomez Santo wants to see me about a matter of "considerable urgency," to use his phrase. I have an 11 o'clock meeting with him today. And then before I have enough time to digest that rare honor, the phone rings again and the voice of his most holiness Father Pedro Ortega Sanchez-Roblés, the Bishop in San Cristóbal de Las Casas asks about my family and wonders if I might find time to come to San Cristóbal for coffee. Solomon this is the person that controls half of Chiapas, especially the forest half that is full of Indians and the refugees from Guatemala. Are you beginning to get the drift?"

"More like an avalanche, Joaquín, go on."

"The gist of it all, I think, is that because of pressures coming out of Mexico City, big-time political pressures, the powers-that-be in Chiapas need to talk to each other and, you know, for Mexicans that's not always easy. They need a middle man to help them save face."

"What's the topic?"

"The environment, can you believe it Solomon; they want to talk to each other about the environment. My guess is that it has to do with the free-trade thing in the works between the U.S., Canada and Mexico. El Presidente wants this deal bad, very bad. The word must have gone out to the hinterlands to get a handle on the green things in your area. Mexico City wants to head off criticism when free trade comes to a vote in the American Congress. The President of Mexico has got enough problems on the border with the maquiladoras dumping everything toxic they can find into the rivers, he doesn't need any more blows from the environmentalists about Mexico slashing and burning the last of the tropical rainforests in North America into dry desert dust."

"How do I fit into all this? What's the big need for me down there?"

114

"To put it bluntly Solomon I need your name. I need a heavy hitter to take this thing out of the local or regional arena and kick ass all the way up the international ladder. I think the time is right to establish an International Center for Tropical Research right here in my backyard. And, Dr. Sol I want to be the one who pulls it off."

"You don't need me then. I am an old washed-up agronomist. The greenies labeled me a disaster for the planet years ago. They think my high input farming has destroyed the planet."

"Solomon listen to me, you're still a hero in Mexico. Rockefeller and those guys still listen to you. Aren't you still on the President's Council for Science and Technology in the States?"

"Sure, for whatever that group is good for. A bunch of office prima donnas that never see the sunshine or put a toe into the earth."

"We need you to help us Solomon. The timing is perfect if we are ever to get a handle on this thing. If we don't, we can kiss it all goodbye.

"Have you got enough rainforest down there to save?"

"I thought you wanted me to save the statistics."

"Don't get cute Joaquín."

"No offense meant Solomon but to answer your question, yes. There is still over 300,000 hectares in the Lacandon Jungle. A good portion to work with. I agree it is not the Amazon, but it is accessible and there is political stability down here now; that is at least for the time being. We do know of a small rebel group in the area but scientists and others can come without fear of being sliced up with machetes."

"But, Solomon there's more to it than that. If I'm reading this whole issue correctly, whoever can put together all the forces to

115

make a change, you know, politics, money, the works; will reap the benefits for their region. I want that to be Mexico in general and Chiapas in particular. I think we can create an ecological model for rainforest preservation down here that could be enlarged and transferred around the tropical world."

"What's in it for you Joaquín? I know you better than you think my boy."

Joaquín lit another cigarette off a burning butt and pushed back in the chair. "That's the personal part, Dr. Sol. As I said before, that is a conversation we can have over a drink when you get here. Let me assure you that I think you will agree with my scheme. Besides all of the arrangements have been made for the Boxxloader Committee's work in two weeks in Chiapas."

"The what?"

Joaquín smiled. He knew the reaction he would get to the announcement.

"I think I can get the Governor to provide the helicopters for an aerial survey."

"Hold it right there Joaquín, what's this about a Boxxloader Committee?"

"Solomon I've already leaked it to the press down here. The story is going to run this afternoon after my meeting with the Governor. You're to lead a group of scientists on a one-week study of the state of Chiapas and propose the solution for deforestation. Even the Mexico City media people are on their way. It is all set."

"Except for one little detail, Joaquín. You've outdone yourself this time my lad. I'm not coming to Chiapas; I'm on my way to Africa."

"Felicia told me you'd say something like that."

"Then Felicia has once again proven herself smarter than you my boy."

"Well, maybe and maybe not Solomon. There's something I haven't told you."

"And, what might that be?"

"Dr. Sol, I think the Governor is going to tell me that El Presidente is about to announce major land reform in Mexico. And not only that, I think he is going to approach you to head up a delegation to propose the form it will take...Solomon, did you hear me?"

"I heard you Joaquín, I just don't believe you."

Joaquín knew how close this was to the old man's heart. He wanted land reform for Mexico more than anything else in the life that remained to him. He once told Joaquín in a bar in Cuernavaca that he would sell his soul to Mephistopheles if he could only bring it about. In Dr.Boxxloader's mind, it was one of the few things that stood in the way of Mexico becoming a first-world country. To him the peasant farming system of ejidos and their inefficiency had long anchored Mexico to a primitive existence and held back production of foodstuffs, in his judgment. Not even Mexico's vast oil riches could overcome the backwardness of agricultural Mexico. Mexico should be exporting food north to the United States and to Europe, but instead they had to import to feed the ever-growing Mexican population.

"My sources are good ones Solomon."

"But Joaquín, I still don't see what this has to do with your rainforest in Chiapas. Enlighten me son."

"Not much if you don't agree to head up my scientific team to study our problem. On the other hand, if you do come and we make the announcement before the President calls you for his personal project, then whatever we decide after that will have the backing of Mexico City. At least that is the way I see it. And Dr. Sol, you know as well as I do that with the blessings of El Presidente we go far, without them we might as well light the match to the next tree ourselves."

"You're playing with some pretty heady stuff Joaquín. Are you sure, you know how to play this game? If you start down this trail you may not be able to turn around."

"I guess now you understand why I need you Dr. Sol."

"I guess I do. You sure know how to tempt an old man."

"Oh, and there's something else. Dr. Emilio Cárdenas has agreed to come."

"Well you little manipulator. How on God's green earth did you get him to come?"

"I told him you were coming."

"I should have known. I guess you know then that he's been tapped to head up the new International Center for Agro Forestry in Africa?"

"Yes. I just found out about that last week. Dr. Sol, that should have been here, not in Africa. But I'm not going to worry about that now. Hell, we'll do him one better before this thing is over."

"You'd better get him on your side my boy. Dr. Cárdenas knows where the money is. But watch him close, he doesn't give things away, you follow me?"

"Like a plow."

"What other little surprises do you have for me?"

"Dr. Simon Blanco is coming from Honduras. I think you know him; he heads the big agriculture school near Tegucigalpa. Been there for years, he's well respected in Latin America."

"Yes, I know him; I thought he'd already retired. You sure are picking some old birds for this roast."

"I've got a couple of youngsters too, by comparison that is. Two gringos are on their way. One is a world-class photographer, done some National Geographic stuff. He'll document the whole process. And the other guy is a burned-out jack-of-all trades that I met a few years ago. He is good at writing and putting together presentations. He did a bunch of ad work for my cattle operations in the States a few years back, good with tying things down and getting a message across. He's been staying on one of my U.S. ranches near San Antonio for the last couple of years mending fences. Kind of a strange guy, unpredictable, but he has some good communication skills we need."

"What's the date Joaquín?"

"Does that mean you'll come to Mexico?"

"Joaquín can't you answer a simple question, what's the date?"

"May twenty-seventh." Joaquín looked over at Jorge for the first time during the long conversation. He snapped a big grin at him. Jorge gave the thumbs up.

"I'll call you back before you leave for your meeting with the Governor."

"Thanks Solomon. Marta's got your plane tickets ready to go out via DHL overnight."

"Don't thank me yet Joaquín. And Joaquín, if I come I want to have a young man down there in Chiapas with me; one of my ABD graduate students. He's something special, an Irish kid with a hell of a past and a great future."

"Anything you want Solomon. You want him to fly down with you?"

"We could do that...no wait, what about your gringos, are they flying down or driving?"

"The photographer is flying in from Phoenix but Andrew, that's the writer, is driving; says he wants to get the feel of Mexico."

"That's exactly what I have in mind for Joy. Think we could get them matched up for the trip?"

"We can try. Andrew is supposed to call me from McAllen, before he makes the crossing at Reynosa. Maybe we can hook them up there. What kind of name is Joy anyway?"

"James Joyce McCarty; his mother named him after the writer. She wanted him to be a writer or something. Instead, he's turned into a damn good scientist. We call him Joy for short. He doesn't like that much, prefers Jimmy, but the name stuck."

"It sounds like you're coming Solomon."

"It's possible. I'll make a call or two. Be back to you in an hour. Hell Joaquín; I don't know why I let you talk me into these hair-brain schemes of yours."

"Sure you do Sol; they keep your life interesting. By the way, how's Barbara?"

"Hell if I know. I haven't seen the poor woman since Valentine's Day. Oh, she's all right. The arthritis is giving her grief. Tell Felicia hello for me and saludos a todos su familia."

"Thanks Solomon. I'll stay by the phone."

DESCENT INTO DARKNESS

PATROCINIO RODOLFO GOMEZ SANTOS' SECRETARY greeted Joaquín and directed him to sit down in one of the plush leather chairs in front of the Governor's desk. She was an attractive woman and added brightness to an otherwise heavy atmosphere.

"Señor, would you care for ¿café con leche?"

"Gracias."

She turned on the cassette player as she left the room and quietly closed the ten-foot-high double doors. The muted sound of an opera began to fill the room.

The Governor's office was on the second floor of the Palacio Gobierno del Estado in the center of the city. On the wall at one end of the conference table hung a huge map of the state of Chiapas. Smaller special statistical maps ran down each side. Joaquín got up and walked across the room to look at the graphics. Above the map, burned in three-inch letters on a dark hardwood plank of mahogany, was the title "*El Nuevo Chiapas 1989-1994.*"

Joaquín remembered well this program's beginning. The Governor had only been in office for two months. It was obvious to all the men of property and money in the state that he was out to make his mark. His vehicle, in this case, would be the national mandate of the Law of Planning, which came out of the Mexican Congress in 1983. The program was supposed to transform Chiapas. Move it and its people into modernity. This would happen through a program of aggressive planning and a rehabilitation campaign for the whole state, all of its people, this time to even include the Indians.

Joaquín had served on one of the agricultural committees formed to provide opinions and ideas to the state planners. His group of ranchers and farmers had done their duty. They had held public meetings in every region of the state, gathered their documentation and written their reports. All of which went to the Governor's planners in this building. Joaquín figured that most of the work ended up in the trash. The final state document contained few of his committee's statistics and only one of their recommendations.

Joaquín continued to scan the small maps while he waited. Chiapas was a diverse place. One of the richest in natural resources and history in all of Mexico. Topography, River Resources, Climate, Soil Types, and Land Use: Potential and Actual, and Ecology were the headings he read. The ecology map was in the bottom right hand corner. Joaquín moved in closer to study it.

The ecological zones in Chiapas were distinguished by what could be produced in each. The Soconusco Valley: coffee, cacao, banana, cotton, tropical fruits. The Coastal Zone produced beef cattle and milk. The Sierra Madres provided coffee and hardwoods. Throughout the Central Valley zone came the corn, the beans and the sugarcane, and on and on, one after another until Joaquín came to the zone that intrigued him most: *La Selva Lacandona*, the last remaining tropical rainforest in North America.

Joaquín had underlined the part in the state plan he wanted to see applied to this zone more than any other. He quoted this part often whenever he spoke on the subject.

...conservar es usar bien. Conservación es sinónimo de aprovechamiento racional, que es decir: aprovechamiento integral sostenido.

...to conserve is to use well. Conservation is synonymous with rational use, that is to say: integrated and sustainable use.

"Muy buenos días Joaquín, es tan bueno verlo." Joaquín felt Patrocinio's hand lay on his shoulder firmly, he turned and the men embraced briefly.

"Come Joaquín let us sit and talk. How is your family?"

"They are all well, and yours Governor?"

"Also very well, thank you. I have been hearing many things about you lately Joaquín. You are making quite a name for yourself in our beloved state. Your agricultural committee is well known in this building and the government. Chiapas owes you a debt for your tireless efforts and we are watching your new organization with a great deal of interest I promise you."

Joaquín sat down and leaned forward to pick up the cup of coffee the secretary had placed on the small table. He tried to identify the tone of Patrocinio's last remark. It could be good that the Governor was recognizing his efforts, but more likely, it was his way of giving him a subtle warning. *Do not go too far without the blessing of this offic*e. Not much of substance happened in Chiapas without it, at least, not in the cities and major towns.

"Joaquín," the Governor lit a cigarette and leaned back against the soft cushion, "let us get right to the matter. As you are aware, the party has begun a major effort in Chiapas to improve our state. We are looking to the future for our people. El Presidente, as you know," Patrocinio looked over his shoulder at a portrait of the President that hung conspicuously over his desk, "supports this work and takes a great interest in Chiapas."

"Yes, I know..."

Patrocinio continued, taking no notice of Joaquín's effort at discussion. "In fact, Joaquín, he called me just a few days ago. El Presidente wished to express his congratulations on our progress, but there is one point of concern both on the part of the President, and myself."

"Concern Governor?"

"Yes Joaquín. We all have a problem with the eastern regions of our state. As you know, it is a very potentially rich area but poorly utilized. Try as we have to integrate this area into our overall plans we continue to experience undue resistance to our programs. I think you know well the source of this resistance; am I correct?"

Joaquín straightened slightly, nervously. He wasn't comfortable yet with the politics at this level. There was something in him that wanted to play the game but something else reminded him that he was not suited for it. He nodded his agreement.

"We have in reality here two problems. The first is that invaders from outside the state are depleting much of our natural resources across our southern and eastern frontier. These Guatemaltecos come to Chiapas, slash, and burn their way through our forest, especially those areas around the Lacandon Jungle. They have no right to be in our country and our state, but they come fleeing their own government and its policies. And to make it worse, they are given shelter and aid by members of the church and refugee organizations that use the plight of these poor people for their own ends."

The opera seemed to getting louder. Joaquín had to strain to hear the words of the Governor.

"Our second problem involves an age-old concern in Mexico Joaquín, one that I know you are personally familiar with. That is the amount of productive land held by the ejidos, in Chiapas mostly by the Indians. Do not misunderstand me, I do not question the policies created by our glorious revolution years ago. It accomplished much-needed land reform in keeping with the times, but now Mexico continues to fall well behind in its ability to provide its people with the agricultural products for a growing population. Moreover, the present reality is that the ejidos are barely capable of supporting their own communities with corn and beans. We have a growing dilemma—one that must be addressed aggressively and solved."

Joaquín took a chance and broke in, "Governor, as you know my committee documented this well in our report to the planning agency."

The Governor's expression grew stern. "Yes, I know this. I also know that you do not understand why our final plans for the state did not reflect your committee's concerns. This is the reason I wished to speak with you today. We have an opportunity to help each other, and our state overcome some of these problems of which I have been speaking. But, in order to accomplish our common goals, we must trust each other, we must learn to cooperate. I hope you agree?"

Joaquín nodded weakly as he tried to calm his mind long enough to utter a simple reply. "Yes, Governor, I do."

"Well then, I must now be very blunt with you. I am well aware of your efforts to organize your fellow producers into a statewide association. I also recognize your desire to preserve the Lacandon Forest, a crown jewel of all of southern Mexico. I know most of what you are doing Joaquín. But, what I do not know is why. What are your motives? You are striking out on your own, and I am afraid that you do not understand the forces that you are dealing with. I want to help you, but I must understand your intentions. Do you follow my meaning señor?"

"Patrocinio," Joaquín tried to sound self-assured but knew his voice had a slight tremble to it, "I must admit that I am slightly confused myself. You seem to be concerned that…that what we are setting out to accomplish may be threatening to the government or interfering in state programs. I must assure you Governor…"

The Governor's cigarette lighter snapped shut with a loud click as he interrupted. "Joaquín permit me a question. Is it not true that you have invited a group of international scientists to Chiapas to study the ecological problems here?"

The Governor's body stiffened noticeably in his chair and he held his cigarette in both hands in front of his mouth. His eyes were dark and their intensity penetrated deeply into Joaquín's consciousness.

"…Yes, Patrocinio, I was meaning to discuss this with you today. We need …"

"And, Joaquín is it also a fact that you have invited, on your own initiative, Dr. Solomon Boxxloader of Texas to lead this prestigious body in its work in Chiapas?"

"Well yes, this is also true Patrocinio." Joaquín didn't try to explain. He realized that the Governor knew most of what he intended to announce to the press at the completion of his meetings with the Governor and later in the day the Bishop of the Catholic Church in San Cristóbal de Las Casas.

"This is my point to you Joaquín. There are many things happening all around you that you are not aware of and which, by your well-meaning interference, can be jeopardized. Let me give you one small example my friend. The problem of land reform is being addressed like never before by our President and our party in Mexico City. And your Dr. Boxxloader may be asked to play a major role in the President's plans. But now you may have involved the good Doctor in a controversial issue in Chiapas. This could very well undermine his credibility in a more crucial question for the future of our country. Do you understand the source of our concern Joaquín?"

"Yes Governor I understand you fully. Let me assure you that it was never my intention to disrupt any plans of the government. My fellow producers and I are only interested in solving a problem of growing concern among all of the people of Chiapas and, indeed, around the world. We feel an urgency to address the cancer that is eating away our rainforest. And that same cancer, unless arrested, is going to make insignificant the other problems of which you express your right concern. Governor I am not a politician. I do not always understand the proper ways, but my motives are not complicated or selfish. I merely wish to be of service in addressing this grave and growing problem."

The Governor took another deep drag from his cigarette and stood up. He exhaled a trail of smoke from each nostril as he slowly walked around to his desk and sat down. "Joaquín, I have one more question for you. Are you going to involve the Catholic Church and the Bishop in your efforts?"

Joaquín had anticipated this question. He was well aware of the conflict between the Church and the State Government in Chiapas. It had a long history that lived into the present and would have much to do with the future. The last Governor had expressed his enmity for the church openly. He proclaimed, on taking office, that one of his greatest problems was the Diocese of San Cristóbal. And the politics had changed little with the new administration.

"Governor you have been candid with me, I shall show you the same courtesy. Yes, I have a meeting with the Bishop this afternoon. His help will be necessary if not crucial. You know as well as I that no one freely moves in these areas of the rainforest or the high mountains without the permission of the Bishop. I must seek his support just as I must have yours."

"Joaquín, I think you are too modest when you say you are not a politician. You show me an understanding that betrays your words. But caution is called for in this matter. You are treading along the edge of the Sumidero Canyon señor. Tenga mucho cuidado that you do not slip over the side, because there is no coming back from that kind of fall."

THE SORCERER

DURING THE FORTY-FIVE MINUTE CLIMB on the highway to San Cristóbal de Las Casas Joaquín kept thinking about Patrocinio's last words. The Governor was certainly right. Anyone who fell over the edge of the gorge at Cañon del Sumidero would not return. It was 950 meters to the waters of the Rio de Grijalva below. Centuries before a thousand Indians had proved that conclusively by committing mass suicide at the Sumidero. They made their final drastic statement rather than submit to their Spanish conquerors. *But why did the Governor use that metaphor?* The thought troubled him.

Without recalling the drive up the mountains onto the Central Mesa of Chiapas, Joaquín drove his Dodge SUV through an ornate masonry arch onto the grounds of the Church of San Juan Don Bosco. He was on time for his interview with the Bishop and he decided to stop thinking about the Governor, to clear his mind for the meeting with the Bishop. He would be meeting with a different kind of power here. The same rules did not apply.

The Bishop represented far more continuity of power, especially in the highlands, than the government ever had or ever hoped to have. Church power had been operating in this region of Mexico since the earliest military incursions of the Spanish four centuries before. The so-called governments of Mexico during this period had slithered through countless revolutions and changed the mantle of rule from Spain to Mexican to Hapsburg Emperor to Revolutionary Mexican while the Church remained the Church, always.

As the various armies of various countries went about militarily subjugating the natives; las curas, the priests, fought another kind of battle. Their objective was to secure the hearts and souls of the indigenos of the region. A battle that was day-to-day and tedious, a battle that Joaquín believed was still being waged. In Joaquín's mind, from this place would come the blessing he most needed if he was to have his dreams for the Lacandon Rainforest.

Father Gonzalo approached and opened the door before the Dodge had completely come to a stop. Vigorously he shook Joaquín's hand as he firmly grabbed the traveler's arm and moved him quickly toward the main chapel. They exchanged animated saludos as they literally jumped the steps to the entrance. Like schoolboys the two climbed the steps arm-in-arm, taking two and three risers at a time until they came under the cover of the portal. Father Gonzalo spun around with a grin as wide as a machete slice through a squash and pointed with his outstretched arm at the grounds of the church compound.

"¡Mira! Joaquín, look, what do you see before you at our humble church?"

Joaquín didn't know how to respond. He saw the same thing he always saw on the grounds of San Juan. Children were playing, teachers and students going and coming from classes and shops. He saw the small vegetable plots where they experimented with many kinds of crops. He saw the animal pens and the methane collection house that trapped the valuable gas made from hog leavings. There was much activity in the building trades evident around the perimeter of the grounds. There seemed to be several new structures in progress. But, by in large, it was the same as he had remembered it from trips before.

"I do not think I understand your question Father," Joaquín responded through a strained smile.

"It is not important, but give it thought while you enjoy your discussion with His Excellency. We will talk again before you leave today. For now let us be on our way. The Bishop will be expecting you." Father Gonzalo again took Joaquín's arm and led him into the main church and around the outside walls to the rectory.

Joaquín had met the Bishop once before quite unexpectedly at a meeting of his ham radio group at the Hotel Palenque. It was the last place he would have expected to meet such a man. But because of their common interest in radios, he was to have an audience with the Bishop to discuss plans for the preservation of the last tropical rainforest remaining in North America: a reminder that the largest questions often turn on small twists of fate.

There was none of the formality that he had expected. The Bishop came to the meeting dressed in slacks and an open-collar white shirt. He had coffee served and he asked Joaquín if Father

Gonzalo could stay during their discussions. Of course, Joaquín agreed.

"So, please, my honored guest, tell me what it is that you wish us to help you with."

"Your Excellency...,"

"Please, Joaquín call me Pedro."

"Yes, of course, thank you." Joaquín felt as nervous as a child in the company of great men. Much more so than with Patrocinio. He wasn't sure why. Perhaps because he knew he needed more from the Bishop than he did from the Governor. A no from this man at this time would stop his plans instantly here in San Cristóbal.

"Well, Father Pedro, as I told you briefly on the phone, I have...or maybe I should say, my organization has become very concerned with what is happening to our natural areas in the state. Our concern is with the continuing destruction of the rainforest regions, most particularly the La Selva Lacandona. We see very little being done to preserve these areas for the future of our own environment and the well-being of our children."

Joaquín was not sure if he meant it about the children, but he figured it would sound right to the good Father. In fact, Joaquín was not too sure about his true feelings for the forest itself. He had never even seen it. Joaquín's involvement had always been detached from the reality of the place itself; confined to the meeting rooms of the Flamboyant Hotel in Tuxtla or cocktail parties in Mexico City.

Joaquín had paused in his description without realizing it.

"Joaquín, whose children are you speaking of?"

"Well, all the children of our state," he responded tentatively.

"I see, please continue."

"Father Pedro as I see it, we are presented with a special opportunity to make progress with this situation. If we can put aside our own interests for awhile, and I speak of everyone involved, I believe we can devise a plan that can preserve this very important natural resource, and at the same time, benefit the people who rely on the forest." Joaquín's voice began to tighten. He wasn't saying what he wanted to say. He turned his gaze to the Savior on the Cross above the doorway.

He desperately wanted to speak with the Bishop not at him. *We have so little time for this, don't you understand what is happening. Don't you care?"* His thoughts almost came out as words but he fought to keep himself under control.

He wanted to be passionate and lecture both of these church men that while they played with their games of power; while the diocese fought the state government and the rich ranchers fought the campesinos for control of the scarce productive lands; while the ecologists fought with business and industry and while the academics fought among themselves over research grants and territories, the small remaining rainforest was being cut at a rate that would finish it in as little as fifteen years. He wanted to jump to his feet and be emotional. Shout for changes in the attitudes that kept them all paralyzed and shackled. He wanted to persuade the lion to lie with the lamb and save something as precious, something as irreplaceable as the Lacandon.

But this is not what he was saying. He had not said it to Patrocinio in the Governor's Palace and he was not saying it now to the Bishop. He was playing it their way. Joaquín did not have the skill with words to be blunt, frank, and forceful. He had been trapped like most of his fellows, trapped by inference and innuendo, by the double meaning of their language, by his own politeness, his inability to force his will or point of view. The need for conciliation overpowered everything else, especially the truth.

Joaquín felt panic swelling up in his chest. His pause was awkward. He couldn't think of what to say next. Suddenly, he had his briefcase on his lap and was fumbling through his papers, looking for his notes of the last meeting of the Consejo. He knew he should have written down what to say but Felicia had scolded him, said that he would offend the Bishop by reading to him.

"Joaquín," the Bishop motioned for Father Gonzalo to retrieve something from his desk. "If you will permit me to interrupt you, I would like to tell you a story."

Joaquín stopped fidgeting and closed his case; nervously he snapped one of the clasps. "Yes of course Father, I was just looking for my notes."

"Joaquín, I do not think you know very much about this region and its people. So perhaps, you are somewhat unfamiliar with the intensity of work that is going on all around you. This is the highlands of Chiapas."

Father Gonzalo handed Joaquín a small map from the folder and passed the remaining papers and reports to the Bishop.

"It extends from here in San Cristóbal east and north across the high mesa. It is the land of the five fertile valleys and the magnificent cloud forests. Mexico's portion ends with a fall of elevation into the Usumacinta River Valley on the frontier with Guatemala. This is where your beautiful Lacandon Rainforest flows into the Petén on the Guatemalan side. The story I wish to relate to you is about the people of this region, the native people that are the descendents of the ancient Maya."

133

MEN TZOTZIL

"JOAQUÍN, SAN LORENZO IS A SMALL PUEBLO in the central highlands of Chiapas. In this place lives a man named Juan Diego Santiago and his family. Juan is a Tzotzil Indian who traces his ancestry back to the classic culture of the Maya, an advanced people that lorded over this land from the Yucatan to Honduras. They were a people who developed a calendar and a numbering system more sophisticated than their contemporaries the Romans."

"This small village is like most of the villages in this area, it is very small and very poor. The streets are of dirt, there are no facilities for sewage, potable water or electricity. And there is little hope for the future among the inhabitants of San Lorenzo."

"The days for Juan are always the same. The same food, the same work in the cornfields and the same lack of meaning that for the father translates into alcoholism."

"For Florencia, Juan's wife, the days are occupied with her family that includes her daughter Catalina who at only twenty-two already has three children and no husband. The man who had fathered the last baby, Roberto, left for Mexico City to find work shortly after the child was born. There is also Margarita, twenty, who is carefree and looking for a husband. Gregorio, the eldest son, helps his father tend the corn and like his father has begun to drink. Then there is Francisco, a boy of twelve that has left school to help with the sheep. And finally José, the youngest of Juan and Florencia's children, is eight. José is the hope of the family. He still attends the small primary school in the village but often misses classes when he is too hungry to leave the house."

"So, Juan Diego Santiago, Florencia, Catalina, Margarita, Gregorio, Francisco, and José are the people of highland Chiapas. They are seventy-five percent of the state's two and a half million inhabitants. They are Indians or mixed bloods, they are rural and they are poor with little prospect for a better future."

"They, like all of the Indians in this region, have been abused, neglected, and often persecuted and incarcerated when they dared to seek a better life for themselves. They are typical of their kind who suffer from the highest rates of infant mortality and disease of any people in Mexico."

"Moreover, in education they too suffer disproportionately. Barely fifteen percent ever finish the meager schooling offered them by the state. In the city of Ocosingo, which is such an important market city for the Indian people of these valleys, the government itself admits statistics of illiteracy of sixty-six percent. "

"The story of Juan and Florencia is also the story of the day-to-day struggle for the basics of survival, enough food, simply basic nutrition. These people subsist on corn, beans and chilies. One in five never consumes meat. And the majority of the others do so only once a week. And that is normally chicken; the beef which is raised in our country, goes north to the McDonalds and the Burger Kings of the United States. "

"In employment it is the same story. Hard work for very little pay. Most trabajadores only make five thousand pesos a day, less than two dollars for ten to fourteen hours on the ranches or on the coffee plantations. This is not even enough to feed one person with a minimal daily ration."

"Then finally there is the matter of human rights or, more correctly, the lack of human rights. The Indians have suffered in this

135

regard since the earliest days of the Spanish conquest. Today they are still shot at from military vehicles and sometimes helicopter gunships. They are incarcerated without cause or recourse. The politically active ones are often *disappeared,* ten of these in the last year alone."

"That brings me to the refugees in this land. Can you imagine coming to a land that I have just described for refuge? That is what the people of Guatemala, El Salvador and other countries of Central America are doing. They come to us for help."

"Not far from San Lorenzo is a camp. The camp is a simple one, an area cut from the edge of the forest. The buildings are also simple. Cane leaf roofs sown into place by thread made from the agave plant. There are no nails in these structures and there are no walls. They are built low to the ground from cane or corn stalks so that the strong winds will not carry them away. The leaves of the cane cover a dirt floor. On these floors at night, lined up in neat rows on simple woven mats, only divided by family affiliations; sleep the people who have fled torture and murder at the hands of their own government."

"During the height of this forced migration came the Guatemaltecos at the rate of one hundred thousand per year. Three fourths of those were women with small children. They were housed in these simple camps with the help of the church and organizations such as the Mexican Committee to Help the Refugees. Today there are still more than twenty thousand of these people scattered among a hundred camps in Chiapas. All of them are near or in the forest areas."

"Like Juan and Florencia in San Lorenzo, these people are Indian. Mostly Quiché or Mam or Kanjobal. They speak one of twenty-two ethnic languages. Very few speak Spanish. In their various languages, they all tell the same horrible stories. Stories of brutality by the soldiers, brothers burned alive, fathers sent to prison for speaking in public about the problems of the workers. Men from the villages who simply are not there the next day following loud noises in the night; men never seen again by their families."

"And, the people who try to aid the refugees and the poor of Chiapas are often labeled by the state government as fomenters of sedition and revolt and are expelled from Mexico. Amidst it all my friend, we work for something better."

LISTENING

"JOAQUÍN I HAVE TRIED TO DESCRIBE to you the people of the place in which you have decided, for whatever reason, to try and make a difference with your life. To make a difference with the tools that you have at your disposal, your intellect, your influence and reputation, your connections and certainly your money. These are things that have been the dearest to you up to this point in your life. But now you wish to add to your list. And you have come to me to seek the help of the Church in your desire, as I assume you have been to the Governor to seek his."

"But before we discuss ways in which we can help one another in our common goal, I will issue you this caution. You are pushing your own view of the world onto the lives of people who may not share that view. You must always be aware that the forests are where people live, Joaquín. These people, like you, wish to share in the bounty of the earth and provide for their families. Moreover, like you, they interpret their surroundings based on their history and their culture. You must always be sensitive to this fact and behave accordingly. You must always show respect and reverence for the ideas and customs of the people who live in the mountains and cloud forests. Their history and experience in this land is far more ancient than your own. If you will do this, I am sure you can satisfy your own hunger and that of the people of the forest as well."

The Bishop shifted his gaze to Father Gonzalo and handed him the folder. "Before we continue with our business Joaquín, I would like for you to accompany Father Gonzalo on a small tour of the facilities we have here at San Juan Don Bosco. We are very proud of our work with the people that I have just spoken with you about. It is important for you to see this. When you are finished please come back and we will take lunch and discuss the remainder of our agenda. I hope this meets with your approval." The Bishop stood up slowly.

"But of course Father Pedro."

"Bueno, hasta de la hora de comida."

Joaquín was a little numbed by the lecture from the Bishop. He was slow to respond to Father Gonzalo's urgings to follow him from the rectory. Finally, he collected himself and fell behind the churchman as they walked out onto the grounds of the compound.

The tour lasted almost an hour. They looked in on shops for woodworking, for metal, for sewing and cooking, for weaving and pottery. There were even modest facilities for computer-based writing and spreadsheets along with a small darkroom for developing and printing film.

From these they ventured through the many small plots of tilled soil and plastic draped greenhouses. Every section cordoned by string boundaries and handmade signs, which declared, for the benefit of the untrained eye, the type of greenery growing within the strings. There were cabbages and lettuce. Beans of every variety and shape. Melons, squashes and cucumbers. In the greenhouses were the flowers. Chrysanthemums, carnations, snapdragons all grew in well-ordered rows of boxes.

Behind the growing plants Father Gonzalo guided Joaquín through the animal areas. Pigs wandered about grunting on concrete floors, floors swept constantly into ground-level aqueducts. The channeled filth collected for fertilizer and to produce methane. Sheep, goats, and even domesticated deer were interspersed with rabbit pens and chicken coups. A few geese roamed freely on the grounds, patrolling diligently for beetles.

Among all of the buildings and facilities, Joaquín was greeted by the stares and the curiosity of the young Indians. They stopped to watch him as he asked questions of Father Gonzalo about their work, about their classes. Joaquín felt good being among them. They seemed contented and unafraid at San Juan. He did too.

"You remember Joaquín when I asked you what you saw here." They were walking back towards the Bishop's residence and had been quiet for several minutes until the Father renewed his earlier question.

"Yes Father, you asked me what I saw at San Juan Don Bosco."

"Well...can you answer me now?" They walked on. Joaquín had to think. He had seen many unexpected things on these grounds. The Bishop had presented him with thoughts that were unexpected as well.

"Father Gonzalo I think I will have to reorder some of my ideas before I can answer you. I believe I see important work at San Juan Don Bosco with these people. I also think that I have not considered the whole issue of the Lacandon. But I am not sure what it is I see here today."

"If you will permit me to say it, I believe you see what all of us want for our lives Joaquín. It is the same for these Indians as it is for El Presidente or for you and your family in Tuxtla. What you see here is hope."

They continued their walk in silence to their lunch.

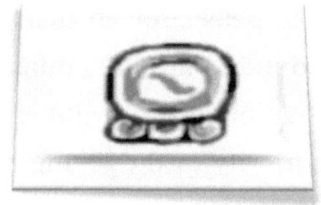

CHAPTER 7

GONE OVER THE LINE

"I'LL BE AT THE MOTEL 6 OUT ON THE 83 by-pass if you happen to need anything," Drew found himself saying reluctantly. "If everything goes the way I've figured, I'll cross the border tomorrow. Sure you are going to be alright?"

Ree and Drew stood in the parking lot of the Tequila Cantina. Ree could see Jane's car on the outside row next to the street. She expected Jane to be inside waiting.

"You've been great Drew. I don't know how to thank you for all you've done."

"Kind of enjoyed the company myself." Chica sat in the driver's seat and watched. "Like I said the Motel 6, it's out on... "

"The 83 Highway cut-off, I know. Jane doesn't live far from there. I think you can see their sign from her block." Ree finished the sentence and forced a grin.

"Listen. I know you didn't ask, but...well, I just think you ought to stay away from this Buddy guy. There is better than that out there. You deserve better than that too. Like I say, I know you didn't ask but well that's my advice, for what it's worth."

"Thanks Drew. You know you have beautiful blue eyes."

Ree's remark stopped Drew cold. "OK...Well, if you ever want to come to Mexico to see the rainforest let me know." Drew turned to open the door but hesitated with his hand on the latch. Chica without command jumped into the back.

Drew spun back around suddenly, took Ree by the shoulders, and pulled her to him. She responded and put her arms around Drew and her head against his shoulder.

"If you need anything call me, OK?"

"Yes, I will. Thanks again."

"De nada. See you."

Ree watched and waved at Drew as he bounced the right rear wheel over the curb and pulled out on South Tenth Street. She smiled as he looked back and shrugged his shoulders at his driving. She picked up her bag and moved toward the deeply carved wooden door of the Cantina.

Narrow bridges

DREW DECIDED TO STOP BY SANBORN'S on his way to the motel. He would need Mexican insurance for the trip and the travel agency always gave you a travel log along with the coverage. The log contained detailed information about road conditions to any destination in Mexico. It helpfully noted all the twists and turns and the unexpected one-lane bridges just around a sharp curve. There was plenty of that kind in Mexico. As the cute little Mexican girl in the office told Drew, the log couldn't tell you about the burro drawn hay cart in the middle of the one-lane bridge but at least it could warn you about the bridge. More than a few gringos had smashed up from a lack of such information.

Besides, it listed all the latest gas stations that had *Magna Sin*. That was what they called unleaded in Mexico. Drew's Jeep ran on that type of gasoline. Anything less than 88 octane and the engine sounded like a hay-baling machine. Mexico had been slow to provide unleaded to all the stations. You could go past ten stations and maybe one would have unleaded. The travel log was a necessity for that bit of info if nothing else.

Drew figured he would spend the evening going over the information from Sanborn's and make note of any potential trouble spots. He was more than a bit nervous about the crossing in the morning and wanted to read the first section that described what to expect at Mexican customs. Drew had crossed many times before but only on foot for the day. This time he was taking his car, a trailer, and what looked like everything he owned, including his dog. He figured he would get some questions about his final destination and his plans from the officials. The way Drew was rigged he knew he would look more than suspicious to the Federales.

Drew checked into the motel and drove around to the back and parked long ways across four spaces just off the highway. He told Chica to get out and go do her number in a scrub field across from the motel. She must have been more than ready because she shot across the road and began sniffing around for the right spot. Drew leaned against the trailer and kept an eye on his dog. He wasn't worried she would run off or anything like that, he just wanted to make sure she did it all before they went up to the room and settled in. That way she wouldn't wake him up scratching at the door at 2 a.m.

Ree came back into his thoughts as he watched Chica. He looked down at the trailer tires and made a mental note that the one on the right rear looked low. "She was nice," Drew said in a low voice. Suddenly he felt lonely. He thought about the Running~Bar Ranch and his life for the last year. It had been quiet, sort of gentle-like. Safe.

Now he was off to Mexico—*his grand adventure.* He remembered Ree's question, *why?* Drew wished he had gotten Jane's number while he had the chance; just to call later and make sure everything was OK. Maybe just to say so long again.

Chica had picked up the scent of some critter and was working the field pretty intensely. Drew pulled the silent whistle on its chain from under his shirt and blew two quick noiseless blasts. The one-inch metal tube didn't make any noise that the human ear could hear but Chica could hear it for almost a mile. They had practiced on the ranch with it. Drew would give Chica the command for stay, usually next to a cedar tree so she could get out of the sun, and then Drew would keep walking. It had taken almost two weeks to get the dog not to follow. But after a while he could get out of sight before he gave the signal with the whistle. Drew got a bigger kick out of the game than did his dog. He enjoyed seeing the little spotted bitch come flying over the hill enthusiastically looking for him.

After Chica got good at this exercise in discipline, Drew would try to hide. It was all he could do not to laugh as Chica raced by his hiding place with her nose to the ground. Most times she only went another twenty yards or so before she would double back and start to work the territory. She always found him without fail. Drew would grab her, roll around in the grass, and tell Chica what a good dog she was.

There was only one time Chica couldn't find him. Drew had climbed a tree and sat down on one of the branches; he leaned against the trunk and tried to blend with the tree bark. He sat still and watched Chica search for almost fifteen minutes before he began to feel sorry for her—she was frantic. So he slid out of the tree and began walking down the cow trail like nothing had happened. Chica caught him before he had gone more than ten paces.

Drew tried to remember Jane's last name. "Chica," he shouted, "vamos a tomar...let's go."

BUENO

DREW TOOK OUT THE PHONE BOOK and looked up the international dialing instructions. It was about ten o'clock and the news was just coming on. The lead story was something about the first swarm of *Killer Bees* discovered on the U.S. side of the border with Mexico. Some farmer had started the engine of his Case tractor and damn near died from the stings. The bees had built a hive on the radiator grill. Drew lowered the volume on the TV; he reckoned he could catch Joaquín at home about now. Drew figured that his Mexican friend was sitting at the dining room table talking to Felicia.

He was. The phone rang just as he was putting the last bite of a honey-soaked sopapillas into his mouth. His wife sat across from

145

her husband smoking one cigarette after another and listening to him as he tediously explained the day's conversations. He went through each one in order, almost word for word. First with the Governor, then the Bishop and finally the late afternoon press conference. Felicia was trying not to interrupt because she could see that Joaquín was still excited. She simply made mental notes of all the hidden meanings she heard in his story. Especially the Governor's reference to the Sumidero Canyon. Felicia saw a dark warning in that one; she was good at seeing dark warnings.

"Bueno," Teri the house cook answered the phone. She was still doing the last of the dinner dishes before going to bed. The young Indian never quit for the day until Joaquín had had his cena and señora had dismissed her.

"Muy buenos noches Teri," Drew spoke a little loud to compensate for the perceived distance from McAllen to Tuxtla and because he was uneasy about speaking Spanish on the phone. Teri recognized Drew's voice and called for Joaquín without answering. She was too shy to try to speak to a norteamericano.

Joaquín rushed to the phone and Felicia began moving plates from the table to the little service window that opened into the kitchen. "Andrew, where in the hell are you?"

"Sitting on the bed at a Motel 6 in McAllen."

"I thought you would be here by now."

Drew could tell Joaquín was excited about something. He could tell because he always ignored the constraints of time when he was excited. He knew damn well that Drew had just left the ranch. Drew had told Ruben to call Tuxtla on the short wave radio the morning he left.

"I've had meetings all day and we are ready to go with the project. I need you here to help me organize the agenda for the Boxxloader Committee. They will start arriving in Chiapas ..."

"The what?" Joaquín didn't bother to answer but kept on.

"... in about a week. We are planning a helicopter surveillance of the whole region and you are going to make a trip into the jungle with Dr. Arturo Argüelles. You'll be going to several pueblos near the Lacandon and end up at the Mayan ruins at Bonampak."

Drew had sat patiently on the bed watching the soundless newscast on Channel 32 while Joaquín rattled on with his excitement. The blond female announcer wore entirely too much lipstick in Drew's opinion and reminded him of those Styrofoam heads they put wigs on at the beauty shop at North Star Mall.

Joaquín was saying something about an ecological model for the world when Drew interrupted him. "Hey...hold on a minute. Save this for when I get there. It's my nickel. I'll be crossing over in the morning. If I'm reading the map Sandorn's gave me correctly, it's about a four-day trip."

"You can make it in three if you drive at night."

"Wow, hold on to your sombrero mi amigo. It says right here in the travel log in big bold type and I quote 'Driving At Night. DON'T'."

"Oh, yes, there talking about the stray animals on the highways at night and the occasional banditos, that's all."

"The banditos?, what's this about..."

"Don't worry about those little things. OK, four days. I will look for you here in four days. Now listen, I've got some company arranged for you on the trip."

"Company? Is she pretty?"

147

"No, no, no, nothing like that. Dr. Boxxloader has a young associate, a graduate student that he wants to have in Tuxtla to help with the research. He thinks it would be a good idea that the young man see a little of Mexico from the ground level so I volunteered your services."

"That's fine by me. Maybe he can help me fight off the banditos, no?"

"Stop with that...you will have no trouble I promise. The student's name is...wait let me get my notebook."

The male counterpart of the female talking Styrofoam head was doing a story on a drug bust just on the U.S. side of the International Bridge. There was a bunch of police with DEA stenciled on their jackets running around a van with guns drawn. Drew wondered how the press knew to be there to capture the action on film.

"The young man's name is James Joyce McCarty. Boxxloader says he has sandy red hair and is about six feet. He will fly in tomorrow morning into McAllen International. You can pick him up on your way to the bridge."

"What time's the flight?"

"It's an American Airlines flight...let's see...flight 1342...gets in at 9:30. He'll meet you at the main entrance. Boxxloader told him to look for a Jeep with trailer. That's right isn't it?"

"Yep, that's it." "

"Did you buy the computer before you left San Antonio?"

"Sure did my friend. A Mac just like we talked about."

"Good. Felicia sends you saludos. How's your money situation?"

"I think under control. I should have plenty to make it to Chiapas. You did say the price of beans and Tequila is pretty cheap in Mexico, right?"

"OK. We'll see you here about Wednesday."

Drew used the remote control to raise the volume on the TV and Chica's ears at the same time. The last story was showing footage of a bus wreck near San Fernando, Mexico about an hour south of Reynosa where Highway 97 turns in the direction of Ciudad Victoria. The bus had matched up nose-to-nose with a fuel tanker. There were no survivors. Beinvenidos a Mexico.

FUZZY-WUZZY WAS A BEAR

JANE AND REE SAT IN THE CANTINA for over two hours after dinner. Jane wanted to know everything about the big fight with Buddy right from the start, but Ree said they needed to catch up on their friendship first. So all through the quesadillas and salsa they told old stories about nursing school and caught up with Jane's life.

Ree's friend kept trying to bring the discussion back to the present. But each time, Ree would ask another question about Jane's mother or her brother Manuel or Jane's ex Rick. And each time Jane would give her a quick run-down and end up by saying something about everything is fine in her life right now.

It was nearly 10 p.m. when Jane finally vigorously said that she wasn't saying another word until she got the whole story. Ree sat back in her seat and cradled her drink. She went over the high spots of the last few months: the fights, the physical abuse, the strain just to keep going. She talked about her guilt. Ree could not explain why she wasn't able to make things different with her and Buddy. Finally, she told Jane she wanted out, away from the whole mess.

By the time she finished they both were a little fuzzy from the Margaritas and Jane was more than a little pissed at Buddy. She told Ree that to her the answer was simple. Ree would have to move to McAllen and they could room together. She said with confidence that a job would be no problem, that nurses could name their own ticket and get it all in South Texas. Jane, with sweeping gestures with her arms, described how they could rearrange her house to fit them both. There was plenty of room she said. Ree could have the guest bedroom. Now that she and Rick had split, Ree could stay with her as long as she wanted. At least until things worked themselves out. Jane was sure of her plan. There would not be any need to discuss it further, she told Ree.

Jane's resolve made Ree feel good and the alcohol made her feel warm. To change her life seemed so easy, too easy. They both laughed about how much fun it all would be—like being in nursing school again. They ordered two more Margaritas and laughed.

RED DOT

THE NIGHT WAS WARM AND HUMID so they rolled the windows down as they drove through the deserted downtown McAllen. It was approaching midnight. The quietness of the city and the rush of air through the car made Ree feel at home. Jane had a Garth Brooks tape in the player. *The Thunder Rolls* gave the interior of the car a feeling that Ree liked. Ree could see her life changing. She hummed along with the song and watched the dark storefronts glide by.

"Hey I've got something of yours," Jane said breaking the mood. She reached behind the driver's seat with her right hand and poked around in her open purse. "Here I think you might want to put this in your bag." She handed the dark grey pistol to Ree handle first.

"Oh, Juanita! I'd forgotten about it." Ree took the gun and held it sideways in her lap. "I had almost forgotten about Buddy all together. What should I do with it? I don't even know how to make it work. I'm not sure I want to."

Ree told Jane how she had meant to kill Savage but couldn't make the gun fire. Jane laughed aloud and said, "That's the spirit girl."

"There's nothing to it honey. See this little button or whatever right here. This one by your thumb." Jane alternated her gaze between the road and the pistol. She reached over and touched the gun's safety. "Just push this up until you see the red dot. That's it. She'll blow somebody to the next life cycle when you pull the trigger."

Ree held the gun up and worked the safety back and forth.

"See how easy it is? Now stick that little kicker in your purse and if the big bad wolf comes again, you can negotiate with a bit more confidence."

Ree slipped the pistol into her purse but kept her hand around the grip.

"Did you ever figure out how the gun got into your house?"

"Beats the hell out of me. Maybe that son-of-a-bitch was trying to scare you or something. Who knows?"

"He used the pistol for that before I left Lancaster." Ree had not told Jane about what had happened in the bathroom. She had just described the fight. Ree knew that Jane would go ballistic if she told her about how Buddy had threatened to kill her with the gun if she left. How he had made her kneel while he undressed and stood over

151

her. How he had raped her with the barrel pressed up against her head while he pulled her head back by her hair. How he had said that, *"You're my woman, forever. Don't ever forget it."*

JANE TURNED INTO THE BACK ALLEY driveway, reached up, and flipped the visor down. She punched the button on the transmitter. Ree could see the garage door three doors down begin to come up. Jane and Ree didn't notice the truck turn in the drive behind them with its lights out. Jane hesitated for a moment until the door finished its up cycle. They pulled into the garage bumping the plastic trash container along the left wall. Bottles rattled across the concrete floor. Jane turned to Ree and they both laughed.

"Guess we better pick those up before I drive over some glass and ruin a tire." Jane left the lights on, opened her door, and pivoted in the seat to get out. The truck tires squealed to a stop with the hood stuck under the path of the garage door, its front bumper almost touching Jane's rear door. "Oh shit!" Jane reached for the transmitter and punched it. The door started down but hung on the hood of the black pickup truck.

Buddy got out of his truck slowly, dramatically.

"Stay in the car Ree, let me talk to him," Jane instructed. Ree felt the same as she did behind the bathroom door—trapped.

Jane swung her legs out and stood up; as she did she kicked a Miller Light bottle against the wall. She took two steps toward the back of the garage as Buddy ducked under the partially closed door.

"Buddy I think you need to get the hell out of here." Jane was a little woman; no more than five foot, but her voice was strong. She showed no fear. Buddy caught her with the full force of the back of his right hand as he swung it across his body. Jane didn't make a sound and fell back against the overturned garbage can.

"You fucking whore! You stay out of this!" Jane sat there dazed. Blood ran over her lower lip and dripped down the front of her blouse, down into her exposed cleavage.

"Ree, get out of the car!"

Ree could see the top of Jane's head. She got out and looked at the man's rage on the other side of the car.

"Buddy, why are you doing this?" she screamed. "Buddy, please leave us alone. I'm not going back with you." She tried to keep her voice from cracking, tried to put some strength to her words.

"Get your ass in the truck Ree. We're getting out of here."

"No. Buddy I'm not going with you. It's over!"

"Like hell you're not. You steal my truck, you kill my dog, you go running off down here with some cowboy and you think I'm going to just let it pass. You must think I'm crazy."

Buddy started around Jane's car. Jane moaned softly but didn't move. Several cans and bottles clattered together as Buddy's boot kicked through the trash.

He had reached Ree's side when she pulled out the pistol and pushed the lever forward. She could see the red dot. Ree squared her shoulders and raised the gun up with both hands trying not to shake. Buddy caught sight of the hole in the end of the barrel.

"Well would you look at this. If it ain't Little Annie Oakley." Buddy made the joke but he stopped short.

"Buddy I mean it. You leave us alone and get out of here right now."

"You think you're going to scare me with my own gun? Put it down or I'll stuff it up your cunt...like I did before."

"Buddy, I mean it. Leave me alone." The tears began streaming down Ree's face. Her hand and the gun were shaking.

"Hey now, be careful with that thing." Buddy lowered his voice. "You better give me that before you shoot yourself." He took another step towards Ree and held up both hands, palms out towards her.

"Don't...Buddy don't come any closer," she said with a determination that made the man hesitate.

"Now Ree, you know you don't want to shoot me. Give me that. I just want to talk to you." Buddy took another step. He was within reach of the gun.

Jane stumbled over the plastic can trying to get up and sputtered Ree's name spitting blood. Ree turned her head quickly and tried to catch a glimpse of her friend. Buddy took advantage and reached up and grabbed the barrel. "OK, you want to shoot me, then do it." He held the gun so that Ree couldn't turn it loose or change the aim. "You think you're so fuckin' brave...shoot me." He jerked the gun in Ree's hands towards his chest. He jerked it again. "Shoot me bitch!"

"Buddy, please stop. Please." Ree tried to lower the gun but he kept it pointed at his heaving chest. Ree could see her panic reflected in Buddy's wild eyes.

The explosion ran around the garage and pounded Ree's ears. There was an acrid smell around her face. She slid into the passenger's side of the black pickup and scooted across behind the wheel. It was still running. The radio was playing an advertisement for Grande Ford. A new Taurus for under factory invoice the voice explained in an affected style.

It was only two blocks up Pecan and two more to Highway 83. There was a hospital on the second exit to the west Ree thought. *Oh my God.*, she whispered. Buddy's eyes were burned into her thoughts. They were wide open. Like saucers, looking straight at the ceiling. There was a cereal box under his head. *Fruit Loops* was colorfully lettered on the top flap.

She noticed the deep scratches on the truck's hood as she passed under the lights at the first corner. *Buddy's going to be really mad about that.* Ree gunned the engine and was on the highway, she could see the hospital in the distance, back off the road behind the Ramada Inn and close to the Motel 6.

IRISH UP

"HELLO THERE. You must be Andrew Cotton?" Drew folded his *U.S.A. Today* and pitched it behind the front seat.

"That's right and you must be Joy or should I say James?" Drew extended his hand across the passenger's seat and flipped the door handle. "Get in."

"Joy is fine. Hope I'm not an inconvenience for you." They shook hands warmly.

"No. It was going to be a long lonely trip without company. Glad to have you. By the way, call me Drew."

"Drew it is then mate. But if you will pardon me, it doesn't look like you're alone. Who's your friend here?"

"Oh, that's Chica. She's my theft insurance." Drew gave Chica the look that meant don't even think about jumping in the front or on the stranger.

155

"She's a dandy." Joy said.

"She's that alright. You ready for the crossing to the land of mystery and adventure?"

"More than ready. Anything to get away from that school for a while. What about the bag? She's still on the curb there."

They both jumped out to collect Joy's duffel bag. "I'm happy you travel light, as you can see we've not a lot of cargo space in the Jeep. Is it all right to pitch it in the trailer? Is there anything you want out of it now?"

"No mate, nothing. The trailer is fine with me."

"I see you haven't lost that good Irish brogue."

"No, not completely. Me mother wouldn't hear of it." Drew liked this kid already. He seemed to be down to earth. He had a maturity that Drew had not expected. The trip was going to be easier with this Irishman along he thought.

Drew went to the back of the trailer and reached for the extra door key he had hidden under the spare tire rack. His fingers probed the recess and he retrieved the black metal box with a magnetic back. The box was open and the key was gone.

"How did this happen?" Drew muttered to himself.

"What's that mate?"

"My spare door key for the trailer is missing. I had an extra key for the trailer door in a box hidden back here. It's not in the box. Must have fallen out on the road. Well I guess it doesn't matter. I've got another one on my key ring in the car. Just a minute."

Drew pushed the key into the door lock and swung the door back still trying to understand how the key disappeared. Chica jumped out of the rear of the Jeep and ran to the door. "What the hell? Chica get your scrawny ass back in the Jeep. Who called you?"

Drew spoke hard to the dog. "Man, what's going on? That's not like her to get down without permission." Chica obeyed. Joy just stood back and watched the mini drama without comment.

In one motion, Drew opened the trailer door and pitched in Joy's bag. He slammed the door and locked it. If anything had fallen or broken, he didn't want to worry with it now. All he wanted was to get through this next part of the trip. Through Mexican customs quickly and get well down the road. Ciudad Victoria was at the end of the first day's mileage quota and they would need to make it there before night. His travel log showed only one trailer park in the city. Drew hoped it would be there. But if it wasn't, they would need some daylight to find a cubbyhole, some place to park for the night.

ONE SIDE AGAINST ANOTHER

THE BRIDGE WAS PACKED. There were at least fifteen cars in front of Drew's Jeep waiting in line to pass through the American side. And, there were five lines on either side of theirs. Drew didn't pay much attention though. The other cars, trucks, busses, vans and foot traffic bunching up all around him didn't interest him just now. Rather he concentrated on watching the U.S. Immigration officers at the checkpoints. The hope was that they wouldn't give him too much hassle. He figured he'd get enough of that on the Mexican side. It was Sunday and maybe it would go easy.

"Good morning. Where you headed on this fine day sir?" The officer smiled while he asked the question but his eyes were moving up and down Drew's rig and then into the back of the Jeep. "Going hunting? What kind of dog is that?"

Drew felt relief instantly. The officer was a friendly sort. Drew always worried that these guys at the border would think he was a drug runner with a Jeep, trailer and all. "She's a blue-heeler. No sir, we're headed down to Chiapas to work on a rainforest project." Drew liked the sound of it; made him feel like some kind of Indiana Jones or something like that.

The blue uniform bent down to look across at Joy. "You fellows got all your papers, passports and insurance and such?"

"Yes sir." Drew looked over at Joy. He had forgotten to ask Joy about his passport. Joy moved his head up and down. He seemed as nervous as Drew did. "Yes sir, I think we're in good shape."

"How about your little friend there; she got her vaccination record?"

"Yes sir." Drew avoided volunteering any details. He simply liked to be friendly. Smile and answer the questions of authorities simply and directly. He was practicing for Mexico.

"OK. Enjoy Mexico. Oh! How long you staying?"

"Six months. We've got visas for six months."

"Well have a good trip. Now pull on across the bridge and follow the signs. You'll have to go in their headquarters to get your visas stamped."

"Thanks a bunch." Drew put the Jeep into gear and pulled slowly through the gate. He was nervous. They drove over the Rio Grande and past a couple of hundred people on foot headed into Reynosa.

The order of the American side gave way to something else as they came into Mexico. In all the times Drew had crossed the border on foot; he was never ready for how quickly the world changed. In no more than five hundred yards, the rules of the North gave way to the rules of the South. And the rules were different. Very different. They appeared, in Drew's opinion, to be made up as the circumstance dictated. Life was so much closer to the edge in Mexico. You had to use your wits to get by.

There were three uniforms directing traffic into one of the twenty or so stalls that lined both sides of the narrow road from the end of the bride into Reynosa proper. The officer closest to Drew pointed him toward the truck side. Drew noticed the forty-five slide action colt stuck down in his belt. He didn't wear a hat and his trousers were a different shade of brown from the shirt. They appeared to be from two different styles of uniforms. Drew caught a glimpse of his badge as they drove close. He would have sworn the shield on his pocket flap was plastic. Drew lost sight of the officer in his outside mirror as he angled the Jeep into the stall. He was afraid he was going to run over the guy's toes as he maneuvered his little train. He tried to pull up as far as possible so the traffic behind could get around the trailer. Drew did not want any trouble.

Another customs official, a woman, met him before he was completely out of the vehicle. She peeled the backing off a small green sticker and placed it on the outside windshield just above the state inspection sticker. It read *Turista, Bienvenidos a México.*

"Por favor, señor, ¿cuanto tiempo vas a pasar en México?

"Seis meses, señora, seis meses. ¿A dónde se va ahora, para la visa?"

"Por allí." She pointed to the main building just across two lanes of vehicles. "¿Señor, un momento...tras cosas en México?"

"¿Cómo?"

"¿Tras materiales a México?"

"Oh...ahh...no señora, no tengo nada pero cosas personales."

"Muy bien, adelante."

"Gracias, come on Joy let's get to the office." Drew didn't wait for any more questions and they moved through a line of cars toward the front door of the customs house.

"I'm glad you speak Spanish Drew," Joy gave Drew a big smile as they walked past three kids selling Chicklets.

"Sí, gracias joven." Drew motioned the shortest of the three over to them at the bottom of the steps to the building and gave him a quarter. Drew watched three Mexican men watch him as the kid handed Drew his box of gum in exchange. The other two gum merchants acted like nothing had happened and stuck out their boxes too.

"No gracias, bastante. Don't let the Spanish fool you Joy. It's not that good. Hopefully, sufficiente, as they say. These people around the frontier are used to dealing with us gringos but when we get to the interior, in particular Chiapas, it may get a little more difficult."

As they pushed through the glass doors Drew noticed a big sign in English at the end of the hall. *Complaints, call toll-free 91-800-00-148.* Drew wondered if Mexico was really changing now that Salinas was the President. He and Joy got in line. While they waited, they looked at each other's passport pictures and had a good-natured chuckle.

Drew felt the roll of cinquenta mil pesos in his pocket. He hoped he wouldn't have to offer a mordida for anything. He hated the mordida system. How do you know what to offer? No one could tell you for sure especially now, with so much talk about changing the corruption in Mexico by the new government. He was afraid he'd get arrested for bribery. The thought of Mexican jails always made Drew doubt his desire to travel in this country. It made his stomach go queasy.

"Buenos días señores. Adelante."

CHAPTER 8

A GIRL IN MY CLOSET

TUNA MOVED PURPOSELY ACROSS THE BRIDGE with his small canvas sack balanced across his narrow shoulders. The Rio Bravo del Norte didn't look any different. Still mud brown. Still dirty. He was very happy to be off the bus. The Greyhound was comfortable but it was hard to sit in the same place for eighteen hours. And there would be at least three times that number to come before he reached the land of his ancestors. Tuna's back hurt. There was a deep ache that he had carried for over a month. He didn't believe it was a muscle pull. The pain was deeper. Somewhere in the organs maybe. He would ask Socorro to put him in balance when he got to Zapata. That is all this pain was he prayed. He was out of balance from the time in the gringo fields of California. From the years in the North.

The Indian dropped his dime into the turnstile and pushed his way into Mexico. He walked past the customs building and the Secretaria de Turismo kiosk and headed for la Calle de Aldama. Tuna weaved through the backed up traffic that did little but crawl all the way to the bridge. Vendors were taking advantage of the stalled cars and putting the hard sell on the drivers, gum and newspapers to the in-coming gringos and fake jewelry and plastic crucifixes to the Mexicans going over to McAllen. There were two kids in the middle of the intersection juggling three dingy yellow rubber balls. La policia for that intersection was talking to a girl next to the liquor store. The traffic officer was oblivious to the chaos in the street.

Tuna jaywalked through a line of cars to clear the traffic and take a short cut on Morelos Street. It would save him three blocks to the bus depot.

An arm came out of the window of a passing Jeep and gently stopped his progress. "Pardón señor." Tuna stopped next to the driver's window and looked at an angle at the gringo who had spoken to him.

"¿Señor, puede decirme?" Tuna didn't answer, but he didn't move on either. ¿Cómo se va a fuera Reynosa a San Fernando, por favor?

"I speak English," Tuna politely responded.

"Great." Drew cut a quick glance at Joy.

"Listen, we're trying to get out of this mess and head to San Fernando. Would you know how to get to Highway 97 from here?" Drew spoke the words slowly and clearly. He did not know whether to believe this pedestrian or not.

Over the horn honking, Tuna began to describe the route past the La Mansion Hotel over the Anzalduas Canal and past the Pemex Refinery. He was about to tell the gringos to watch for the Plaza Santa Fe Bullring when Drew interrupted him.

"Hey listen. We will pay you to ride with us and show us the way. What do you say?"

Tuna looked toward Chapa Street two blocks up Zaragoza to give him a bit of time to think over the offer from the stranger.

Finally he said, "OK, señor, I will help you find a way out of this traffic. Go down this street."

Tuna did a better job than the traffic cop and stopped the cars and directed the Jeep and trailer out of the jam. When they had reached the second block away from the bridge, Tuna waved for Drew to turn at the next corner. Joy squeezed between the seats and Drew motioned for Tuna to jump in his place. The little Indian was almost in the Jeep when he noticed Chica.

"¿El perro no muerde, no?"

"No she doesn't bite. Come on hop in."

Tuna directed the caravan through every twisting block of Reynosa, past the Deposito de Cerveza and by the La Mansion and Elegante Hotels. He pointed to the bus station next to the supermarket just before they reached the canal. Tuna already liked these gringos. They were very friendly, not at all formal or stuffy. They smiled every time they asked him a question. Tuna also liked his role as guide. He waved his arm out the window and showed them how the coyotes sometimes dropped their little pollitos off on the south side of the Anzalduas Canal. They told the dumb ones, the first timers, that the canal is the Rio Bravo he explained. Tuna said it was so sad to see these people who have traveled so far think

164

they are in the United States after they wade through the open sewer of the canal. There are many dishonest and cruel men he tells Joy in the back.

Drew asked him how he came to speak English so well and Tuna responded with a short explanation of his first trip to the United States and his work in California. He said with no small pride that he had his Green Card and was legal in the United States. But now, he is returning to his home in Zapata deep in the land of his birth. As the Jeep passed the Morelos Monument, Tuna described his village. Drew noticed the Pemex station with a hand painted sign that read Magna Sin.

"Let's gas up here before we hit the highway," he said.

Drew pulled up to the green pump and the attendant pulled out the nozzle and asked if they wanted Magna.

"Sí, lleno, por favor," Drew answered as he got out.

Tuna got out too and started around the front of the Jeep. He pointed to the bullring and said that Drew will see the sign to Ciudad Victoria and San Fernando when he reaches that point.

"Say, my friend. What is your name?"

They call me Tuna, señor. My friends call me Tuna.

"Tuna? Like Charley the Tuna...never mind...listen Tuna I've got an idea. Where is this place Zapata, your home?"

"Many kilometers to the south, señor." Tuna pointed in the same direction as before, towards the bullring.

"Where in the south?"

"In the state of Chiapas," Tuna answered.

"Drew, call me Drew. Chiapas! Did you say Chiapas?' he snaped a quick look over in the direction of Joy, "We're going to Chiapas."

"Sí señor."

"Hell amigo, you can ride with us, no?"

Drew didn't wait for Tuna to answer, but turned and stuck his head into the driver's side of the Jeep and began explaining to Joy that someone like Tuna would be a great asset for the first-time travelers in Mexico. He asked Joy for his opinion. Joy was sitting on Drew's duffel bag and was wondering about how much room they had when Drew said he had a jump seat behind the spare tire and that Tuna could ride in it. Joy agreed.

"So, what do you think? You want to ride with a couple of gringos down to Chiapas?"

I DON'T THINK WE'RE IN KANSAS ANYMORE

DREW, AND JOY WITH TUNA NESTLED IN THE JUMP SEAT cleared the intersection at Mexican Highway 40 and fell behind an overloaded cement truck on 97 as it lumbered across the narrow bridge and past the village of Colonia del Banco. Highway 97 is the longest straight highway in all of Mexico. It runs like a taut string to the El Tejon Junction ninety-seven kilometers into the interior.

Drew's travel log said that there would be little or nothing to see along this way. A few settlements with names of Alfredo Bonfil, El Porvenir, Ejido Florida del Norte and Aquila Azteca. The whole stretch of road was a narrow two-lane highway with no shoulders. Nowhere to pull off, not that anyone would want to.

There was only one place ahead where they would have to stop. Drew wanted to get it behind them as soon as possible so he could stop thinking about the Mexican officials for a while. That was the customs stop at the twenty-six kilometer marker. Drew asked Tuna if he knew anything about it. Over the soft roar of the highway noise, Tuna said he had never gone through the point in a car, only on a bus. He didn't know about those men there. Drew didn't either and that's what bothered him, keeping him from feeling relaxed, excited about the adventure. Customs at the border was different. He was nervous but he could still see his home turf. This checkpoint was well out of sight of the U.S. Consulate in Reynosa.

Drew never could understand why he was so nervous about Mexican officials. His travel log had reassured him. It painted a positive picture of the Mexican police as men who were often helpful to turistas. Drew wanted to believe the benign description but couldn't shake the mental images from the movie portrayals and books about Mexico. And, then there were the jokes Joaquín liked to make about the Mexican police. How all Mexicans hated them. Hate was not strong enough, how they despised them. It was this image that worried Drew. The image of la Policia as men who still routinely tortured their prisoners. Men in uniform with pistols jammed into their belts who took delight in putting cattle prods to a man's testicles or his tongue, pain with no lingering physical marks. Men, who concoct a mixture of chili powder and place it in a bottle of Tehuacán, a carbonated mineral water sold all over the country. The mixture then shaken and forced up the nostrils of the victim. Drew had read that there is always a confession, a confession to anything, after this technique.

Maybe the others were thinking the same. The Jeep was quiet except for the noise of the wind. Chica even had settled down. She didn't take her eyes off Tuna. Tuna likewise was uneasy with the little dog. He did not try to make friends. Drew glanced at his key ring and the missing trailer door key came back to his thoughts. He didn't like the fact that he couldn't figure out how it had come out of the little magnetic metal box he had securely slid under one of the spare tire cross members. He had never known the box to come open like that. It must have been when they crossed the bar ditch after the blowout below George West he thought. It didn't make any sense otherwise.

"What the hell was that?" Joy shouted as he spun to look back over his shoulder.

"That, my friend was a vibradora. The gentler cousin of the tope. The customs station is about a mile up ahead. Those things are designed to slow us down. Maybe even wake you up on this straight stretch of road," Drew explained.

There was a whole section in the travel log about the topes. The raised asphalt or concrete that were used in U.S. shopping centers to keep hot-rodders from running over old ladies coming out of Neiman's. They were used by the Mexicans to slow down all traffic around any kind of settlement. The book had described them as *speed bumps with a desire for revenge. If you do not slow down, they will tear your suspension apart.* He now was beginning to understand what the warning meant. If the topes were worse than the vibradoras he would definitely slow down to a crawl before he tried to cross one.

THE SECOND TEST

THE RED LIGHT WAS BURNING ON THE HIGHWAY crossover. Drew figured this meant all vehicles were to stop for inspection. He slowed the Jeep to less than ten miles-an-hour and pulled up behind a pickup loaded with hogs waiting to clear the station.

"What do we need to show here mate." Joy reached under the seat and pulled out his brown leather document folder.

"I guess our visa and other papers, quien sabe?"

There were two young kids in the back of the truck in front of the Jeep. They were sitting next to a mama sow and the girl had a piglet in her lap. The pickup pulled on through, waved on by one of the three officials. Drew thought the customs building looked like an old gas station. The kind you still see in the rural parts of Texas. Those with two pumps under an overhang attached to a small blockhouse with a screen front door. The only thing missing here was the Royal Crown Cola sign in the window.

One of the customs agents was sitting in a lawn chair next to the front door. He was holding a clipboard. Both of the other men walked to either side of the Jeep. No one was smiling.

"Buenos días, su papeles." Drew noticed there was no por favor attached to the order. He handed the officer his visa. Joy did the same on his side. The customs agent studied the papers but didn't ask any questions. He bent down and looked across at Joy and then he turned his head toward Tuna.

"Estaciónalo allí, señor." He pointed to a graveled strip just out from under the overhang. Drew's heart added a few beats per minute to its rhythm and he could feel the pounding in his throat. He pulled slowly to the spot as instructed.

"What's going on?" Joy whispered without turning his head toward Drew.

"Beats me. Tuna... ¿hay problema?"

"I don't know señor."

The brown shirted men in tandem followed and walked up both sides of the trailer and then the Jeep. They went to the front

169

and the one with two yellow ribbons on his shoulders motioned for them to get out of the vehicle and come to them. Drew grabbed the black canvas passport bag that hung from a string around the rear view mirror. They all got out. Drew ordered Chica to stay and prayed she would obey.

"Necesito a ver tu pasaporte, su papeles de seguro y para el perro." The other official took Tuna by the arm and walked him back behind the trailer. Drew watched them move away as he opened his folder and handed the items requested over to the official. The grim-faced officer looked at the passport for what seemed like a full minute. He studied the picture and then Drew's face. Finally, he handed it all back and repeated the process with Joy. Drew did not say a word. He noticed that there were large sweat rings under both of Joy's arms, but the kid looked calm otherwise.

The double yellow ribbon official handed Joy's papers back and started around the Jeep to the passenger's side.

"Por favor, abre la puerta." He pointed to the door on the trailer. Drew was glad to hear a please for this request. He pitched his papers in the driver's seat, took the key out of the ignition, and sorted through the ring for the door key. He thought about the missing key again as he half jogged around the front of the Jeep towards the agent standing by the door making a note on his clipboard.

"Dispénseme señor," Drew pushed the key into the lock and opened the door. He jumped up over the single step, into the trailer. He reached down and grabbed Joy's duffel and pitched it towards the back of the small interior. When he did, he saw it. The black bag. It was lying on the upper bunk right above the couch. It was Ree's

170

bag. Drew's mind raced. How did that get there? Ree had it when she left him at the Tequila Cantina, he was sure. But there it was. Drew backed up to the closet door and politely motioned the agent to come in.

The customs official placed his right foot on the metal step, leaned into the trailer and looked toward the back. "¿Qué es en el compartamento?" He pointed to the trap door under the couch.

"Solo cosas personales." Drew tried his best to speak good Spanish.

The agent took another step and squeezed between Drew and the little sink and counter that made up the kitchen. There was barely room but Drew didn't move away from the closet door. He tried to shield the agent from seeing the doorknob.

"¿Y aquí?" the official said pointing at the cabinet.

"Just... I mean....solo platos y otra cosas par la cocina señor."

The official reached up and pulled at the door above the kitchen counter but it was stuck. He pulled harder. When it suddenly released two hard plastic plates slid out and crashed in the sink. The dirty water glass in the sink broke. Drew jumped in his skin. He heard a small gasp behind him. He wanted to say a few cuss words but he suppressed the urge.

The customs official looked at Drew and shrugged his shoulders slightly. Drew noticed a slight smile. The official took two steps and was back outside. Tuna was already in the Jeep sitting in the jump seat. Chica had moved over and had her head between his feet.

Nobody said a word or dared to look back as they jumped the small ridge that marked the end of the gravel and the road surface. They jiggled across the vibradora on the south entrance to the customs station and began to build up speed to the eighty-eight kilometer-per-hour limit. Drew thought now he knew what had happened to the key, but he decided to wait until San Fernando to make sure. He wanted away from the customs station at the twenty-six kilometer mark. He pressed hard on the gas pedal.

THE TRIO DROVE PAST THE BUS STOP at El Tepehuaje and Joy noticed the microwave tower up on the hill. He made some comment about the contrast between that sign of modern communication and the primitive appearance of all the pueblos they had sped past in the last hour. Drew just nodded but didn't answer. He hadn't been able to think about anything besides what he suspected he would find in the trailer when they stopped in San Fernando. The town was in the middle of a prime agricultural area, which Drew could tell by the number of grain trucks that kept his speed at half the limit. He looked at the gas gauge and decided they could make Ciudad Victoria with no problem. He drove by a Pemex station going into town.

"Let's stop here and grab a bite; might not get another chance before Victoria." Drew handed Joy the travel log. "See what you can find in here. Anything but Chinese." Drew meant it as a joke but Joy didn't seem to get it and seriously went about the task.

"The guide says there is a good place next to the La Hacienda Hotel. Says try the caldo de res. Enough garlic to frighten Dracula it suggests."

"Sounds fine to me. Where is it?"

172

"About a half mile up this road. I think I see the sign. Better move to the right. You'll have to go around that plaza." Joy waved his hand to give guidance.

They parked the rig right in front of the hotel behind an aged Greyhound tour bus. Eight or so senior citizens were looking at brochures or something next to the front door. Drew hoped they were on their way out and not in. He didn't want to spend too much daylight eating lunch. There were still three hours of road surface before they would reach Ciudad Victoria.

Joy got out and held the seat forward for Tuna.

"Joy you and Tuna go on in and save me a place. I want to check something out." Drew took his keys and found the one for the trailer door.

Drew stood in front of the door for a second. He knocked. It opened slightly.

"I thought you were here. I saw your bag back at the customs station. What in the holy mother of hell's fire is going on Ree?"

Drew bent over slightly to clear the shelf above the small dining table and slid in across from the stowaway. She was shaking. Her eyes were swollen, red, and slightly glazed. Ree looked at Drew for a moment and then put her forehead down on her arms and began to cry softly.

Drew wanted to be mad. After all, Ree had put them in a dangerous position with customs. She was in Mexico illegally. No visa and Drew assumed no passport. If they had found her in the closet they would all be in deep shit. In spite of that, he didn't feel mad. In fact, he was glad she was sitting across from him now. He reached over, put his hand on her arm, and again asked Ree what was going on, but softer this time.

Ree raised her face, looked at Drew intensely, and released the twenty-megaton bomb.

"I think I killed Buddy." She didn't bother to wipe the rivulets from under her eyes and put her head back down on her arms.

Drew just sat there. His mind moved in several directions at once but got nowhere. There was just too much to absorb from that one simple statement of fact. Too many variables too fast. It was a puzzle of a thousand pieces dumped on the table all at once. All that seemed to be clear was the image of Ree standing at his table at the Dairy Queen back in Texas. Then he saw her walking back to the Jeep in front of the Firestone Tire Store. He saw Ree combing out; her wet hair at the Lemon Grove.

"Do you want to tell me about it now?"

Drew sucked in a deep breath and put both hands behind his head and tried to bend backwards to stretch. He knocked the curtain rod off its track. The sunlight poured in through the gap.

"I'm so scared," Ree whimpered.

Drew maneuvered out from under the table and took the one step over to the sink. He pulled the dishrag from its hanger and used the hand pump to bring a trickle of water from the five-gallon plastic tank under the sink.

"Here. Wipe your face. Lets' go get a bowl of soup in the hotel. There are a couple of people you need to meet."

Drew suddenly felt in control.

Ree rose, took the towel and began to compliantly rub her eyes.

"Drew what am I going to do?"

"You know that's the second time you've asked me that question. The first time I told you to go to Mexico. Well it seems you took that advice." Drew didn't smile but his look was soft, there was

174

no tension over his eyes. "So maybe I can give you some more. First, let's get you something to eat. How long you been in here?"

"Since late last night. I..."

"Save it. Stop thinking about it right now. Just think about how hungry you are, and how the chilies in the soup are going to clear out your sinuses. That's enough for the moment. I hope you're ready for Mexico.

"Sure. The soup sounds wonderful. I'll have to let you know about Mexico," they both smiled finally.

ASK ME NO QUESTIONS AND I'LL TELL YOU NO LIES

DREW WASN'T SURE ABOUT THE PRESENT REALITY. Three days before he had left Bulverde and started his journey to southern Mexico, alone. The trip had taken him two years to plan. He had tried to think through every possible situation, every conceivable detail.

Now he had three passengers as they drove into the Victoria RV Park on Calle Periferico. Drew suspected it had something to do with Mexico.

There were some heavy thunderstorms dancing over the mountains back to the west. The first leg was complete with no trouble, that is, if you didn't count Ree and the blown tire. Actually, they were ahead of schedule. The lightning flashes were bright and spectacular but the thunder did not follow. It was a long way to the mountains Drew figured even though their magnificent mass looked very close. He wasn't accustomed to mountains, just the low contours of the Texas Hill Country.

Drew tried to decide which space to pull into. The park looked deserted except for a couple of travel trailers that were on blocks near the house at the front gate. They looked permanent; probably some gringo who came and liked the climate, the Mexican pace or something and stayed. Joy wondered aloud if the park was open. There didn't seem to be anyone around.

Drew said, "It is now."

Drew had made a joke out of Ree's sudden appearance at lunch back in San Fernando. He didn't want to try and explain something he didn't yet understand himself. He didn't feel he owed Joy an explanation anyway. He was getting a free ride, as was Tuna. Drew simply introduced the strange woman and said that he had found a stowaway and would make her walk the plank as soon as they were safe in port. Drew winked at Joy and hoped the kid would not ask any questions over their meal. Joy complied admirably. At the counter on the way out Drew paid the check and whispered to Joy that Ree was an old girlfriend and he would tell him the story later. Joy again politely nodded.

Since there were only seats for three in the Jeep and Ree made four, Drew asked her to ride in the trailer to Victoria. They would figure out something different that night. Ree seemed to like the idea. She appeared grateful not to have to join in the conversations of the road. She squeezed Drew's arm as she climbed up the step and thanked him for the soup.

"I feel better," was all she said and closed the door.

Joy came back from the house at the front of the RV Park and said he could not get anybody to answer the door. He said that there was somebody in the house because he could hear music but no one responded to his knocks. Drew said they would probably come around later and collect the fee before dark. Drew had Tuna block the trailer tires and he and Joy lifted the hitch off the ball. He figured they'd need to make a run to the store later to buy some ice and beer. It would be too much trouble to pull the trailer.

For the rest of the afternoon everybody took things easy. Tuna played chase the ball with Chica. They were now amazingly great friends after being in such close proximity on the long drive from Reynosa. Joy sat under a tree and read some scientific journal he had brought along. Drew could see by the title it had something to do with crops in Latin America or something similar. Ree stayed close to the trailer and Drew pulled out his red chair and watched the lightning show up in the mountains. The thunderheads were still climbing and he hoped the bad weather stayed up in the heights. He was a bit anxious to get Ree's story but decided not to rush it. In the meantime, he made an effort to push the words *killed Buddy* out of his thoughts.

DEAD OR ALIVE

"MIND IF I JOIN YOU?" Drew looked up and Ree was standing next to him. "Here I brought you a beer."

"Thanks. The mountains are kind of nice aren't they?"

"Yes, they are."

The two sat in silence and watched one of the three storms that were torturing the peaks go into its last life cycle. It made an anvil at the top and began to spread and turn a brilliant white. The sun, well below to the west, made the water vapor almost too bright to look at. It was rapidly becoming an umbrella over the other thunderheads that continued to puff up and climb towards the bigger and older brother. The lightning continued to dance around each group. Occasionally a jagged bolt made the jump from one to the other.

"I suppose you're wondering about all this?"

Drew hesitated slightly but then answered. "You might say that. Here you take the chair and I'll prop up against the tree." Drew sat down in a half lotus and secured the beer can in the well created by his legs.

Ree tried to describe the sequence of events from the time she and Drew had separated in McAllen without breaking into tears. She did a good job up until she started talking about Buddy knocking Jane down. Drew just let her cry. After a bit, he handed her his bandana. She took a deep breath and rubbed her eyes, and then continued her story.

Drew followed everything she said except the part right after the gun went off and Buddy sprawled on his back next to Jane's car. He tried to form a mental picture but somehow he couldn't see Buddy's image. It made it hard for Drew to think about the scene. Instead, he found himself creating quick mental scenarios of what to do now rather than worry about what had happened.

"So how did you get to the Motel 6 and in the trailer?"

This part did not make any sense. Ree said she just panicked as she approached the hospital. That's when she saw the motel across from the building complex and her last conversation with Drew came to mind. From the parking lot near the hospital's emergency entrance she could see the Jeep and trailer parked along the road. Ree said she was shaking really bad. She just stood there. Suddenly, somebody from behind touched her on the shoulder and she jumped and let out a short scream. The guy jumped as well and nervously asked her if she was alright.

That was when she started towards the trailer. She told Drew she was praying that he would be there. She could not even remember why she had come to the hospital because she wasn't hurt. She didn't understand herself what happened after that. All she could recall was that she had knocked on the trailer door several times. Finally, she walked to the back and got the key from the little box under the spare tire. She had remembered seeing Drew get it from there when they had the flat on 281. Ree said she slept the rest of the night. "Strangely," she went on, "I felt really safe there. It was small and dark but very comfortable. I just wanted to stay in that little space forever."

The next thing she knew the trailer was rolling. Ree said she couldn't make herself get off the couch. She stayed wrapped up in the small Indian blanket she had taken out of the storage bin in the closet. Then she realized they had crossed the border. She could hear people speaking Spanish all around the trailer and horns honking. There was just a lot of noise.

"I panicked and got in the closet."

"You know you could have got us all in big trouble back at the customs stop?" Drew made a conscious effort at sounding stern. He wasn't very good at it though. Never had been, so he made a mental note to himself to drop the tone.

"Yes. I guess I did know. But I was scared. Scared that you didn't know I was there. I think I was more frightened that you would get in trouble than me. And I couldn't help thinking about Jane. Drew, I've made such a mess. Everybody around me is getting hurt."

Drew could tell that Ree was about to break down again so he interrupted that process.

"OK. Let me see if I have this straight. You don't really know what happened to Buddy because you left right after the gun went off, right?"

"Yes, that's right."

"OK. So, he could be dead or alive. As far as you know, he could be following you right now?"

"I suppose. But, Drew, I saw blood."

"I know, I know. But that's all you know. It could have been a flesh wound. You have no way of knowing for sure, right?"

"Yes, you're right."

"Well, then let's not worry about that part. What we have to think about is what you do now. Wait a minute. Before we do that, I want to say something for you to stick in your sack and remember every time you start blaming yourself for what has happened the last few days. That is simply this. What has happened is the result of an irrational, violent man. A man who is bordering on evil. If Buddy hadn't beat and raped you in the first place; if he hadn't followed you to McAllen; if he hadn't tried to intimidate you in Jane's garage, and if he hadn't threatened to kill you, you wouldn't be in this spot. OK?"

"OK."

"OK. So the question is what now? Let me go over the facts. Nothing but the facts ma'am." Drew tried to make a joke and change the mood from despair to hope.

"First, you are in Mexico illegally. No passport. No visa. Nada. You do have your driver's license I hope?"

"Yes, it's in my bag."

"By the way, how'd you get your bag?"

"It was slung over my shoulder when I got out of Jane's car."

"Oh. Well good. At least we can prove you're a U.S. citizen. Second, I can't turn around and take you back to the border. We, that is Joy and I, have to be in Chiapas on Wednesday. That's a given. So we can either go find a U.S. Consulate or you can ride with us to Tuxtla-Gutiérrez and we can deal with it when we get there."

"Drew, what if Buddy's dead?"

"I thought we had settled that point. It is an unknown. And, even if he is it's self defense. Don't worry about that jerk. Agreed?"

"Agreed."

"OK, here's what I think we should do."

Ree sat back in the chair. She felt relief that Drew was taking control, safe like in the trailer. She saw Weaver in his eyes more than ever.

"You come with us on the trip. Hey, look at it as a great opportunity to see Mexico with a charming fellow, right? We will get there in two more days and we'll ask Joaquín to help us with the Mexican officials. He is a man with money in Mexico. That should take care of that part of the problem. If we go to the officials now, you may get tangled up in the bureaucracy and never heard from again. And, we'll make some calls and find out what happened to Buddy. How does that sound?"

"What if we are stopped or have to go through customs again?"

"There is no more customs between here and there. They are only near the borders. And, hey, we got through the last one didn't we? We are going to have to tell Joy and Tuna a little of what's going on. At least the part about you not having a visa. I'll just tell them you're an ex-girlfriend who couldn't live without me so you followed me to Mexico."

"Maybe some of that is true?" Ree flashed something like a smile for the first time since they began to talk.

"OK, it's settled. Now get into that kitchen and cook diner woman!" Drew smiled broadly.

Drew got to his feet, squatted in front of Ree and put his hands on her knees. He made her look into his eyes.

"Look, this is something that will work out for the best. Believe that. Sometimes breaking with an old life can be pure hell. Nevertheless, in a few weeks, it will be history and you will be better for it. Now, do the best you can to let things move along without force. Just take advantage of this situation. You are among friends. You are on a grand adventure through the land of mystery and enchantment if you can believe the brochures. You're going to be all right. Right?"

"Did I ever tell you that you have beautiful blue eyes?"

"No, I don't think you have. But feel free anytime."

CHAPTER 9

IT'S ALL SCIENCE TO ME

DR. BOXXLOADER'S AVIACSA FLIGHT from Mexico City came in low over the mountains and lined up for the final approach to the tabletop Tuxtla airport. He had a window seat but it did not furnish much of view. Nothing on the ground was visible. All he saw was the smoke that followed the contours of the valley like a mantle. The valley farmers were burning their fields. It was May and the rainy season would begin soon. If their prayers to the Virgin were answered, next month the long growing season would begin. The nitrogen from the burned material would be carried by the water into the top layers of soil. The mixture would provide for a good harvest in the fall, or so they all prayed.

The State Government of Chiapas prohibited the burning of crop residue but the farmers did it anyway. Their fathers had and their fathers before them. The farmers in Mexico had always burned. It was the only way to control the bugs and the weeds. The use of expensive northern manufactured pesticides and herbicides was not possible. These farmers did not have money for the extravagance that science dictated. If the people were to eat, the government would have to let the old crops burn and everyone must put up with the smoke and the haze. It was as indispensable as the dirt.

A moment after Boxxloader caught sight of the landing strip the wheels emitted a squeal as rubber abruptly kissed the concrete runway. He was happy to be on solid ground. Even after all the years of flying, he still did not relish coming in blind to an airport. The British built jet of the Mexican airline reached the end of the runway and turned around on the cul-de-sac. Slowly the plane retraced its route and taxied toward the main terminal. Everything on the ground appeared brown and stunted. What little vegetation he could see from the window was dead or dying. The rains would be welcomed as always when they finally came.

The pilot cut the engines and everyone stood up at once in the cabin. Boxxloader was practically the last one to leave the jet. He descended the portable stairs to the tarmac just ahead of the two pilots and a couple of young flight attendants. As his feet touched the last step, he could see Joaquín coming to greet him, weaving his way through the small groups of arrivals and the hugs and kisses. The good doctor braced himself as much for the week to come as for Joaquín. As he watched the anxious man race his way he suddenly wished he had gone on to Africa. There were many problems there too, but they were old problems. Problems he was used to. He took a deep breath and forced a smile.

HERE WE GO AGAIN

IN THE SHORT FIFTEEN-MINUTE DRIVE FROM THE AIRPORT to the Flamboyant Hotel, Joaquín had spoken of his dream, the non-existent International Center for Tropical Research, he repeated it three times. Dr. Boxxloader just listened. Already the pace was frantic. He knew it would be this way. He knew it because he knew his host too well. Grand ideas. Sweeping generalities. Unwillingness to accept any contrary proposals. Stubbornness. Unrealistic expectations. A man with a good heart. These were all qualities Boxxloader had had to deal with while Joaquín worked for him in agricultural research years ago. Boxxloader never was able to make the changes in Joaquín that would be necessary for him to be a scientist. He never could convince the young man that the scientific community did not take well to pressure and simple force of will. It wanted methodology, patience, thoroughness of technique, detachment from the thing investigated, rational positive thinking. Everything that Joaquín couldn't or refused to do. Joaquín could not sit and watch the glacier move. He had to push it. Help it along toward what he often called God's purpose. Boxxloader looked at his animated chauffeur, as excited as he had ever seen him, determined as always to have his way.

The old man had hoped he would get a chance to read the background material in his room that afternoon before they began work. He should have known better. Jorge, Joaquín's segundo, met them at the door of the hotel and took the one suitcase from Joaquín as he hurriedly explained that Jorge would take care of the check-in and that their first meeting was already arranged. To protest would be futile Boxxloader concluded.

There were four long meeting tables arranged in a square. Most of the chairs were already filled except for three at the lead table along the blackboard. Boxxloader knew about half of the people in the room. The ones he recognized were all agricultural scientists of one persuasion or another. Some he liked others he did not. Some he had worked with over the many years in Mexico and others were of the new generation. A generation, for the most part, that did not agree with his methods. He was familiar with their arguments, but as he took his place he knew he'd get another dose soon enough.

Boxxloader began removing his papers from a well-worn briefcase when he thought to inquire about his young protégé. Joaquín took delight in explaining that it had been taken care of and that Mr. McCarty would be arriving tomorrow, Wednesday, with Andrew Cotton. Boxxloader appeared pleased with the news. With the faces he saw around the table he knew this would be Joy's big chance to rub elbows with the people who could make his transition from graduate school to field research a much easier journey. The kid deserved it. Just then, a hand came down on his shoulder.

"Bienvenidos, viejo."

Boxxloader strained to look up and over his shoulder. To his delight, the round, deeply tanned face of Dr. Blanco greeted him.

"Well look at this will you. Joaquín told me he had put the con on you. I am glad you're here. How's your lovely wife Eva?" Boxxloader scooted his chair back and stood up embracing his friend.

"She's doing very well, thank you for asking Sol. The woman is looking forward to my retirement though."

"Yes, I can imagine. I've heard you're going to finally exit Honduras and move back to Kansas after all these years."

"Could be. We will have to see. There's another two months before I have to make that decision."

The harsh squeal of the amplifier as hotel maintenance tried to adjust the volume on the microphone interrupted the two men's reunion. Everyone groaned. Dr. Blanco quickly shook hands with his old friend and asked Boxxloader to join him for a drink that evening before supper. Boxxloader nodded his acceptance and Blanco returned to his seat. Joaquín nervously shuffled papers on the podium. He tapped the microphone and cleared his throat. The milling around and various conversations began to subside and the room finally settled.

CHIAPAS AWAITS ITS FATE

DR. EMILIO CÁRDENAS SHOOK HANDS with the governor and excused himself for having to leave. He tried to explain diplomatically that he was scheduled for another engagement. He did not mention the Boxxloader committee but he did not have to. The Governor was well aware of the proceedings about to begin at the Flamboyant.

Dr. Cárdenas was pleased. He and the Governor had had a good meeting. The Governor said he certainly understood his involvement in his state. That he was more than happy to have such a distinguished body of scientists from all around the world here in Chiapas. The problems of the rainforest were serious and must be confronted forcibly he said. He welcomed the expertise and concern for Mexico and for Chiapas.

Cárdenas looked at his watch as he gave the taxi driver his instructions. He would be a few minutes late but the meeting with the Governor had been necessary. Cárdenas had arrived a day early for the opportunity to meet with him. His appointment as the Director of the International Center for Agro Forestry in Kenya necessitated that he become as much a diplomat as a scientist. Moreover, if Cárdenas wanted to establish an extension station in Chiapas it would require the Governor's blessing; much more so than he would need that of Sr. Villa's or Dr. Boxxloader's for that matter. Still, he hated being late for meetings.

Joaquín broke off briefly his opening remarks as he watched Dr. Cárdenas push through the double doors of the meeting room. All eyes turned to watch the prominent scientist take his place at the lead table. He hurriedly apologized and begged Joaquín please to continue. Joaquín offered a welcome but was puzzled by Dr. Cárdenas' late arrival. Joaquín knew he was not on the *Aviacsa* flight with Dr. Sol and that was the only scheduled one until *Mexicana* came in later that night. He made a note on his opening speech to ask Cárdenas about his late arrival. Several of the men around the table silently acknowledged Cárdenas with hand gestures. He graciously returned the acknowledgements.

"Well," Joaquín began, "we are all here now. So please permit me a few comments about our purpose and then I will brief you on the week's plan for action. As you can see, we have put the plan on the chalkboard behind me. Everyone will get a copy of the itinerary after the meeting"

Joaquín tucked the first page of his remarks under the stack and looked at the heading on the second page, *History, Goals and Purpose*. He methodically perused the room at the eighteen faces. All but one was a biological scientist of some shade. He had worked for nearly two years to bring these men to Chiapas. As he looked toward Dr. Boxxloader to his right, Boxxloader was whispering something to Cárdenas. Joaquín immediately recalled Dr. Sol's words on the phone: *Are you sure you know how to play this game? If you start down this trail, you may not be able to turn around.*

Joaquín cleared his throat and began his lecture, "Maybe I should begin with a little history." Joaquín felt the perspiration begin to form a wet circle under both arms.

During his presentation of the history leading to this day, Joaquín avoided the use of international center like the plague. He didn't want to excite the old doctor unnecessarily; not just yet. Once he slipped up and referred to his plan as an international model of forest preservation and reclamation but Boxxloader didn't seem to notice. If Joaquín could have seen his eyes, he would have noticed that the old doctor was catching a nap.

"So, gentlemen, these events of the last year have led us to this meeting and to your involvement in our study. Over the course of the next week, we will make a concerted effort to present this body with as much evidence and practical observation of the regional situation as time permits. From this, we, as a group, will formulate a plan of action to meet this challenge with the rainforest that remains in Chiapas and, hopefully, by extension, to the other threatened forests around the tropical world."

Joaquín was feeling good about the words he was using. They seemed to flow from a source not of his making. He could not remember a time when he felt more comfortable at the speaker's podium.

"Before I explain the agenda, I would like to close my opening remarks with a call to your heart as well as your mind." Joaquín slipped the last sheet of paper on which he had written this appeal.

He knew he would have to read this part. He could not speak these words spontaneously from the heart. They didn't reside there. The source was his intellect. He took a sip of water trying to control a slight handshake, and then began his summation.

> *As all of you are aware, the ecological deterioration of our planet has become a world concern. Complicated and costly ecological programs in one country are not effective on a world basis unless other countries can take similar actions.*

> *Those who, for many reasons, cannot, or will not act otherwise are seriously damaging the air and water we all must have. It is no longer sufficient to legislate, educate or appeal to conscience if we do not all take the same concerted course. The evidence of ozone layer destruction and global warming are very convincing examples of local action which have global repercussion.*

> *The destruction of the rainforest and the resulting worldwide climatic effects are sufficiently documented. This terrible destruction is often associated with irrational behavior by those causing the damage. It is this aspect of the problem that makes it readily impossible to resolve.*

> *It is true that past uses of tropical resources gave origin to these destructive processes, but today it is the social and economic destitution of the local populations that continues to drive the forest from existence. Only if we*

attend to this root cause can we expect to implement a permanent solution.

The state of Chiapas is a microcosm of this phenomenon. The destruction of the vast tropical resources in our region has left behind a system of subsistence agriculture, which does not generate surpluses nor even provide adequately for the ever-growing population. Indeed, the pressure on the remaining jungle is great. It is not enough that governments have begun to act. The complete disappearance of these magnificent forests is simply a matter of time unless we deal directly with the human misery that drives this destructive process.

"Gentlemen, that concludes my remarks. Again, I thank all of you for taking the time from your busy professional lives to come to our part of the world and offer us the value of your expertise and experience. Now let's take a short break for coffee and pastries before we continue."

Joaquín hurriedly stuffed his speech into a manila folder and went to sit down next to Boxxloader. He wanted feedback on his remarks. Before he could sit, a hand touched his shoulder. The stranger introduced himself as Dr. Arturo Alvarez. He explained that he had come to the meeting not as an invited participant, but as an observer at the request of the Governor of Tabasco. He said that the Governor of Chiapas had called his counterpart in the neighboring state to invite his participation. Joaquín was more than a little surprised. The Governor had not informed him, but he let it pass. Alvarez asked if they might have a word together after the

191

formalities were complete. He believed he had something important to discuss with Joaquín about his project. Alvarez then commented on the opening speech. He said he had a strong feeling that the two men shared much in common concerning the true causes of the deterioration of the rainforest in the south of Mexico. Dr. Alvarez then politely said he recognized Joaquín had much to attend to and would wait to resume their discussion later.

The group spent the afternoon discussing their agenda for the week's fact-finding activities. Joaquín went over each day in detail. Too much detail for most around the table. He was barely into the second day's fly-over of the southeastern part of the state, the area that contained the ecological reserves of Laguna Belgica and El Ocote, when Dr. Cárdenas recommended that Joaquín save the details for the trip itself. He believed these men could follow the instructions on the written agenda and didn't need Joaquín's detailed explanation. Several voices arose in agreement with Cárdenas' observation. Dr. Mañcheco added that they were all anxious to renew or make acquaintance with other members of the committee. That best could be accomplished in the bar of the hotel he noted. Again, comments of agreement came from several points around the room.

With that, the meeting began to break up into isolated conversations. Joaquín knew he had lost control. He felt a flash of self-doubt about the whole plan. Cárdenas had upset Joaquín's agenda with a simple comment. Several of the scientists had begun to get out of their chairs when Boxxloader stood up and, without the microphone, asked the group to remain seated for a few minutes. He then turned to Joaquín and gestured politely for permission to take the floor. Joaquín felt relieved and sat down.

Everyone returned to their seats and cut short their conversations. Boxxloader picked up one of the printed agendas from the table next to the speaker's podium and looked at it before beginning.

"It says here that the *Boxxloader Committee* will conduct a survey of the present situation in Chiapas concerning the rapid destruction of the Lacandon Rainforest and then will make recommendations for remedying the problem."

He took a few seconds to let that soak in to his colleagues before he continued.

"I wish to make four points about that statement. First, there is no such thing as a Boxxloader Committee. I will act as lead scientist for this brief study and will lend my name to the cause, but we are in the same boat here. I am not in charge. For the second point, Joaquín in his opening remarks didn't once mention the words International Center for Tropical Research, but I can tell you all that's what he has in mind and I will oppose such a bureaucracy. He thinks just because we did it in food grains in Mexico forty years ago and had some success in raising crop yields around the world that we can do the same for the tropical forests. I have told him I won't support such an idea."

Boxxloader looked at Joaquín just for a second to underscore his words. Joaquín only smiled and didn't look back.

"But just because I don't support the creation of another layer of bureaucracy, don't any of you in this room think for one minute that I do not take our work here in Chiapas seriously. Gentlemen, remember that while we are out and about this beautiful and ancient land, flying in government helicopters over hill and dale, being fed graciously at night and treated like some visiting royalty;

193

that a hectare of primal tropical rainforest is disappearing every minute that we tarry. And along with it some one hundred species a day will go extinct around the world. I am sure we will hear a lot more about this during our deliberations. But suffice it to say at this juncture, that I will not tolerate in my presence anything less than the utmost seriousness in the efforts to study this problem in detail and to make clear and doable recommendations."

Boxxloader let his words float out over the room and settle for almost thirty seconds.

"My final point is related to point three. When we come back together at the end of our survey work in seven days, I want this body to be prepared to give some sound and objective descriptions of the root causes of rainforest destruction in Chiapas and to offer concrete action plans for making an impact on the problem in the shortest possible time. If I hear one of you propose a research project, I will personally throw you out of the meeting. And yes, one other thing, Joaquín has worked his butt off the last few months to get us down here, and the least we can do is listen to his agenda." Dr. Boxxloader sat down abruptly and motioned for Joaquín to proceed.

Dr. Cárdenas spoke as Joaquín was standing up to continue. "Excuse me Joaquín, a word before we continue. I know most of you in this room know Dr. Solomon Boxxloader personally. Many of you have worked with him over the years in projects all over this planet. All of us respect and admire the many years of dedication and uncommon insight he has brought to the field of agricultural science. I even see two members of this committee who owe their careers to this man. But, with this in mind, and with the utmost respect I must contradict Dr. Boxxloader. There is a certain lack of logic between the first point he made and his last threat to personally and bodily eject anyone who proposes more research. I submit that Dr. Boxxloader is, indeed, in charge."

The whole room broke into applause and laughter. Cárdenas had demonstrated his skills of diplomacy. Joaquín waited for the room to settle. It would be a long wait.

THE MAN FROM TABASCO

ARTURO ALVAREZ APPEARED TO BE A YOUNG MAN. Joaquín thought a little too young to have all the credentials and experience he had just outlined over three rounds of Scotch Whiskey. But he couldn't help thinking that this Alvarez, if legitimate, would make a good director for his International Center. And, Joaquín liked his quiet, self-assured manner. He was Mexican but there wasn't any of the normal over-educated bravado in him; probably due to his taking his Ph.D. in Australia. Dr. Alvarez even had a slight Aussie slant to his Spanish. It gave his voice a worldly resonance.

"Do you speak English Dr. Alvarez?"

"Yes I do, although I am not comfortable in its nuances. And I would appreciate it very much if you would call me Arturo."

"Certainly. So, how long did you say that you have been applying this technical transfer technique to the campesino communities in Tabasco?"

"We will celebrate our tenth anniversary next month. We have documented our work every step of the way. We believe we know what works and what doesn't because we have experienced both. I think I can show your committee a view of the problem you are addressing in the next week that you will not see in any other place on your itinerary. I am absolutely positive you will not see the same level of accomplishment at any of the government-run operations that I see you have on your schedule."

"Why is that Arturo?"

"Because," he hesitated to collect himself, "may I speak frankly?"

"Please, by all means."

"Because, the government does not understand the people of this region. They are still trying to carry out the conquest of these native people five centuries after the Spanish first landed on the shores of the Yucatan Peninsula. They only think in terms of technology. That is the government's god. Production, greater yields, better plant genetics, these are their criteria for success. But they are only mechanical criteria; platforms for statistics. They have no respect, and in most cases, no understanding of the traditions of these people. People who can trace their cultural roots in this land back over two thousand years."

Joaquín felt the rise of emotional temperature in Arturo as he spoke. It reminded him of the conversation with the Bishop in San Cristóbal only a few days before. There too the emphasis was on the people and their unique and traditional ways. But this was not what Joaquín had envisioned when he started. He sought a scientific solution. The men that were to participate in the upcoming study were scientists and science was what they produced. They would propose scientific solutions to what they all believed were merely scientific problems. Dr. Boxxloader would see to that; and, Joaquín believed, that the International Center would institutionalize the result of that science.

"What are you suggesting?" Joaquín glanced across the crowded hotel bar and noted that Dr. Boxxloader, Dr. Emilio

Cárdenas and Dr. Blanco were having an intense discussion at a corner table. He suddenly felt left out and wished to be at their table. He needed to know what those men were discussing.

"Only this," Arturo continued, "bring your committee to our facilities during your study week. Let me and my staff make a presentation and demonstrate the successes we have experienced in both the technical and cultural arenas where we have worked with the peasant farmer in the rainforest regions. If nothing else, it will give your group a better perspective of the problems in southern Mexico. It can serve to provide a balance and complement your emphasis on technical solutions." Arturo sat back and sipped his drink. His eyes were locked on his tablemate.

"Let me study our itinerary Dr. Alvarez and discuss it with Dr. Boxxloader. What day would be to your liking?"

"My entire staff is at your disposal Joaquín. We will adjust to your schedule."

"That is very gracious. I will tell you in the morning our decision. You are staying in the hotel tonight aren't you?"

"Yes. I am in room 146."

MY SIDE YOUR SIDE

THE MARIMBAS WERE PLAYING TOO LOUD for Boxxloader's taste. He sat looking at his glass of red wine. He did not respond directly to what Dr. Cárdenas had just said. Both Cárdenas and Blanco let the old man think. Boxxloader was tired of all these intrigues. He had always fought his way through them before. You had to if you wished to get anything accomplished. He had played these games for fifty years, but never gotten used to it. *What was the purpose?* So much greed, so much deceit, so much waste. Egos, reputations,

197

associations, recognition; this was the ugly side of the world of science. *To hell with it!* Boxxloader wanted to go home and rest. He wanted to board a train and watch the countryside slowly pass outside the window. Watch the countryside of Mexico pass by the window and feel no responsibility for it or its people.

"Cárdenas, why didn't you tell me this before we came to Chiapas?" Boxxloader finally spoke. There was a hard edge to his question.

"I just found out myself two days before I left the U.S. Hell man, nobody can ever catch up with you anyway. You know that."

"Director of the International Center for Agroforestry in Nairobi, Kenya. Very impressive title my friend." There was sarcasm laced into Boxxloader's words. "The fourteenth center. Another layer of bureaucracy. But, I suppose, Cárdenas that is not important to you, is it?"

"Boxxloader why don't you come down off your Nobel high horse for this once? What makes you think we cannot have an impact on the world deforestation problem? At least now we will have some money to work with—we will have the mandate to pursue a solution."

"Yes, my distinguished friend, you will have a mandate and you will have something else as well. You will have administrative paper work up to your ear lobes. You will spend your days manipulating budgets, making presentations to the money sources, kissing every corporate butt or slimy ambassador with an official inflated ego from here to Bonn. In the first two years, you will turn out reams of paper detailing in the most obscure language your staff can create, some esoteric proposal to save the rainforests. You will preside in some kind of anointed pomp over innumerable staff meetings of countless sycophants whose only desire is to someday knock you off your throne and claim the jeweled headdress for themselves. Oh, and every now in then you will publish some report or other to justify all the resources used. Justify your existence at all cost."

Simon Blanco put his hand on his old friend's arm.

"You sound pretty bitter Solomon," Cárdenas did not respond to Boxxloader's attack.

"You're damn right." Boxxloader took a slow deep swallow of his wine and held up the glass to signal the joven for another.

"As a practical matter, Cárdenas what do we do about this work we have to do here? What about Joaquín; what do we tell him? Even though I have told the stubborn son-of-a-bitch not to expect an International Center for Chiapas, he ignores me. His whole purpose is for this to happen. Now that is impossible. What do we tell him and when?"

"May I suggest something?" Blanco asked looking between the two scientists. Both men signaled their approval.

"The fact that the outcome has to exclude the possibility of establishing an International Center in Mexico does not in any way diminish the importance of our work here. In some ways, it enhances it. Dr. Cárdenas is now in a position to provide help and resources to Chiapas that would have not been possible otherwise. Now that he knows he will have to develop a worldwide program for reversing the trend of rainforest destruction, he can use this experience to his advantage and, hopefully, to the advantage of this region. He has a unique opportunity to gather data and have the opinions of other scientists to help determine with this meeting what a program for the future should entail. He will see firsthand what is needed for this particular area of Mexico. Other than the problem of dealing with one man's ego and desires, I do not see our work here changed in the slightest. Boxxloader, you can deal with Joaquín as you see fit. For now, at least, I think we should proceed."

"Yes, Solomon. That is exactly what we should do," Cárdenas raised a toast to Blanco as he spoke. "In fact, let me tell you one other small piece of information of which you may not be aware. Simon's logic is right on target, because in my briefcase, I have brought to this meeting a rough outline of a new program that will be proposed to several United Nation funding agencies. My staff and I will propose a Worldwide Program for Alternatives to Traditional Slash and Burn Agriculture. Moreover, the important part of this proposal is that it will establish experimental stations in eight sites throughout the tropical world. Obviously, one of those sites could very well be here in Chiapas near the Lacandon Rainforest.

Boxxloader interrupted the monologue. "It sounds like to me Cárdenas that you have already worked this whole problem out in your own mind. Am I right?"

"Solomon, my friend, let us get through this week and discuss it at our deliberations for solutions with the entire group."

Boxxloader did not like Cárdenas calling him his friend, but he nodded his approval and sipped his wine.

CHAPTER 10

"SO, WHAT'S THE FOCUS OF YOUR GRADUATE WORK?" Drew asked.

Veracruz was more than two hours behind them. They felt, if not rested then eager. All the Chiapas-bound travelers had agreed to make the push to Tuxtla-Gutiérrez today. The night before had been one of the more comfortable on their journey south. They had parked the trailer in the parking lot of the Hotel Mocambo and paid the thirty thousand pesos to use the facilities of the luxury hotel. The hotel sat on a hill overlooking the seawall and the green waters of the Golfo de Mexico. The tourist season was still a month off so they had the two-acre covered swimming pool to themselves, almost. The mosquitoes enjoyed the party as well.

The accommodations would have been perfect if it were not for the grain trucks that stopped a couple of hundred feet from their location at the red sign on the busy highway. Drew easily recalled after the all night audio tutorial that most of the trucks had five low gears and six medium ones. Usually the trucks got out of hearing range after the sixth change. After about an hour, the patterns became more or less rhythmic and they all slept in spite of the bizarre music.

"Traditional agriculture. Traditional agriculture," Joy repeated, "that is my field of study."

"What kind of agriculture?" As he sped down the main road, Drew watched the loaded cane truck move at right angles to their trajectory. The truck had cane stacked at least three feet above the sideboards. Drew couldn't believe the load stayed on the truck. He also wondered if the driver planned to stop or would simply pull onto the highway. The convergent vehicles were synchronized to reach the juncture at the same time.

"Traditional agriculture. The cultivation techniques of traditional or native cultures. My focus is on Latin America."

Drew decided to tempt fate and pushed a little harder on the gas pedal. He couldn't believe how bold he had become on these Mexican roadways in only three day's time. It was like a game. If you didn't take the same chances that the Mexicans did you'd probably be dead before they were. Everyone drove the same. Crazy. So you copied their techniques. A wide range of headlight and horn signals, most of which Drew didn't understand yet, usually preceded one of a variety of suicidal acts.

"You think that guy in the cane truck is going to stop?" Joy glanced in its direction.

"I guess," Drew responded trying to sound unconcerned.

"In fact, my dissertation was on the growing impact of slash-and-burn cultivation." Joy too was becoming cavalier about the highway danger.

202

The truck stopped and sent a cloud of dust from under its wheels drifting lazily across the highway. The Jeep train cut the drift in half.

"That must be why the old doctor wants you down there for this project, right? I mean, isn't slash-and-stomp or whatever you call it, one of the things eating all the trees?"

"That's it."

"Well then, since I'm going to have to understand all this stuff to be able to write something intelligent in the proposals for money, why don't you give me a little education on the subject? Wait a minute professor. Before we get started, I'm going to stop at that roadside fruit stand. Let's get one of those pineapples—give us a chance to check on Ree and Tuna in the trailer."

Everything seemed to have calmed down after Ciudad Victoria. Ree had accepted Drew's suggestions and took to the trip better than he had figured. She and Tuna were becoming buddies. Ree couldn't seem to get enough of Tuna's stories, the descriptions of his village in Mexico. The life he lived in the fields of California. The trips back and forth across the muddy and polluted Rio Grande. The little Indian enjoyed telling them too. Drew was glad that they were riding in the trailer. There was more room than in the back of the Jeep, and it kept Ree out of harm's way. Chica joined them. Drew figured that if he didn't watch it, he would lose his dog to one or the other of his trailer passengers. Ree and Tuna both gave her more attention in one day on the road than Drew did in a month of Sundays.

They all sat on some crates under a shade tree next to the fruit venders make-shift stand. Tuna had borrowed the vendor's machete and had skillfully used the big knife to render the yellow fruit into even rings. Drew passed his knife back to Ree and she cut the rings into bite-size chunks. With some reluctance, Drew asked Ree how she felt. She responded with a smile and said she was doing fine. She was learning so much about Mexico and the Indians from Tuna. Drew noticed a brightness about her he hadn't seen before. It made the woman more attractive than ever, he thought.

"I don't know if we will make it to Tuxtla today or not. I think I've underestimated the time to drive from Veracruz to Joaquín's place. We'll see where we are by two o'clock and make our decision then about where to stay."

Drew pitched a small piece of pineapple at Chica. The dog took one reluctant sniff of the yellow fragment and walked away leaving it for the flies.

"You know Drew, if we cross over to the Pacific side there's a place on the ocean that a couple of the guys from graduate school told me was great. Big surf and beautiful beaches. I think it's called something like Puerto Salina or something like that. It's right on the Pacific." Joy went to get the map out of the Jeep.

While he was gone Tuna said he believed that Joy meant Salina Cruz.

"Yeah, here it is Salina Cruz. It's not too far north of the Arriga junction. Have we got time to check it out?"

"I think so. We'll just have to decide whether to go to Villahermosa and go south over the mountains to Tuxtla or to cross over to the Pacific side and go east. Six of one and a half dozen of the other as I see it. A night on the beach doesn't sound so bad. What do you guys think?" Drew looked at Ree who didn't answer.

"Well, we will be at the fork at Acuyacan in about thirty minutes. We'll flip a coin there. That's where we will have to decide. ¿Listo?"

GO TO SCHOOL

"SLASH-AND-BURN CULTIVATION WAS AS OLD as the Maya civilizations in tropical Mexico and Central America," Joy explained as they headed for Acuyacan.

"The technique is simple enough. The vegetation on a small land plot, usually about a hectare, or two-and-a-half acres, is cut. Trees, vines, anything and everything are felled. Then the Indians let the material dry. Once it's dry they burn it. The burning releases the nutrients from the trees and other plant matter that is then used by the crops when planted—which is almost always corn. For one to two years, the subsistence farmer raises and harvests his maize, corn, as we know it, from this small jungle plot. Because the soils are very thin with very small traces of plant nutrients of their own, the nutrients from the burned vegetation are quickly depleted. Thus, the migrating cultivator has to move to another area and repeat the process. Once the soil has recovered, a process that can take from eight to twenty years, the process is repeated."

"Researchers conclude that slash-and-burn agriculture is one of the four major causes of rainforest destruction around the world. Along with international logging, fuel wood collection and capricious western consumption of forest products; almost 82,000 acres of tropicjal forest disappear each day. A forest the size of the state of Delaware vanishes each month."

Joy explained what was being lost in this natural world holocaust. He said that of the estimated 30 million species that share our planet with us, 50 percent, perhaps even 90 percent, are found in the tropical forests. It took nature at least 100 million years to create this diverse richness. Man, on the other hand, is currently forcing into extinction several hundred species a day. Some scientists have called it the greatest extinction event since the dinosaurs disappeared from the earth.

"And, with this destruction," Joy said, "we are endangering our own survival beyond anything we have seen since man walked out of the caves. For example, many of the miracle drugs and cures we rely on to treat our ailments have come directly from the cornucopia of the forest. Quinine for malaria, cortisone for arthritis, fever, allergies and the like. Alkaloids from the rosy periwinkle have produced major breakthroughs in the treatment of some cancers. And, this is not to mention that a full 80 percent of what we eat in our so-called modern world originated in the tropics."

"But, what has most of the scientific community concerned is atmospheric stability. They feel that is the greatest danger to the future of mankind."

By the time, Joy had finished detailing the relationship of carbon dioxide to the burning of fossil fuels and its relationship to increased atmospheric gases and the *greenhouse effect*, Drew had a headache.

"Hold it right there Einstein," Drew interrupted Joy's trance-like performance. Joy was just beginning the *albedo effect*, something about increased solar reflection caused by the burning of rainforests.

"Look I'm going to have to take your word for most of this scientific mumbo-jumbo. We poor political philosopher types never could get through elementary physics so most of this stuff is passing right through the right ear and on out the driver's window."

Joy laughed but protested. "Hey, you can get your hands around this Drew. Look, let me put it metaphorically."

"You do that my young friend, us old guys like stories."

"Think of the rainforest as the lungs of our planet. All of the green matter that makes up these forests, the leaves and the like, are talented little entities. They are just full of chlorophyll, and chlorophyll's talent is that it captures the sunlight and breaks the light energy into hydrogen and, guess what? oxygen. I think you see the importance of that chemical, right?" Joy waited for Drew to nod.

"This all happens during the daylight hours naturally. And, as if the oxygen wasn't enough this process produces stored energy in the plant such as starches and sugars. The stuff you like to eat. So, if you haven't guessed, we are very dependent on this process of plants for our existence. Basically the tropical biological mass exchanges in a constant cycle, taking and storing carbon dioxide from the atmosphere and giving back oxygen and storing energy in the form of sugars. Get it?"

"I think so. We need them there forests."

"Right."

"So where does native agriculture fit into the equation? Hey, how do you like that, you've got me talking that science lingo." Drew chuckled.

"You'll be a pro before we get to Tuxtla. I'll give you a new insight every hundred miles and maybe you can give me some of that political jargon in return."

"Don't count on it. I've been away from that world for nearly fifteen years. Oligarchy and the Hatch Act are about all I remember. Drew hesitated. "I suppose, if you pressed me a little, we could discuss the role of power in all of this. Seems to me power always plays some part in any equation. "

Drew let his mind think back to the days he worked on his master's degree. At that time he dreamed of teaching college. That was his goal. But the inner-office politics of the university had beat him down to his knees and he decided to give it up and go out to the real world.

"You know Joy, maybe what we will find in Chiapas is as much a political problem as a scientific one, you suppose?"

"I don't doubt it my friend."

Drew was taking some pleasure from their far ranging conversation as the caravan smoothly rolled south. "Do you think that the group of scientists that Boxxloader and Joaquín have brought to Chiapas is going to be able to propose some real solutions to what's going on with the slash-and-burn thing that you describe? Or do you think their perspective will be too narrow to grasp the bigger picture? What's really going on? Is it really just a question of, what did you call them, migrant cultivators?"

"I don't know Drew. That's part of it. A big part. But, I don't know. Maybe that's why Joaquín wants your help?"

"You flatter me my young Irishman. No, Joaquín wants me there to do yeoman work. The guy hates to write anything or organize anything. He's too nervous for all that. He simply wants to talk. Let others put it down on paper."

"But hey, don't the scribes of history in the end write what they want?"

208

"Oh, now you want to get philosophical with me. You know, I haven't talked with an intellectual in so long I had forgotten it could be fun. Looks like the Acuyacan junction up ahead, you agree?"

"Yep, that's it. See the sign on the right?"

"Sure do amigo. Decision time. What's it going to be? The northern route or do we cross over to the Pacific side and dip our toes in the great ocean?"

Joy looked at the map. "You know it has been way too long since I've put my digits into the cold waters of the Pacific Ocean. My vote is to take the Pacific route."

"Too bad you didn't bring your surfboard. OK, let's do it. It's for sure we can't make Tuxtla by nightfall anyway. Might as well see something of the interior. Why don't you mark the route. There's a highlighter in the glove box somewhere. Lets' stop up here and get some frescos and stretch our legs before the crossing. We need to check on our friends in the trailer. They may be having too much fun."

Drew noticed a sign just on the other side of the highway cut-off. In crude hand written letters it read *Hay Cerveza y Refrescos*. He pulled the Jeep off the road. As they got out the trailer door opened and Tuna stuck his head out. Drew motioned for them to come out. While they waited for Ree and Tuna to catch up Drew looked across the top of the Jeep at Joy.

"Say Joy, you mentioned something about the Maya when you started. I guess since you studied how the Indians cultivated their crops, you must know something about their culture, right?"

"I do. Cultural anthropology is my minor in graduate school."

"Well, I read a book once about how their cities all disappeared suddenly or something like that. I don't remember exactly. But I do remember being fascinated by their development of the calendar and other stuff."

"You're right. They were amazing people. You talk about political organization. They had it."

"Let's talk about that when we get back on the road."

"Sure. It's one of my favorite subjects anyway. And, by the way Drew, there are still over 4 million people in Mexico and Central America that trace their ancestry back to those ancient civilizations."

MEN OF CORN

"HOMBRES DE MAÍZ. I THINK THEY SAY MEN OF CORN in English. That's how my people are called in Zapata señorita." Tuna had never been alone and this close to a gringa before. It made him a little nervous.

"That's strange. Why men of corn?" It was the same for Ree. She had never known an Indian from the United States, let alone one from such an exotic place as southern Mexico. Talking helped take her mind off the troubles she had run from in the North. It helped to talk and learn something from someone so different than she had ever known.

"Because the Maya are made of corn señorita. I am made of the sacred corn." Tuna held out is arm and pinched the skin near his shoulder. He smiled but Ree could sense he wasn't making a joke.

BLOOD MORTAR

"THE QUICHÉ MAYA ARE THE ONES I have read the most about. There mainly in the highlands of Guatemala, and if we happen to wonder near the Usumacinta River that divides Guatemala and Chiapas we may meet some Quiché. More likely though it will be Tzotziles and

Tzetales. Although the general public, if they know of the Maya at all, think of it as a dead culture. One that disappeared long before the Spanish claimed to have discovered America. But actually, the Maya or their descendents who speak one of the many Mayan dialects still thrive all throughout southern Mexico and Central America. I've seen estimates of 4 to 5 million. Far from a vanished culture, wouldn't you say?"

Drew listened to Joy and sipped the mineral water he had bought. He wondered if this whole rainforest project was going to be more complicated than he wanted. Well if it was, he'd just head it all back north.

"You see the archaeologists think the Maya originated a millennium before Christ," Joy went on, "although their highest cultural peak was around 900 A.D. Anyway, in the Maya cosmology the whole thing began with nothing but water covered with sky. No earth, no animals or plants, nothing but water and sky. Then the gods created land. Some called it the back of a turtle or maybe a caiman. Once they had the land, the Maya gods began to create the trees the bushes, the animals. The guardians of life came in many forms, but it all was in darkness at this point. However, the gods were a little disappointed with just birds that squawked and monkeys that howled in the trees. They wanted something more sophisticated, I guess you might say. So they created man."

Joy took a deep breath. "First they tried to make men out of animals. That didn't work. I don't remember why. So they tried clay, then wood, but nothing worked. Then the story goes the gods took white corn and yellow corn from inside some sacred mountain. A female god then ground the corn nine times and from this meal, the gods molded the flesh of man. Water was used to create the first

211

blood. You see blood to the Maya is very sacred. It's like a mortar of their ritual life. It holds everything together. Blood and corn; you understand, flesh and blood. So you see when the descendents of the Maya plant corn, which is the primary staple in their diet, they are planting souls, not just grain"

Drew interrupted. "What about human sacrifice? Seems like I remember reading somewhere they liked to throw virgins off cliffs or something like that?"

"I don't know about the virgin stuff, but they did practice human sacrifice. I think they used captured nobles from other clans or tribes or cities. One source I read, described the priest and four assistants, called Chacs, performed what we would call open heart surgery. Except in this case the patient never survived the procedure. A shaman type of priest then read the insides of the guy sacrificed for signs of the future."

"Kind of bloodthirsty wouldn't you say?'

"Oh, that's not the end of it. They practiced self-mutilation too. The nobility especially. They would take needles or stingray spines and stick them through their ears, cheeks, lips or tongue. The guys would puncture the skin of their penis and let the blood spatter onto some paper or use it to anoint an idol so that the future could be revealed."

Drew took his eyes off the road and fixed them on Joy. "You think we are likely to run into any of these ancestors who still stick things in their dicks? Or, maybe more importantly, in others peoples' dicks?"

"You never know what you'll find out there in the jungle." Joy seemed to take some delight in the speculation. Drew grinned but the story did add a little anxiety to his private thoughts.

"I could talk about these cultures for the rest of the way to Tuxtla. But, the important thing to remember is that the Maya are not a dead culture. Oh, their great civilization more or less disappeared but the people didn't. They changed and evolved like the rest of us. But they are still there, along with much of their customs and beliefs. Remember, when we come into contact, hopefully, in the next few weeks, that the practices you will be privileged to see go back for millenniums. In some cases very little has changed."

"It sounds like you admire these people Joy?"

"I do in a way. But up to now it has only been through books. Finally I'm getting a chance to see some of what I have read. I expect to learn a great deal more."

"You don't sound like the typical know-it-all scientist to me. I thought you would be anxious to transplant all you've learned about agriculture to these poor folks in the jungle. Isn't that the point of all your schooling? You said that the way these people raise corn is one of the main causes of the destruction of the rainforest, right?"

"It's not that simple Drew; nothing ever is. But to answer your question, I have to say yes and no. Slash-and-burn agriculture in and of itself is not the reason the jungle is disappearing. There's a lot more to it. Population increase, forced migration across borders, the way governments control land distribution, international markets, and national policies toward human rights. We're talking about a fabric with many colors of thread woven into a complex pattern. Everything connected to everything else. You have to be very careful. If you pull a loose thread out you may unravel the whole cloth. You follow?"

"You know Joy, you seem a little too smart for your age my young friend." Drew grinned. "I didn't think Irishmen were that smart to begin with and now you impress me with all this knowledge and a sensitivity that I thought only liberal arts majors had. How do you account for that?"

"Oh, I don't know. I'm not sure you're right to begin with. At least not about the Irishmen. I guess if there is any answer to your question it would be because I have worked with Dr. Boxxloader for the last four years. He pushes his students to take a universal view. Plus, I grew up a Catholic in Northern Ireland. That whole country is a running argument about right and wrong, church and state, and prejudice and tolerance. You either think a lot or you hide. I chose to think and to learn and, I guess, not to judge too quickly."

"Well, Joy, I've got a sneaking suspicion that your view is going to get a good test before we're through with this trip."

Montañas peligrosas

THE SURF'S POUNDING WAS HYPNOTIC. The trip over the mountains to the Pacific side had been long and hard. Ree and Tuna both had been sick to their stomach from the unrelenting change of directions over the serpentine mountain roads. All they could do was hold on as the trailer whipped back and forth. Ree felt sorry for Tuna. His brown skin was a nauseous shade of green. Tuna felt embarrassed every time he threw up into the yellow bucket that Ree had given him from the pantry. She was sick but not that sick. But there wasn't anything else she could do for the young Indian.

Drew and Joy had ceased their conversations when they reached the mountains. It took all the concentration Drew could muster to keep the Jeep moving around the curves. The Mexican government had invested a small fortune in the 'curves peligrosas' signs that seemed to be every hundred yards for the two hours it took to climb up and then descend the Sierra Atravesada Mountains. Drew said more than one prayer there would be no trouble with the hitch that coupled the trailer to the Jeep. He had invested in extra-heavy-duty safety chains, but then he hadn't expected to be carrying passengers. If the hitch broke now they would lose more than dishes at the bottom of some canyon, but their luck held.

Drew and Ree now leaned against the trailer and looked out on the Pacific. It was the first time they had been alone since the RV Park at Ciudad Victoria. Joy and Tuna had put up the small tent and were settled in for the night. Drew could here Joy asking Tuna questions about his village. Drew figured the Irishman was in hog heaven. He had something live from a part of the world he had spent years only reading about.

The moon was as bright as Drew could ever remember. It came from behind the trailer and reflected off the waves as they broke several hundred yards from the shore. Drew watched the phosphorus in the water paint patterns in the foam. It took his thoughts back nearly thirty years. He was a 19-year-old sailor stationed at NAS Coronado just across the bay from San Diego. Then he had spent all his free time watching the ocean. The waves and the sounds surrounding him now recalled the loneliness of that time in his life. The ocean had helped to lessen the sting. Funny, the ocean had not changed in all that time. It had not changed one bit. The waves came as they had 30 years before. Still they worked their magic, their spell. It was one constant that Drew had forgotten about.

"How you doing Ree. Are you alright?"

Ree was in a trance of her own. The power of the sound had captured her as well.

"You know what Tuna says he's made of?" Her voice was still and smooth. She didn't look at Drew but continued to watch the surf. Drew could see that her eyes were filled with moisture. They didn't produce tears but were heavy with liquid. "Masa. Tuna says he's made of masa."

"Masa, did you say masa?"

"Yes, ground corn. You know, what they make tortillas out of. That's called masa."

"I really like Tuna, Ree said. "He has a way of seeing life that I've never known. I don't think I know how to explain it."

Ree fell silent for a moment. Drew didn't interrupt the peace.

"He's just so quiet and gentle. When he speaks he looks like a kid but he seems to know everything about himself. There doesn't seem to be any tension in him. And I found out something else about him."

"What's that?"

"He's dying."

"Dying!"

"He has oat cell."

"What's that?"

"Cancer. One of the most deadly varieties. Once it spreads there is not much the medical people can do. It's just everywhere. Chemotherapy or radiation just can't cope with that type of cancer."

Did he tell you all this?"

"No. But he showed me a diagnosis report that they gave him from some clinic he went to in California. He worked in the vegetable fields there."

"You think it's one of those cases where the chemicals they use in those fields caused it?"

"I don't know. But Drew he is just so peaceful about it. He says when he gets back to Zapata he will be back in balance. He told me about a woman in their village, I think he said her name is Socorro. Tuna believes she can help him lose the sickness he carries. I forgot what he called her. Something like cure."

"Curandera. North American Indians call them medicine women; Mexicans call them curanderas."

"Yes, that's it. Tuna says she can call his animal spirit back to fight the invader in his body. He told me that when they are born they are born with an animal spirit, as well as with a human spirit. The two spirits coexist in their body from birth. I think he called it a nahual. Does that sound right, a nahual? When they reach adulthood their parents tell them what their animal spirit is. The nahual is his shadow. It goes with him everywhere. He thinks he has lost contact with his animal spirit. Tuna thinks it is why he has this sickness."

Drew noticed that Ree was really working at sorting out what she had learned from Tuna on the trip over the mountains. He wondered why she wasn't talking about what had happened in McAllen. It was if that was a million miles away, in another place and time—now umimportant.

"It's kind of like his soul, this animal side. Tuna says if one of his people needs to kill an animal they have to ask its permission, because it has a human double somewhere and the double would be very angry if permission had not been granted. He said that trees can also be nahuals. They are chosen by their ancestors, these trees. Tuna says there are beautiful trees where he lives. When they cut a tree they ask its permission, just like the animals. You know what his animal spirit is?"

"I have no idea."

"It's an owl."

"An owl? he told you that?"

"Yeah, he did. He said when he became a man his father told him that the owl had been with him since birth, and would be with him until he died. His father told him that the owl would show Tuna his nature. From then on Tuna was to sit and listen when he came upon the owl. To be quiet and let his animal spirit teach him about his human ways. He said it is how he learned that concentration was his nature. He used this concentration to learn English and the ways of the gringo. When it was very difficult, which it was most of the time, he recalled the optimism and enthusiasm that is the owl in him. Then he would continue with the work, tirelessly. Drew his English is very simple, but it is very good. He says just what he wants."

"You're kind of taken with this little guy aren't you?"

Ree seemed to think about it as if she had not thought about how she felt about Tuna.

"You know how he got his name? Tuna. Doesn't that sound like an unusual name?" Drew didn't ask but simply turned his palms up and shrugged his shoulders.

"You should know this one, you being a cowboy and all that. Tuna is what they call the fruit of the prickly pear cactus. That little glob that grows on the petal or whatever you call those ear-like parts with the stickers. I didn't know it, but that part is like a fruit you can eat. And that's what they do. They eat it. Tuna said that they ate so many of them when they walked from Texas to California. Can you imagine? Three of them walked all the way to California to pick crops to send money back home. Anyway they ate the little tunas as they crossed places like New Mexico and Arizona. It was usually Tuna who picked them as they moved through the desert at night. He put them in a cloth sack he had tied with a string around his neck. When they stopped during the daylight, to rest, they peeled the tunas and ate them. That's how they started calling him Tuna. Pretty neat, huh?"

"What's his real name?"

"That's funny. I didn't ask him." Drew felt Ree slump a little more against his shoulder. He heard a faint push of air from her. A full minute or more passed before she said, "I'm doing OK."

"Good."

SURPRISE, SURPRISE

ALL WAS SET. Joaquín had made most of the arrangements from his home in Tuxtla and what was left to do could easily be attended to. Boxxloader's group would take the Pemex and government helicopters. They would over fly the forest reserves in the east, El Ocote and Laguna Belgica. They would witness the patches of denuded forest within the reserve confines; see the destruction despite the official proclamation without enforcement. They would see from above the hydroelectrical dams at Malpaso and Peñitas that supplied much of the power for Mexico. Power at the expense of vast inundated forests. They would visit every agricultural experiment station and every reserve in the state within the next seven days. They would meet with the governors of Tabasco and Chiapas. They would see the latest scientific experiments in crop production and alternative agriculture. They would visit Dr. Alvarez's facilities to hear his ideas on working with the campesinos. It would all end with two days of meetings with the farmers and ranchers in Palenque and Tapachula; the citizen input part. It was all set to begin with the first light of day.

Boxxloader sipped his wine on the couch while Joaquín argued on the phone with the hotel manager at Palenque. He was trying to get a discount. The manager wasn't buying the argument that these were government sanctioned programs and that the Governor would take it as a personal favor. All he wanted was a few thousand pesos off the room rate. The manager countered with complimentary cocktails on their arrival, but that was as far as he would go. Joaquín thanked him for the small concession, and suggested that a free breakfast buffet would be a goodwill gesture that he wouldn't forget. Surely the manager was aware that they held producer meetings in his city every three months. Joaquín could arrange for some of those meetings to be in the hotel if only the manager would cooperate on this one occasion. Boxxloader considered Joaquín the winner when he noticed a broad smile come across his face as he hung up the phone.

Felicia moved around the dining room in the main house nervously. She liked Boxxloader, but getting ready for the lunch with so many people interrupted her routine. She could not sit still for more than a few minutes. Joaquín didn't help matters by asking her between every phone call if things were ready. She tried to be polite to Boxxloader and not show her irritation with her husband, but it was hard. She just wished this whole week was over and

220

everyone had gone back to where they came from. She hated all the disruptions to her life; to her family. She had never understood why Joaquín wanted to open their life up to so much complication. But she would honor her promise. He had asked her to please support him with this work. He needed it. He needed to be successful with it. And, to be successful, he needed his wife to support him. Without that, he would fail again. Felicia didn't think she could bare another failure on the part of her husband so she said she would go along for one year. No more than that, only one year. But that had been almost two years ago. She now was very nervous about the lunch today.

She had just asked Dr. Boxxloader if he would like some more wine before the other guests arrived when the dogs began to raise a chorus of barking out near the front gate. Felicia bent down to look through the window. She could see Drew's Jeep and trailer with someone opening the gate to let it pass. Felicia motioned for Joaquín to get off the phone. He kept talking. Teri came out of the kitchen and asked the señora if she was to serve the re-fried black beans with slices of avocado and lemon. Felicia replied quickly and went to the front door to call Domingo. She wanted the dogs put in the back. Too many strange people at the ranch today she thought. Demasiado extranjeros.

Drew pulled the rig up to the front of the house. The bougainvillea was blooming around the arched front entrance. Little houses filled with birds of all kinds lined the gravel driveway. Every tree and bush was perfectly trimmed. There was nothing out of place. Old Javier was smoothing the gravel at the far end of the drive. He looked up and smiled but did not stop his raking. Drew heard Felicia shout someone's name as he and Joy got out of the

Jeep. Joy spotted Dr. Boxxloader coming through the door and seemed to be relieved to see his face. Joaquín and Felicia followed. Everyone hugged. Joaquín looked at his watch and noted the time of arrival. He pointed to it and commented that they were right on time. Lunch would be in a half an hour.

Enrique, Joaquín's favorite driver, came from inside the covered carport. He had the broad grin he always wore when guests were at the ranch.

"¿El equipaje señor?" Enrique held out his hand to Drew. Drew shook the young Mexican's hand and asked him not to worry about the baggage for the present.

Drew figured he might as well get it over with quickly so he walked along the trailer and knocked on the door. He called out that they had arrived in Tuxtla. Ree opened the door and stepped out on the gravel and said something back to Tuna who followed. Drew glanced back at the greeting party. He could see Felicia was still smiling with her face half-turned toward Joy but her gaze directed towards the new people exiting the trailer. Drew knew from experience that Felicia was a woman who didn't like surprises; particularly female ones. He braced himself.

As Drew escorted Ree forward for introductions, Tuna remained back by the door. He looked around like a man just let out of prison. He was trying to get his bearings, to put his body into a place. Drew called out to Joy and motioned for him to go get the Indian. Drew could tell by Joy's hand gestures to Boxxloader that he was already beginning to tell him about Tuna. He was repeating to Boxxloader the same thing he had told Drew on the last leg of the trip. Tuna would be their advisor on matters related to the Indians and the rainforest. Joy was convinced that they had a bridge in

Tuna. A unique bridge between what is the unknowable about the Indians and their ways, their customs, their attitudes, and the unrelenting objective scientific approach of the committee.

Drew figured he'd let Joy and Boxxloader handle this one. Right now Drew was beginning to dread what was about to happen, or what he assumed was about to happen, by the stare that was coming his way from both Felicia and Joaquín. Boxxloader was the first one to step forward to greet the female stranger.

OUCH!

THE LUNCH WENT WELL ENOUGH. In fact, Felicia had appeared to be understanding of all the surprises. She had Teri and Dori make extra places on the coffee table, although Drew could tell she didn't like the idea of Tuna eating in her house. Everyone wanted to hear how the trip had gone. Dr. Cárdenas and Dr. Blanco had listened politely as Joy described his conversations with Tuna, but they didn't prolong the topic with questions. All in all the meal was pleasant.

It was the meeting in Joaquín's study that afternoon that had been awkward and testing. It started with Joaquín quietly asking Drew to come with him. He said he needed to tell him about the accommodations for Drew and Joy and the schedule of activities that would begin tomorrow early.

Once they had moved to the study at the other end of the house and settled into the overstuffed white leather couch it began like a rocket launch. It wasn't so much the tone but the string of expletives in Spanish that caught Drew off guard.

"¿Qué coño te pasa? Chinga madre pendejo. ¿Quien es la puta? ¡Me mandó pa'l carajo!" Drew had to finally shout at Joaquín to calm down and listen. He had to do it twice. He had never seen him this way.

It took almost an hour to recount the whole tale, from George West to the customs station well inside Mexico. The only part he left out was about Ree shooting Buddy. He couldn't bring himself to pull that one out of the bag, not just yet. Not after Joaquín's temper tantrum. Joaquín had managed to listen to Drew without interrupting for only the last thirty minutes. But that was only after Drew had threatened to turn the whole damn caravan about and head back that afternoon. He figured that he was too much a part of the plan for Joaquín to let anything interfere with it now.

He was right. Joaquín finally agreed to help with Ree's visa, but only after they got back from the committee's work in a week. She would just have to sit tight at the house in Tuxtla until they had completed their task.

Then all hell broke loose. Again. Felicia came through the door and it started all over. She didn't want an explanation. She just wanted that woman, as she called Ree, out of her house! Joaquín made an effort to intervene but Felicia would have none of it. Drew had never seen her stomp her feet, but he saw it now. To Drew's amazement Joaquín began to take Drew's side. It was he and Felicia toe-to-toe in the middle of the room shouting at each other. Most of it was in a Spanish that blazed by Drew's ears without leaving any meaning, just a strident ring. He was glad that he wasn't the target for the moment.

Drew wondered what Ree was doing. Probably having a nice conversation with Joy and Boxxloader over a cerveza unaware of the volcanic explosion not far away. It's where Drew wished he was. The battle raged. Drew heard enough words to understand that the subject was now on Tuna. Drew stood up and walked around the two and went to the door of the study. Joaquín looked up and motioned for him to wait. He didn't. He wanted that beer. He needed some quiet to think.

Boxxloader moved over on the couch and motioned for Drew to sit next to him. Drew obliged and asked how the old professor had been since the meeting in College Station. They both commented on how quickly the year had passed.

"Joy tells me you guys discussed a little politics on the trip down here. I didn't realize you had that kind of background. You never mentioned it when you came to the meeting with Joaquín." Drew noticed that Boxxloader inflected the question in a way that signaled he wanted to talk about it. It wasn't just polite conversation.

"I didn't think it had a place in that meeting. You were all discussing soils, grain varieties and reforestation. I just didn't see the connection."

"Do you see it know?" The old man's question was delivered along with an intense stare that gave emphasis to his words.

"Yes, at least based on what Joy and I have discussed. Dr. Boxxloader, your young scientist here has a good understanding of this place and its people. I was impressed."

"That's why I wanted him here Andrew." The old professor looked at Joy and then his eyes went to Tuna who was sitting on a straight-back chair in the far corner of the room. Then he looked at Ree.

"If the young lady will excuse us and our conversation for a minute, I would like to tell you what I feel needs to happen in the next two weeks and why it will not." Ree politely nodded and Drew

225

caught her glance and slight smile. He could tell she was taken with Boxxloader as much as Drew was. In that instant, looking on the two of them, Drew knew what to do about Ree. He turned his attention back to Boxxloader.

Boxxloader took a drink from his wine glass and raised his right hand and pointed to Tuna who sat still in his chair. "You see your young Indian friend there Drew; he has the answers we need for our work. He is the future of these rainforests, if there is to be a future. He and his people can tell us how to manage them, how to preserve them and, most importantly, how to respect them. His people and their ancestors have lived with this forest for millenniums. But sadly, or maybe more correctly, tragically, he will not help us. He will hold his secrets from us. His people have learned not to trust us in the last few centuries. They will quietly let us destroy them and their world, and at the same time our own, without a word. What is more tragic than that?"

Boxxloader seemed to slouch more in the couch, his shoulders slumping into the soft cushions.

"The ultimate tragedy is the so-called men of science, with maybe the exception of this young man," he pointed his glass at Joy, "will not even attempt to get the answer. We will pontificate our imagined solutions that are full of self-serving outcomes. Solutions that are based on a foundation of values that is no more applicable to the salvation for the world's great rainforests than English is applicable to speak to the headman of this young Indian's village. We are as disconnected from the reality of the forest and the wisdom of the people who live there today as the Spaniards were from the Maya who greeted them when they landed at the Yucatan peninsula over five hundred years ago. Do you follow my message?"

Drew didn't speak he just looked into Boxxloader's eyes and did not waver.

"It will be you and Joy who will have the best chance to bring to this work some knowledge from the forest. This will be your job. The rest of us have too much invested. There is too much history in our methods, in our reputations. We are all bound up like pigs going to slaughter."

With that he stopped. The room was silent. Drew noticed that Boxxloader and Tuna were looking at each other. There was little he could make out of their expressions, but he felt something of the intensity.

"Ah! Joaquín. Here you are. Have you told our young explorers about their mission?"

CHAPTER 11

A JUNGLE CALL

"JANE! ... JUANITA IS THAT REALLY YOU?" Ree talked to Jane for almost an hour. Drew could tell by Ree's half of the conversation that it was both good and surprising news. Finally, she laughed and slapped her leg. With tears streaming over her cheeks she said goodbye. Drew waited with patience to hear the report, but Ree just sat still on the couch staring at him with a slight grin pasted to her face. The longer she looked at him the heavier and faster the tears came.

There was no sound with them, only small droplets creating wet circles on the legs of Ree's jeans.

Then Ree did something that surprised Drew a little, but at the same time it pleased him greatly. She wiped her face, stood up and without a word she sat down on his lap. Both arms circled around his neck and held on with enough force that made Drew issue a slight groan. He could feel the wetness on the back of his neck. Ree did not speak, and Drew didn't disturb the spell.

He could hear the men in the front room rehashing the plans for tomorrow. Joaquín's nervous chatter came through above the others. Every so often Boxxloader would make a point or ask a question, mostly to Joy. Ree's weight felt good to Drew, as she seemed to relax every muscle and slumped against him. His right leg was starting to go to sleep but he wasn't going to upset the healing going on.

Instead, he just sat there holding the woman and going over in his mind the outline for the next week that Joaquín had described. It all sounded like something out of a movie. The ground party, as Joaquín had called it, would leave in the morning for Ocosingo. Drew was to take his Jeep. Joy and Tuna would ride with Drew. Boxxloader and Joy had convinced Joaquín of the utility of having Tuna go along. After all, he spoke two of the Indian languages of the region, Quiché and Tzotiles. And, he spoke English. A combination of tongues that no one else in the group could equal. Jorge, Joaquín's right-hand man, would follow in his four-wheel-drive wagon and the photographer JonKing would come with him. That is, if he arrived tonight as scheduled on the flight from Mexico City.

The entourage would climb the mountain road 190 out of Tuxtla just after dawn and meet up with Raymundo Salazar and Santiago Villereal in San Cristóbal de Las Casas. Raymundo would represent the Catholic Church and Santiago the Government. Their escort would help guarantee the safety of the party as it moved through the small Indian settlements in and around the Lacandon Jungle. Drew felt good about the arrangements. They would have extra seats available in the second car for any last-minute passengers.

The group would have their breakfast in San Cristóbal and then make the two-hour pass through the highlands to Ocosingo. There the entire party would meet with the priest and the mayor in the city and obtain their blessings for the trip. Joaquín had jokingly said to Drew that both the Governor and the Bishop had told him that some people who went "back there," as he called it, without the understanding of these people seemed to get lost. Sometimes never found. Joaquín thought that was funny. Drew did not share in the humor.

The entire ground party would spend the night in Ocosingo; Joaquín had an old shortwave radio buddy that had agreed to open his house to the group. He had promised Joaquín he would feed them well the next morning. After breakfast they would pick up their supplies and start toward San Quintín. According to the map Joy had, they would find the pueblo at the end of a hundred and forty kilometers of road that would begin as pavement in Ocosingo and then quickly turn to gravel only a few kilometers from the city. The same road would just as quickly change to dirt after they left the last village of any size at Patihuitz. If the rains began early the dirt would likely become mud the farther they traveled.

The ground entourage would be on this road for two days. The first night they would have to ask permission from the village of Soledad to hang their hemacas and mesquito nets in one of the community buildings. Raymundo and Santiago should be able, Joaquín explained, to arrange for this permission with no trouble. The group would spend the next night in San Quintín. Joaquín said that there was a ham radio station in the pueblo and they could make contact back with the other group. By that time, the airborne group would have arrived at the city of Palenque.

The following morning the ground party would make the final walk with their supplies to the last Indian pueblo before entering the Montes Azules Reserve and La Selva Lacandona. The pueblo would be Zapata.

Drew looked at Tuna and mouthed the question across the room, "That's your Zapata?" Tuna nodded back that it was. Drew got lost in that thought for a minute. His mind wandered back to the encounter with the owl on the Running~Bar and he almost missed the next part of Joaquín's explanation. The part about the ground party making a three-day walk across the Lacandona for a rendezvous with the other scientists. That group, led by Boxxloader, would include Cárdenas, Blanco and the others. They would take the easy way in and fly via helicopters from Palenque to the Mayan ruins at Bonampak. By that time they would have completed their fly-over of the entire region and concluded their fact-finding meetings. The ground party would complement what Boxxloader's group had learned with observations from the rainforest itself. Joaquín explained that if the ground party was lucky it would make contact with the small tribe of Lacandon Maya.

Drew had made some half-hearted statement that he was just the grant writer followed by an equally weak question about whether he needed to go on the trip at all. Everybody ignored it. Joy came over and pointed to his marked course so that Drew could see the whole picture. He saw it but he wasn't sure he liked what he saw.

ME TOO

REE FINALLY PUSHED BACK. "Am I killing you?"

"Just my right leg, but you don't have to get up," Drew let his thoughts about the rainforest trip move through his consciousness. "You want to tell me the good news?"

"How do you know it's good news?"

"Isn't it?"

"It's a strange story. Life is so funny. Juanita's all right and so is Buddy, at least as far as Jane knows. I didn't kill anybody. I'm not in trouble. All the way down here I have kept it out of my head, but something always hurt in my stomach. I guess I expected the worst. That has been my life the last few years, expecting the worst.

"Tell me what happened."

"Jane says that when she got up, just after I left in Buddy's truck, Buddy was sitting on the back of her car on the trunk. He had a handkerchief stuck inside his shirt under a big spot of blood. He had the pistol stuck in his belt. She didn't say anything to him. For some reason, she said she was not mad at Buddy. She opened his shirt and took the handkerchief away from his wound. It looked nasty but she could see that it was not serious. The bullet had gone clean through his shoulder. A good amount of blood, but no major damage. Then Buddy just started sobbing. She told him they had better go the hospital but he would not hear of it. She led Buddy into the house and cleaned his wound the best she could. The real danger was infection. Jane had seen these types of wounds before. She patched it the best she could."

"Jane couldn't believe how calm he was. He just talked about me. Said he was so sorry for all the trouble he had made. All he wanted was to talk to me. About that time, the cops came to the house. A neighbor must have heard the commotion and called them. Buddy said that he had accidentally shot himself. Jane said they actually believed his story. The cop looked at Jane hard. Her lip was still puffed up. He asked her if she was all right. Jane said she was, so the cop left. He didn't even fill out a report."

"They talked for over two hours after that.

"How did she know about me?"

"Well you big dummy. I told Jane. I told her all about how kind you had been to me. You know, the ride, the advice, all of it. Oh, and I told her about your trip to Mexico and Joaquín and Tuxtla. After all, we talked forever at that bar after you dropped me off."

"How about that. I didn't know you cared." Drew squeezed Ree around the waist slightly. "You think she told Buddy?"

"What do you mean? You mean told him about where you were staying in McAllen?"

"That, and about me telling you that you ought to go to Mexico with me."

"You think he might follow me here. You've got to be kidding. Jane said he was very sorry about everything. Besides, he wouldn't come all the way to Mexico after me. You don't think so, do you?"

"Stranger things have happened in this world. I was just curious. You know, I'm a cautious kind of guy."

233

As it turned out, Drew was glad that he hadn't told Joaquín about the shooting. Now he would not have to explain anything about what had happened. All they had to do now was get Ree a visa. She would be home free.

"What happened to Buddy after they had their talk?"

"He figured from what Jane had told him that his truck might be at the Motel 6 and that I might have gone to get your help. Jane wouldn't let him go. She made him lie down on the couch and he passed out. She said she stood there and just looked at the man. She couldn't believe she had not told the cop about his harassment and about the assault. I told her it was the nurturing spirit of the nurse in her. I've got the same problem."

"That's not the problem Ree. The problem is you just pick jerks to nurture." Ree paused at the notion but then went on with her explanation.

"Anyway, the next morning Jane took him over to the Motel 6. You had already pulled out. Jane took Buddy to get his truck and he left. Jane had told him to go to a doctor to have his wound redressed. She even gave him the name of one of the doctors she knew. One she could explain about the gunshot wound without causing a hassle. He did not say a thing. Not goodbye. Kiss my ass. Nothing. Jane couldn't understand what I ever saw in the psycho anyway."

"Wasn't Jane worried about what happened to you?"

"She was. But she figured since I had the truck I would at least go somewhere safe. She thought I might have headed back to Canton to my folks."

"What about your folks. Don't you imagine they're about out of their minds with worry?"

234

"I'm sure they are. Jane was going to call them for me and try to explain everything."

"Even about where you are now?"

"I'll call Mom in a little while to let them know I'm all right."

"What do you want to do about staying here until we get back from the Lacandon?" Felicia's words echoed in his ears as he waited for Ree to answer. This wasn't going to be easy no matter the response. He knew Felicia well enough to know that she could be stubborn. If she did not want Ree in her house, it would not happen.

"We will be gone about a week or so. Joaquín cannot help you with the visa until we get back. And, you cannot fly back until we get you legal. So, you're going to have to cool your heels for awhile."

"When are you leaving?" Ree's voice took on a little of the hoarseness that Drew had learned to recognize as nervousness.

"Early..."

"I'm going with you."

"Ree, I don't think you realize where we're going. It's not going to be very comfortable or, even safe for that matter. Joaquín has a ranch about thirty minutes from here. I think you could stay there. There are people there to take..."

"No Drew. I am going with you. Is Tuna going?" Drew could see it wouldn't be worthwhile to argue with Ree at the moment. He shifted her weight from one side of his leg to the other.

"Yes, Tuna and Joy are going to ride with me. Believe it or not, we are going to Tuna's pueblo near the rainforest. Tuna is going to be sort of a native guide. Strange how things work out. Anyway, that pretty well fills the Jeep. So you see?" Drew assumed his logic

235

would be enough to win the argument, but as was usually the case with women, he was wrong.

"Drew listen to me. The last week has made me feel like I have died. The old Ree is dead. Now I have a chance to start my life again and I want something different. I am not going to find it waiting to catch a plane back to what I left. I want to go with you. I want to see what it is you came here for. You said you came here by choice to give something back. I'm not sure you weren't running too. Maybe it was a little more planned, but running just the same. Let me come with you. I want to meet Tuna's people. I want to experience something new." Ree stopped and got up. She turned and stood facing Drew looking down at his face. "I'm going with you."

8x10 GLOSSY

EVERYBODY LIKED THE TALL AND LANKY JONKING. His long sandy hair was always combed back into a ponytail that he tied with a blue rubber band. The kind paperboys wrapped around the Sunday editions of the newspapers. He had more pockets in his fatigues than Drew had ever seen. Every one of them seemed to be stuffed with something. Drew later discovered that JonKing could carry nearly two hundred rolls of film along with enough plastic sheeting to get himself and his cameras out of the rain in an emergency. The camera that hung from his neck looked like it had seen better days. The icon Canon, just above the telephoto lens that protruded about three inches from the base, was worn to almost anonymity.

The army issue jungle boots and the pronounced limp on the left leg made Drew suspect that JonKing was a Vietnam vet. He looked about the right age. But, what Drew really liked about the photographer was that he was experienced. He had been to where they were going. He knew what was there. They all sat on the big porch and watched the lightning behind the mountain range that ringed the valley at Rancho Julieta. JonKing was entertaining all listeners as they drank the Corona's they had bought in Ocozocoaútla on the way to the ranch. There was plenty of room for everyone to be comfortable for this night; three bedrooms, all with two beds.

JonKing explained that he had been lead photographer on a trip down the Usumacinta River only five years before. He said they had gone there to do a story for the *Geographic* about the river valley as the ancient seat of a once proud Mayan civilization. The project had quickly become an exposé of the refugee problem with Indians being driven out of the Petén in Guatemala and fleeing into the jungles of Chiapas and southern Mexico. That besides being held captive for a couple of days by members of the Fuerza Armadas Rebeldes, one of the guerrilla groups fighting in Guatemala, the trip had been a revelation. He had always wanted to come back and do it again.

Everyone except Tuna kept JonKing at his stories for several hours. Joy particularly wanted to know as much about the jungle and the Indians as this storyteller could describe. Drew just listened but he could not get the guerrillas out of his thoughts. Joy, the prototypic scientist, asked the better questions. He wanted to know what JonKing thought was the primary reason for the loss of rainforests in Mexico and Guatemala.

JonKing swung in the hammock strung across the porch and took a long sip from his beer bottle before he answered. He then launched into an hour of what Drew thought was a coherent explanation of the population pressures on the rainforest. Slowly he told of the government programs, on both sides of the Usumacinta River, that encouraged migration into the river valley. The random movement of the Indians helps the governments of Mexico and Guatemala cope with the land scarcity in the other parts. He said all these people want is a little land to grow their corn and raise their families. Many of them come to the rainforest to escape the soldiers. The guerillas had told them that the soldiers were afraid of the jungle. "This is our territory," they had boasted while displaying their automatic weapons with pride.

"It has been estimated," JonKing explained, "that some two hundred thousand have moved from Guatemala to escape persecution into the remote areas of Chiapas. They look for land, for a small piece to farm. In most cases, that land is hacked out of the forest."

He went on to explain there were other reasons for the rainforest destruction as well. "Illegal logging in some areas still goes on. In spite of the laws, there are still mahogany and other precious hardwoods coming from that region. A little mordita, a bribe at the border, and the loggers can move their contraband lumber from Guatemala to Mexico then on north to the markets in the United States. We are going to see much of the same thing when we get to the Lacandon." He moved farther down in the hemaca and sipped on the beer.

Then JonKing interrupted his explanation for a second and politely asked Joy to fetch him another Corona. He took another long swallow, letting the liquid fill his cheeks like small balloons before he swallowed. He looked at Drew and said the real danger is coming though. He had seen it developing when he was there the last time. We would see a lot more of it when we go back in the next week. Drew asked him what he meant. JonKing said just one word. "Pemex," before he swung his lanky frame out of the hammock and walked out into the yard. He headed over to where a peacock was perched in a mango tree. Drew could tell he was thinking about retrieving his camera and going to work.

CHAPTER 12

SOCORRO

THE SCENE COULD HAVE FROM A HOLLYWOOD B movie. Stick houses
with thatch roofs, a dirt road with pigs that appeared unafraid of
the horn blasts, and inquisitive and penetrating black eyes staring
from every angle and corner. Men dressed in plain and simply cut
white trousers and shirts—all carrying machetes in their hands or
strapped to their sides. Human figures which melded with the
jungle like animals as strangers approached.

The caravan had been at it for over two days. All had hoped to
be in Zapata by now, but within five miles of the goal was an
obstacle. To reach San Quintín and then Zapata, they would have to
walk leaving the vehicles back at the last river crossing. The bridge
had been washed out since the end of the last rainy season, six

months ago. Six mud-brown men were digging out all that was left of the original concrete in knee deep slime.

Santiago had negotiated a deal with the locals. All of the supplies, including the three cases of Coors beer, were loaded on the backs of men no taller than Ree. She and Drew stood and watched as the little men were loaded with impossible loads on their backs. Brightly colored cords were stretched around the assorted boxes, duffel bags, ice chests and across their foreheads. The last two days and nights had been just like this, filled with a new adventure at each turn of the road.

The mountains, for Ree, topped the list. She had never seen mountains like these. Vaguely she recalled those of Colorado, on a vacation long ago. She was just a kid then and and viewed the tops from the valleys looking up. But this time, she had ridden over the rough roads in the tops. For most of the ride, Ree stared out of the passenger side of the Jeep looking over the edge of the gorge that seemed to drop forever to the Jíjate River below. She couldn't decide whether to be scared or not.

Raymundo said that they were lucky that the serious rains had not started. The roads were in passable shape. About two more weeks was his estimate. They had two more weeks to complete their business and come down from the mountains. After that the only way out would be by helicopter; the roads would be gooey mud for the next five months.

Every time the road widened a little in the mountains there seemed to be a group of thatch houses scattered around a few central buildings. Since the party had departed Tuxtla they had spent the night at two of the settlements, Betania and Soledad. They hung their hammocks in what the leader of the ejidos called a school. To Ree it was only a roof of thatch covering a dirt floor. The few chairs and desks she saw were stacked in the corner. They didn't appear to be used.

Now nearing their destination the line of hikers topped a hill and came to a small mesa that gave a panoramic view of the valley. They began to walk in what appeared to be wheel ruts that extended for several hundred yards. Ree was curious and quickened her pace to catch up with Tuna.

"What are these ruts?" She pointed and spun around and walked backward for a few paces directing Tuna to look back along the trail in the clearing.

"This is a landing strip," Tuna answered. "There is a man from Ocosingo that will fly the touristas here to see the jungle. He lands on these strips here in San Quintín and then some of the men from Zapata take them on to Laguna Miramar to see the beautiful lake at the edge of the rainforest. It is about one-hour from our ejido, señorita. I will take you there myself while you stay with us."

"How much farther to your village?"

"Not far. Ten minutes more. Are you tired of this walking?"

"No, not at all. This is such a lovely place. It is like a place in a dream." Tuna didn't reply, so Ree wondered whether he understood her allusion.

Ree noticed that JonKing was moving in front of the group taking pictures. First of the entire line with its components of gringos, Mexicans and Indian bearers intermixed, and then a close-up of each individual as they passed. Ree wished she could send the image he took of her back to Mom and Dad. She would enjoy seeing the faces of two people who never left Kaufman County. Here was their daughter in another world. Ree could not help the smile. She was in another world. A better world than she had known for a long time.

COLORES

ZAPATA WAS DIFFERENT FROM THE PUEBLOS the group had seen on the road from Ocosingo. Here there was a large group of Indians waiting on the path that led into a large broad area that provided the center of the pueblo. Men and women were staring at the approaching column. Ree could see five or six men who looked like a welcoming party all dressed the same in brilliant red-striped pants and shirts that reminded her of old cowboy movies. Every man wore a western style straw hat. They were all short, like Tuna.

The women were so brilliant in their dress. Intense colors of flowers cascaded from their shoulders. Red, yellow, violet and orange ran in wide vertical stripes from the top of bare feet to their waist. They, like the men, stood quietly and just watched and waited. Some propped their face in one hand with its attached arm resting comfortably on the other in the crook of their hip. Many of the women had a sling of the same cloth as their skirts around their shoulder. The sack looked to be filled to capacity. Only black tuffs of hair protruding from the decorated fabric gave a hint as to the cargo.

As the procession neared the waiting assemblage, Ree watched Tuna slowly move his position to the lead. When he passed Drew, she saw him gesturing and talking to Drew before their arrival. Suddenly the march stopped and Tuna vigorously embraced the head men of the village. Their exchange went quickly and one-by-one the visitors, beginning with Raymundo and Santiago, moved forward and spoke briefly to the elders. There was an extra long

243

time in the introductions of Joy and Drew, Ree noticed. Ree was happy to see Drew shake hands energetically with what she figured was the head man. The excitement of the small group seemed to be spontaneous and spread to each connecting cluster of Indians. Suddenly everybody was talking and pointing. The villagers began to collapse slowly but steadily onto the visitors until all Ree could see was a sea of undulating color. Drew, JonKing, Joy and the rest were lost, swallowed up by the vivid undulating paint.

The light touch to Ree's elbow from behind made her jump.

"I'm sorry señorita. I didn't mean to scare you. I want you to meet my sister." Ree had not seen Tuna break free from the gathering.

"She is the little jewel of my family. Her Indian name is Xucane, but we call her Estrellita. It means Little Star. She will walk with you to our pueblo. Is this all right?"

Ree didn't respond. The beauty of the child and her intense black eyes seemed to capture Ree completely. Ree had never imagined that children in such a place as this jungle could be so appealing. Ree reached out her hand to the girl but stopped short of touching. Estrellita didn't show the same reserve. She grabbed Ree's hand and began to pull her towards the others.

"Yes, I think that will be just fine Tuna," Ree said as she was being pulled away.

Everything seemed to begin to move in mass along dirt trails laid out in uniform grids like the small towns all over the world. There were fences made of sticks between the thatched-roof houses. Every family decorated their places with small unique specialties. Pots of all shapes and kind hung on racks next to the front door, or rather front opening. No door. No lock. Just an opening. Flowers were everywhere. Even the trees, big or small, were covered with the colors. The pinks and violets dominated, but there were yellows and jade greens too. Ree noted that many of the trees were full of fruit. She recognized the lemons and limes, but was unsure about some of the others. The air was full of sound. The calls of birds seemed to come from all directions with patterns of no pattern. For a minute Ree thought she heard what sounded like a roar, or maybe a scream. The call was somewhere in between the two. If she would have to guess, Ree thought it was some kind of big cat like a panther she had seen in the Marsalis Street Zoo in Dallas. Ree looked for some sign of concern from the people around her but none was evident.

Ree felt like she was a participant in a parade as the crowd moved up a slight incline that suddenly broke into a large central square. The public place was situated on top of a rise that gave a view of the surrounding mountains. Except for a few large covered areas, the center was grass, lush green and comfortable. Estrellita pulled Ree along just behind, talking continuously, pointing and laughing. Ree wished she understood the beautiful child's words. They flowed from her happy face like water over a fall. They sounded so joyful, light, and full of description. Occasionally the young girl flashed her gleeful small eyes at Ree. Every time she did, Ree felt a feeling of inexplicable joy.

Finally, the procession came to the entrance of a building that was screened on all sides and covered with a tin roof. Only the small group of men that had greeted Tuna moved through the door. They turned and with grand sweeping gestures bid the strangers to enter. Ree could see the leaders directing the bearers to place the bundles belonging to her group in one corner of the building.

Estrellita led Ree to the door but would not go through the opening. Ree stepped in but was reluctant to release the warm delicate hand that had brought her here. When the girl pulled free, Ree moved toward Drew watching her little guide run to a group of women standing in front of a small hut just off the open area. Ree could see Estrellita waving her arms at them and talking rapidly. The women did not appear to be listening. They just stood and intently watched the activities around the central building.

"Well, what do you think?" Drew put his arm lightly around Ree's shoulders and pulled her away from the crush of bodies around a table at the entrance end of the large rectangular building.

"You're going to think I'm crazy, but I feel strange. I mean, I feel like I've come home for the first time in my life."

"Maybe you have." Drew increased the pressure of his arm slightly on Ree's shoulders and looked directly into her face. "They do make you feel special don't they?"

"Did you see the little girl that held my hand up the trail?"

"Yeah. She's a cutie."

"That's Tuna's sister. I guess that's Tuna's family standing over there by that house." Ree tried to point without being too obvious.

"I think you're right." Drew looked for a moment toward the women.

"Let's move away from the front. I need to explain what's going to happen in the next few days." Drew reached and took Ree's hand and led her to a small bench about midway between the door and what appeared to be a storage area in the back. The bench was right up against the screen. Drew sat down and pulled Ree down next to him.

"I've been talking with Raymundo and JonKing. They both say that you should stay here in Zapata while we make the trip to the Maya ruins at Bonampak." Drew paused waiting for a reaction but Ree did not give one.

"They say there are some unknowns in the Lacandon Rainforest that...well, it would just be better if you waited here. We will be back in a week. Three days to the ruins through the jungle, two days of meetings and then the helicopters will bring us back here." Drew paused. "OK?"

"OK."

"You mean OK, really?"

"Yes. OK, really." Ree looked at Drew and nodded. "Really," she repeated through a grin. "You know five minutes ago I would have argued with you. I mean I've come this far. And, in a way I would like to go with you. But, there is something about this place that makes me want to know it better. Maybe it is that little girl. Maybe I'm a little tired. I don't know. Yes, it's OK."

They both watched the milling around in the front of the building for a few minutes. It looked like the people were preparing to have a meeting. Raymundo and Santiago were talking with the leaders and Joy and JonKing were getting the translation from Tuna.

"Where will I stay?" Ree broke the silence.

"Oh, we'll find you a nice tree someplace to hang your hemaca." Drew didn't smile.

"Come on, be serious."

"I am serious." Drew stood up and offered his hand. "Come on let's go talk to Tuna."

"SOCORRO, HER NAME IS SOCORRO. She is our healer. She will take good care of you until we return from the Lacandon, señorita."

"Where is she Tuna?" Ree looked around the inside of the simple hut with its dirt floor and one crude table in the far corner. The table was covered with several pots in a random order; all of clay and painted, except one. It was graphite black and big. Water stood almost to its brim. All along one wall hung rows of bundled and dried plants; their seed heads hanging down and their stems bound with root string. There was no other evidence of furniture or comfort except for the small altar in a dark corner opposite the cooking area. On it, Ree could see brilliantly colored feathers and two small figures back-to-back. Both figures appeared to be the same, a mirror image.

"She is in the jungle señorita. The old woman goes everyday to collect her medicine. She will know you are here, though. Socorro knows everything that happens in this place even without the seeing."

"Socorro lives alone? Alone here in this hut?"

"Sí. She has never had a family. She was always too busy with the others of the community. With their babies and sicknesses. With their futures and their pasts. Socorro is the only one in our pueblo who can talk with the ancestors. She knows where we came from and where we are going. She takes care of our ceremonies, the ceremonies of birth and death, the ceremonies of the sowing and harvest, the marriage ceremony. All of these Socorro must help us with. She is a very busy woman señorita."

"She is your doctor too Tuna?" Ree asked as she stared at the altar.

"Oh yes. She will see to my sickness when I return from Bonampak. Now that I am here, I think she will cure me. Then I can live a normal life with my people. I can get married and have my new face."

Ree turned and looked at Tuna and tried not to grin. "You're new what?"

"My new face. My son who is my face for the pueblo when I am no longer here to help and work for my community. This is important for me and for everyone. I must make a new face."

Ree jumped. The hand, like that of the child before, had touched her so lightly that when she finally recognized its pressure on the back of her arm it gave her a start.

"This is Socorro señorita. This is our curandera. Please permit me to explain to her who you are." Tuna spoke for several minutes in his Tzotzil tongue. Ree could only watch the woman as Tuna explained. She listened with her eyes fixed on the stranger. They were dark like Estrellita. Her eyes were encircled with small areas of white that contrasted with the black like lint on black velvet. Ree tried to maintain contact with the old woman's eyes but she could not. They were too strong in their attachment. Ree alternated her gaze by looking out the front opening of the hut and then back to Tuna trying to seem attentive on Tuna's words as if she understood what he was saying. She took quick glances at Socorro thinking that the smile that was plastered to her own face must seem ridiculous. But the old woman never turned her gaze or changed her expression.

Ree suddenly noticed how much the old woman reminded her of the child Estrellita. The inquisitive gentleness was the same. The appearance of serenity was the same. The beauty was the same.

Then she recalled she has seen of these traits in Tuna. They all seemed so alike. Her mind began to struggle to remember the others she had seen while walking to the center of the pueblo. Ree tried to bring a picture of their faces forward in her mind's eye. She wondered if they all had that same appearance. Ree could still hear Tuna speaking. His words came to her as almost poetry and spoken verse rather than speech. She let her sight fix on the light in the opening and listened.

Then Ree felt the same touch she had felt a few minutes before. This time she recognized it and did not flinch. Socorro took Ree's hands in her own and turned the much taller woman to face her. Her expression was still the same, blank but not threatening, not judging. The curandera turned Ree's hand over and looked down at the palms. She studied both with her thumbs, rubbing with a slight pressure that moved over the lines and felt the peaks and valleys of her palms.

Ree could feel something warm move through her. The image of an old woman about to die came with such reality she jerked her hands slightly but Socorro held them firmly, but with no tension. Ree could see vividly the old woman. Ree had spent almost an hour at the hospital holding the dying woman's hand and rubbing gently. Letting the warmth go from her body to the her. It was the same here and now with Socorro. Except this time the warmth was flowing into Ree so abruptly that she felt flush. Socorro must have felt the slight shiver in Ree's body as well because she smiled into Ree's eyes and turned and walked to the darkest corner of the hut. When she returned she pulled the rebozo softly around Ree's shoulders. The cloth was finely woven and its colors were as intense as anything Ree had seen in the pueblo. Socorro's smile remained.

Returning the smile, Ree sensed tears in her eyes. She turned to Tuna, "What did you tell her?"

"I told her that you were a healer like her. That you could teach her about the medicine of the North. That you could help her. We have a small clinic here. It is on the other side of the open area." Tuna walked to the opening and pointed directly across from Socorro's dwelling. "The government put it there two years before. There are many medicines and things in the building, but we do not use what is there. It is too strange to us. Too much bother. I told her that you knew about these things and could show her."

"Oh, Tuna...I don't..."

"Señorita, I have spent enough years in the North that I understand that we need some of the things that are from there. Some of the medicines can help us greatly. But we need to understand how to use them. The government just brings these things and leaves them here. They make no effort to help us understand. The Indians do not trust the people who bring these things so they do not trust the things that they bring. I have told Socorro that you can be trusted and that we have an opportunity to learn about what is good in that building and what is not. Do you understand?"

Ree hesitated for a moment trying to absorb Tuna's words. Finally she said, "Yes, I understand. But, I am only a nurse, not a doctor. And besides, I don't speak your language. How would I would I make myself understood?"

Tuna walked over to Ree and took her hand, which surprised her a little. He held out his other hand to Socorro who responded

251

immediately. "You are used to telling only with your words, but that is just one way. We understand many ways to share ourselves. I think that this old woman is very wise and understands many things. I think she will understand what you show her. I think she will know the difference between what is right for us and what is not. Will you try?"

Ree felt warm with the many-colored shawl around her. The shivers had vanished. She felt just as she had with the young girl. "I will try," she said softly looking at Socorro.

THE ORACLE OF THE BLACK STONES

THE MEETING HAD GONE WELL ENOUGH. Drew picked up enough of the Spanish to tell that. On one side of the table was the one they called the Maestro. He was clearly in charge and did most of the talking. To his right and left were two others. Drew thought the one on the far end, the one who said nothing but wore a baseball cap that read Special Forces, was the one he would like to get to know better. He was steady. Lean and hard looking. His machete leaned lightly against his thigh as he listened without expression to the exchanges.

On the other side were Raymundo and Santiago sitting together in the middle. Drew and Joy were on either side of them while JonKing moved around the building, quietly documenting the proceedings with his camera. The spectators lined up on each side of the building, on the outside of the screened wire. They watched everything without emotion. Merely stood and watched. Drew couldn't help but think that they reminded him of the couch-potato kids in his country. Those who could sit, like a stone, and watch some silly flickering image on the TV for hour upon hour. Watching

252

without comment or emotion, burning less energy than if they were asleep.

Tuna with Ree following, entered the covering. Ree came and sat on a bench just behind Drew and Tuna moved to do the same behind the Maestro. Drew noticed that the old woman called Socorro was standing half in the doorway. The small cloth sack she wore around her neck caught his eye. It reminded him of the spirit bag he wore around his.

From what Drew could tell Raymundo was negotiating for a couple of guides to lead the way through the Lacandon to Bonampak. As Raymundo had explained to Drew on the trip from Ocosingo, even though the great rainforest was only half its original size it was still a formidable piece of vegetative tangle, especially if they were unlucky enough to be caught there when the rains started. Raymundo said that a compass heading might get them through to the Mayan ruins at Bonampak, but he for one didn't want to take any chances. They had two days to get there for the meeting. Two days to walk thirty miles—miles of verdant tangle and body-hugging thickness.

Judging by the way the silent one with the machete kept nodding Drew was sure he would be one of those that pointed out the trail. Drew figured he was unhappy about something because he kept pointing to Ree and shaking his head. Raymundo turned and glanced at her as well, and Drew could tell he was explaining that she would not be going with the group but would wait here until they returned. The machete man calmed and didn't speak again. A little brown man to the Maestro's right must have made a joke at Ree's expense because everybody except Drew and Joy laughed.

253

The joke completed the negotiations and the Maestro made a slight gesture towards the door. Socorro moved to Drew's end of the table. Without any introduction the curandera sat down, removed the sack from her neck and laid it with the open end towards her. All talking ceased and all the leadership seemed to lose their expressions. The laughing eyes changed to black holes.

Drew got the feeling that something important was about to happen. Joy must have had the same feeling because he quietly got up and moved to the bench next to Ree right behind Drew. He could see much better from there. Drew could tell by the excited look on his face that the young man was in field research heaven.

Tuna moved quietly like Joy. He came to the right side of Socorro and just slightly behind her. As the woman began removing small stones, one of them jade, she looked at Drew and seemed to stop in mid-action. At first he thought maybe he had done something to disturb her, but he had not moved or uttered a word. He could tell when the old woman had looked into his eyes she had reacted to something. Tuna, who had his hand resting on the woman's shoulder, must have sensed something as well because he too looked at Drew in a way that Drew had never seen before. His eyes were wide open and fixed with a look of surprise. Socorro went through the beginning of what Drew figured must be a ceremony of some kind. She never diverted her eyes from him.

She then took another five small stones from the sack and arranged four of them in a pattern. From what Drew could tell they seemed to lay roughly on the cardinal points of a compass. The fifth stone, which was black, glassy and shaped like a point, she positioned in the center. Next, she placed something in a small rock bowl and lit it with a match. Drew noticed that the matches looked just like the kitchen matches he used at home. Then she began to speak, more a chant than spoken word. Drew noticed that all of the little faces that had been staring through the screen were gone. He had not remembered hearing them leaving, but they were nowhere to be seen.

The woman still had her eyes on Drew. For some reason her intense gaze did not make him nervous. In fact, it made him feel a part of what was happening. The chanting went on for five minutes or more and then Socorro poured a pile of corn seeds next to the small rock circle. Finally, she diverted her eyes to the pile. With her right hand, palm down and fingers spread, she moved her hand over the corn seeds and mixed them. All the while, she kept whispering. Drew suddenly became aware of thunder in the distance. He tried not to be obvious when he looked past the woman to see the massive build-up of thunderheads. It was in the direction of the forest. The direction he assumed they were to go tomorrow morning. The lightning began to dance continuously through the tops of the gray mass that seemed to be boiling.

Then Tuna came to Drew's right side and slightly behind. Drew felt the slight weight of his hand on his shoulder. The touch brought on a sudden remembrance; it flashed through his head like the lightning flashing through the distant cloud mass. Drew could again feel his baptismal. It was the same experience. He had been too young then to know what all of it meant, the language, the icons, the water running down from his head into his eyes. Just like now, he did not know what all these strange signs meant, the calls, and the language. But there was no doubt, it was the same feeling. He was being brought into a circle. Made part of a larger whole. A participant. And as before, without being asked.

Socorro grabbed a fistful of the corn seeds and with her left hand gently pushed the remaining ones to the side. Then she began slowly sorting the seeds from her right hand into lots of four arranging each into parallel rows beginning with the top left corner. When she finished she had 17 divisions of four, and one of two seeds. She placed a single seed just below the division of three. All the while that she built the pattern, Socorro seemed to be speaking directly to the objects before her. Drew recognized one phrase he heard several times during the placing of the corn seeds. *Ma ban la ri mentira; ma ban la ri mentira.* He understood *mentira*. It was Spanish for lie. But that was all he could make out.

Drew could see the woman was now counting the small divisions. She started in the corner, with the first one she had placed. As she touched each one separately, she spoke several names. Drew figured she was counting. As she reached the last division, Socorro again raised her eyes to meet Drew's. She seemed to be telling him something. Somehow he could see the flashes of lightning behind the woman without breaking eye contact. The faint rumbling of thunder was beginning to reach his ears again. Drew could feel Tuna's hand slightly change pressure on his shoulder. Socorro continued speaking. Random images were coming into Drew's head quickly. Almost at once he saw his grandmother, a toy gun he had lost at a 25-cent movie in the Airway Theater a million years ago, snow on army tanks, the eyes of the owl from the ranch in Texas. But it didn't seem strange at all. He did not feel that he was hallucinating or seeing visions. He just seemed to be remembering things at random; out of context, like a dream. But he wasn't dreaming, or at least he didn't think he was.

A clap of thunder, immediate and very near, broke the spell. Drew jumped and lost his balance on the bench. Tuna caught him before he fell backwards. Drew heard the laughter.

XIBALBA'S CALL

"WHAT WAS THAT ALL ABOUT?" Drew sat with a beer in his hand leaning against one of the corner posts. Tuna sat on a bench opposite with Ree and Joy on either side.

"Whatever it was it sure set you off mate," Joy smiled and coaxed the others to laugh with a broad grin. "I think it was a divination for the trip," he continued, looking at Tuna for some recognition.

"Yes, it was that," Tuna's voice was soft but with no hesitation, almost reverent in tone. "We believe that the difference between ourselves and the animals is we must ask permission when we go on a journey away from our place, our pueblo and our people. We want the approval of our gods so that nothing bad will happen to us. This is most true when we venture into the darkness of the forest. In the forest, there are powerful things that can do us harm. We cannot, like the animals, simply wander without permission. That was the purpose of Socorro's borrowing of the forces." He stopped for a second. "You saw and heard the lightning? It was speaking of these things from the forest. Speaking through the days that the woman was counting. This was the way of our Mayan ancestors."

Drew was content to let it rest there, but Joy had to ask. "Well, what did they say about the walk to Bonampak? Is everything on the up?"

Tuna sat quietly for a second too long. "Is there something wrong?" Ree asked as she put her hand on Tuna's arm and leaned forward to see the young Indian's eyes. She shot a quick glance as if to ask him the same question.

"Why did Socorro stare at Drew for so long during the ceremony? She almost put him into a trance."

Drew got up and moved away from the group just as JonKing sent a flash that covered the small gathering with an intense illumination.

Ree, without lifting her hand from Tuna's arm, shifted from her seat next to him to where Drew had vacated. She asked him again, "What is it? What did the old woman say? Tuna, you are our friend. Tell us."

JonKing sat down on the bench next to Joy. "I've got some great shots..." Ree looked at him and JonKing realized he was butting into something. He mouthed the words, "Oh, sorry."

"Tuna?" Ree said again. She could see Drew moving out the door and walking slowly, out to the middle of the common green area.

Tuna finally looked up at Ree. "She said that Drew has been sent here. The messenger from *Xibalba* called him to this place and to the Lacandon Forest. That is why she looked strongly at him. She could see that it was so. She could see it in his eyes. Now Drew knows it. He knows he has been called to this place. He saw it too in Socorro."

"What is this, this...how did you say it?"

"It is the *Xibalba* señorita. It is the place of the lords of the night. The *underground.*

"Is the messenger an owl?" Joy joined in with his question.

258

"Wait a minute! Would somebody explain to me what this underground stuff is? And, why Drew?" Ree leaned back against the post and crossed her arms.

Joy could see that Tuna was very nervous and that he didn't want to try to explain these things to Ree. "Let me see if I can throw a bit of light on this." Joy looked at Tuna, "Is it the same *Xibalba* that is in the *Popol Vuh*, the ancient Counsel Book?" He waited for a response.

Tuna didn't speak, but seemed surprised that Joy spoke of the Book. He nodded his agreement.

"I studied this in an anthropology course on native cultures in Mesoamerica. It has been nearly three years ago, but I think I can give you a fair account. First things first. This book, if I remember correctly is called an *ibal*, a seeing instrument. You know, for seeing the future from wise writings of one's ancestors and seers; that kind of thing. It is not a crystal ball or some metaphysical telescope in this case. It is a book. This book is like the creation story. Events that happened before the first sunrise. This is all coming back to me pretty good. Maybe because I am right here in the middle of it."

"Anyway, I guess Socorro is what they call a *daykeeper*. She keeps all this mythology alive." Joy hoped Tuna did not understand the word mythology. He didn't want to offend him.

"Socorro was borrowing from the forces," he went on, "in this case, from the forces behind the Counsel Book. She did it by counting the days on their Sacred Calendar. They used the same one for the last 2,000 years. I think it has 260 days. Each day has a god associated with it, and each god can tell you something about what the future holds. Kind of like astrology. You do read your horoscope don't you?"

"Joy, don't make this too complicated. Just explain to me what all this has to do with Drew and this *Xibalba* place, or thing, whatever it is."

"Sure. *Xibalba* is what we would call Hell, the bad place where you go when you die. But to the Maya it wasn't that simple. There was a lot of wisdom to be gained from the lords who lived below. You could go down to *Xibalba* and if you were smart enough you could get back out; with knowledge of how to live this life above. I think the owls can help you get back above in one piece, something like that."

"OK, stop right there," Ree demanded. "What is all this about the owl? Tuna, isn't that your other spirit, the one you were born with?"

Joy did not wait for Tuna to acknowledge Ree's question.

"The owl is the messenger from the Lords of the Underground. They come calling when the Lords would like to see somebody. There are four of these little winged harbingers. I don't recall all their names, but one of them was just a skull with wings. How would you like to get a message from those birds?"

Joy seemed to be enjoying his lecture. He didn't believe in any of it. But, it did make good story telling.

"I still don't see what this has to do with Drew. I mean he has never been to this place before. He doesn't know anything about this Mayan thing."

"That's one I can't help you with. All I can say is that you can find several authors, both scientific and popular that believe that all life, all matter I should say, is interconnected. Who knows? Two weeks ago you wouldn't have thought you would be in this remote

Mexican ejido talking about the Lords of the Underground would you?"

"No. I guess not. But, if all this is true, what would they want with Drew?"

"Who knows? Maybe we will find out soon enough. Right mate?" Joy nudged Tuna. Tuna didn't answer.

RENDEZVOUS

The Vietnam surplus helicopters repainted with government and Pemex colors and logos descended in a gentle glide path over the luxuriant green canopy. As the altitude dropped, Boxxloader began to make out certain detail in the sea of trees that stretched beyond the horizon in all directions. Differences from what at five thousand feet had appeared only as homogeny. He and his entourage had left the airport in Palenque only an hour before. Boxxloader could still taste the bitter breakfast coffee when he belched.

CHAPTER 13

THE FACE THAT APPEARED AMONG THE TANGLE of vines and broad leaves was more pleading than sinister. The eyes, overburdened with a heavy protruding rock brow, balanced the wide gaping mouth in a grotesque symmetry. The lush profusion of vegetation had all but made the strange face unrecognizable as the small group passed within 20 feet. They would have missed it altogether if Chica had not shot off the trail, jumped into the mouth opening and barked, proudly announcing her discovery.

It was a find too good not to linger. The two Indian guides from Zapata had worked for ten minutes to chop at the vine and bromeliad snarl that bedecked and obscured the jungle face. Now it was obvious. The giant rock figure, which had been reclaimed by the jungle and the dense foliage centuries before, was part of a larger structure. Ancient cieba trees extended their reach more than

150 feet above the jungle floor now grew out of what must have been the top of the head. JonKing was setting up a small remote flash unit to try to direct more light onto the massive front for a photograph. It was late afternoon and the small group was on their second day out of Zapata.

Drew sat down on the ground and leaned against his backpack. He squirmed free from the shoulder straps and unscrewed the plastic lid off his water bag.

"Tuna, what is this place?" Tuna didn't answer.

"It looks like some kind of mask. Almost like a big snake with its mouth wide open. Big sucker isn't it?" Joy offered his assessment. "Most of the pyramid structures of the classic Maya had large faces attached to the steps at different levels. I bet that's what this is." Chica was still at the opening. She had penetrated a few feet, and Drew thought about calling her out but let her be.

"How much further to Bonampak?" Drew tried once again to get Tuna to respond. He seemed fixated on the steady rectangular eyes that now peered so steadily at the party of explorers. "We are close. Maybe two hours. I will ask Xiloj." Tuna moved toward the one in the Special Forces ball cap but didn't take his eyes from the stone stare.

"What do you think Joy? Should we just set up camp here tonight and move on to the meeting early in the morning? It seems to me that we might not be able to get JonKing away from this place for awhile anyway. I certainly don't want to run out of daylight on the trail." Drew seemed to answer his on question as he began to unlace the first few eyelets of his boots and get comfortable.

"I think we've found something with this mask," Joy said. "Who knows, maybe we'll be famous. Maybe this is the only thing showing of some once great Mayan city. Camp here...I'm for that," Joy headed for JonKing. Drew could tell he was more than a bit worked up over the prospect of discovery.

"Xijol says I am right. Not too far. We could be there before dark." Tuna squatted down to Drew's eye level as he delivered his message.

"Tell him we will set up our camp here tonight. The morning's soon enough to get to that bunch of long-winded scientists. All of us gringos are a tad tuckered." Drew slid down a few inches more on his pack. He was almost lying down on the soft floor of the rainforest.

"Did Xiloj know of this place?"

Tuna again was slow to respond. He looked back at the sculpture, which seemed to have grown in size since they had first seen it. Finally Tuna said. "No. He does not remember this place. But he said that he believes it is the mask of the dark corner that José kept telling him about."

"José?"

"José is a Lacandon Indian. He lives in this rainforest, close to Bonampak in a pueblo called Nahal. José takes tourists through the forest for money. His people are from the ancient Maya who lived here in the far away times. The ones who built these things." Tuna pointed across his body with his right hand at the stone face. "José knows of these places."

JonKing came up and put his camera bag down. He folded his lanky legs up under him and jackknifed down to a kneeling position. "Up for a little exploring Drew?"

"Exploring what?"

264

"The cave," was JonKing's short response offered almost as a challenge. Joy had joined them but didn't sit.

"Do you know something that I don't? What cave are we talking about?"

JonKing seemed to enjoy the moment of drama and slowly raised his hands to form an interlocked finger support for the back of his head. "The one that leads down from the mouth of our *cuello amigo* there. That cave."

Drew was taken by surprise at the suggestion. "You mean that thing leads to something?"

Joy butted in, "Yeah, Drew...it's..."

"Either it's a cave or the stone man has a mighty deep gullet," JonKing said reclaiming the conversation. "For my part, I can see another *National Geographic* spread down that hole. You up for it?"

"I don't mean to be overly cautious but don't you think we are a little ill-equipped to be plunging down some dark passage to who knows what?"

"I've got my photo equipment lights and we don't have to go too far in. Just far enough to see if we have anything. If we do, we can get some help from the bunch at Bonampak tomorrow. But, we need to at least check it out. "

"That must mean you want me to go first?" Drew raised forward and began to re-lace his boots.

"I'll be right behind you with the camera. You're going to be famous man."

"Sure. We'll only go in as far as the length of that rope. No further. Tuna pitch me the rope."

"I can live with that." JonKing began to rummage around in his bag.

Drew pulled out his neck chain from inside his shirt and blew on the small noiseless whistler. He watched the mouth hole of the stone face. He waited 30 seconds and blew the whistle again. The Zapata men watched the opening with him. Suddenly Chica exploded out of the black and charged through the vines to Drew's side. "Well it's about time. What's down there girl? Any demons or monsters?"

If there were, they didn't seem to bother the dog. Drew could tell Chica sensed the adventure as much as Joy did. Her tail betrayed her agitation.

"OK JonKing let's take a look. Joy you and Tuna sit in those big beautiful eyeholes and shine some light down the passageway for us. Above all, keep a hold of the end of that rope just in case we need to come out of that thing fast. You got that?" Drew pitched the knotted end of the rope to Joy.

"Hey mate, why don't you let me take the plunge?"

"I want some young legs that can run like hell for help if need be. Besides, why would I let some fresh-face college kid get all the glory?" Drew smiled and started for the opening. Joy didn't protest.

JonKing crawled through first on his hands and knees. "Hey Drew you can almost stand up once you get through the opening. Let me make a few passes with the light before you come in."

Drew wrapped the rope around his waist and tied a bowline while he waited. The echo effect of JonKing's voice came out of the mouth hole. "Pitch in your machete Drew. There are only a few vines growing across what may be a passage."

Drew and the others could just see JonKing's back as he took swipes with the long knife. Chica took advantage of the opening when it got larger and jumped by Drew. She squirted out of sight

266

within a second. Drew called her name, but there wasn't much conviction in his call. Chica didn't come back into the light and Drew didn't pay any more attention to the dog.

"Come on in my friend, the water's fine." JonKing put the light up under his chin so that Drew could see him plainly, framed against what looked like a masonry wall.

"Here take the end of this rope and tie yourself to something in the real world." Drew pitched the other end to Joy. "Don't let go boys." He slid on his back over the smooth stone through the entrance. Just as he was getting his bearing the flash caught him square and everything went black.

"Thanks a lot. Now you're going to have to wait until I can see my hand in front of my face before we can make the discovery of the century."

"Just thought I'd get a shot of the next Indiana Jones. You know you sort of look like old Indiana."

"Yeah, right. And I bet we find the Holy Grail down there too, guarded by some Nazi death squad."

"Never can tell. Never can tell."

"Señor Drew, Señor Xijol says you and Señor JonKing *tengan cuidado*, take much care. There may be things in there. Things..."

"Don't you worry Tuna; care is exactly what we are going to take. You just don't let go of that rope, you hear?"

"Sí señor, I will hold it *muy fuerte. Tómalo muy fuerte. Pero, tú debes recordar las palabras de Socorro. Tenga cuidado señor.*"

"Come on. Chica just came back out of some passage. This damn thing looks like it goes forever." JonKing was becoming impatient. He took a couple of steps deeper holding his light at the level of his forehead probing the darkness for whatever the darkness would give up.

BOXXLOADER SAT IN A LAWN CHAIR next to the massive stone stele covered top to bottom by enigmatic glyphs. He gazed with a kind of hypnotic fixation on the pinnacle of the pyramid that rose at least 150 feet above the grassy area leading to its steps. A small pamphlet put out by the government lay across his lap. The title simply read Bonampak. He could not imagine how such a place could have ever been built. According to the literature, it was constructed without the use of any tools that we take for granted in our own time. The pulley and the wheel were unknown to these people. Yet they built these great cities in some of the most inhospitable jungle on the planet. They moved these giant stones, one onto the other, and capped them above the tallest treetops with beautiful corbelled arches leading to narrow rooms for their priests and gods. Then, as if to taunt further generations, these ancient people developed the only known complete writing system in primitive Mesoamerica and left its evidence in stone; glyphs of stone that experts only now were beginning to extract meaning. Messages from a millennium past; messages that appeared to hold secrets from another world and from another time.

Boxxloader considered what those old ones might say about his work in this place at this time. Would they know what would save this rainforest from the destructive forces of modern times and the greed of man? Would they be better at it than he and his fellows? He wondered. The pamphlet explained that the current theory was that the Maya didn't vanish, but merely dispersed. Abandoning the cities that had become unworkable. Cities that were crowded and captured in perpetual warring with neighbors and ruled by an overgrown class of priests and nobles producing nothing but their own perpetuation in power. Would they have a message for him? What would they say about the men gathered here in this long ago forsaken stronghold?

"¿Qué piensas mi amigo?" Boxxloader felt the hand and heard the voice of Dr. Blanco.

"Oh! You startled me a little." Blanco moved around to face Boxxloader and squatted down on the stone ledge that formed a border around the stele.

"I was sort of lost in my wonderings. I wonder if the ancients who created this place could help us with our deliberations. Everyone has a different notion about what causes the destruction here and, of course, a different solution. Then we have all the egos and jealousies and the small battles for position that are always going on among these so-called men of science. At my age I have lost my patience with the bickering. I would like to leave it behind, for the younger ones."

"Yes, I understand. I suppose both of us should have retired from this menagerie a long time ago, but nevertheless, here we are. Moreover, you must try to bring something from this opportunity. As we have seen in the last few days, the destruction is real and extensive and it shows no signs of abatement. There will reach a time, and I am afraid that time is now for this small rainforest, when we either take drastic measures to prevent further devastation or we must let it go. The time for planning and debate is gone. It is important that actions be taken."

Boxxloader shifted his weight in the chair and re-crossed his legs. "Of course you are right, but you understand as well as I Simon, that makes little difference when it comes to producing desired results. Look at these ruins, my friend. Do you not see the same lesson here? Do you think that these people, who had the intelligence to build these cities, to carve these magnificent glyphs in stone and to record their thoughts and deeds didn't see the same destruction that we see now? Speak of the same dire consequences? But, as you can see, they too were unable to stop it. Their civilization disappeared from the face of the earth. At least in this form."

"So, what do we do? What do we say this morning as our discussions begin? What wisdom are you going to give us to use for the search for a favorable outcome Dr. Sol?"

"Simon if you keep that up I'm going to turn the whole damn thing over to you and get that young helicopter pilot to take me back to Palenque, send for Barbara and give that woman a vacation that she has long deserved. To hell with the bunch of you."

"Now Solomon. Don't get so testy so early. There's still a long day to go. I'm putting my money on your leadership. By the way I noticed Joaquín finally flew in late yesterday afternoon. Has he calmed down?"

"Who knows? I think so. I'm just hoping he and Cárdenas won't start up again at the meeting. I swear I'll crown both of those hard heads if they so much as look cross-eyed at one another."

"Maybe you should threaten them with the same fate as those poor bastards in the murals painted in that ruin. It looks like the Maya were a little bloodthirsty. Did you see the guy with his fingernails pulled out?"

"Yes, but I prefer the beheading method they used on the other one. That befits Cárdenas better I suppose." The two men shared the laugh and then fell silent staring at the decayed grandeur all around them.

Blanco, after a few minutes, broached the subject that Boxxloader didn't want to face. "Are you going to support Cárdenas' Slash & Burn proposal? You must agree it is the only one that is organized and has much of a chance of being tried. By that I mean funded."

"I know what you mean." Boxxloader lifted himself up out of the chair and took several steps around the stone monument. He reached out his bony hand and placed his finger tips against one of the bas-relief figures. He rubbed it gently. "Simon, I've got a strange premonition. I think there is an answer right here to our question. I just don't know what it is yet. Why don't we give it a little time to reveal itself before we make a commitment? What do you say to that my old colleague? Some science, huh?" Boxxloader dropped his hand to his side and turned without waiting for Blanco's answer. Walking slowly towards the meeting tent.

Boxxloader had almost made it to the group when Blanco saw a line of men move out of the deep forest just off to the right. He figured they were the group that had taken the trek through the Lacandon Selva. He thought that they seemed to be moving quickly for men that had been walking through thick jungle for two days. The two in the front were waving and went into almost a trot as they moved toward Boxxloader and the others.

WHERE THE LIGHT FROM THE STROBES FAILED TO REACH; it was dark, very dark. The two explorers had already made one 60-degree turn to the left and now, within no more than ten feet, they were faced with another but this time to the right. Drew kept making the comment that the walls were so smooth. Far too smooth to be the inside of a cave. When he put the light close to the surface it seemed to be whitewashed—cracks criss-crossed like veins through a dried-up creek bottom into intricate designs. *Someone had built this passage* Drew thought.

JonKing asked Drew to hold both of the strobes over his head while facing down what appeared to be a straight stretch of corridor. He wanted to get a perspective shot. As the photographer did his work, Drew felt the slight rush of air coming from the direction they had traveled. It seemed to pulsate; almost like breathing, in and out. Drew asked JonKing if he noticed the air movement, but he ignored the question and pushed Drew's right arm higher adjusting the angle of the light through the darkness.

Drew could feel the gentle tug on the rope as he moved in a slight crouch behind JonKing. It felt comforting to keep his connection with the outside. Then they came to another turn, but Drew could see immediately that it was a fork, the second passage going off at a 45-degree angle to the first. The two debated which way to go, with JonKing pointing to the right and Drew pointing to the left at the same time. JonKing tried to make some kind of joke about the high road and low road, but Drew just pointed in the direction of JonKing's preference. After all, he told him what difference does it make? JonKing started off and took about two steps when Drew heard him say something. It sounded more like a gasp than a phrase.

"What is it? See something?" Drew poked him in the back with the end of the light. JonKing didn't move for almost ten seconds, Drew could see his light moving in what looked like circles. When he finally moved it was backwards. He backed up but never turned around, just retraced his steps. When he had cleared the corner, he turned to face Drew. The normal sleepy look that was JonKing's countenance was transposed with eyes that seemed to be double their normal size.

"Holy mother of Jesus!! Holy mother..."

"What the hell is it? You're scaring me you son-of-a-bitch. What is it?" Drew redirected his light around his partner and leaned sideways to try to get a look.

"Listen man...holy shit! ...we have just discovered the mother lode you mother-fucker...the fucking mother load."

"What the hell are you talking about?" Drew could tell that the man's mind was racing like some Richard Petty car at Daytona. JonKing was trying to let his words catch up with his thoughts.

"Holy...OK, listen. Drew there's writing all over that wall around that corner ... it's everywhere."

"What do you mean writing? You mean like graffiti or..."

"For crying out loud where in the hell do you think you are? New York City? This is no fuckin' subway. This is a Mayan temple, or cave or something and we have just discovered something no one in this modern age has ever seen. I'm telling you Drew we have stumbled on to something momentous."

"Well for Christ sakes, let's take a look." Drew made a move to go around his companion. JonKing's arm stopped him.

"What happens after we leave this place? You know, what do we tell the others?"

"Come on; let's just see what's here." He pushed through the arm restraint and took a couple of cautious steps that brought him to the corner.

"WHO STAYED BEHIND? You did leave someone there at the entrance in case he came out?" Boxxloader motioned toward Joaquín to come to his side. He continued, "I don't think I understand. You mean Cotton just wandered off in that damn cave and got lost?"

"No, not exactly. We had made our second trip in and had doubled the ropes so we could explore farther. I was busy taking Polaroid's of as many of the inscriptions as I could when Drew decided to backtrack a little and take a look down the other passageway. The one that went off in a different direction."

JonKing paused a minute while he dug through his deck of photos that would show the intersection. He finally found the one he wanted and placed it on the table in front of Boxxloader.

"He took his dog with him. He said he would whistle every few minutes just to keep in touch."

"How much rope did he have?" Joaquín asked leaning over Boxxloader's shoulder to get a look at the photo.

"About the same as I had. We had tied two of our ropes together. I'd say about 200 feet or so." JonKing took a long drink of water from a canteen. "Like I said, I kept at the photography. I'm not sure when I stopped hearing his calls." JonKing slumped in a lawn chair. "We called and called for several hours. We never got a response. Tuna went back in with me a couple of more times. We found the end of Drew's rope and it had been untied. I figure he must have seen something that he wanted to get a better look at so he untied the rope. "

Boxxloader kept at the questioning, but now directed it to Joy. "What about the dog? Did she ever show up, son?" Joy seemed a little surprised that he was being asked and stumbled over his words for a second.

"Uh...yes...yes Chica was with him, but she never came out either. Dr. Boxxloader we did everything ...."

"I understand that. What we have to figure out is what to do now." Boxxloader turned his head to the side. "Joaquín do we call the Mexican government in on this?" Before Joaquín had a chance to answer Boxxloader turned to JonKing again. "You never told me who you left behind. Who was it?" Joaquín held his response and looked at the photographer as well.

"The Indian kid, Tuna. He said he would wait."

"OK Joaquín what about the government?"

"Well we can...but...I think..."

"No," Boxxloader butted in, "we had better take some action on our own." Boxxloader sent a finger out towards Xiloj and his partner from Zapata, "can these boys get us back to the spot?" JonKing and Joy both nodded in unison.

"There's a field archaeological team just up the Usumacinta River near Yaxchilán." Joaquín glanced around at the various faces as he made the statement. He noticed that JonKing had put his collection of Polaroid's back in his bag. "Those archeologists know something about these kinds of places; maybe they could help? We could send the helicopter for them. It wouldn't take more than 30 minutes."

"Good idea. Do you think the helicopter could get us back there faster?" JonKing asked.

"The jungle's too thick. You would never get anybody to the ground."

"OK then, get that pilot on his way. We'll leave as soon as the dirt diggers get here." Boxxloader motioned for the photos when Cárdenas distracted his attention.

"Doctor, what about the meeting? We were scheduled to begin our deliberations this morning. We only have the two days before many of us must leave."

"I know that Emilio. I think then it would be appropriate for you and Dr. Blanco to co-chair the proceedings in my absence." Joaquín was quick to object.

"But, Dr. Sol, you don't have to go. I believe these other men can handle the search. You are needed..."

It came like summer lightning, "Damn it! Wasn't Andrew your friend?" he paused for the statement to sink in. "Whatever recommendations that need to be made from our work can be offered by the rest of the group. We have more pressing and immediate work now." Boxxloader turned his gaze towards Dr. Blanco. "Simon you can help with this until I get back, and Joaquín, you can certainly stay here if you would prefer."

"Yes, of course Dr. Sol, Emilio and I can see to things. But, I must say I too share a little concern for you. It is a hard walk in this jungle."

Boxxloader ignored the comment, "OK, then it is settled. Joy pack us plenty of water and see if you can round me up an extra hemaca for tonight." Joy answered with a nod and turned quickly to carry out his assignment. "Now, Mr. Photographer come with me please. Damn it Joaquín get your ass in gear. Get that helicopter out of here!"

"XBALANQUE." DR. HENRY MERCHANT SAID it at least three times as he shuffled the Polaroid's like playing cards. Boxxloader thought he looked too young to be in charge of a major dig at Piedras Niegras, the archeological site he and his colleagues from Yale were excavating just up river from Yaxchilan. They had been at it for almost five years. He had insisted that they take the time to study the photographs before heading out. He said there might be clues as to how to search for the man lost among the passages in the cave. Although Dr. Merchant didn't think that this was a cave, more correctly he speculated it was likely a pyramid long since reclaimed by the jungle.

As he made one identification after another he pronounced the names with almost a laugh in his voice. Everyone could tell he was excited. *Hunahpu* and *Xbalanque*. He spoke these two names several times, as he read aloud what sounded like dates or some form of counting. Sometimes he even used his fingers to count backwards. Nobody had the slightest idea what he was doing.

Finally Boxxloader showed his impatience. He repeated the question to Joaquín several times, the last time loud enough so Dr. Merchant noticed.

"Is everything ready to go?" Boxxloader almost shouted.

Dr. Merchant motioned for Boxxloader to take a look at something. Joy, as inconspicuously as possible, squeezed in close enough to get a look over Boxxloader's shoulder.

The archaeologist laid out ten of the photos lined up two abreast. He pointed to the one at the top left and began his explanation.

"You see this set of glyphs. These over this lintel. If I'm even half right they identify this as the entrance to the underground described in the Mayan Counsel Book."

"The Popol Vuh, Dr. Merchant." Joy couldn't help himself.

"Exactly. Merchant seemed to be both a little surprised by Joy's knowledge and yet pleased to have an understanding mind amidst the group.

"According to the Mayan cosmology there are 13 layers or levels of heaven and nine of hell. The earth's surface is the first layer in both directions. You see these inscriptions here? They, gave this place the name of *Xibalba*. It is the entrance to the Mayan underground. Most of these others along this right side are glyphs naming the various gods to be found down these passages. I am certain about two of them. This one is *One Death* and the other, just opposite, is *Seven Death*.

Now look at these two photos," he put his fingers on the two about half-way down and slid them out away from the others.

"This is what has me believing we may have something earth-shaking to the world's archeological community. The first one is numbers. You see this series of bars and dots? That was their counting system. Even though it looks primitive to us now, it was vastly superior to anything in the world of the time. This, by the way, was from about 300 A.D. to 900 A.D. on our calendar. These numbers do something that I have never seen on any of the other forms where they are normally found, such as the one behind us here at Bonampak." Merchant picked up one particular Polaroid and handed it to Boxxloader. Everyone pushed around to get a look.

"You see that series of five glyphs and the Mayan numbers along them?" He waited for a few seconds. "That date is the date in the Mayan Long Count Calendar, a very accurate one incidentally. That is supposed to signify the end of the world. It reads 13.0.0.0.0. The little shell you see is the sign for zero. We have been able to correlate that date to our own calendar. We believe it corresponds to the date of December 21, 2012. Not so far away." Dr. Merchant stopped and let the group pass around the photo.

Boxxloader spoke up, "Dr. Merchant, you'll have to excuse me, I'm not exactly seeing the significance here."

"Well sir, it's just a hunch. Until we get there and I can see these inscriptions in context, I can only guess. But, if I'm right, and that's a big if, this pyramid or cave or combination of the two may well hold something that scientists and Mayanists all over the world have hoped would someday be found. This could very well be the resting place of the original *Popol Vuh*, the sacred text of the Classic Maya. Many of us have long argued that an original text must exist somewhere. We have only had the crude copy that was found in a church long after the Spanish conquest in Guatemala. That copy was a translation, not the original Maya writings that you see evidenced in these photos. If your man in that cave has stumbled onto the *Popul Vuh*, whether he is found alive or dead, he will go down in history as one of the most fortunate explorers in the long search for this Mayan mystery."

"I'm sure if given the choice he would just as soon suffer a little less fame and a little more life. In that regard, we have spent as much time in speculation as we should. I think we need to be on our way. Joy, Joaquín, are we ready?"

Joaquín moved around from behind Boxxloader and nodded. "Yes Dr. Sol we are ready."

"Very well then: Joy, you and the young man from Zapata lead on. Let's go and extract our man Cotton from *Xibalba*."

THROUGH THE HOLE IN THE WORLD

Tuna tried to sit still but he was nervous. It had seemed too long since the rest of the party had left for Bonampak. He wanted them to get back. He wanted to find Drew. Socorro had been right again. She saw things so clearly. Tuna kept thinking he should go get her from Zapata and bring her here. She would be able to see where Drew had gone. She could call to him as no one else could. Tuna knew Socorro could get him back into the light. If only she were here. After all, Socorro had known that Drew had been brought to this place. She knew that Drew had no choice. It was the call from the messengers.

Tuna tried not to think about being alone here. There was something very frightful that appeared to hang around the mouth of the cave, but he couldn't move away. If he did, he might not hear if Drew called out. The noise of the Lacandon seemed so loud. The birds, the insects and the frogs kept up a constant chorus. Tuna reminded himself over and over, *I cannot leave la boca del cuello, I must find the courage and stay close.*

Tuna fixated on the scream that came from deep in the jungle. He knew it to be of the Howler monkey. He had heard them all of his life. They always made him think of the Jaguar, the Lord of the Dark. At least it was daylight now and he was more than glad.

280

Just as another unsettling scream echoed through the trees something wedged between his arm and side from behind. Tuna reacted instinctively and jumped to his feet. He lost his balance and slid on leaves and wet vines for almost 20 feet, and then came to rest against the trunk of a Guanacaste tree. The bump to his head brought stars. His vision was clearing when he felt something wet against his cheek.

"*Chinga madre* Chica, where did you come from?" Tuna slipped again as he tried to regain his equilibrium and get to his feet. Chica did her little dance of excitement as she circled the wobbly Indian.

"Where's Drew Chica? Come perrita. Come show me where Drew is." Tuna began to move back to the stone orifice. Chica ran through his legs and beat him to the opening. He could tell she knew what she was doing as she moved in and out of the hole in short, determined bursts. He grabbed the bulky flashlight sitting on the rock ledge, next to his seat, and decided to follow the dog. He cautiously took a moment to tie the loose end of the rope around his waist and moved into the black hole. He did not like this place.

"Chica, ven acá, where are you perrita? Again the dog came into view and again she shot forward, out of the light's eye. Each time Tuna called she came back within sight, but just long enough so that he could be sure of his direction. It was damp. Tuna could feel the wetness on the wall surfaces as he put his hand against them for balance. His senses kept telling him that there was a breath moving in and out of the passage. He felt the movement, the cooling on the back of his neck and then on his face. This place was alive. He knew it.

Every time he rounded a new corner, Tuna pulled the rope slack to him. He wanted to make sure it was secure, not tangled or snagged. It marked his trail for the way out. He wondered why Drew would untie it.

The writings were everywhere; almost solid on the walls and ceilings. Tuna knew the ancients had put them there. They had left them for the future. He wished he knew their meaning. He wished he could see into the minds of his ancestors. Such wisdom he would be able to find there. Such stories. Tuna realized he had stopped walking and was staring at the marks and signs. Chica barked. The echo off the walls made it difficult to determine where the sound came from.

"Chica, ven acá, Chica." Tuna called several times before she came from around a corner. Chica moved up right in front of Tuna and sat down.

"Are we there?" Chica just looked at him. Her tail lightly dusted the soft dirt carpet. Tuna scanned the walls and the ceiling for some clue. Again, he asked, "Is this the place?" He pulled at the rope to see how much slack there was. There was none. This must have been where Drew untied it. Tuna again looked all around at the writings. He couldn't see any signs that would tell him. He looked again at the dog sitting at his feet for some direction. She looked back at him as if it was clear how to proceed. She seemed to be waiting for Tuna to take the lead. He slowly shined the flashlight out along the walls. The little carved mask was finally caught in the beam and its low relief face became apparent. It had a nose that curved like a corkscrew and a tip that grotesquely pointed to Tuna's left. When he followed the direction of the paint he saw that there was still another corner a few feet beyond the end of the rope. Chica barked and made him jump. She seemed to be getting irritated.

"OK, show me perrita, Where is Drew?" Chica continued to stare at him.

Tuna pulled at the rope hoping for a bit more length. He wanted to see just around the corner and to what the mask was pointing. Tuna fumbled to undo the knot that secured the lifeline. With her patience seemingly exhausted, Chica raced ahead around the corner. Tuna called her back, but she had disappeared. Tuna carefully laid the rope down making sure the end was in the center of the passageway. He took a small rock and rested the rope's end on the stone. He figured if the flashlight failed, he could feel his way to the end and follow it out of this place. He turned and took a step towards the corner, but something made him stop and look back. Tuna let the beam of light again find the end of the rope under its stone altar. He wanted to make sure it was really there.

The corner was a bit narrower than the others. Two stones lay across the floor. They didn't completely block the way, but a high step was required to clear them. Tuna thought they appeared to have been recently moved. He wondered if it had been Drew. "Chica!" he called again.

Tuna stuck his head forward over the stones and directed his light out into the new darkness. More of the same it seemed. More writing. Then he noticed something which appeared out of place. It was very small in the distance. Brown maybe. It was lying on the floor and there was something larger just to its right that looked to be black. Tuna deliberately moved the illuminating beacon, slowly tracing the edges of both objects. Then two glaring reflections came back. Tuna's muscles tightened all over his body until he realized it was Chica sitting next to the two objects. She was calmly gazing back at Tuna.

Tuna didn't really want to go any further, but the two things were only about ten feet over the rock obstacles. He put one leg over the rocks. Chica barked twice. "OK. OK. I'm coming." Tuna pulled the other leg behind him then leaned back through the hole. Again, he felt the breath coming around the corner. He inched forward, painting the surfaces with his flashlight.

The brown thing was Drew's spirit pouch. Tuna turned it over in his hands. The soft leather was so smooth it had a gleam to it. Tuna knew this bag. He had noticed it on the trip from Reynosa when Drew took his shirt off to get cool. "Chica, this is Drew's, no?"

Tuna sat down next to the black thing that was a small opening in the floor. It was only about a foot, maybe a foot and a half wide. Tuna could feel the air rising up through it. Like the air around the corner it pulsated back and forth with a rhythm. The edges of the hole were not round but square. Tuna felt along the outline. It was made of thick stones.

Tuna pushed his light over the edge. Another bark shattered the quiet. "This is the place, no?" Tuna tried to reassure the dog that he understood. "You have done good, perrita, very good." Tuna slipped Drew's pouch in his belt and tied the string around a belt loop. He leaned forward enough to peer down in the blackness. He pulled back with a sharp jerk and scooted away from the opening. He felt as if he was about to fall. Tuna just sat there for a long while. He could feel his heart working hard in his chest. With a bit more caution, Tuna again leaned over the hole. He stuck the end of the flashlight in and tried to focus on the reflection. All he could make out was an inky blackness. Then he realized what he was seeing was water. Still and calm. Because the opening restricted his field of vision, he couldn't tell how far the water extended. He could see inverted columns of mineral deposits hanging from the ceiling off to one side. They appeared to be dripping liquid into the pool below. His flashlight caught the pearl ends which sent back a twinkling message. Chica nudged his backside and Tuna overreacted. The momentum of his backward jerk sent him onto his back. "Chica, tenga cuidado," was all he could think to say to the dog that seemed to be getting more nervous.

As he laid there for a minute, he felt the breath pass him again. Then he thought he heard something. He tried to calm himself. He wasn't sure that the call or whatever it was had been from outside. He sat himself up as quietly as he could. Tuna extended his arm and rested his hand on the back of the dog. Chica felt reassuring. She gave a steady comfort in her closeness. Tuna listened with everything he had. Just as he let out a sigh, he thought he heard the sound repeated. But he wasn't sure. He listened again.

There. He heard it again. Tuna caught the sound. It was clearer this time. He pulled Chica close and held her tightly. The dog returned the attention by licking Tuna's bare arm. Tuna sensed that Drew's dog was listening too. The slight noise came again but a bit louder. But, that was it. Tuna strained to hear the sound but it never came again.

For a long minute Tuna sat still. The flashlight seemed to be getting dimmer so he clicked it off. The darkness closed in around him like a thick wool blanket. Almost instantly, the surroundings seem to come alive. Tuna thought he could feel something begin to move. He snapped on the light again and did a 360-degree search. There was nothing except the breathing. Then his light hit on the square stones just a few feet beyond the hole. As he let the light play over the new shape, Tuna could see that what must have been its lid was lying against a larger box. He thought about going to look inside but the light reduced its intensity by almost half. Tuna moved quickly back to the corner and stepped over the stones. He looked back, "Chica, come quickly." He didn't wait to see if she responded before searching for the rope. His heart felt relief as he grabbed the end and tied it snuggly around his waist.

"Chica, perrita, ven acá, ahorita," he shouted. Tuna immediately began to reel in the rope and follow its directions. Suddenly he wanted out of this place. He wanted to see the jungle and hear the birds. He stopped and looked back, letting the weak light go back down the passage. Chica was not there. Tuna called again but did not wait. He pulled harder on the rope and moved slightly bent at the waist along the passage. From behind him, he thought he heard a splash and hesitated. He thought about going back to see if the dog was coming. The light gave in to the darkness of the cave. Tuna began pulling himself along and inched his way forward, feeling his way along the damp walls.

I'VE FALLEN AND CAN'T GET UP

DREW SAT STILL. He heard a splash. He was certain he heard something. For a few seconds, it took his mind off his condition. He flipped the light on and called out. Now that he could see, he checked the strange thing he had held on to as he had fallen through the passage. Even when he hit the water he had not let go of it. Now the ancient object sat next to him on the little dry strip of land he had found after wading for what seemed like forever.

There had been no way to go back. He had stood in the waist-deep limpid waters and looked up after he recovered from the surprise of the fall. Drew could see the hole but there was no way to reach it. He had felt fortunate for an instant. At least he hadn't been badly hurt. He had clung to his flashlight and the book-like object he had picked up from the stone box. Now, as he stood in the water, he quickly realized that he was trapped. Drew shined the light back up into the opening overhead and could see Chica. He tried several times to get her to go get help. But she only looked at him and moved nervously around the opening. Drew could see she was trying to figure a way to get down to him. He kept telling her no. After a couple of minutes he decided he had better move out of sight. Before he moved away from the hole he realized he needed to leave some sign. He removed the pouch from around his neck.

The first toss was awkward and the small leather bag bounced off the ceiling and fell back into his face. Drew had to scramble to keep it from falling into the water. He had tucked the relic under his arm and the flashlight was pushed down the front of his pants with the lens pointing up to the hole. He took a long look at the hole before he made the second toss. The concentration paid off. The pouch went through the opening and didn't return. Drew spoke again to Chica. "Go get Tuna Chica. Get Tuna!"

"Shit man. What have you gotten into now," he repeated the question several times as he began to wade through the water. His light found what looked like shoreline a hundred feet or so downstream. He could hear Chica barking as he moved away. He was scared. The thought of never getting out of this place became uncomfortably real. He called out again. "Chica, go get Tuna!" he kept wading toward what seemed more like dry land the closer he got.

Drew wasn't sure how long he had been down here. He wished he hadn't stopped wearing his chronograph years ago. He figured it had been a while though. His clothes were almost dry.

"OK, you son-of-a-bitch are you just going to sit here and wait to die?" He spoke harshly trying to vent his anger. He called out reflexively to his dog hoping that she was the splash he heard. He wished the little bitch was with him. Looking back, he wondered why he had not coaxed her to jump down to him. At least he would have some company.

"That's it...let's go," Drew said a loud as he stood up and reached down to get the book. "OK, you came in this way so let's go out this way." Drew swung the light in a big arc in the direction he decided to try. There appeared to be a dry route along what he had determined was an underground river. His steps were deliberate. "I'll walk until the light runs out, or I get out. This water has to come in from somewhere. Probably just up ahead."

Drew turned around at the waist without stopping and called again. He let the light go back to search for the dog. It sent back two gleaming flashes. Drew stopped dead in his tracks. He called another time. He heard the splashing. Then Chica came running into the beam shaking the water from her thick coat.

"Well you little bitch, it's about time."

A COLD WIND BLOWS

"WHAT IS HAPPENING TUNA?" Ree greeted the young Tzotlil as he scrambled from the mouth of the cave. She stood next to Socorro with José a few steps behind the old woman.

"Señorita, "Tuna lifted himself up to his feet, "what are you doing here?"

288

"What are you doing with Drew's spirit bag?" Ree pointed at the leather sack dangling from Tuna's belt.

Tuna grabbed it self-consciously and handed it to Ree. "He is in the cave. We cannot find him. The others went for help. I went in to look with Chica but I could not find him. He has been in there for a long time. I have been waiting for the others to return."

"Where is Chica now?"

Tuna turned at the waist and pointed back into the opening, "She is still in there. She won't come out. I called her, but she won't come out."

Socorro stepped forward and put her hand lightly on the back of Ree's arm. She began to speak to Tuna, softly. Tuna took a couple of steps back and sat down on the ledge leading up to the face. Ree came over and sat down next to him. Socorro kept speaking in a steady, almost chant-like speech. She spoke for several minutes before she abruptly stopped.

"What did she say Tuna?"

"She told me that she had brought you here because you are needed. She heard it spoken two times since we all left Zapata for Bonampak. She says that you and José must go find Drew."

Ree interrupted, "You mean he is alright? How can Socorro know?"

"Señorita, I don't know how this woman knows these things but she does. She talks with the ancients, she knows." Tuna spoke with Socorro again. This time Ree could tell he was asking questions and receiving answers. When they stopped Ree looked expectantly at Tuna.

"You said that Socorro said that I must go find Drew. Does she mean in the cave?" Ree looked around at the wide mouth that gaped behind her.

"Sí, señorita, but not in the cave. You must go with José. He knows where to look. He will take you. She calls it the place of the black road. José knows this place. She says you will find Drew there."

"I want you to come with us Tuna. I can't even talk to José. Please come with me?" Tuna said something to the old woman. Ree figured he was repeating what she had just requested.

The curandera became somewhat agitated. Her reaction surprised Ree. Socorro spoke very quickly to Tuna. Ree could tell there was force behind her words. "What is it?" Ree asked Tuna as soon as the old woman went quiet.

"I don't understand it. She says that I am to wait here. To give the men who will come the pouch and to tell them of my search behind the face. Nothing more. She says that they are not to know that you came to look in another place for the *gringo*." Ree didn't know how to react. She sat quietly alongside Tuna.

"There is something else señorita. She says that before you left Zapata there was a sign that was meant for you. It came in the night, through the *palapa*, while you were sleeping." Tuna paused and looked at Socorro. He spoke a few words to her and she responded. "Socorro said that she felt a cold wind blow through the opening on the north side. It blew past her and around the inside of the *palapa*. The cold kept circling, looking at everything around the room; it even stayed over Socorro for a while. Then it left her and continued its search until it found the corner where you were sleeping. She said the wind rustled the clothes that you had hanging over your hemaca slowly with its nudging. Then the wind lay down with you. It was then she also felt you had to come here. The *gringo* was in need of you and you were in need of him. That is why she brought you here."

"What does she mean Tuna? What is this sign; what does it mean?"

"The old one is not sure. I only know that you must do this. You must do what she says. Socorro likes you. She speaks these things because of that. I know this. And she believes strongly that Drew was sent here. Will you go, like she says?"

"Yes, I'll go," Ree looked at Socorro who said nothing and returned the gaze. "I am scared a little Tuna. Can I trust José?"

"Yes. José is a Lacandon. He knows the place that Socorro describes. He knows how to find it in this jungle. They have lived in these forests forever and share its secrets with no one from the outside unless they are given permission by the ancients."

Ree looked at José. He was even shorter than Tuna and wore only a long white sack-like covering. His hair was long and loose. It forged a deep black trail to his waist. He carried only a diminutive cloth pouch tied with a vivid string draped over his shoulder. His right arm was prolonged by a machete. It appeared shorter than most of those she had seen. The handle was made of a red wood that shone through his fingers. His face had hardly an expression and he never took his eyes off her.

LOST AND FOUND

DR. MERCHANT CAME OUT OF THE MOUTH OF THE CAVE so quickly that he scraped his forehead on the stone. He was wiping the blood away with a bandana as he approached Dr. Boxxloader. The old man had sat down under a tree and was sipping water from a canteen. He hadn't moved from the spot for nearly two hours. The walk in had absorbed most of the septuagenarian's strength. Joaquín had used the time while they waited, chattering an argument for his plan for the forest. Boxxloader had tried to convince Joaquín that they would sort that all out when they returned to the Bonampak meeting, but Joaquín kept at it. Boxxloader changed his strategy and simply ignored the harangue. Nonetheless, he was happy to see Dr. Merchant rustling toward them. Boxxloader figured by the look on his face that he had some news.

Dr. Merchant squatted on his haunches and tried to catch his breath so he could speak. "See this," he held out his hand and turned around a small piece of what appeared to be pottery. Boxxloader took it and raised his head so that his bifocals could help him make sense of the object.

"What is this? What about Mr. Cotton? Are there any signs? Did you find the hole that the young Indian told us about?"

"Oh yes, we found the hole. And we could see the underground river below. There is no sign of him though. It seems that he must have fallen or jumped down through that opening. There is no way to tell. We lowered Joy down through the hole and he looked around but we found nothing."

Boxxloader turned to Joaquín, "Maybe we should have notified the government."

Dr. Merchant interrupted, "It wouldn't have made any difference. There is only so much you can do. If he hit that river and had the wind knocked out of him, he could have floated downstream who knows how far. It looks like the water moves with a current. It could be strong enough to move a body."

"You think he's dead?" Joaquín asked.

"Who knows? It depends on what happened when he fell or jumped, or whatever he did. There is no sign; at least that we can see. There is no sign of blood or clothing or anything for that matter. The man just disappeared through that opening in the floor of the passageway."

Boxxloader raised the little bowl, "What about this? What is it? Does it tell you anything?"

"Along with the other things we see in there, it tells me that we have discovered something here that could be extremely important. It confirms what I suspected from the pictures. This is a special place. Everything in that cave or structure says that this was the entrance to *Xibalba*, the Mayan underground. This was the end of the black road to the Mayan hell. In addition, where Cotton went through the floor was a box-like stone carrier. That's where this little piece came from." Dr. Merchant pointed at the object that Boxxloader still rotated through his fingers. "It's an incense burner. From what I can tell it is from the classic period of the Maya. Somewhere between 250 A.D. and 900 A.D. Anyway whatever was in that stone box has been removed, and, I think recently. My guess is that your man found it and took it with him." Dr. Merchant shifted his weight.

"Any idea what was in the box Doctor?" Joaquín's curiosity had been piqued.

"An idea anyway. It's almost too fantastic to believe. But if I'm right and Cotton did remove what was in the stone box then we really need to find him."

Boxxloader thought for a moment, "Dr. Merchant we have to find him regardless."

"Yes, of course, I understand. I didn't mean to imply otherwise. But I think that Mr. Cotton may have come across the ancient text that I spoke to you about back at Bonampak. I will need some more time to study closely the drawings, but I'm sure this place has not been disturbed up until just a few hours ago by your people. A few of my colleagues and me have long felt the Popul Vuh in its original form lay hidden in these jungles. The evidence is growing stronger by the minute. I don't know why Mr. Cotton would take it with him, but he has something of great importance. I'm sure of it."

"So what now?"

"With your permission I would like to let Joy and the young Indian...what's his name?"

"Tuna, at least that's what Joy and the rest call him."

"Yes, Tuna. We would like to drop the two of them into the opening that I have described to you. Maybe they can find some sign when they reach the base that we cannot see from looking down. Joy wanted to go before I came out, but I felt we needed to proceed cautiously."

"Dr. Merchant," Boxxloader cleared his throat, "Dr. just how important is this book that you hope or think Drew Cotton might have? Exactly what is the significance of this Popo Boo?"

"Popol Vuh. To those of us of archaeology it is comparable to the Rosetta Stone. It could provide the key just as that great discovery provided Jean-Francois Champollion the help he needed in breaking the code of Egyptian hieroglyphic writing. If, as we suspect, the original was written in a forerunner of the Chol language, a language still spoken in this region, it would give us a complete story to follow. This is in contrast to the written record that survived which is very fragmented."

Merchant moved over and sat down next to Boxxloader. "And there is something else. We hope that it will help us understand the mystery that has perplexed most of us in this field for almost as long as the Mayan culture has been studied. That is what happened to these great cities? What happened to make such a great culture that had achieved so much disappear? Why did their cities cease to function? What were the causes? You see some suspect, including yours truly, that there are lessons for the modern era in what happened to the Maya. A people who could build such magnificent structures without the benefit of metal and the wheel, who conceived of and used the concept of zero in their very sophisticated mathematics and calendrics, must have some vital secrets to reveal. I believe the Counsel Book could very well provide us some definitive answers to these mysteries." Merchant paused.

"And, I bet it would be worth a lot of money, no?" Joaquín stood up to face the two seated men. Boxxloader looked at him for a moment.

"OK, let the boys go for a short distance to see what they can discover." Boxxloader grunted as he raised himself, "What if they find nothing, then what?"

"Then I'm afraid Dr. Boxxloader your man is lost to the cave. I can tell you right now that the Mexicans won't help us. Oh, they will be sympathetic, but that's about all. Mr. Cotton is simply another gringo who took his chances in this remote jungle and lost. They don't have the resources or the will to mount any kind of search. Do I make myself clear?" Dr. Merchant looked between both Boxxloader and Joaquín.

"Painfully clear. OK, then let's get to it. Tell those men to be careful. We damn sure don't want to lose anymore down that black hole." Boxxloader took a few steps toward the face. He stopped and turned to Joaquín, "Did you bring that little radio of yours?"

"Yes, it's right here in my satchel. Why?"

"Can you reach Bonampak with it?" Without waiting he continued, "Get Blanco or Cárdenas on it for me." He then rotated his eyes to Merchant.

"Merchant, Joaquín and I will take one of the young Indians with us and go back to Bonampak. I don't see how we can be much use to you here and we have important business to conclude. We will leave Joaquín's little radio with you so you can keep us up to date with the progress."

"That won't be necessary. I have a radio with me. But you can do one favor for me if you will. Have the helicopter pilot go back to Piedras Negras and get the people whose names I am going to write down."

BEE IN YOUR BONNET

DREW WAS HUNGRY. But at least he was outside.

"Chica what about this jungle?" he asked his dog. "Is it great or what?" Drew rubbed the back of the little dog's neck. He couldn't remember feeling this alive. Everywhere he looked there was green tangle. The birds incessantly sang every kind of song imaginable. One sounded like a faucet dripping; another like the brakes on an old worn-out bus. Drew leaned against the trunk of a tree and looked back at the opening that he could barely make out. While it was no more than fifty feet away, it seemed to melt into the jungle covering. Someone coming down a trail would never see it. But from the other side the light came pouring in.

He had just kept walking. Drew had no idea how far. And then there it was, just as easy as walking out of a building. Drew sat under the tree and tried to recall how many turns he had made. At one point, he had felt that he was turning back on himself. But he never rediscovered one of the small rock triangles he had stacked every couple of hundred feet to mark his passage. He wondered what had made him make the right decisions about his direction.

"*Así es la vida,*" he said to Chica and laughed. "You know old girl it's nice to reborn."

For the first time since he lifted it out of the stone box, Drew let himself study the ancient thing that rested next to his knee. It was some kind of book. Most of the covering had fallen away when the water hit it. It felt like hard leather to Drew's touch, but he knew it wasn't leather. It felt almost like wood, like a thin veneer. He picked the oblong shape up and rotated it in his hands; looking for markings on the outside. There were none. Drew could see that it had some kind of structure, almost like pages except they were folded like an accordion, one back onto the other in a continuous fold. The binding was still intact and solid. He thought about breaking them and opening it to get a look inside, but decided to wait. As his eyes worked over his find, suddenly he felt intensely alone.

"Wonder if they're looking for us Chica?" Drew looked up through the canopy. He reckoned it was sometime either right before or just after noon. He made a sighting on the sun's angle and decided he would wait a few minutes to get the direction of movement. Drew knew they had gone from west to east on the trip in. Once he knew which way east was he would try to go back west on that tact. Except it was hard to keep your bearings in the rainforest. Often the sun disappeared all together. It would be easy to move in a circle. "But what choice do we have?" He enunciated his thoughts. Chica just stared and waited as she always did. Drew kept thinking about the beef jerky he had in his pack. He was really getting hungry.

Drew felt the canopy close over him again. It seemed to be getting dark, very quickly.

"Hell, it's going to rain," he could feel the humidity close in around him. There wasn't any thunder but he knew it was going to rain. The jungle was closing in fast. Drew pushed himself up. He bent over to stretch his legs and picked up the book. He eyed the opening and made the decision to move back under its sanctuary and wait out the downpour. The last thing he wanted was to get drenched again.

"Come on Chica. Let's get back in the hole before we get laundered." Drew slid the book under his arm and the pair moved toward the refuge.

His weather forecast proved correct. Drew had no more crawled through the vine-covered hole than the faucet turned to full open. Drew stuck his cupped hands out of the opening as the lightning cracked in sudden and violent outbursts. The water tasted good. He drank several handfuls. It helped with the hunger. He noticed the stream at his feet that had guided him out of the underground. The water began to rise rapidly and make noise as it rushed by.

The rain showed no signs of letting up soon, so Drew moved a few steps back from the opening and pushed the flashlight lever to on. He had not paid much attention to his surroundings on his way out. He had been eager to move to the light and free himself from the cave, but now he could see that the room just inside the opening was large. He let the illumination advance along the walls at eye level. The enclosure was almost circular. There was plenty of dry dirt on both sides of the small stream that cut the open space roughly in half.

Drew momentarily put the light on Chica who was slapping at the stream with one paw and taking bites out of the water. He turned the light back to continue his survey work. Stalactites or stalagmites, he could never remember which, hung thickly from the ceiling. Some of the larger ones, Drew figured were at least 10-to-15 feet long. Where they attached to the roof of the cave they were as thick as the biggest trees out in the rainforest. Nearly all had thick fuzzy coverings. The smaller ones reflected the beam of the flashlight and glistened. Drew wondered what could grow in this darkness.

"Come on Chica girl, let's take a few more steps back and look around," Drew stooped over and picked up the book, he tucked it under his arm. He pointed his light in front and followed the natural direction of the water course. About one hundred feet farther in, Drew could see a small quiet pool formed just before the water disappeared around a corner. He took a couple of steps in that direction. He looked back over his shoulder and could see the rain was as heavy as ever.

When Drew and Chica reached the small, translucent pool Drew bent over and agitated the water. Chica took that to mean playtime and repeated her strange paw slapping in the water. The water was as green as jade and its clear color made Drew think of the streams flowing over limestone beds back in the Texas Hill Country. In both places, the water was clean and pure. The only difference was the temperature. This water was warm and the streams in Texas were cold. Drew put another handful to his mouth. The taste was as good as the rainwater. It was sweet.

Drew rose up and started back toward the light of the opening. He just let his flashlight play against the walls. He could see his way toward the light without it. The strobe seemed to stop itself on another small hole just a few feet from the water's edge. Drew followed the light's path to take a closer look. He called back to his dog who was still making splashes in the pool.

The hole was almost shoulder high and about a foot wide. Drew leaned forward at the waist and tried to stick his arm with the flashlight and his head through the opening. He couldn't get them both in at the same time. As he pulled his arm out the end caught on the rock and he reflexively pulled back with a jerk. Two big stones came with his arm and Drew had to jump back to keep the rocks from rolling across his feet. When he looked back, the hole was now doubled in width and height. He stepped over the debris and looked in. This time he could see clearly through the opening.

And there it was; another huge chamber. Another grotto, the ceiling covered with the growing mineral structures. But there was no pool of water in this one and the roof seemed to grow to the floor. Several of the inverted encrustations formed giant pillars that looked to support the roof. Drew had to duck slightly to push into the gigantic room. He had just come up straight when his light revealed a spectacle that made him suck air into his lungs in two short bursts. Scattered everywhere around the support post were dozens of pottery vessels and what appeared to be incense burners.

Miniature *metates* and *manos* were mixed in with the objects. Everything seemed to be arranged and ordered. Chica jumped in behind Drew and bumped into the back of his leg. He didn't pay her any attention and kept moving the illumination over the ancient exhibit.

Drew had to crawl over several piles of fallen rocks and the muddy clay made him slide to his knees a couple of times. When he reached the base of the stone pillar, he could see that all of the archaeological remains were intact and undisturbed. He didn't touch anything. There were beautifully carved stone cylinders with many of the same markings he had seen in the passageways of the jungle face. One of the larger vessels was brightly painted with a bizarre figure of a man-like creature with a long unnatural nose. He sat on what Drew reckoned was a throne with many more human-like men circling around and on their knees.

Under what looked like a throne created by the stone support, Drew could see a squared out chamber about a foot across and about as deep. For some reason, he took the book and pushed it in. It fit like hand in glove. As he slid it in, he noticed several insects pass through his light. He could hear the buzzing of more than one around his head. He had almost taken the book back out of the hole when the noise suddenly became louder. The buzzing in his ears grew rapidly.

Drew scrambled to his feet and swatted a couple of times at the menace. Suddenly, the pain shot from behind his right ear and he saw the beam of light fill with flying objects. He heard Chica bark somewhere near Drew and himself shouting as he fell across the rocks and fought to regain his footing. He scrambled toward the opening flailing his left arm as much as he could. He kept hearing his own voice scream and mingle with Chica's strident barking. He heard himself say "Help me! Help me! Please God help me! They're killing me!"

He dived through the chamber's entrance and struggled on his hands and knees toward the beautiful warm pool of water. As his right arm advanced in front of the left, the flashlight revealed his arm covered with a fur like substance that moved. Chica was right next to him, he could hear her clearly. She sounded like she did when she battled with other bitch dogs on the ranch to protect her pups. Drew thought he felt her weight on his back as he made a decisive effort to get into the water.

The darkness enclosed him as he immersed under the warm liquid. He clutched at the flashlight and deliberately brushed at the furry covering on his arms. He rose above the water's surface and sucked in a quick breath and went back under.

It was getting darker. He no longer heard the barking. There was a little pain, but Drew didn't think it was too bad. He sensed he had broken the surface for air, but strangely he couldn't feel the water. He was glad because he didn't want to get wet again. All went dark.

CHAPTER 14

JOAQUÍN SAT TO BOXXLOADER'S LEFT AND LISTENED patiently as Dr. Cárdenas began his presentation. Joaquín recognized that he had already lost his dream even before the first words were delivered. He did not have the influence to persuade the others to see the logic in his approach. Cárdenas was too well known, had too much influence and too many credentials. In the final analysis, Joaquín was only an interested layman, not a member of the scientific fraternity or of the stature of the next Director of the Center for Tropical Research in Africa. There was little Joaquín could do now that Dr. Sol had abandoned him too. He would have to admit to Felicia that he had failed again. Joaquín counted the freckles on the back of his hands and listened without hearing.

Cárdenas stood at the end of the folding table. He had moved his chair to one side and laid his notes in front of him. "What we have seen here in Chiapas is actually no different than what I and others of you have witnessed in the rainforests of the Amazon and of Zaire," he began. "Everywhere we look in the tropical world, we witness a combination of factors that cumulatively are taking the tropical forests at the rate of an acre a second. And, unfortunately, that rate is accelerating."

"Before I outline my recommendations for an action program permit me a moment to summarize the situation. First globally. The world's inventory of rainforest comprises approximately 6 percent of the surface of the earth. Within this relatively small percentage of surface area up to 30 million species reside; this is as much as 90 percent of all species. Even though in reality we know so little about this mysterious biome, we are paying witness to its death. Through a combination of disastrous and wasteful human actions we are removing permanently some 46,500 square miles of forest cover globally every year. This is an area roughly the size of the country of Nepal. Put another way, some 19 million trees are felled annually, most of them similar to the trees that surround us now in this remote and stupendous setting. Since 1940, I have seen estimates that human kind has cleared a full 40 percent of our forest cover from the planet. Let me emphasize here the process to replenish these forests requires centuries to complete. In effect, once the forests are cut and the land lay waste the forests are gone. Destroyed for ourselves and our heritage."

Cárdenas paused for a moment to sip from a water glass before continuing. "What then are the implications of widespread and continuous destruction of our tropical forests? Various environmental groups, even some in the scientific community, are calling this issue the sleeper issue of our century. Others rate it as the greatest calamity since the last Ice Age. A threat to our very survival as a species, second only to thermonuclear war. Dramatic speculation possibly, but certainly the statistics and the data gathered have sounded a most strident alarm. We ourselves in this past week, due to the foresight of our friend Sr. Joaquín Villa, have had the opportunity to witness firsthand the very destruction that often we only abstractly contemplate through the field work of a few. We cannot deny the consequences that we have seen in Mexico. And, I assure you, it is the same in practically all similar regions of the globe."

"So, what is to be done? What remedies should this body recommend for the immediate and concrete action to be taken by the governments involved and appropriate NGO's?"

Cárdenas paused again. "But before I attempt to answer that question, let me make something official. I have been selected to head an international consortium of scientists and national research organizations to confront boldly the threat that I have just outlined. Our organization will transcend national boundaries, thus our name The Global Research in Agro Forestry Board or, if you prefer, GRAB. GRAB expects to be funded completely through the United Nations and therefore we are anticipating considerable stability in our research efforts for several years to come. With this economic predictability, it is my hope that we will be able to approach this problem in a comprehensive manner. Not as is the case today where fragmented efforts are uncoordinated and scattered throughout the tropical zones. The only result of which is inefficiency and poor communication between the participants."

305

"Now gentlemen, that brings me to the here and now. What to recommend as a product of our work here in Chiapas this past week. Before we began this effort, I made a call on the Governor of Chiapas, and I am pleased to announce that he has graciously agreed to support the program I have just described. In exchange for this vital commitment of cooperation, we at the new GRAB organization will recommend to our board of directors and to our funding agencies, that Chiapas, and the Lacandon Selva be designated a benchmark site for our global program. I firmly believe this designation will draw resources to the vital work in saving this last remaining tropical forest in North America. There will be recognition by the world community that this place exists and has great value to the world. This is essential if we are to have the any chance of success here."

"I make the recommendation to Dr. Boxxloader and to everyone here that we put in writing that Chiapas be included in this new global program and that the local governing bodies in cooperation and deliberation with the NGO's of the region exhibit through proclamation their intentions of cooperation and support. Thank you gentlemen. I will certainly entertain any questions or points of discussion."

From the rear of the room came a response, "Dr. Cárdenas, I would ..." Boxxloader stood abruptly and interrupted the questioner.

"Obviously, Dr. Cárdenas, you have given this considerable preparation and thought. I, for one, had no idea the efforts of a world organization was in the works, let alone so far advanced. It certainly sounds well thought out. As you and most of the others here are well aware, I do not believe the solution to many of these world problems lies in the creation of another layer of bureaucracy. But for the moment, I will attempt to set my biases aside. Permit me to ask a question Dr. Cárdenas."

"Certainly Dr."

"What, in your judgment is the time frame for translating the process of organization building, funding attraction, research gathering, scientific analysis, field testing and validation, information dissemination and, finally, practical change of behavior and practices to the immediate on-going deforestation that we have all seen in graphic detail this week?

"Dr. Boxxloader I don't think ..."

Boxxloader again interrupted, "Please, humor an old man, will you Emilio. First answer my question before you go on the defensive. What is your time line for this GRAB bag program?" Boxxloader smiled at his play on words.

Cárdenas noted the sarcasm with a change in tone. "I am glad you have set aside your biases Dr. Boxxloader. As I noted, we have to go through the process of securing funding, and you, my good friend, are as knowledgeable in these matters as any of us. You know that the first year will be spent attracting the necessary long-term funding for our program. Of course, at the same time we will be attempting to build our organization and to attract top-notch people. I am confident that in the two subsequent years after the first funding cycle begins we will be able to select and put into place our benchmark sites around the world. From there..."

"So, three years and we get a benchmark site, is that correct?"

Dr. Cárdenas hesitated. He knew well where this was leading, but he could not stop the train.

"Yes, basically. From that point, we will begin to gather our data. Let me emphasize, we will not be starting from ground zero. There are years of research already accomplished. Our task will be to assimilate this data into our own effort."

"Maybe you have just made the point that I am leading to Emilio. You say you will incorporate into your own methods the years, let me emphasize this, years of research that already exists. What do you suppose will be happening here and other similar locales as you gather yourself together? Do you suppose that the rate of deforestation you so adeptly describe will not be ongoing in those years? And, what about the next three years. The buildup period you describe. What happens while you are raising money for your people, your organization, your buildings, your computers, your vehicles, your employee benefit packages? Dr. Cárdenas, are we to believe that during these years the destruction here and other points in the tropical world will hold itself in abeyance until you are finally ready to take real, concrete steps to alleviate the cause of the destruction?" Boxxloader stopped and waited.

Dr. Cárdenas folded his file folder gently and diverted his eyes from Boxxloader. He made a deliberate show of placing his pen in his shirt pocket and his manila folder in a small leather bag. He appeared to signal that his work was complete.

"Just what would the good doctor have us do? I think it is somewhat ironic that you question our proposal for establishing good science to attack a global problem. Ironic in that you, my dear friend, have spent your many productive years in the field of agricultural science in empire building yourself. You have been given..."

"Dr. Cárdenas," Boxxloader started to speak.

"No, wait a minute Solomon. You must let me make my counterpoint." Boxxloader relented and touched the eraser end of his pencil to his lips and nodded toward his colleague.

"As I was about to say, you have been recognized over the last forty years for your important work in extending the availability of good crop science to many parts of the world that were in desperate need of increasing their production just to feed their growing numbers. You were only able to accomplish what you did because of the so-called bureaucracy that was created around your initial work. That bureaucracy channeled all of its efforts and successes, if I might add, under the heading of Dr. Solomon Boxxloader. You my friend have shelves of awards and prizes to validate my point. Now, am I to believe that you, of all people, suddenly have seen the errors of your ways and are here to tell us that our methods, our approaches are no longer valid? That they are no longer feasible? Is this the message contained in your point?"

"Exactly Dr. Cárdenas." Boxxloader raised himself forward in his chair before continuing. "That is precisely what I am saying. The approaches you outline will no longer serve the ends we wish to achieve. For one simple, unavoidable reason." The eyes of the old man moved around the table and fell for an instant on each man there. "Time."

"I beg your pardon sir?" Cárdenas asked.

"Time. We do not have the time necessary for your approach. You are correct Emilio. I have benefited in my career and my life from the fact that I have been surrounded by many talented individuals operating within the structures of a large and well-funded organization. And you are also correct when you say that I have reaped the benefits. But I will tell you this. I have grown, by the years of experience you point out, to see the mistakes we made. I see the monster that was created by my science, by my own ambition. Our mistakes are my mistakes. I accept that. But, I will not acquiesce again to the same mistakes. And my dear colleague, you do not have the time to build this global response to the problem of deforestation. And, even if you did, your approach is incomplete and doomed to failure. Just as my own work is so roundly criticized. Why? Because we only addressed a portion of the problem. Its symptoms rather than the disease."

"Well then Dr. Boxxloader could you please give us the benefit of your insight. What is the proper course for us to take?" Cárdenas barely contained his anger. He was a master at the game being played and painted his question with a slight coating of sarcasm.

"I'm not sure I know the answer to your question Emilio. The reason is perhaps I, like most of us at this table, are thinking about global problems in old and outmoded ways. So, no matter how hard we work towards possible solutions, they are incomplete and, ultimately ineffectual." Boxxloader stood up from his chair slowly and began to walk behind the men seated at the rectangular table.

"We need, no we must, take a different perspective of the situation we have found in Mexico. We must stop the pretense that solutions to these very complex problems can be dictated from on high and merely passed down to the people and organizations that live with the problems on a daily basis. We only have the remainder of this afternoon to put forth a recommendation. As the Chairman and the one who must sign his name to our collective document, I will refuse to do so unless we have something different from what I have heard here today. I will not lend my name to a new bureaucracy. Not for my friend Joaquín or for my colleague Emilio

Cárdenas. For in both instances we would be building the same monster. You are both not thinking beyond your own narrow interests. You are not, indeed, representing a real solution, but, merely business as usual. And business as usual will only provide us with more of the same destruction of the natural environment. The Lacandon Rainforest must have a say in this matter or the Lacandon Rainforest will cease to exist in a short 10 to 15 years."

The room was ghostly still. No one appeared ready to move.

Finally Boxxloader intervened. "This is what I want from you after we return from lunch. Anyone who can provide an alternative to what I have described can have the floor for 15 minutes. If we do not hear any alternatives, I will disband this group with no final message. We will all simply return to our worlds and conduct our business as usual. So, time for lunch. Dr. Alvarez, I'd like to speak with you and Joaquín for a moment. Thank you. Enjoy your lunch gentlemen."

MOON POX

"HOW DO YOU FEEL?"

"Ree is that you?" Drew turned his head towards the voice and tried to open his eyes. "I can't see very well."

"I guess not. Your eyes are almost swollen shut. The bees really worked you over. Do you hurt?" Ree took a wet cloth and gently wiped the ooze that came from pox-like swellings on Drew's face.

"No. Not really. Where are we? Ouch!"

"I'm sorry. We're in the Lacandon village. You're in José's hut. We brought you here after we found you in the cave. José, Joy, Tuna and I. I'll explain it all later. I'm going to put a little more of this goo

311

on your face. Socorro made it out of some roots. It really seems to help the swelling."

"Ree, how did you get here? I thought..."

"It's a long story...boy you're ugly. Your face looks like the moon on a bright night. Here, turn this way."

"Thanks a lot. You wouldn't be so pretty yourself if you had been made into a pin cushion. Where's Chica? Is she all right? I could hear her barking before the lights went out." Drew squirmed a little up in the hammock.

"Drew, I don't know how to say this except to say it. We found her a few feet from you. She died in the attack. She was covered with stingers. Joy said that's what probably saved you. Chica diverted most of the bees to herself."

Drew could hear the birds calling from outside. He took a deep breath. Ree wiped the moisture from the side of his face as it ran toward his ears.

"Where is she? What did you do with her?"

"Tuna and José wrapped her in some broad leaves. They brought her back with us. She's buried close by. I'll show you when you can get up. José even brought a small stone from inside the cave and made a marker. Tuna said the Lacandon people of this village think Chica is a heroine. They placed incense to burn at the marker."

Drew grunted and raised himself in the hemaca.

"What are you doing? Lie back down you idiot!"

"Nurse, I want to go see where they put my dog."

Drew swung his legs over the side of the colorful woven fabric and felt for the dirt floor.

"Take me there."

"Come on Drew, don't get up. You should see how bad you look." Ree put her hand lightly on his shoulder.

"Hell lady, you should feel how bad I feel. No, I want to get up and move around. Where's Tuna?...and Joy? Did they come with you here?"

"Tuna's here somewhere, he and Socorro, but Joy headed back to the cave right after we got you here. Another guide was going to take him back. Seems there are some archaeologist types there searching for you. Joy wanted to tell them you were alive and safe."

Ree moved her hands under Drew's arms; she could see he was determined.

Drew stood still for a second. He wobbled a little around center. "Did anyone look around in the cave when you found me? "

"No, we just bundled you up and headed back here as fast as we could. We thought you were going to die. We weren't in the mood for siteseeing." Ree smiled broadly. "As a matter of fact, José was really nervous about being in that place to begin with. He kept talking to Tuna. I could tell he was scared."

"Get Tuna for me. I need to talk to both of you about something. Let's go out to where Chica is buried. Don't bring anyone else." Drew took a couple of steps and put his hands softly to his face.

"This thing on my shoulders feels like a basketball."

"A basketball is pretty compared to what it looks like."

Drew leaned against the front opening. "Just go get Tuna. You can save the wisecracks. Whatever happened to sympathetic nurses anyway? I thought you were supposed to comfort the sick?"

"You're thinking of mothers. I'll be back in a minute. Don't go exploring, stay right here."

"Very funny."

"TELL ME EXACTLY HOW YOU FOUND ME." Drew looked at Tuna but Ree answered.

"José and I found you first about an hour after we left Socorro at the face entrance. Then Tuna, Joy and the rest of the men that had been searching for you from Bonampak showed up."

Ree squatted down next to the small stone headstone buried in the fresh-turned soil. The ashes of incense were still emitting a fragrance but no smoke.

"Yes. Señorita, that is right."

Tuna stood facing Drew with his hands clasped in front of his waist. Then we started to look for you, señor. We went into the darkness, but you were not there. I was frightened of that place. But Joy and JonKing were there too. And the officials outside said we could go into the hole we found. I told them about your spirit pouch that I found next to the hole, and about the dog. Joy wanted to go in right when we got to the hole, but we had to wait for permission from the officials."

"What officials Tuna, you mean Mexican police?"

"No señor. They were..."

Ree took over. "The men you were supposed to meet with in Bonampak. Dr. Boxxloader and Sr. Villa came back with JonKing and the guides from Zapata. Joy told me they had another man, a Dr. Merchant with them. He's an archaeologist from some place near Bonampak. Because of all the inscriptions and stuff on the walls, they thought he could help find you. According to Joy, this Merchant fellow knows a lot about these kinds of things."

"Dr. Merchant, where is he now?" Drew kept trying to open his eyes a little wider as the swelling lessened.

"I'm not sure. Still back at the cave I guess. Joy said he was really excited about what had been found. In fact, Joy thought this Dr. Merchant was more excited about the things inside the cave than he was about finding you. Merchant was directing JonKing on how to take the pictures of the drawings and stuff. He said something about a stone box near the place they found your pouch. You know what that is?"

"What did he say? About the box I mean."

"I don't remember exactly. Tuna do you remember? You were there."

Tuna thought for a second. Drew couldn't tell if he was only trying to remember or possibly deciding what to say. Drew pushed the point.

"Tuna, que dijo este hombre, diga me por favor, es muy importante mi compañero."

"He said that you had the thing that was in the, how do you call, la caja piedra?"

Drew answered quickly, "the stone box."

"Yes señor. He said you had what was in this box."

"Did he say what he thought that was?"

"No, not to us."

"But Joy knew what he meant," Ree added, "Joy told me you will be famous on the way back here."

"Yes señor," Tuna added enthusiastically, "the same thing he tells me when we walk along the dark river in the ground."

"We have to go back to the place you found me. Tuna can José take us there now?"

"Whoa! cowboy. You're not in any shape to be playing Indiana. The nurse isn't going to permit any adventures until that swelling goes down."

Drew ignored Ree's remark and turned to Tuna, "Go get José and bring him here."

"Sí señor."

When the young Indian was on his way, Drew turned back to Ree.

"Listen to me carefully Ree. I've got to go back. It doesn't matter how I feel. I've got to go back before this Dr. Merchant has a chance to do his work."

"I don't think I understand. What do you think he will find?"

"I'm not sure myself. I found something. He's right about that. It looked like a book. I had it with me when I fell through that hole in the floor. And I had it until right before the bees got to me. It is back there. I know where it is."

Drew took a couple of steps in a small circle. Ree could tell he was trying to collect his thoughts.

"I'm not sure why, but I have to get to this thing before the others. Something tells me that it is important for Tuna's people and the Lacandones. These Indians. This is too strange to believe I know. I am not sure I believe it either."

Drew repeated his little circular dance. "You remember when you asked me back in Texas why I was coming to Mexico?"

"Yes, I remember. You said to save the rainforest.

"I know now that wasn't it. There was something else. It was that message I got before I left." Drew had enlarged his circle and was walking slowly around the tiny grave.

When Drew didn't continue Ree asked, "You mean the message from your friends in Tuxtla?"

"No." Drew stopped and turned to face Ree.

"You're going to think the bees have got into my brain, but it was a message from an owl. I can see it as clear as I did my own death when I lay in that pool. The owl told me to come here."

Ree reached out and cradled Drew's puffed-up hands in her own. "I believe you Drew."

"The old woman that brought me to find you, she knew it also. You know she did. She saw it in your eyes before you left Zapata. She told me that you needed me and to go find you. She knows you have found something too."

Ree took Drew's hands away from her face but didn't release them. "There is something going on here, with both of us that we can't understand. If you think you must go back for whatever it is you left back there in that place in the earth, I think you should. I think we must go back together."

"Good." Drew looked over his shoulder. Back towards the pueblo. He could see Tuna leading José towards them. There was someone else coming as well. Drew could only see that he was very short and dressed in a long white garment. It was the same as most of the Lacandones wore. To Drew it looked like a night shirt. There were no designs or markings on the fabric. Simply white and long.

"There's something else that Socorro said she sees." Drew turned his attention back to Ree. "What's that?"

"She thinks there is trouble coming for me. She says I need you to help me."

"What do you think that means?"

317

"I'm not sure. There's only one kind of trouble that I know of..." Ree cut off her sentence.

"You think our friend has followed you all the way here? I find that a little hard to believe; don't you?"

"Yes."

"Señor Drew; I have brought José as you asked." The three short men stood across from Drew and Ree, on the other side of the tiny grave. The stranger sprinkled some dust-like substance over the turned earth, but he didn't speak. He looked at Drew with eyes that were badly crossed. Drew couldn't focus on his face so he looked away at José who stood motionless. "Tuna, will José take us back to the cave?"

"Si señor. But they say that we must purify the underground when we get there. This man," Tuna motioned toward the cross-eyed little man, "is their *h-man*."

"What?"

"His name is Maxímon señor. He is their priest. He will explain to you and I will translate his words."

As Tuna turned to the odd little man, Socorro appeared on the trail and quietly joined them. Drew held his question until she had reached them. She walked around to the side that Drew and Ree were on and moved calmly between them. The old curandera softly took Drew's arm and indicated she wanted him to face her. Drew complied and looked over the top of the short woman at Ree. He gave a facial sign the best he could, silently asking Ree what was going on. Ree responded with a slight shrug.

Socorro had some more of the sticky stuff Drew had felt on his face when he first woke up after the bee attack. It smelled like allspice to him and was cool as Socorro smoothed it evenly in a thin layer over his forehead and down around his eyes and cheeks. Drew stood there patiently until she had finished. He smiled a thank you and straightened up.

"OK Tuna, what's the deal with the priest?" Before Tuna could answer, Socorro interrupted again. She said a few words to Tuna.

Drew looked around at her and then to Tuna, "What?"

"I do not have time to explain now. Socorro says they come. We must go to the cave before they reach us."

Maxímon and José turned to walk back along the trail.

"Tuna, where are they going?"

"To get the others. We will go now."

Tuna turned to leave and Socorro started around Chica's marker. She stopped and looked back at Ree and smiled. Drew and Ree followed.

Drew turned his head as they walked and looked back over his shoulder, "What others?"

"Beats me," Ree answered.

Down to cases

"WELL, YOU BOTH HEARD DR. CÁRDENAS. I don't have to ask how Joaquín feels about Emilio's plans for Chiapas, but I am curious about your feelings Dr. Alvarez. What do you think?"

"Dr. Boxxloader my feelings are probably as predictable as Sr. Villa's. I cannot support the solutions to our problems in tropical Mexico that come to us from outside. Maybe it's my ego or my national pride, but we have had these programs brought to us before. And quite frankly, they do not achieve much progress. This is even truer as it applies to the Indians. They do not trust their own government or, sadly to say, many of their Mexican compatriots.

They have lived with discrimination and persecution for centuries in these regions. Anyone coming to them with promises of a better life frightens them. Oh, they always smile and nod in agreement. But they never support the programs. Do you understand?"

"Of course I do Dr. Alvarez. I have seen the same thing in my own work around the world. The solutions we bring to these people are all too often one-sided. They are technical solutions. We seem to ignore the social and spiritual aspects of the problem. We come to change things to fit our own model of how the world should be, not to adapt better ways into local customs and practices."

"I absolutely agree. I think you saw when you visited our facilities in Tabasco that we are trying to make the changes that will increase yields in agricultural production by integrating the new methods into the community as a whole. It is the only way. The truth is we may be too late, but still, it is the only way."

"OK, this is what I will support. If you two are willing to cooperate, and make a presentation to the group after lunch, I will force the others to go along and sign our recommendations. Do I have your agreement?"

Alvarez indicated his but Joaquín hesitated. "Dr. Sol, I do not understand what you are suggesting. I did not..."

"I told you I wouldn't support your scheme for an International Research Center in Chiapas and I said exactly the same thing to our friend Cárdenas. I think you heard him say that he has the support of the Governor for his program. This means your idea is dead."

"Yes...but."

"But nothing! Cardenas's program, even with the support of the government, is doomed to failure and eventual obscurity. You know as well as I do, if not better, that without the blessing of the

Catholic Church in these mountains nothing of substance is ever going to happen. I think the Bishop has made that clear to you. So let Cárdenas play his empire building games all he wishes. In four or five years, he might have something going, but it won't amount to much." Boxxloader continued as he took another breath.

"So, what we have to do is start right now in these jungles to address the real reasons the forest is being cut. And that my good friends, from what we have seen is no giant mystery. The forest is being cut to raise corn. Cut to feed a rapidly expanding population of both the locals and the refugees that have fled the political persecution in places like Guatemala and El Salvador. Joaquín are you with me?" Boxxloader waited. Joaquín knew better than to argue with the old man so he simply nodded.

"Joaquín I want you to underwrite a small grant to one of the local communities. Someplace like where that young Indian was from, what's his name?...yes Tuna. Yes, some place like Zapata. I want you to go back to the Bishop and tell him you will fund a start-up project in one of the Indian communities if you can get his blessing and support. Can you do that Joaquín?"

"I guess. How much money are you talking about?"

"At least a hundred thousand. What do you think Alvarez, can we get things rolling with that amount?"

"Yes if we have the support of the locals."

"Wait a minute!" Joaquín raised his voice. "I can't put up that kind of money."

"Yes you can." Boxxloader didn't hesitate. "Don't panic. Let me finish with the first part and I'll show you how this will work." Boxxloader settled back in his chair and intertwined his fingers just under his chin.

"Dr. Alvarez, if our friend here can buy permission to work in this area from the church with his generous contribution," Boxxloader let an almost imperceptible smile cross his lips before he continued, "then will you agree to be the Director of the project for one year?"

"Well..."

Boxxloader interrupted, "With no salary of course." Dr. Boxxloader made eye contact with Joaquín and then locked his gaze on Alvarez and waited.

"Señor, you are asking much of me. You must understand that I have my own work in Tabasco. It is a long hard journey to this remote region of Chiapas. There are many obstacles to working in such a place. For one it is very hard to get good, knowledgeable people to come here, and..."

"Yes, Dr. Alvarez, I know. I have worked under these same limitations all my life."

"I merely wish to make clear my position. I do not want to start something here that cannot be finished. These people have been lied to and disappointed too many times. We have to be able to carry through with what we begin. We must be able to build a trust with the peoples of these mountains."

"I understand. So it is settled. You Joaquín will secure our start-up capital and access, and you Dr. Alvarez will lend your knowledge and experience to help us get organized. Now, this is what I will do when our group reconvenes after lunch."

CHICKEN FEATHERS, WHAT DO I DO?

JOY WAS IN THE PUEBLO WHEN THEY REACHED JOSÉ'S STICK HUT.

"What are you doing here? I thought you went to tell everyone that I am still among the living?"

"Hey mate, I'm not sure you are. You don't look so good."

"Yeah, so I've been told."

"I did go back and tell Dr. Merchant that you are safe. He sent me back to tell you that he will be on his way as soon as colleagues of his arrive. He's not very far away."

Drew grinned. "It's good to see you Irish. Thanks for the rescue."

"It wasn't me mate. Your good-looking friend there is the one who dragged your worthless hide out of that pond. You should have seen all the stingers in your face. You looked like me granny's sewing ball. How do you feel?" Joy moved closer to inspect the damage.

Drew just waved off the question and turned to Tuna, "Let's get started."

"Where to Drew?" Joy pulled back and looked quizzically between Drew and Tuna.

"Back to the scene of the crime. Joy you stick with me. I need to talk to you about something."

"Sure mate. I'll just buzz around you like a bee at the hive."

Drew tried to look angry at the humor, but it was no use.

There were thirteen of them in all. Maxímon took the lead. They were all dressed in the same white cloth sacks. Each one carried a cloth bag draped on a string from their shoulders and a chicken tied by the feet balanced by a bundle of corn on the other end of a rope. These too were draped over their shoulders. Maxímon also had a small turkey tied along with the chicken.

Drew couldn't help thinking they looked like the seven dwarfs plus six as they moved through the thick rainforest. They were all miniature compared to him and Joy; almost a half-a-foot shorter than Ree. José and Tuna came next in the line that ducked and dodged its way through the tangle. Although every one of the Indians had machetes they rarely made a cut. They could usually bend forward slightly and slide through the growth. Unfortunately, the gringos weren't so lucky. Drew winced each time one the branches or vines scraped across his face or arms. He was glad to know they were not far from the cave.

Drew tried a couple of times to turn and ask Joy about this Dr. Merchant fellow, but it was too difficult to talk and keep pace with the ones in front. So he focused his awareness on the sounds of the forest. They were constant and varied. As they broke into the small clearing where Drew had sat under the tree, he figured that he had heard more than 30 different birdcalls over the hour they had walked through the forest.

He was just about to tell Joy of his scientific observation when Maxímon and the six other dwarfs came in a tight circle around Drew and Joy. They all sat down. Maxímon motioned for Tuna and Ree to come inside the circle and he said something to Tuna. Socorro did not join them, but sat down and crossed her legs immediately behind Maxímon.

"He asks us all to sit with them," Tuna explained. "Maxímon will speak for the rest."

Drew started to ask Tuna what was going on in English, but decided to simply let things unfold as they would. His face hurt but he could tell the swelling had gone down as he gently passed his fingers over his tender skin.

As Maxímon pulled a small *incendiario* from his bag and lit incense, Drew looked back at the dark opening. He could hear insects humming. Then the images came, one quickly upon another. The gaping dark mouth in the grotesque jungle stone face; the writings on the walls; untying the rope; Chica splashing in the green pool.

Drew felt sadness suddenly. It came over him like a too warm blanket in a summer sleep. Drew pulled his gaze away from the hole and forced himself to watch Maxímon's hands. Drew again softly ran his fingertips over his face and thought about the sound of the first few bees as they came from the hole. He could see the book, barely visible in the recess under the stone throne.

Drew was only faintly aware of the priest's words. He wondered how long he had been speaking. He turned his head and tried to focus on Tuna.

Tuna's voice became clearer.

"Maxímon says they are very grateful for your long journey from the North and for traveling the Black Road. The messenger, the great monstrous owl has brought you to find the thing we lost many cycles ago and to endure the blackest night in the dark house. You have survived. You have come back from the anger of the Lords of the Underground. You have endured the attacks of the terrible wasps and you still have your heart. Our ancestors have always told us that when we are ready the thing that was lost will return. We will then be able to see the changes that are coming."

Maxímon spoke slowly, in a kind of singsong rhythm. Drew thought he was almost singing his message. The other priests hummed very lowly in harmonious accompaniment.

"We are also grateful, " Tuna translated, "that you have given a sacrifice to the White Sparkstriker of the *adoratori;* the keeper of the cave. The small, brave animal will become stone in the ground and will live with the others in that place."

With those words the old priest passed a small object around the circle. Each of the seven priests took it in turn and said a few words. When the object came to Drew, he held it in his palm and turned the stone carving around in his fingers. It was a four-legged animal.

"Now we must go to the cave. Without delay we must carry on our ceremonies. The Chacs of the rain have been violated. The guardians must be appeased. We must ask them to forgive us, and you, our friend for the disturbance. This must be done so they will not harm you or take the rain from us and not kill our crops bringing hardship upon all of our people."

Maxímon was the first to stand up. Slowly, in unison, the others followed and began to retrieve their small bags and to drape the birds tied with rope over their shoulders. Tuna got up along with Ree and Joy. Drew sat for a moment and looked at the stone animal.

"Come-on mate." Joy reached under Drew's arm to help him up. "Feel like another look at the inside of that place?"

"Do you and Tuna understand what they are talking about? Do you know what they mean by the thing I am supposed to have found in that place?"

Joy answered, "Let me guess. You found something in that stone box, and you know where it is in the cave. Am I warm?" Joy looked at Tuna and back to Ree.

Drew thought a second. "And if I did, what was it?"

326

"The Popol Vuh. None other than the original Book of Counsel of the Quiché Maya written in the ancient hieroglyphic text. At least that is what Dr. Merchant thinks you found. I suspect it is what the priest is talking about too. All eyes are on you mate. It's your game of cricket my lumpy-face friend."

Drew looked at Ree. He wondered if she had said anything to Joy about the book.

"Tell me about this Merchant fellow Joy."

"He's an archaeologist. A pretty savvy one from all appearances. He thinks you have found the Popol Vuh. The guy can read those inscriptions like you would the New York Times. That's why he is desperate to talk to you."

"You said he's on his way?"

"Well, he was coming to the Lacandon village. He's probably there right now wondering where we are. The guy has got the scent. He'll find you soon, of that I'm sure. You want to let me in on any secrets mate?"

"It doesn't seem like much of a secret," Drew pulled the spirit pouch on its leather string out of his shirt. He stuck both fingers in the top and expended the opening. Drew pushed the small stone animal in with the other tiny artifacts and pulled the drawstring tight.

"The book is in the cave. I was putting it in a safe place when the bees got after me. Do you think they have found it?

"No," Joy looked at Tuna and Ree for confirmation. "I don't see how. In the first place it's dark in there. As soon as we found you we just brought you right out. As far as I know, no one has been in there since we left."

"Did you tell Merchant about this entrance?"

"Yes, in a vague sort of way. I told him how we got out. But he doesn't have the foggiest idea where it is. He will come to the same spot where Tuna and I found you if he follows the route we took. You remember all the little rock triangles you built as a road map don't you?"

"Sure, I remember."

Ree joined in, "What's all the mystery about? What's the harm if Dr. Merchant finds out where this book is located?'

"I'm not exactly sure myself. Maybe no harm at all. On the other hand, I can't help thinking if he does locate the book that it will disappear into some museum or, worse, into the private collection of some rich international antiquities dealer."

Drew took a couple of steps toward the entrance and then stopped and turned back to the others.

"Jesus Christ, I don't know. For some reason, I am beginning to believe that I was really supposed to find this thing. Why? Hell if I know. I never have believed in this hocus-pocus stuff. But, for the love of the Irish, this time...I just don't know."

"Thanks mate for the concern. Let me to give you one idea, OK?"

"Sure. Shoot."

"It's what Maxímon said. He said that you have found for them something their people had lost many cycles ago. This book still belongs to these people. Their Mayan ancestors wrote this thing centuries ago. It is their history. Their heritage. Maxímon said it was the proper time." Joy hesitated but Drew kept silent.

"It goes hand in glove with your feeling that you were somehow directed to be in this place at this time. They believe that in the cycle of life there is divine intervention. Your arrival did not surprise Maxímon in the least. He believes you found it because his gods directed you to do so."

Drew nodded. "The priest doesn't feel that way about Dr. Merchant or the rest, right?"

"That's it mate. That's why he is so grateful to you. Do you know why they would have never discovered the Popol Vuh on their own? Because the place you went through is their equivalent of Hell. How many people would choose to take a trip to Hell? You have made it through the mythical underground. You and that little dog are like St. George. You faced down the big bad dragon mate and saved the fair damsel. You brought back the Holy Grail. You're a real hero."

"Yeah sure. Except this time the fair damsel saved me."

"Details, details. Who cares? You've got what legends are made of. That's the point. So now, what are you going to do?"

"I'm going to tell you where it is and go home. That's what I'm going to do."

"Oh no you don't. You paid the price and you get the glory. That's only fair, right Ree?" Joy turned and broke from the tight little circle of discussion.

"What are you going to do?" Ree quietly repeated the question.

Drew looked at the ground and pushed a small beetle along with the toe of his boot. Finally he looked up and let the black insect go on its way.

"Since Joy isn't going to let me punt, I'm not sure. You have any ideas?" Drew put his arm around Ree's shoulder. "I'm not kidding. I'm still your patient. What do I do nurse?"

"Ask Maxímon."

"What?"

"Ask Maxímon. Let's see what they are doing in the cave with the ceremony. Then get Tuna to help you talk with the old priest. Ask him what to do about the book. Like Joy said, the book really belongs to these people."

"You know for a girl you're pretty smart. What do you think Tuna? Is that what I should do about this book?"

"I will help you talk to Maxímon but it is for you to decide."

"OK, so be it. Let's go see what happens next."

WATCH THE SMOKE

THE TORCHES PAINTED THE AREA AROUND THE POOL in an undulating glow that made the walls move back and forth. With the breathing of the cave. Drew began to feel uneasy. Not so much about the cave itself, strangely the enclosed space made him feel protected, but it was the notion of the stinging bees. Every time the book came to mind, the bees came with it. He looked around for the opening that led to the hiding place. *Why don't these people know about the entrance to the altar? Maybe the old priest is right, maybe this place is protected.*

Maxímon and the others were moving around the pool into a circle. Drew and the rest were in the shadows watching in the diffused light the thirteen prepare a small make-shift altar from loose rocks picked up from around the green water. Drew scanned the rock walls again. No opening. It had to be right here.

"Wait!" The single word echoed around the chamber and came back. "Tuna, tell Maxímon to stop. Tell him I need to talk with him before they begin."

They sat in a tight circle for over an hour and talked. Maxímon had lit a bowl of copal that gave off a sweet smell and raised a column of smoke that swayed back and forth like the pendulum of a

330

clock. Maxímon patiently listened saying nothing, until Drew was finished with the story of how he came to find the book and his journey down the underground river. Drew was ready to tell him about the other grand chamber he had found; with the throne and the altar. About the book now protected by the bees, when Maxímon interrupted.

Tuna translated his words carefully.

"Maxímon says he is frightened by what Drew is about to tell him. His people are frightened because they believe they know what the book will reveal. He says that if they do not listen to you they will not have to know what is to follow. They can avoid the teachings if they do not see them. They can live without the certainty of the end."

"The end? What's he mean by that?"

"I don't know señor. But Maxímon has decided you must continue your story."

Drew sat still for a moment and watched the smoke rising. He realized that the priest was giving him the option of revealing the location of the ancient text. Drew could tell that Maxímon really was frightened of what he was about to hear.

Drew turned his head and looked back down the passageway in the area he thought the entrance to the chamber might be. He explained what had happened. Maxímon listened with no emotion. When Drew had finished, the priest closed his eyes and chanted a few words that Tuna said that he didn't understand.

When Maxímon was through he started to stand up, but changed his mind and slumped back down. He said a few words loud enough that the others could hear. In response, Socorro came to the small circle and folded to her knees next to Maxímon. They talked without looking at each other for a time. Then the priest turned his face towards Tuna but kept his eyes on Drew as he spoke. He kept at it for what seemed like hours without pause. At last he stopped. Tuna began the translation.

"This is hard for me to explain señor, but I will try. The priest says you must take the Book. He says that you have the wisdom of the cave now. The *balams,* the guardians, they have entrusted you with the knowledge of the underground and the knowledge of the future. It is yours, not ours. He would like you to share the wisdom with them. But, even this is yours to decide."

"What is he talking about? Tell Maxímon that I found this book by accident. It is theirs. It belongs to him, to his people. Look, I will show them where it is. But it is theirs. Tell him exactly what I said, make him understand. Tell the priest that I won't tell the gringo scientist where it is. Just make sure he understands that they have to get the book away from here."

Drew waited as he imagined how Tuna would phrase all of his instructions. This Indian language was strange. The guttural stops reminded him of the German he had taken in college. The words were nothing like Spanish or anything else. Tuna and the priest talked first one then the other, for what seemed like a long time. When they stopped Maxímon stood up. He reached into his sack, took out a seedpod of some kind, and began to rattle and hum a chant. Slowly, he took steps toward his fellows. Socorro fell in behind him and echoed his sounds. The music they created set the pace of their steps.

Tuna didn't speak until Maxímon had moved away. He was smiling slightly. "Señor, Maxímon says you are now a *balam* in the eyes of his people. You are a guardian."

Drew looked at Tuna waiting for more, but Tuna left it at that, as if it was perfectly clear. "Great! That is just great. I am now a *balam*. You think you could tell me what that means?" Drew didn't like the sarcasms he heard in his voice. He motioned for Joy to join them.

"I want Joy to hear this. He knows more about this stuff than I do."

"What's up mate? Did the old priest tell you what to do with the book?' Joy moved his gaze quickly between Tuna and Drew. Drew hesitated "I'm a *balam* guys."

"Did you say *balam*?" Joy said the word comfortably.

"That's right. Maxímon tells Tuna that I'm a *balam,* and that is not all. I am the keeper of the Book, if that is what I found. Maxímon doesn't want it. He says it is my responsibility. Do you believe this? What is a *balam* anyway?"

"I think it is something that protects the sacredness of this place and its contents. Maybe because you survived you are one."

Drew lowered his chin to his chest and looked at the sand-like soil he was sitting on for a moment.

"Tuna, you've got to convince Maxímon and the whole priestly bunch that I can't do what they ask." Drew offered a pleading look to Joy before he continued. "Help me tell them. I don't even know what's in the damn book. I never even opened it. For all I know, it may not even be the Book." Drew let out a long sigh. He spoke under his breath, to himself. "Damn it, I should have just shot that damn owl and left it at that."

Joy was quick to pick up on Drew's last words, "What owl?'

"Nothing. It's a long story." Drew began to rub his forehead with both hands. He noticed Ree was watching.

"The swelling seems to be almost gone." Other than the remaining crusty residue of the salve medicine Socorro had applied, Drew's fingers felt normal contours. "What am I going to do now?"

Tuna spoke up before the others could answer, "There is something else Maxímon said señor."

"What's that?"

"He told me that you will have to stay here and he will teach you to interpret the words of the Book of Counsel. He will make you a *Daykeeper* and he will help you see the future. You can tell them these things when you learn to read The Book."

"Mate, how lucky can you get. They're going to make a gringo into a Mayan priest. You've hit the jackpot." Drew held up his hand to stop Joy's enthusiastic outburst.

"First, I'm a *balam* or some such thing. Now they want me to be a *Daykeeper*, whatever that is. And all this because I was so wise that I untied my lifeline in a dark unexplored cave which led me to fall through a hole and get stung nearly to death by a bunch of pissed-off bees. Then I lose the best dog I've ever had in my life to this hell hole. And now these little men in white sheets want me to live and learn to be a Mayan priest so that I can read a book that tells them of the end of the world. You're right Joy; I'm the luckiest son-of-a-bitch on the planet. That's good ole Irish logic for you."

"You did come here looking for some meaning in your life," Ree intervened pacing her words evenly, with a strength that caught Drew off guard. "It may not have been exactly what you had in mind when you left your life in Texas."

Drew sat quietly without saying anything for a while. "Tuna, you said something a minute ago I don't understand. You said that I could tell them about the future when I learn to read the words of the Book. Isn't that right?"

"Sí señor."

"Why don't they read the words for themselves? I mean ..."

"Wait a second Tuna. Let me guess," Joy jumped up on his young legs and squatted like a baseball catcher.

"They can't read the ancient texts right?" Tuna didn't answer, only nodded. "Don't you see Drew? This book is no good to them because they have lost the ability to read it. Like all of the glyphs in the cave and on all of the Mayan ruins in these jungles, they don't have the foggiest of what they mean. People like Dr. Merchant can read these things better than the very descendants of the people who wrote them."

With those words he did a spin on the balls of his feet, a full 360 degrees. When he came back to a stop Joy jumped up and shouted, "That's it! That's it!" The words went off down the river and came back in several repeating echoes.

"What's got into you Irish?"

"Listen! Drew listen to me carefully. You can't imagine what a position you are in. You are a living Rosetta Stone. Think about that for a second. You, Andrew Grady Cotton, a broke down city planner or almost political scientist or want-a-be cowboy, have been dropped like some cosmic messenger between the hard science of a man like Dr. Merchant and the ancient spiritual understanding and wisdom of a priest who is a descendent of the Mayan ancients. Oh Mary! I can't believe this! What irony."

Joy couldn't contain his energy. He walked away several steps from the group.

Drew shouted after him, "Come back here Mr. Blarney." Drew got to his feet and looked down at Ree, "You follow this?"

"I think so."

"Look Drew," Joy came back and started again, "don't you see? Maxímon knows in his blood the meaning of that text. He doesn't have to read it. He just knows. But then, all of a sudden, here it is. The writings of his long-dead ancestors. Wouldn't you want to know? But, guess what, ironically the only one that can read these strange drawings, even though not perfectly, is someone like Dr. Merchant. A scientist who thinks like a scientist with facts and theories. To him the world is reducible to parts and pieces. Mechanics. There is no spirit. I should know, I'm training to be one of them."

"Do you really think Maxímon will trust what Merchant tells his people. That is, if he would bother to tell them anything in the first place. Hell-fire mate, they're just Indians in his eyes. But then you come onto the scene cowboy, according to Socorro, sent by a messenger. Believe it or not, that's what they think. Then to top it all you go through Hell and pay the price. Since the Lords of the Underground didn't do you in these people believe that the Lords must have a purpose for you."

Everybody fell silent. The distant chanting continued, filling the space with a slight vibration.

Ree took a step toward Drew and put out her hand. "What are you thinking?"

Drew took her hand and looked into Ree's eyes. "Just wondering."

"About what?"

"Wondering whether Mayan priests have to be celibate." The corners of his mouth turned upward. He turned his eyes from Ree, "Joy will you hang around these parts for awhile to help me out?"

"Do bees sting mate?"

Drew turned back to Ree. "What about you? What's your plan lady?"

"I'm not sure. Suppose I'll have to go back to the real world sooner or later."

"Tuna get Maxímon. Tell him I want to show them where the book is. Alright you guys, come on. There's another hole along that wall somewhere."

Joy picked up two torches and handed one to Drew.

Drew pulled Ree's arm to follow. "Let's talk about your real world when we get back to Tuxtla. I might have a suggestion."

"Really?"

"Really."

CHAPTER 15

SUMIDERO

"WHAT DID MERCHANT SAY? Did he find the boy?"

"Yes, they found him."

"Is he OK?"

"Merchant's not sure. He thinks so."

"What's that mean? What's Mr. Cotton's condition?"

"Joaquín spoke slowly, "Dr. Merchant knows where he is, but he hasn't actually seen him. He said that Joy came back to the cave from a forest pueblo and reported that Andrew was safe. Joy said that he was insect bit or something, but he's alive."

"Where is the closest place we can land your Cessna out there?"

"They have a small dirt strip just outside San Quintín."

"And how far is that from where he is?"

"Not sure, but I don't think it's too far."

"Good. Get back to Merchant on your radio and let's see if we can get Cotton back to Zapata. We'll pick him up there when we fly out of here. It would be wise to get him back and have a doctor take a look at him in Tuxtla muy pronto."

"That plane of yours, will it get us both out of here, right? I mean it can get over the tops of the trees? The strip looks pretty short to me." Boxxloader slid some papers back into a manila folder and stood up.

"It got me here didn't it?"

"Coming down Joaquín is a little easier than going up, no?"

"Some."

"Go get Alvarez. Let's get this thing over with. And Joaquín, find Blanco and tell him to round up the others and make sure Cárdenas gets to the meeting. I want to finish this committee stuff quickly and get out of here before Cárdenas has too much of a chance to play politics with the others. Oh, and Joaquín, can you radio back to Felicia in Tuxtla?"

"Yes, of course."

"Ask her if she would humor an old man one more night. I would love to eat some of Teri's black beans and quesadillas one more time before I head back to the States. I've still got to get on to Africa sometime."

"Sure, she'll be happy to do that for you."

"Joaquín. One other thing."

"Yes."

"You know Cárdenas isn't going to be too happy about what we are about to do. You understand that don't you?"

"Yes, I know. I'm not exactly happy about it myself."

"He could make trouble for you with the Governor here in Chiapas."

"Yes, I figure he probably will. He will not like the competition with his program that the Church will bring. The Governor will not like it either. But you know Mexico Dr. Sol. What can I do? Either we try to make a difference or we don't. Qué sera, no?"

Boxxloader finished stowing his documents.

"You really wanted that International Center for Chiapas didn't you? You know, we never did have that drink. Were you ever going to tell me the real reason for all of this down here?" Boxxloader stopped for a second. "You want to tell me now? Before we set all of this in motion."

"What's the use?" Joaquín started to walk away and then hesitated. He looked back at the old professor over his shoulder. "I suppose God changed his mind. I'll get the others."

Boxxloader watched his former student walk away, Joaquín's shoulders slumped a bit more than usual.

SWEEP UP BEFORE YOU GO

DR. MERCHANT WAS SITTING ON A SMALL STOOL and JonKing had the line framed in his 400 millimeter lens as the men broke through the clearing and walked onto the common area of the small pueblo. Drew knew who the stranger was from the logic of it. Joy saw him too and he turned his head without breaking stride and looked back mouthing Merchant's name. Drew shook his head slightly in recognition.

All the wide-eyed children stopped their play and stared with dark eyes as the line from the jungle passed. The women kept their heads down sneaking furtive angled glances, seeing but not being seen.

The air was thick, humidity hung about bodies like fog on a pond. The early afternoon sun attacked everything under its domain giving it the feel of a sauna.

Drew carried his fatigue like a sack. He was breathing heavy and suffering from a mild onslaught of asthma. A cold beer and a hemaca sounded very good to him but that would have to come later. Tiredness had pushed up his legs into his lower back, and now that he could see Merchant, he felt the weariness move into his shoulders.

As Dr. Merchant approached, Drew's thoughts drifted back to the ceremonies under the torch light in the cave that had moved in slow motion. He had imagined the Lacandon priest would go ballistic when they saw the altar of the ancients but that did not happen. The thirteen men shrouded in their white sacks gathered staidly, equidistant around the tower of the natural altar and went about their priestly business. They removed objects from their cotton bolsas and placed each thing carefully at the base.

Just out of the torch light, Drew, Joy and Ree stood watching. Tuna and Socorro stood just behind the priests but took no part. Drew kept his eyes glued on the altar. He waited for the bees to return and to scatter all of them like chaff before a stiff wind. The stone column that rose to the cave's ceiling was much bigger than he recalled. With the surrounding light and men moving under its mass, Drew could see nature's throne carved out of pitted rock. From where he stood, he could make out the dark opening at the base. He took Joy's arm and pointed at it. Joy asked if that's where he had hidden the book. Drew nodded that it was.

Joy stepped out of the shadows and said something to Tuna. They both came back and joined Ree and Drew. Joy wanted a description. They had barely turned back toward the altar when it began.

Tuna sat on his haunches. Everyone followed his cue. A curious prayer-like chant began to fill the chamber from all of the Indians seated cross-legged around the altar. Maxímon moved slowly among them swinging a metal box in a pendulum motion dispersing the smoke of incense.

Tuna softly repeated the melodic words of the prayer song as they were sung. "Lords, come these ones of the corn humbly. In the three we honor the thrice honored. The words come to the Lords, my Lord K'ulu Balam greatly named as the ancestor of the men of corn. The creator of the wooden people. The cooler of the warmth, my Lord be honored."

Twenty-seven times the words were repeated. Tuna said they would placate the gods who have been offended by the disturbance to the peacefulness in the darkness of The Underground. The priests paused only long enough between chants to take a drink from small gourds of a bittersweet beverage made from corn gruel and honey. Then they resumed the chanting.

Joy was getting anxious. He wanted to know when they would retrieve the book. Tuna said he didn't know. That it all must be done in the proper way. Maxímon would determine that. He would take the book from the altar when it was the proper time.

Drew had drifted off to sleep as the chants droned on. He was dreaming of the croaking sounds that the frogs made as they anticipated the rain. Maxímon's hand touched his forehead lightly. Drew came back suddenly and he saw seven boys now seated between the thirteen priests. They were imitating the frogs and tree toads of the rainforest. Tuna whispered that they were earthly messengers from Chac the maker of the rain. The croaks were interspersed with the priestly chants that continued. It was a chorus of high-pitched croaking and clicking, punctuated by the monotonous prayers of the elders.

Tuna whispered that it was time to see The Book. He said that Maxímon would lead. Drew couldn't help but ask about the bees. As if he understood, Maxímon spoke to him. Tuna translated.

"There are no bees in the altar. The old priest says the Lord of the Sun has released the terrible wasps from his service. They now have retired to the forest."

Drew reluctantly moved to the altar with Maxímon. They walked into the circle. The chants and croaking went on without notice of their movement. Two stone steps were visible. Drew didn't remember them. He took the first and his eyes made contact with the treasure. This he did remember. The binding was just like before. He looked at Maxímon seeking permission, but Maxímon's eyes were also on the hole. Drew looked back toward Joy, Tuna, and Ree. They were not there. They were lost in the shadows. The pumping in his chest was uncomfortable, but as he became aware of the pressure it melded with the clicks and frog sounds and disappeared.

Drew wanted, needed directions. His request went unanswered. He was offered no signal; black eyes simply stared at the ground. There was no sound to be heard, no look to be seen, and no connection to be made. Drew bent slightly at the waist and grasped the bound book with both hands. He heard the bark of a dog outside the cave. The chanting and croaking and clicking started again but there were no bees.

The sweeping went on for at least an hour. Everyone swept with the bush branches. Tuna said it was urgent to sweep the evil spirits from the grotto. Joy swept the fastest of them all. Everyone paused at the entrance. Tuna said the priests would seal it with their words. No one may enter this place for two passings of the moon hence, Tuna explained as Maxímon led again the prayers. Whoever would enter before then would be at grave risk from the guardians. They all gathered to leave.

May I see it?

"MR. COTTON. I PRESUME?" Merchant said in greeting. Drew and Joy made momentary eye contact and exchanged smiles at the use of the phrase.

"Yes, that's right. Dr. Merchant?" The two men shook hands.

"Good to see that you are all right. Do you need medical attention?"

"No, thank you. I have my private nurse with me.

"Now that I've seen you for myself let me contact Dr. Boxxloader back at Bonampak. They are anxious to hear. I believe they are planning to fly in to San Quintín and pick you up."

"Oh?"

"Sr. Villa has his plane at the ruins. Let me confirm. It'll only take a minute. I'm very anxious to speak with you about your experience."

"Dr. Merchant, if you will excuse me, I am a little tired. Let me catch my breath and get a bit of sleep."

"Certainly. It's just that I believe we have made a very important discovery, or rather, I should say, you have made a very important discovery. We need to make plans. You understand, I'm sure?"

"I'll meet with you in an hour. Come to the hut of José. It is the third one over this rise."

"Very well Mr. Cotton. Oh! Mr. Cotton. Do you have it with you?"

"In an hour Doctor."

"But, of course."

SOBREVIVENCIA

ALVAREZ WAS CONCISE AND EFFICIENT, he didn't waste words. The idea would be considerably simpler than Dr. Cárdenas's. No global strategy. No swarm of technicians. No extended research. Although he did not say it, no bureaucracy.

He described the problem in one word. Sobrevivencia. "The rainforest are disappearing because the people in and around them, the indígenas, cut the trees to make land to grow corn. They cut them to build shelter. They cut them to fuel their cooking fires or to shield the bodies of their children from the mountain cold. They do these things to survive," he explained. "They do these things for their families. It's that simple." he said.

"But when they cut the trees," Alvarez continued, "the wooden people as they call themselves, they do something the commercial loggers in every rainforest from the Amazon to Sarawak do not do. They ask for permission. Not permission as we normally think of it. Not the permission of the government or the state. They ask the permission of the tree. They pray to its spirit, its essence. They seek its willingness to sacrifice so that the family of the indígeno might use it and survive."

Dr. Alvarez paused for a long moment before he continued.

"Don't you see gentlemen? There is little utility in talking global warming to these people. There is no use in pleading with them not to cut the trees because the hole in the ozone is ruining vacation spots. They do not know of the melting ice cap and the rise in ocean levels that may, according to some doomsday scenarios, inundate the great coastal cities of the United States and Europe. They cannot count the one hundred species a day that scientists say are being driven into extinction. These are arguments for lecture halls, for stimulating banter at cocktail parties, for fund raising presentation to patriarchal foundations."

"To make matters worse, we have in the last two decades created tremendous pressure on the capacity of the region with uncontrolled population growth, and exacerbated the situation further with refugees fleeing persecution and war in Guatemala. For over five hundred years, the Indians have been driven deeper into the mountains and have been expected to survive on their own. They have been allowed to occupy the land that no one else wanted. It was jungle, the green hell. But now we are slowly coming to the conclusion that the green hell is vital to the survival of us all. Now we are suddenly interested."

Alvarez had become agitated as he spoke but he calmed himself before he continued. "It is about preserving a way of life and a forest. It is literally about survival. That's it. That is the problem as I see it."

Dr. Emilio Cárdenas shifted his chin from his left hand to his right. Dr. Boxxloader didn't wait for any other comment.

"So what do you propose we do? What do you want the Boxxloader Committee to recommend to the government here and to the outside world?"

Alvarez hesitated a moment without offering a response. He folded his manila folder and sat down.

"We ask these people in the highlands and in these forests. We ask the people for the solution." He paused again, for nearly thirty seconds.

"We ask their permission to come and help. We bring people here and have them stay for a time to gain local wisdom. We observe and learn. Then we apply the full range of knowledge from our own research and what we know will work. Apply it only where appropriate. And where it is not, we use what these people know of this world. In short, we look at the plight of the Lacandon Selva through the eyes of the indígenos, we listen with their ears, we touch with their hands and we feel with their hearts, this place."

"I think then, and only then, we will be able to bring resources to the situation. Maybe that resource is as simple as a better way to store the grain. Maybe it's a water wheel to mill the sugar cane or corn. Maybe it is a solar cooker or composter. Simple, useful and appropriate technology is what I propose. With their permission and help, together we can discover a better way in the forest."

"Bravo! Bravo!" Cárdenas got up from his chair and moved to the front.

"A very stirring delivery my friend; very stirring indeed. There is only one minor flaw in your plan."

Boxxloader interceded on Alvarez's behalf, "And that is?"

"There will be no money for this approach. There will be no support from the government. There will be no recognition for the people who come here to work. That is, assuming you can attract competent people for such work. These Indians, of whom you so graciously speak, in reality have no say in the matter; they are pawns to the ebb and flow of world politics. A world that has long ago discounted any value that they may possess. Harsh words to your sympathetic ears I suspect, but the truth nevertheless. In the words of the accountant they are marginal. How do they put it? Externalities. Dr. Alvarez, in short, these people that you, quite nobly I concede, wish to enlist in your crusade do not, like the world you put them in for all intents and purposes, exist."

Dr. Cárdenas sat down. The drone of the tree cicadas outside was heard by all for the first time in nearly an hour. Before Boxxloader or any other spoke Cárdenas spoke again.

"Dr. Alvarez, please do not take my comments as an attack on your person or your reputation. That it is not my intention. Merely I disagree with your logic and your approach. Even though, I must concede that your facilities and work in Macuspana are impressive and inspirational. For this, I salute you señor. But I believe you are fundamentally wrong. You are attempting to treat a global hemorrhage with a band-aid. The only chance we have, the only chance, is to bring into play all of the resources available from the very sources that you accuse of being callous and unfeeling."

Cárdenas stopped and then looked at Dr. Boxxloader. He went on. "So let us complete our work quickly. I wish to return to Tuxtla as soon as possible. I'm sure we all have other pressing business to attend to, yes?"

"I suppose we do," Boxxloader responded. "Dr. Alvarez, Joaquín do you have anything to add?"

Dr. Alvarez stood up to collect his papers and then stopped himself. "I would like to make one final comment Dr. Boxxloader."

"Certainly."

"I believe that when all of our technologies have been tried, all of our chemicals used and all of our machines exhausted, they will still plant their rows of corn asking permission of the sun and the earth to produce their sustenance. They will remain."

Bitchy bitchy

INTRODUCTIONS HAD BEEN MADE ALL AROUND before they all gathered around a table with two split log benches arranged opposite one another. Merchant sat on one, Drew on the other. Joy on Drew's right and Ree on his left. JonKing sat to the side with his long legs crossed straight out in front, his camera rested in his lap. Merchant had a young graduate assistant next to him. He introduced her but Drew didn't catch the name. He thought it sounded Russian. She looked a little ragged out. She stared at the floor and didn't speak. Her stringy hair formed a privacy curtain over her features.

Tuna and Socorro stood near in the opening, their features invisible, with the sun forming a halo around their bodies. Two dogs reclined just inside the shade of the thatch covering. José stood on one leg against a frame timber in the shadow of the corner. The smolder from the cooking fire rose next to him. The smoke looking for an opening in the thatch.

Dr. Merchant said Sr. Villa and Dr. Boxxloader would be at the small airstrip in a couple of hours. They wanted Drew to fly back to Tuxtla-Gutiérrez with them. They thought a doctor should look at his injuries and make sure he was all right. With that piece of business over he said he would like to hear the story.

But before Drew could begin, Merchant thought of something else. "Oh, I almost forgot. Ms. Taylor, Sr. Villa also sent a message for you. He said to tell you that your brother had arrived in Tuxtla and would wait for you there."

"My brother?"

"Yes." Ree and Drew looked at each other.

"Now Mr. Cotton, please tell me about the cave."

Drew tried to give a shortened version of what happened but the archaeologist insisted on hearing it all. He was polite and listened. He saved his questions. Sporadically he made notes in a black leather covered pad. He made a pronounced gesture every time he closed it, like he had recorded some important fact for posterity. He always stuck the pencil behind his right ear. All but the eraser disappeared in his bushy, gray streaked brown hair. Although he smiled, Drew didn't like the appearance of it. For that matter, he didn't like the man.

"Why did you go back?" Merchant asked.

Drew was honest and he did not try to conceal anything. He went into as much detail as he thought necessary. Merchant wrote furiously as Drew described the Book. He attempted to create a verbal picture of the ceremony and the appearance of the natural throne in the chamber. Twice Drew asked Joy to fill in.

"Where is it Mr. Cotton?" Dr. Merchant finally asked the long anticipated question. The graduate assistant suddenly looked up.

"You mean the Book? Drew responded."

"Yes, the Popol Vuh. Is it here?" The interjected question of the grad assistant came across as edgy and cold. Drew noticed that Merchant touched her briefly with as little movement as possible.

"As you might expect Mr. Cotton, we are a bit anxious to get a look at it. I think you can appreciate our excitement."

"That I can Doctor."

"So?"

"So, it's not here," Drew said with little emotion.

JonKing recrossed his legs like pine boards. One old worn-out Vietnam issued boot on top of the other. He put his camera on the bench next to him and took out his Camel filters. He and Drew locked gazes as he blew out the first puff of smoke. One of the dogs barked and ran outside. Everyone jumped.

"It's safe," Drew said.

"I beg your pardon?"

"I said it was safe, Dr. Merchant."

"Mr. Cotton maybe I need to explain something to you." The smile was gone. "The Popol Vuh is potentially the most important antiquity of the entire scientific exploration of the Mayan culture. If the book is as complete as I believe it to be, based on your description, we will finally be able to interpret the Mayan language in its entirety. Can you grasp the significance of that Mr. Cotton?"

"Yes."

"Well?"

Well what?

"Look. There is something else that you should be aware of Mr. Cotton." Drew was glad he never told Dr. Merchant to call him Drew. The graduate assistant stood up and moved behind the bench. She stood straight as a Marine sergeant with her arms at her

351

side. Drew cut his eyes up at her and noted the aggression in her eyes.

"What you have does not belong to you. Fact of the matter, it does not belong to any of us. The Popol Vuh is covered by Mexican law. It is a found antiquity, which means it belongs to the Mexican government. Follow me?"

Professor Merchant waited for a response, but Drew didn't offer one. Merchant finally went on. "Furthermore, if you do not turn this over to us you will be in violation of the law. Does the old priest have it?"

"No."

Dr. Merchant exhaled long and hard. He looked first at Joy then at Ree, and finally at JonKing. Whatever he was looking for he didn't find. "The rest of you know that the authorities will consider you all accessories in this matter, don't you?"

Drew made an attempt to explain. He said that he realized how important his find was, and that everything was all a bit overwhelming.

With that comment, the graduate assistant took two quick steps over the bench and stood over Drew. "You have no idea what you're talking about. Who do you think you are? What makes you think you have a right to the Book? We can get you put so deep in a Mexican jail that any light you see will look like stars and take about as long to reach you. Now where is the Book?"

Merchant didn't intervene.

"Dr. Merchant I have a plan of action I would like to discuss," Drew finally said never taking his eyes off the graduate assistant standing over him. "But first, if you don't get this rag out of my face I'm going to knock it on its academic ass.

Merchant jumped up as if someone had spilled hot coffee in his lap. "Now! Now! Come on! There's no need for this." He instructed the woman to sit down in a stern voice.

It took Drew only about two minutes to outline his plan. He had no sooner finished his suggestions when he heard the Cessna 182 power up and come in low over Zapata. It was a good excuse to end the meeting Drew thought. "Sounds like we have guests," he said. Ree followed close behind as did Joy and they all vacated the hut.

Dr. Merchant tried to stop Drew from leaving with another question, but the three left the hut.

GEAR UP, FLAPS DOWN

WELL MY BOY LOOK AT YOU? Jokes were passed around at Drew's expense. Drew just grinned and backed up to the sleek Cessna's fuselage and rubbed on the identification letters POM-42.

Boxxloader congratulated Dr. Merchant on the rescue. Merchant began to explain that he couldn't take the credit but Boxxloader wasn't interested in detail and walked away. The professor wrapped Joy in his arms and gave him a strong hug. They walked a few feet away from the group arm-in-arm.

Joaquín made a cursory inquiry into Drew's state of health. Drew responded in kind. Acting as if Drew had been a part of the committee for the last week, Joaquín began reiterating point by point the changes that had been made from the original plan. They would write a grant to the Rockefeller Foundation immediately, he said. Dr. Boxxloader would guarantee acceptance. He had already talked to the Mexican rep via radio patch from Bonampak to Mexico City. Drew pretended to listen.

Joaquín was still talking when Drew noticed Cárdenas talking with Dr. Merchant and JonKing near the plane. Drew could see Dr. Merchant motion with his head toward his direction underscoring his words with gestures. Cárdenas looked his way as well.

Ree had joined Joy and Boxxloader. They had moved under the shade of a tree and were laughing. Joy was frantically swinging his arms around his head. Drew figured he was telling Boxxloader about the bees and the book.

Drew wanted to join the fun. Ree looked comfortable as he watched her help Joy out with the explanation he was giving the old man. She had adapted to this place better than he had. The serape she wore around her shoulders must have been a gift from Socorro, he thought. Drew was anxious to spend some alone time with her and find out what she was going to do. He wondered what she thought about his suggestion to Dr. Merchant. Joaquín was still talking but Drew wasn't paying any attention. He was slowly moving towards the shade trees and Joaquín, caught up in his own schemes, was moving with him. Suddenly a word caught in Drew's ear. He stopped and turned with a jerk.

"What did you say?"

"About the computers? I said..."

"No. About Ree's brother?"

"Oh! Him. I just said that Felicia told me on the radio this morning that we had better get that man out of her life or there would be hell to pay. You know she's still upset you brought that woman with you."

"Her name is Ree."

"Yes. But really Drew the brother has caused Felicia some headaches."

"What kind of headaches?"

"He just comes by the ranchito several times a day and wants to know if you have returned yet. She said he frightens Domingo and the other servants. He has a pistola in his belt. She saw it once when she talked with him at the second gate. Felicia says. Tenga cuidado. You know how Felicia can be, no?"

"Yes, I know."

"I've got the woman's visa."

Joaquín could see that he had surprised Drew. "I got notified it was waiting in Tuxtla by radio. I know those people at the consulate." Drew noted the pride in Joaquín look and words.

"So now she can go back to the United States as soon as we get back to Tuxtla. She can take that brother with her, no?"

Drew started to tell him that he didn't think she had a brother, but thought better of it.

They were almost to Boxxloader and his party under the trees when Joaquín stopped him again.

"You will ride back with us in my airplane. The others can get the cars and drive back as they came, via Ocosingo. We must start quickly because of Cárdenas. I will explain further when we get back."

"I'm riding back with the others. I'll meet you in Tuxtla in two days. We need to talk about some things, Joaquín, and I need the time to think. A lot has happened since we last talked."

"No, no, no! You have to come back with us! We will leave in a few minutes and be back in Tuxtla in an hour. A doctor needs to look at you."

Drew knew that Joaquín only thought of the doctor as an argument.

"No. I'll see you in two days. He started walking toward Ree and looked back over his shoulder. "Two days," Drew said emphatically.

Joaquín started to follow, but Cárdenas with Dr. Merchant at his heels stopped him. Drew didn't hear any of it.

Dr. Boxxloader shook Drew's hand again. "They've been telling me about your adventures Andrew. I'm envious. You know they make movies out of these kinds of stories."

"Yeah, horror flicks."

"Dr. Boxxloader would you have a minute to talk with me and Joy about something?" Drew looked at Joy and Joy nodded. "We may be in a little trouble over this adventure as you call it."

"Oh really. What kind?"

"If you will, Dr. Boxxloader..."

"That's Sol. Call me Sol. At my age I've gotten pretty sick of all the formality."

"OK, Sol. Ree, maybe you had better come with us. Let's go back to Zapata."

As they walked away Drew and Boxxloader noticed Joaquín and Cárdenas waving them to come to the plane. Boxxloader ignored them and so did Drew.

"What kind of trouble son?" he asked. "Joy tells me you're some kind of holy man now. What kind of trouble could a holy man have?"

Drew didn't answer. He didn't even smile.

They met the graduate assistant on the trail as they approached Socorro's hut. She didn't look up. Nobody spoke.

"Who is that?" Boxxloader said under his breath looking back.

"That's part of what we want to talk to you about," Joy said.

¿SON TODOS LISTOS?

THEY WATCHED THE PLANE STRUGGLE INTO THE SKY from the porch of the tiendita at the end of the rutted runway. Everybody sipped on Coca-Cola from a bottle. Drew could tell by the sound of the engine that Joaquín had overloaded the Cessna once again. They all stepped off the low porch and looked at the plane ascend. None of the men in the plane waved at those on the ground. Everybody on the ground waved at those in the plane. Drew could see Dr. Merchant in the back seat.

"Did you see that streamer coming from the right side of the plane?" Drew leaned hard against Joy and made him spill Coke on the front of his shirt.

"Hey! See what mate?"

Drew watched the plane reach an angle just above the horizon were it appeared to stop in mid-air. He could follow the thin line of mist from just behind the wing next to the cabin almost to the runway. "Oh, nothing," he said finally. "Never mind. Hey Irish, you spilled Coke on your shirt."

"No kidding."

Merchant's graduate assistant stood like a sentry a few yards away from the rest.

"What next mate?" Joy asked.

"JonKing!" Drew stepped back onto the porch, handed his empty to an Indian boy with only one arm, turned, and began walking in the opposite direction from where the graduate assistant stood. "JonKing, let's talk."

Joy hung close to Drew's side as he turned and waved for Ree and Tuna to follow. They all settled under the umbrella of a guanacaste tree. Drew leaned his back against the trunk.

"I think I'm in deep shit," he said. No one offered argument. "My bet is that the next time we see Dr. Merchant he will be with Federales. Little Miss Sunshine over there is going to stay and work on Maxímon after we leave."

"You don't think that Merchant bought your idea?"

"No. If he had he wouldn't be in that plane to Tuxtla-Gutiérrez. He only wants the Book. No substitutes."

JonKing squatted and lit a Camel. "From my perspective, I thought it was a good compromise. I mean, Merchant and his Mayanist get the pictures of the book and Maxímon's people get to keep the original. Sounded fair to me."

"Yeah, fair. But fairness is an alien concept to those archaeologists. They want artifacts with their science not morals. The desires of Maxímon do not show up in their rulebook." Drew exchanged the right foot with the left against the tree and picked up a dry stem of grass. He stuck it between his teeth.

He continued, "We're not going to wait for his decision or permission. I'm going to protect my ace in the hole." He looked down at his boots and took the grass stem out of his mouth.

"JonKing I've got to have your word that I can trust you on this one. You follow?" Drew looked out of the shade to the landing strip. He could no longer see the graduate assistant. His eyes scanned the area. "Do I have it?"

"Of course, you've got it. But, I want something in return. If I'm going to a Mexican jail I want a little compensation."

"You're not going to any Mexican jail. None of us are. Instead, we're going to be a day late back to Tuxtla. JonKing, how much film do you have left?"

"What kind?"

"All kinds."

"Well, I'll have to do a quick inventory but I think I have enough 35 mm to do another *National Geographic* feature and a few flats of Polaroid, why?"

"Good. Tuna I need you to find a way to lead our graduate assistant friend on a wild goose chase through the Selva for a few hours. Do you understand?"

"Yes señor. I will talk to José."

"Tuna tell Maxímon to meet us in front of Socorro's hut as soon as José gets Natasha away from the pueblo. Tell him we are going to the lugar del escondido, ¿entiendes?"

"Sí señor, perfectamente."

"Bueno."

"What about the others, Santiago and those guys from Bonampak," Joy said.

"Let them go on back to Ocosingo. You, me, Ree and JonKing can ride back in the Jeep tomorrow. Tuna is going to stay here."

"We're going to photograph the entire Popol Vuh in 35 mm film. That's your *Geographic* layout JonKing along with the pictures you took in the cave. Got it?"

"Now you're talking man," he said and lit another Camel off the short butt that still burned.

"We'll do some sampling with the Polaroid. JonKing, you will take those out on the next plane back to the States as soon as we set foot in Tuxtla. A few teasers for the folks back home. Follow?" A chorus of head bobbing signaled universal agreement.

"The Book will not leave these people. The science crowd can have the photographic evidence. The world gets the knowledge of the Mayan people and I get to keep my vows to Maxímon, and they keep what belongs to them. No gringo or Mexican museum for the Popol Vuh. It is going to live and teach were it began. Who knows, we might actually learn something ourselves."

When Drew paused Ree walked up to him and put her arms around him and pulled him to her.

"Hey, hey, hey! What's this?" She didn't answer and after a moment she turned and walked back out into the sunlight and looked towards the mountains that ringed the Lacandon Selva.

Joy broke the scene. "What about the Mexican authorities Drew? They might not think your idea is so great."

"Probably not. We will just have to play it out and see." He turned to JonKing. "How much clout do you think the *Geographic* can offer us?"

"Just don't tell the Mexicans where it is when they torture you. I think in the long run the whole scientific and journalistic communities will make such a stink that you'll survive."

"Thanks for the encouragement. I feel a lot better. No matter, we're going to do it. ¿Son todos listos?"

Joy wrapped his arm around Drew as they joined Ree in the sun. "Un gran adventura, ¿no?"

"Your Spanish is getting better Irish."

"Sí señor, por cierto... padre."

THEY LET JONKING OFF AT THE AIRPORT. Drew gave him a thumbs up. The lanky photographer did the same and pushed backward through the double glass doors into the lobby of the Tuxtla-Gutiérrez International Airport.

Drew let Joy out in front of the Flamboyant Hotel and asked him to get rooms. He and Ree would be back after they visited Joaquín and Felicia in a couple of hours.

"You ready for this?" he said.

Ree only shook her head in agreement but didn't speak.

"You scared?"

She looked back from watching Joy disappear into the Flamboyant and gazed through the caked mud-covered windshield. "I think you asked me that once before."

"That I did. A few light years ago, back in a strange place called Alice, Texas if my memory serves me right."

"It does sir." She turned and met his eyes. "It does."

She smiled the way he liked to see her smile.

"You could stay here with Joy and let me slay the dragon for you. I'll get your visa from Joaquín and tomorrow we can get you on a plane back to the North Country. You wouldn't have to face Buddy again."

"You've got your own dragons to slay Sir Drew."

"That's my concern."

"Thanks. But if the son-of-a-bitch is going to follow me all the way to southern Mexico, what's next. I had better get it behind me."

"I reckon. What's the plan?"

"I don't know. Just make it up as I go."

"OK señorita, vámonos a matar el dragón."

MUY TRISTE

THE OUTER GATE WAS CHAINED AND LOCKED. No sign of anyone in or around the compound. No gardener, no stable people, no housekeepers moving between buildings with laundry or brooms and mops. Nothing stirred as Drew and Ree peered down the quarter mile of tree-lined driveway that terminated at the second gate. From what Drew could see, it looked closed and chained too.

"I've never seen this gate locked before. Wonder what's going on. Let me check the lock to see if it's fastened," Drew said as he got out.

Ree watched him pull at the steel links and saw that they didn't budge. She felt a slight tremble and her forearms were blanketed with chill bumps. She was glad the gates were locked. She figured it meant that Buddy wasn't here.

Drew walked around to her side and leaned down to Ree's eye level. "I'm going to jump the gate and walk down to the main house." He looked quickly down the entrance road and then back at Ree. "Something's going on. I'll be back in a minute. You be all right waiting here?"

"Sure."

Ree could see Drew talking with Domingo through the bars of the second gate. Domingo opened it after a word or two and both of the figures disappeared from her view behind the lemon trees and bougainvillea. Ree passed the time looking through Drew's Pemex road map of Mexico. She let her fingers follow the route from Reynosa to Tuxtla. She wondered how many miles they had come. Drew had told her but she couldn't remember. It looked like a long way. Then she tried to locate Zapata and the Lacandon Rainforest and any other names she had heard over the last two weeks. She located Ocosingo but Zapata wasn't there. And what she thought might be the jungle was labeled Montes Azules. Ree didn't know what that meant. The Mayan ruins at Bonampak were on the map. She wanted to see that place sometime.

Drew's boots made a thump as he jumped back over the front gate. Ree looked up as Drew slid into the driver's seat. He was holding a white envelope. She could see Andrew Cotton written on one side.

"This is really strange," he said.

"What is? That was Domingo you spoke with, right?"

"Yes."

"What did he say? Where is everybody?"

"He wouldn't say for sure, just that there was no one here. He said señora had left this for me." Drew held up the envelope.

"What about Buddy. Did he say anything about Buddy?"

"I asked him. He just said no aquí, no aquí. Not here. He seemed really nervous. I've never seen Domingo nervous. Like I said, it's strange."

"Why don't you open the envelope?"

The letter was written on two pages of yellow paper in Spanish. Drew read it aloud, translating as he went,

> To our friend Andrew,
> I am very sorry. I have gone to Mexico City to be with family. There is no one to receive you at the ranch. I hope that you will be able to care for yourself.
> It has been a terrible day in my life and I am very sad. The day that has passed will forever change my family and

the lives of many people who knew Joaquín and Dr. Solomon Boxxloader and the two other men. I will not write the details of the accident here, Jorge will explain to you whatever you wish to know. Jorge will be at the office in town.

I am very sad this day Andrew. There was not even a piece of Joaquín to take with me for the burial next to his father and his mother in Mexico City.

I think in a way I caused this to happen. I told Joaquín on the radio before he left the ruins of Bonampak that he would have to stop these games he played with these men of science. He would only fail again. I told him that he must let this Dr. Cárdenas have his way. He was very disturbed with me on the radio after I told him these things. I should have waited for him to return home before I said these things to him. I was wrong and I will have to live with that.

It is over now. It has happened for whatever reason and we will have to live with the way things will be from this time on.

I must also tell you that I had the authorities arrest that woman's brother. I had no choice in this matter. He came to my house after I received the terrible news about my husband and screamed terrible things at us. He is an ugly man. He is in jail in the city. You should have not brought that woman to my house. You brought her trouble with you.

I have placed in the envelope the woman's visa that Joaquín had arranged with the Mexican authorities.

Everything is in order and she will have no trouble in passing from Mexico. Her brother is a different matter. I would like to thank you for the help you gave my husband.I have enclosed a check for some money. It should be enough to get you home.

With much affection,
Felicia Sanchez Gonzalo Villa

Drew removed the visa and the check. He looked at the letter for a moment and slid it back into the envelope.

"What does it mean?" Ree said.

Drew put his hand on the ignition keys and looked down at the silver Un Peso coin dated 1944, that hung from a silver chain. "You know Joaquín gave me this for my birthday a few years back," he said as he fingered the coin. He started the Jeep and backed out into the road and headed back toward the city center.

As they bounced over the first of four topes that slowed traffic in front of the Pemex refinery, Ree repeated her question.

"I think we better go talk with Jorge," Drew said.

POPPA-OSCAR-MIKE

JORGE FILLED IN MOST OF THE GAPS. At least as far as anyone knew.

"The only piece they found was a wing. A campesino riding a burro close to the edge of the Sumidero Canyon had spotted something silver with POM in blue letters floating in the Grijalva nine hundred meters below. He had sent his hijo the five miles to the highway to get help."

Jorge said that is all they recovered. The river is very deep and inaccessible at that point. It would have been impossible to search the bottom.

"There was no debris, no bodies, nothing else. Just the wing." Jorge noted that the authorities said there were still many alligators in the river. They probably disposed of the remains.

Drew asked Jorge about the cause of the crash but he said they couldn't be sure. Jorge knew that Joaquín had had trouble with a fuel line on his way to Palenque for the meeting. Joaquín had wanted to have it checked out but there was no one there who could see to such a problem on a Cessna. Joaquín had decided that he would wait until he returned to his mechanic in Tuxtla. Drew didn't bother to mention the stream of fuel mist he saw when the four left the dirt landing strip near San Quintín.

How they ended up in the river at the bottom of the Sumidero Canyon was another matter. Jorge could not be sure but he knew that sometimes Joaquín liked to fly his guests along the river in between the vertical walls of the canyon. Joaquín would always wear his cap that displayed *Top Gun* embroidered on the front when he did these things. "¿Quien sabe?"

The two talked for a long while and drank two pots of coffee that Annabel graciously provided. She and Marta sat with them and listened as Jorge spoke his broken English and Drew asked questions in Spanish. It was a habit they started sometime back to give them both a chance to practice. Every once in awhile Drew would go over what Jorge had said with Ree.

They talked about what would happen now with the rainforest work. Jorge described what had been decided before the group left

Bonampak. About the small project Joaquín would fund in Zapata and modeled after the work of the Catholic Church in San Cristóbal.

"But now," Jorge said, "I don't know. There is no money without Joaquín. There is only enough for two more weeks for the office, for our salaries. There is no direction for us, he said sadly. "La Señora no tiene interés."

Drew saw the moisture well into the man's eyes but no tears fell. Marta got up abruptly and went and sat in front of her computer starring into the screen. Drew looked into the black hole of his coffee cup and gave Jorge some time.

Without being asked Jorge mentioned Ree's brother. Drew explained that the man was not her brother. Jorge said that the Federales had charged the man with being a narcotraficante. They found a pistola on him that was a favorite of the Columbians and gringos who transported drogas through the Tuxtla Airport. They said he was a suspected to have taken part in a recent shoot-out with the Federal Police in Veracruz. They had found the fresh wound in his shoulder and that they had found toll-road receipts in his pickup that put him in Veracruz at the time of the gunfight. Jorge said it was very serious for the man and advised Ree to stay away from him because she might be suspect as well. Jorge asked her if she had her visa. She told him she did and thanked him for the help.

They all sat without speaking and drank the last of the cold coffee. After a while, Drew pushed his chair back and extended his hand to Jorge. "Gracias por todo señor," he said.

"De nada."

Drew said hasta luego to Annabel and Marta then he and Ree walked out into the bright sun and the intense traffic noise on Calle

B. Domínguez. There was a giant thunderhead building back towards the mountains. It had a huge ball at the top that was as white as white gets. Bigger than anything Drew had ever seen in Texas. He wondered how far away it was. Probably farther than it looked. Ree noticed it too.

"Is it going to rain?" Ree asked.

"Somewhere," Drew said.

ONE MORE WINE STAIN ON A WHITE SHIRT

"UNO MÁS TEQUILA POR FAVOR." All three had had enough but no one suggested they quit. The straight shots of José Cuervo Tradicional had ceased to have a bite. Only the salt and lime had a taste.

"Irish you look a little drunk amigo," Drew said.

"Kind of like the pot calling the kettle black ain't it mate?"

The bar was quiet. The five-member traditional music group had given up on the three remaining patrons nearly an hour before and packed their flutes, tar drums and assortment of idiophones. They came by and shook hands before they went across the hall to the Cafe Macaw to look for request buyers.

Drew knew he would be sick before morning, but he didn't care. The Mexican tequila just tasted too good to worry about such things—to worry about the future.

"It doesn't make any sense," Joy said for the third time since the band left. "How can four men like that just not exist anymore? Dr. Boxxloader did so much good in his life. They all did."

Drew and Ree ignored him. They had talked it out with no resolution. There wasn't any resolution as to the why. These men, famous or otherwise, were simply not here any longer. Nothing more to say about it.

"Drew." Ree quietly asked.

"What?"

"I'm staying in Mexico for a while."

"Sure you are."

"No, I'm serious. I'm staying. I'm going back to Zapata and work with Socorro. I've got six months on my visa. I'm going to help as best that I can."

"Well, well, if you're not harder to get rid of than a wine stain on a white shirt."

Drew downed another shot and sucked on a lime for a chaser as he felt the bittersweet liquid burn all the way into his stomach. He blinked and looked across the table at Ree, "Do you need a priest?"

Ree took her time in responding. "Maybe. Is he celibate?"

"We will have to ask Maxímon."

"We'll ask him tomorrow," Ree said.

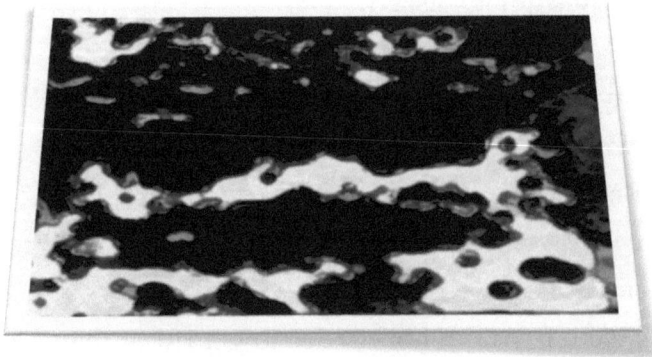

EPILOGUE

REMEMBER THE OWL

I HELD THE TELEGRAM IN MY HAND as Ree and Joy came from the hotel toward the Jeep. It was a cryptic note from JonKing. He had sent it from the States the night before. It had only two lines: *The film is in the can, stop. Go pick up the package at the Tuxtla airport, stop.* It was signed, JonKing, a friend of the owl.

"What do you make of this?" I said as I handed the message to Joy who was climbing in the back jump seat.

"What's that Drew?" Ree said.

"A telegram from JonKing. They had it for me when I checked out. What do you think Joy?"

"It appears our famed photo guy has completed his mission. I have no clue as to the package part. Maybe we should go find out," Joy passed the note to Ree.

"That's just what I intend to do. You guys ready for the Mexican adventure part two?"

"Ready Teddy," Joy said.

"What about you nurse?"

"Ready. Let's go back to the jungle and help our friends," Ree displayed a broad exuberant smile. "Now that you're a priest, do you want to say a prayer before we head to San Quintín?"

"I would but I don't know the words yet. Maybe Maxímon will teach me one or two when we get there."

As we drove west on Highway 190 out of Tuxtla-Gutierrez toward the airport, I couldn't help thinking how much had happened since I left Texas. I looked at Ree but she was looking out the passenger window and didn't notice my stare. She's a pretty lady I thought. Especially now that she is free from her past—from that invisible ball and chain that Buddy had strung around her neck.

It's so funny how this life works. If I had known beforehand that this woman with all her baggage was waiting for me at the DQ that day, I would have probably just driven straight on, avoided the complications. But now, in light of what happened to us over the last couple of months, I wouldn't have it any other way. I think back now to all my planning, my cautious preparation for coming to Mexico. What a joke.

"Joy," I hollered over the wind noise to the back of the Jeep.

"Yeah, Drew."

"Do you think I was supposed to be here for all of this? I mean the book and all that."

Joy didn't answer right away but scooted forward a bit so that his face was between me and Ree. He put his hand on my shoulder. "You damn right mate."

Ree turned her face toward me. "You damn right mate," she echoed.

We drove up to the cargo ramp behind the terminal and we all decided to go have a look at what JonKing had sent along from the States. Joy thought it had to be some prints from the book. Ree said she didn't think so. That old dog is too mysterious for that, she had noted. There was something else afoot she thought.

I handed the telegram to a young woman at the counter and she had me fill out a form with my name and address. The name part went well but when I came to the address I hesitated.

I turned to Ree, "What the hell is my address now?"

"San Quintín," is all she said.

"San Quintín it is." That 's what I wrote and handed it back to the woman.

She disappeared through a set of swinging doors and was gone for several minutes. When she came back she had a small box with holes in the sides and a handle on the top. The attendant was grinning broadly and speaking to the box. I must say it looked a little weird.

Ree snapped as to what the package was before Joy or I did and was practically jumping up and down. The woman set it down on the counter and asked me to sign the form. I did.

"Open it Drew," Ree practically shouted.

"Yeah mate, let's have a look see."

I was just about to comply when the attendant handed me a note that she explained came with the box. It had my name on the envelope.

"This must be from JonKing," I said as I broke the seal.

"Well Drew. What does it say," Ree said."

"OK, let's see."

To my friends in Chiapas,

Since you idiots are going to be jungle nuts, I thought you might need a new protector. That is in case the bees get after you. JonKing, hope to see you again soon.

Ree had opened the box as I read the note and turned to face Joy and me. "Look at this boys."

She held a ball of soft fur with a soft brown nose cradled contentedly in her arms. "Drew, it looks like you've got a new trail buddy." Ree held out the pup to me and I took the young dog and held it up in the air.

"Well would you look at this? What have we here? You're definitely a cow dog if I have ever seen one and a little boy to boot. What do you guys make of this?"

Ree reached out to take the pup back and again held it close to her body. "What are you going to call this little fellow?"

"Don't know, got to think on it a bit. Looks like there's going to be four of us on this trip."

Drew handed the box back to the attendant as he admired Ree with the new pup. Finally, he turned to face Joy. "Do you still want to go with us Joy? What about your studies? What's up with that?"

The three headed out to the parking lot and Joy answered Drew's questions as they made their way to the Jeep.

"Drew, now that Professor Boxxloader is gone I don't see that there is any hurry to get back to the school. I'll have to find a new advisor when I get back anyway. The way I see it is that what I will learn here trumps anything else I could possibly do. Hell man, this is going to be my dissertation, I just know it."

"OK then. It's a deal. I think we're set. Joaquin left me enough money to see us by for at least the six months we've got on our visas. So let's do this thing."

As they reached the highway again and turned back east, Drew pulled off the side of the road.

"Ree, hand me the pup." Ree did as Drew asked and Drew again held the young dog up in front of him, just over the steering wheel. "I know what I'm going to call this new one."

"What's that," Joy asked.

"Chico. His name is Chico."

Ree reached out and took the pup back. "Chico it is then," she said.